The Life After Life Chronicles

by Andy Zach

Zombie Turkeys
My Undead Mother-in-law
Paranormal Privateers

Paranormal Privateers

Andy Zach

Reviews of *Zombie Turkeys,* Volume 1 of Life After Life Chronicles:

"This book will not only make you laugh out loud, you will be surprised at the tender moments! You'll fly right through it and want more. Mr. Zach has a sense of humor we all need!"- Goodreads

"The yarn is fast-moving from start to finish, opening with the first attack of carnivorous red-eyed wild turkeys very difficult to kill. They can quickly resurrect after death and grow back cut-off limbs. They're led by a tom full of confidence as Zach gives us this tom's perspectives from time to time as he builds his flock into the tens of thousands throughout Illinois and beyond." - Author Dr. Wesley Britton, BookPleasures.com

"Zombie Turkeys is definitely not your typical zombie book. Instead, it is a parody of the standard zombie book, and as such may even be destined for cult status." - Amazon

"I am not one for . . . zombie material, but this was a very entertaining book. The satire kept me reading. Being from Central Illinois I was quite familiar with much of the locations mentioned in the book. I look forward to what is next." - Amazon

"I loved every gobbling, clucking page of this book. It's this hilarious and insane story that wonderfully hits all the right zombie outbreak tropes I love, but done with turkeys and thanksgiving themes. SO FUNNY! I could read about heroic turkey farmers making chipper-shredder last stands for just about forever.!" – Amazon

Reviews of *My Undead Mother-in-law,* Volume 2 of Life After Life Chronicles:

"I am a huge zombie fan, I had thought the genre had worked itself out for a while and then I read this book. I think I have been scarred for life! I foresee months if not years of counseling in my future." – Author Greg Aldridge, Goodreads.com

"Who hasn't had mother in law issues? Well, what if your mother in law was a zombie?

And yet our hero is a zombie avenging evil with her zombie turkeys, bulls, and corgis--all under her command.

Hilarious and heart warming at the same time. The perfect wedding shower gift for the new bride. . . . Can't wait for Andy's next adventure!"

Jacqueline Gillam Fairchild--author Estate of Mind, The Scrap Book Trilogy – Amazon

"This is the kind of mother-in-law we all need--one who can take over a flock of zombie turkeys by tearing the lead turkey into bite-sized pieces. This is just as good as "Zombie Turkeys," folks! Andy Zack is an amazing author! Hope he writes another story soon!" – Amazon

"My Undead Mother-In-Law, while not publicized as a YA story, should appeal to a generation for whom blogging is part of their daily life. Zach even asked a less than famous blogger to write the humorous "Foreword" to the book. That's really what any reader needs to enjoy this strange yarn—a sense of humor and a willingness to lose yourself in a world that never was and never will be. But a world that seems likely to appear once again in yet another sequel." - Author Dr. Wesley Britton, BookPleasures.com

Paranormal Privateers:
The Adventures of the Undead

Copyright © 2018 by Andy Zach

First Edition, 2018

Cover Illustration and jacket design: Sean Patrick Flanagan
Edited by: Dori Harrell
Formatting by Rik - Wild Seas Formatting
Published by: Jule Inc.

PO Box 10705
Peoria, Illinois 61612
zombieturkeys.com
jms61614-andyzach@yahoo.com
andyzach.net

ISBN: 978-0-9978234-1-7

Published in the United States of America

Dedicated to International Justice Mission and their battle against human slavery

Acknowledgments

I must acknowledge my awesome illustrator. Sean Flanagan, who created the book art. Once more, he has exceeded my expectations.

Next, let me mention my children, Tori, Olivia, Ray, and daughter-in-law Jacki. They listened to excerpts and refined my ideas.

My editor Dori Harrell managed to meet my tight deadlines without complaining and again improved my writing while cheering me on to completion.

I thank my advanced reader Ann Keeran, who gave me valuable feedback on my second draft.

Finally, I always have my wife, Julie. She patiently listens to me explode with laughter as I read my own jokes to her, and then she suggests how the story could be better.

Foreword

Finally that high-and-mighty novelist Andy Zach asked me to write a foreword to his book. It's about time he tapped a true professional, and Pulitzer Prize winner, like me. I don't know if he would have even thought of it if I hadn't badgered him after he asked my husband, Sam Melvin, to write the foreword to his first novel, *Zombie Turkeys.*

Not that Sam did a bad job—it just didn't ring with the professionalism that I bring to the table as the leading publisher of zombie news in America and the world, the *Midley Beacon.* It's only appropriate the creator of zombie news journalism should tell about the foremost comic paranormal animal author Dr. Andy Zach.

Dr. Zach, dripping with undue modesty, never mentions his doctorate in animal revivification from the Cambridge College of Paranormal Animals. I feel obligated to note this omission. But any attentive reader of his paranormal animal documentaries in his Life after Life Chronicles will detect his careful and exact attention to detail describing zombiism in animals and humans. After the latest apocalypse, several universities hoped to award him honorary degrees in paranormal science based on his books, but he declined.

Even I, editor and publisher, must tip my hat to his prose. More than once I've met a tight deadline by cutting and pasting from his novels into a last-minute news story or editorial to meet a minimum word requirement.

You should now be properly prepared as a reader for his latest book, *Paranormal Privateers.*

—Lisa Melvin, publisher and founder of the *Midley Beacon,* foremost paranormal animal and zombie news source

It is always darkest just before the day dawneth.
—A Pisgah Sight of Palestine (1650)

Chapter 1

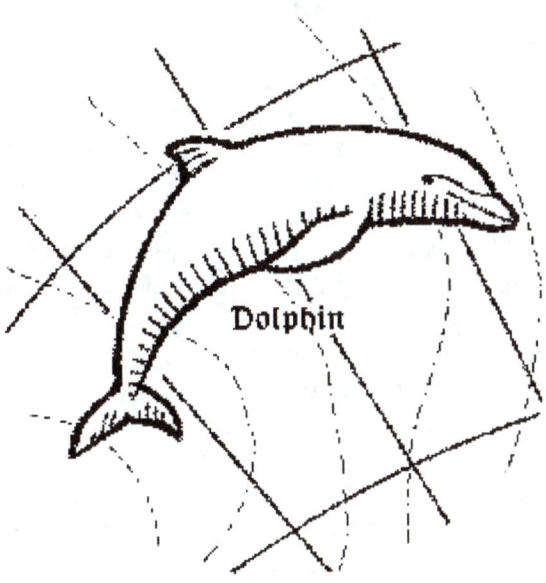

Dolphin

Somalia

Dirac sighed with relief when the US flag came down and the surrender flag went up on the mast of the titanic luxury yacht. He didn't mind firing rounds from his AK-47 over their heads, but he hated killing people. He knew they were only infidels, but they were still people.

Inhaling the salted breeze, he grinned back at Muhammed. He cheered and laughed in his seat behind the M2 machine gun in the bow of the boat they used to patrol the coasts and fishing waters of Somalia. The sun gleamed off his white teeth.

"Look, Dirac!" he said. "They're stopping!"

True enough. The bow wave ceased as he watched. A pod of dolphins ended their sporting on the wave and submerged. The gleaming white yacht loomed above them. What were they doing in the fishing waters of Somalia? He couldn't imagine the wealth on board. Enough for their whole village to eat well for a year!

Their supreme leader, Omar Ogala, organized Somali fishermen and former coast guard sailors to patrol their fishing waters. He ordered them to capture any fishing or cargo vessels they spotted. He told them the Americans and Europeans no longer cared about Somalia with the other crises around the world and they could defend their coasts from foreign competition—and dumpers. Many foreign nations, knowing Somalia's military weakness, sent cargo ships full of pollutants and dumped them into their waters.

Dirac never expected to see a luxury ship here. It was as big as a cruise liner, but apparently a private yacht. He'd seen one once before when an Arab sheik visited Mogadishu. This one was three times the size! The owner would pay big to get it back. Maybe even a billion dollars? He couldn't imagine that much money, and he was good with numbers. Let's see: fourteen million people lived in Somalia. Divide a billion dollars among them would give each about seventy dollars. Unbelievable. A family of five could live comfortably for a year on that!

He came along as a navigator, fighter, and boarder, guiding their boat along the shore of Somalia and into the Arabian Gulf for several days, before leading them back. Besides Muhammed and him, there was Zahi, another fighter and boarder, and Ali, their captain.

"Dirac," Ali said, "you and Zahi board this ship and take the helm. You will follow us back to Hobyo. Muhammed and I will stay on the boat and keep the machine gun on them."

"Yes, sir," he said.

Ali took the megaphone they carried for ship-to-ship communication. "Let us board! Let us board! Or we will gun your ship!"

Dirac didn't understand English, of course, but he knew what Ali was saying. Ali was the only one who knew any English.

"Don't shoot! Give us time! We have to get our ladder!" Surprisingly, the person spoke in Arabic. Good Arabic too, but with a strange Saudi and European accent. More surprisingly, it was a woman, a blonde, from what he could see of the figure leaning over the railing far above us. He kept a close watch on her. Strictly for security purposes, of course.

They kept their boat about fifty meters away from the ship and watched the crew scurry about the many decks. Dirac counted five including the main deck, and there were at least three more decks below the main one.

Finally a rope ladder unrolled from the main deck, perhaps ten meters above them. They came close to the ship. A pod of dolphins flashed under their boat. Then they leapt out of the water and into it.

Only, they weren't the dolphins he had seen earlier. Four people in green wet suits landed with heavy thumps in Dirac's boat. They had no breathing equipment, not even snorkels. They took off their goggles, and their eyes shone bright red in the sun.

"Zombies!" Ali cried. "Shoot them!"

Automatically Dirac sprayed the nearest with his AK-47. He heard the others fire too. Muhammed shot the largest one with the big .50-caliber machine gun. That could cut a man in two.

Dozens of red craters appeared in the green wet suit of the one Dirac shot. But she—a white, brown-haired woman—didn't go down. Her brows furrowed in anger, and shouting in English, she ripped the gun from his hand and threw it into the ocean. He was like a baby with a rattle taken by his parent. The other zombies did the same, except the big one. He grabbed the barrel of the machine gun in both hands and wrenched it from Muhammed. Dirac could hear the zombie's flesh sizzle on the hot barrel. Then the big zombie bent the barrel into a right angle. Rubbing his hands together afterward, the burned skin fell on the deck of their boat. Pink skin showed on his palms.

He was enormous, bigger than two Somalis put together. His red eyes looked out of his calm, square face. The bullets from the machine gun had sliced the wet suit open across his chest, and more pink skin showed in the gap. As he watched, brown hair grew.

The fighters were all struck dumb with shock and terror. Then the woman Dirac had shot called up to the blond woman on the main deck. She yelled down in Arabic, "All of you, lie down on the deck, and you will live."

They quickly obeyed.

Dirac heard a splash. Apparently, she'd dived into the water. She then leapt from the water and landed in their boat.

"I will direct you, and you will listen and obey," said a tall, shapely blond woman with bright-red eyes. She asked each of their names and roles and plans for taking the yacht. She consulted briefly in English with the others. "Very well, we will follow through with your plans. Dirac and Zahi will come on board with us. Ali and Muhammed will stay in the boat, and we'll all go to Hobyo."

Numbly, Dirac climbed the rope ladder to the deck, following Zahi. He tried to process all he had learned in the few minutes of their aborted attack. *They hijacked us. But they're zombies! They want to follow our plan. But they're zombies! We're going to Hobyo. But they're zombies! What will happen there? But they're zombies!*

He tried to remember everything he'd heard or read about zombies. They were some kind of Western fad, and then they'd become real. They fought in the US and in England. They were fast and superstrong, just as he'd seen in the last few minutes. And they regenerated. Quickly. Even from death!

Zahi went over the railing and onto the main deck. Dirac followed him, looking around. A crowd of people greeted them, led by the red-eyed man and the woman he had shot. They talked in English among themselves, and most held phones.

He heard a female voice behind him, the translator from the boat. She spoke in English to the crowd and then to them in Arabic.

"I'll translate for you, but most people have English-to-Arabic translator apps on their phones. Please be patient and answer any questions we have. We have a lot to learn from you before we get to Hobyo."

Her words barely registered as Dirac's eyes feasted on her curvy figure under her wet suit. He tore his gaze off her figure to her eyes. They shone bright red under a broad brow, with blond eyelashes and a square chin. She could be a marble idol from a Greek temple. A zombie goddess.

"What are your plans when you get to Hobyo?" he asked.

"Why, we'll be kidnapped and held for ransom!" She smiled.

It was the most terrifying thing Dirac had ever seen.

"My name is Sharon. Let me show you the ship and your quarters, Dirac and Zahi."

To the aft on the main deck was a beautiful swimming pool overlooking the transom dock between the two outside hulls. Dirac marveled at the luxurious wooden paneling on the inside.

More wonders followed. They climbed marble—marble!—steps to the next deck. Many rich staterooms surrounded the enclosed atrium. Ahead was a movie theater.

"Here's your room. You and Zahi will stay here." She went to the adjacent room and called out in English. An adorable little dog ran to her and jumped three feet into her arms. Its eyes glowed blood red too.

"This is Her Majesty Margaret—Maggie, for short. She'll be your personal escort." She grinned and spoke to the dog in English. "She only understands English, but she knows to follow you wherever you go. She'll make sure you don't do anything bad."

"How?" Dirac asked.

"Watch." Sharon went into the stateroom and came out with a meat-covered bone. It was nearly as big as the dog!

The dog sat and watched her with beady red eyes, its whole body quivering. Sharon tossed the huge bone to the dog. Before it hit the ground, the dog leapt, grabbed the meat, and with a shake of its head, ripped it from the bone. It gulped and grabbed another bite. Before Dirac's eyes, in less than a minute it stripped the meat from the bone and began gnawing. Sharon spoke again, and it stopped.

"Maggie's a great guard dog, but she's the kind to bite first and ask questions later. Don't provoke her by going into other people's rooms, striking people, or damaging anything. Her bite is *much* worse than her bark."

"Uh, will you keep her fed?" he asked.

Sharon looked at her watch. "Oh, it's time for their feeding. Let's watch!"

Sharon led them down to the main deck, then to a set of stairs going to the transom dock. A ten-meter boat nestled there with its catch of fish.

"Watch!" She pointed to the deck of the boat.

The men dumped their net full of fish. A ten-foot shark wriggled out, still snapping. The fishermen gaffed it in the gills with a hook and swung it to the deck next to the dock. A howl of barking and yipping came down the stairs. Forty, fifty, a hundred of the zombie corgis attacked the thrashing shark. It didn't thrash long. After the corgis gobbled for a minute, only a skeleton remained.

"Allah deliver us!" Zahi gasped.

Dirac never knew him to be pious, but he sounded devout, for a change.

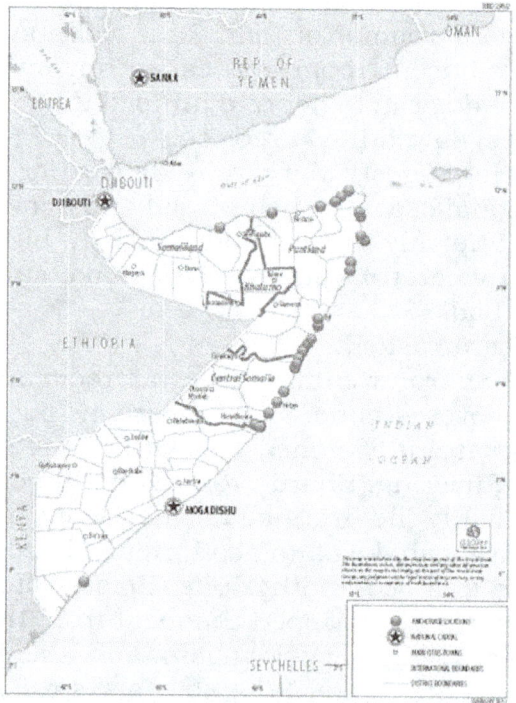

Sharon's red eyes glinted as she said, "I'd be really careful not to provoke Maggie. These doggies can smell blood anywhere on the ship, and they all come running. I've got things to do now. I'll give you these and go." She handed them each a phone and showed them how to use the translator app.

"Just speak Arabic into it, and out comes English. Try it."

"Who can I ask to give us a tour?" Dirac asked.

Out came English gibberish.

"Allah akbar!" Zahi said. He still sounded devout. Maybe he was reforming. Out came "Allah, gobbly-gook."

"Good. You've got it! Have fun exploring! Lunch is in an hour, on the deck above you." She walked away.

The dog eyed them redly.

"Good doggie!" Dirac said into the translator. The English noise came out, but the dog's watchfulness didn't change.

* * *

I saw Sharon enter the video conference room.

"Everyone's here now, General," said my wife, Diane Newby, in her normal, cheery voice.

My eyes feasted upon my wife of thirty years. How far we'd come from Gary, Indiana, where I wooed and wed her!

General Ramon Figeroa, assistant head of the National Security Agency, looked out from the huge screen mounted on the bulkhead at one side of the conference table. We conferred daily before lunch to apprise him of developments and to receive any intelligence pertinent to our assignment. Around the table, looking at him were Diane and me on one side. We'd turned zombie three years ago, after the zombie turkey apocalypse. You can read all about it in the *Midley Beacon* online archives or in Andy Zach's book *Zombie Turkeys*.

At the next side of the table sat our friends, Sam and Lisa Melvin, fellow zombies and owners of the *Midley Beacon*, the worldwide authority for all zombie news.

On the fourth side of the rich wooden table sat Lulu Gutierrez and her friend Sharon Windham. They'd become our loyal bodyguards after Diane saved their lives from sharks during a battle on this very yacht. They, in turn, saved Diane's life. We were embedded with US Marines at the time, assaulting the last hideout of Sid Boffin, a reclusive billionaire and criminal megalomaniac. The *Midley Beacon* documented it all just this spring, so you're probably familiar with the whole story. If you've been living on Mars and missed the story, get a copy of Andy Zach's book *My Undead Mother-in-Law*. The title refers to Diane, of course. I guess that makes me, George Newby, the undead father-in-law.

These daily meetings had become routine since the *Resolute Too*'s commissioning as a US privateer at the beginning of the year, three months ago. Our letter of marque, issued by the US Congress and signed by President Trump, hung on the conference room wall. The ship's name came from me. I researched the history of US privateers. There was a dirigible in World War II named the *Resolute*. Technically, it wasn't a privateer, but it was a privately owned craft directed by the navy to watch the West Coast for subs, so it was almost a privateer. Diane added the "Too," and we had a name for the yacht.

I vividly remember the rechristening of the yacht, formerly named *Rule Britannia*, in January in New Orleans.

Diane had held the bottle of champagne at the boat dock and smashed it against the prow. The sheet covering the new name had slipped down, revealing *Resolute Too*— and the figurehead.

"George, is that supposed to be me?" Diane yelled in excitement.

"Of course, Diane. Can't you see the resemblance?"

"Yes, in the face. She even has cat's-eye glasses just like me. But she's too buxom."

"Oh, I don't think so." I knew that part of her anatomy very well. The sculptor had actually made Diane's waist narrower, which made her seem more buxom, but I hadn't wanted to point that out.

General Figeroa interrupted my reminiscence. "You're all looking fit and tan today."

He usually conducted our daily meetings casually. He'd done that for the past three years we'd worked with him against Sid Boffin.

"Have we got news for you!" Diane said, enthusiastic as usual.

"Did you find Somali pirates?"

"They found us! They tried to hijack the ship, and then we hijacked them."

"How will you find the leader behind the pirates?"

That was the key question and was the reason we were here off the coast of Somalia. As privateers, we were not in the direct chain of command of the military. We reported to the president, who'd made General Figeroa his liaison to the *Resolute Too.*

"That's next on the agenda," I said. "We're acting like they have control of the ship, and we're following them to Hobyo, a fishing port. We'll be there tonight. We'll go in as their hostages and hope to get to Omar Ogala."

"I can't imagine anyone holding you hostage, George. Or Diane. Still, do you have a backup plan?"

"To make sure, we're also taking Lulu and Sharon as 'hostages.' Meanwhile, Sam and Lisa will remain on the ship in case we need further reinforcements. They have the V-22 and our zombie animal backups."

"That'll do it. I assume you'll spring free when you meet Ogala?"

"Yup."

"When will you complete the operation?"

"We'll be there tonight. Then we have to meet Ogala, who'll determine our ransom and use our phones to call. That's their usual protocol. It'll probably be after midnight after we tie up all the loose ends."

"Call me when you're done, no later than tomorrow morning."

"Will do."

"Figeroa, out."

Later that afternoon, Diane and I sat in our stateroom, awaiting our arrival at Hobyo. Diane knit a complex afghan for our bed. A skull and crossbones with cat's-eye glasses and red eyes decorated it. She found knitting very relaxing.

I scrapbooked. I'd found out about it by reading the Scrapbook series by Jackie Gillam-Fairchild. Diane and I went to Her Majesty's Tearoom in Dunlap, Illinois, and I saw it there. I loved saving and collecting things and organizing everything into a timeline. I found scrapbooking a great way to unwind after a hard day fighting criminals.

Into the scrapbook, I taped an AK-47 bullet, a piece of my burned skin, and a splinter that had entered my hand from the pirate's boat. I was trying to figure out what else to add, when there was a knock on our door.

I opened it, and it was Dirac and Zahi. Dirac spoke into his phone. "Could we see your stateroom? We're taking a tour of your ship."

"Of course!" Diane gushed. "Here. Have some cookies!"

Diane loved baking and giving away her goodies. They each took a chocolate chip cookie, tried a nibble, and then wolfed it down.

"What is that?" Dirac asked into his phone, pointing at the scrapbook.

I explained scrapbooking to him through my phone app. Then I took a picture of him and Zahi eating cookies. I printed it out on photo paper and taped it into my book. "There. Do you see how it works?"

"That's great! I'd like to try that!"

"Sure. I have lots of blank ones." I gave him one, along with tape and glue, some African and sea-based stickers, and a coaster from our stateroom. It had the Jolly Roger with cat's-eye glasses on it. "You can put anything in it. Here are some ideas."

They thanked us and went to their room to scrapbook.

* * *

"We're here!" Lulu Gutierrez announced from our stateroom doorway. Her dark-brown eyes gleamed with excitement.

I looked up from my book *From Good to Great*. Diane had finishing knitting the paranormal Jolly Rogers bed cover and was sorting through her recipes.

I glanced at the clock: 11:00 p.m. East African time. "You ready, Diane?"

"Sure. This'll be a new experience—the first time I've been held hostage! I'm eager to try it!"

We weren't wearing our Kevlar armor, nor taking any weapons, to maintain the image of helpless hostages. We'd decided to wear just basic US clothing: jeans and T-shirts. Certainly, we hadn't needed our armor when we took over the Somali boat.

We also put in our contact lenses that hid our red eyes. They hampered our night vision, which we'd received when we became zombies.

Sharon waited for us at the railing, as well as Dirac and Zahi. I heard the boat's motor, smelled the warm salt air, and saw a few lights in the small fishing village a half mile away.

"Let's go." I descended the rope ladder.

* * *

Dirac followed the four zombies down the rope ladder, and Zahi trailed him. They'd been given AK-47s from the ship's armory. The zombies didn't look nearly as fearsome without their red eyes—except George. His fingers were thick as a tent stake, and he still seemed like he could break any of the Somali fighters in half with his bare hands.

Of course he could. They probably all could. Dirac had to remember that.

Zahi and he hadn't had a chance to plan how to signal that their "hostages" were not actually hostages but were severe threats to their nation's coast guard. He hoped Ali and Muhammed had a plan. He'd watch what Ali did.

They all assembled in the boat. Ali held an AK-47. "Zip-tie them all!" he shouted.

That was their normal practice. Dirac watched Ali carefully as they zip-tied the four hostages. He didn't show fear but seemed on edge.

"Gather their phones!" They did, following their standard operating procedure with hostages.

"Ali, how will we tell the base?" Dirac whispered in his ear as they cruised to the dock. The only one he had to worry about was Sharon hearing him, and she was in the bow with the other hostages, guarded by Muhammed. They sat in the stern, ten meters away.

"Leave it to me," he said.

He looked directly into his eyes and seemed confident. Dirac relaxed.

The other vessels in their fleet were docked there: two more ten-meter boats with machine guns and the thirty-meter "mothership" they used when they traveled far into the Arabian Gulf.

"Ho there, Ali!" yelled the dockmaster, Bashiir. "You've caught a big fish tonight!"

"Bigger than you know, Bashiir!" Ali called back. "We've got four hostages. Do you have guards ready?"

"Yeah, we're ready for them."

They tied to the dock and climbed onshore. Four local fishermen armed with AK-47s met them, cheering and blustering.

"Look how white they are!"

"Are they all Americans?"

"They look rich!"

"We'll get a lot for them!"

"Quiet, all of you!" Ali commanded. "We have to take these four to Supreme Leader Ogala tonight. Get the truck."

Once the truck pulled up to the shore, Ali directed the four prisoners, Zahi, and Muhammed into the back of the truck. I climbed into the cab and drove, and Ali sat beside me.

As soon as we were off, headed for Haradhere two hours away, I asked Ali, "What's the plan?"

"This." He pulled out his phone and called the supreme leader.

"Sir, we've got four rich prisoners. Millionaires, maybe billionaires... Yes, we also have their ship, a luxury yacht... We'll be at headquarters in an hour, hour and a half... Yes, sir, I'll do that... One more thing you should know... They're zombies... Yes, just like the ones in the US... Superstrong and fast... We have them in zip ties, but I don't think they'll hold them. OK, I'll drive there."

"What did the supreme leader say?"

"He wants us to park in his private garage. He'll hold them securely there."

"I don't know how."

"I don't either. But I trust our leader. He's really smart."

After a fast, bumpy trip to Haradhere, instead of going to the main compound, Ali drove around back to the leader's house. It was large and heavily fortified, with an underground garage. Inside the garage, instead of the supreme leader's luxury cars sat a metal shipping container.

The truck backed up to the open end of the container. Muhammed and Zahi pushed the hostages into the container with their rifles. The door was slammed, bolted shut, and locked with a heavy padlock.

Omar Ogala entered. A tall, burly man, he carried a grenade launcher. "I had your backs, men, in case they jumped you." His round face and bald head showed a grim smile. "I'm proud of you for bringing them in. Zombies are no joke. Cabdi, come here."

Cabdi, the supreme leader's chief bodyguard, stepped up carrying a rocket launcher. It didn't carry the normal antitank shell, but a bulkier one Dirac didn't recognize.

"Ali, you open the feeding door, and then Cabdi will fire in."

"Supreme Leader, are you going to kill them?" Dirac asked. That wasn't their usual procedure for hostages. They kept them alive to prevent an undue military response and to maximize the ransom.

"You're Dirac, aren't you? No, the rocket shell won't kill them, probably. It's a fléchette shell with salt water, to dezombify them. Don't worry about killing them. Worry about them staying alive and zombie."

Ali opened the small steel door on the bottom of one side of the shipping container, used for feeding prisoners. As soon as he unlatched it, he slid it up enough for the shell to enter, and Cabdi fired.

Even outside the container, the exploding shell made Dirac's ears ring.

"Check and see if you got them. If not, fire another shell."

Cabdi rotated a steel disk above the feeding door and peered into the smoky darkness. He shone a flashlight in, then closed it.

"The women are gathered around the man who caught it," he reported to Ogala.

"Fire another shell. We can't leave any in a zombie state."

Ali opened the door again, and again the concussion battered his ears. What was it like inside there? How could they still be alive?

"Check again."

Peering in, Cabdi reported, "They're all down, and they're all bloody."

"Good. That'll hold them. Now let's go to my conference room and call for ransom. You've got the phones, Ali?"

"Right here, Supreme Leader."

"Whose cell will you use?"

"It doesn't matter. They all gave the same number to call for ransom."

"So they're all in this together. It'll probably be some lawyer or insurance agent of theirs. I hope they have enough insurance!" Ogala laughed.

"How much will you demand, Supreme Leader?" Dirac asked.

"One billion dollars—each. And another billion for the ship. How'd you like to use that to patrol our coasts, Dirac?"

"I'd love it, but we can use the money more."

"Right you are. The people of Somalia need help. This could put us over the top and fund a full-time, official navy. That would supply thousands of jobs. We can also build an industry here."

"Inshallah," Dirac murmured fervently. "Let it be God's will."

They all settled in the conference room. "You do the call, Ali. You have the best English."

"Yes, sir."

"Put it on speakerphone."

"Corporate legal office, how can I help you?"

"We have arrested George and Diane Newby, Sharon Wyndham, and Lulu Gutierrez for trespassing in Somali waters. You must pay one billion dollars for each for us to release them. For the ship, *Resolute Too*, you will pay another billion."

"I don't believe you. Put them on the phone."

"They resisted, and we had to knock them out."

"Fat chance. They're zombies! You're bluffing."

"They're locked in prison, and we knocked them out with salt water. You know that kills the zombie germ that regenerates them. Now, quit arguing and send the money! It must be US cash and bills of fifty dollars or less. Drop it off at Hobyo Airport."

"It'll take at least a day to get the money and another to fly the cash there."

"We'll keep them safe for at least two days. Don't try any military force, or we'll kill them immediately. We'll burn them with napalm. Even zombies can't take that."

"OK! You know this much cash will weigh tons. Even using fifty-dollar bills, that'll be a hundred million bills. That's a hundred tons."

"Let me check." Turning to Omar Ogala, Ali said, "The weight of the bills is a hundred tons."

"A hundred thousand kilos? That's within the capacity of a 747 freighter. Tell them to hire one and land it at Aden Adde International Airport in Mogadishu. I'll take it from there."

Ali relayed the message in English.

"Also tell them we'll check all the counts, and if there is any shortage, no one is released!"

Ali also repeated that.

"This'll take at least a week! We have to get the cash and rent the plane."

"We have time. We have plenty of salt water to keep the zombies down. Your week begins now." Ali hung up.

Chapter 2

Haradhere

The reek of high explosive hung in the black cargo container as I awoke. My whole body ached like a two-a-day football practice followed by a sound beating. I knew that meant I was no longer a zombie.

My last memory was shielding the women with my body. Where were they? Where was Diane?

"Diane?" My voice came out as a croak.

Someone groaned in the dark. "Is that you, Diane?"

"No, it's Lulu. Diane's here. You awake, Diane?"

"Oooh," Diane moaned.

I felt grit, dirt, fléchettes, and blood on the bottom of the container as I crawled to her voice.

"I'm here, honey." I took her into my arms. She felt small—and bloody. "Are you OK?"

"I hurt all over. I haven't felt this bad since we battled the zombie ninjas and I got impaled with the naginata."

"They must have used fléchette rockets."

"Yes, they shot you, and then they shot us. Lulu, Sharon, how are you doing?"

"I've been better," Lulu said.

"This is what we signed up for when we became your bodyguards. We haven't done too well so far," Sharon said. She sounded...good.

"Sharon, are you still a zombie?" I asked.

"No and yes. I lost my zombie infection and power—and then I reinfected myself with my zombie blood capsule as soon as I awoke a couple of minutes ago."

"I forgot mine! It's been so long since I was in battle. I left it in my room."

"You can have mine, Diane," I offered.

"No worries. Sharon and I both carry spares."

We all injected the blood capsules. They looked like EpiPens, used to treat anaphylactic shock from allergic reactions to bee stings. Punching the capsule into one's leg shot a milliliter of blood through a needle into your bloodstream.

The zombie bacteria doubled in quantity every twenty minutes. When it encountered damaged tissue, it replaced it by copying the DNA into itself. Over time, a zombie would become almost entirely this replicated tissue. The zombie tissue was twice as strong as normal tissue. The muscle fibers flexed twice as fast. Even one's skin became as tough as nails.

That was how we survived the saltwater fléchettes. Although they killed the bacteria in the blood, it took a while to kill all the bacteria. The surviving bacteria patched us up enough to live—and then it died. Whoever planned our capture—probably Ogala—knew a lot about zombies.

"I'm glad they didn't think to search us for our capsules," I commented.

"Perhaps they didn't know about the technology?" Lulu speculated.

"They should!" Diane insisted. "I helped invent that with Maggie, my daughter-in-law, three years ago when we first began fighting for zombie rights!"

"But, dear," I murmured, "Zombies are mostly confined to the US, where people have a right to be a zombie. The rest of the world, especially a backwater like Somalia, doesn't know all the tech that goes with us. They fear zombies, like the old US, and don't allow us to immigrate or any zombie blood to be transported."

"Hah!" Diane snorted. "Do you know how many millions of dosages of blood we've shipped around the world in the past three years?"

"Yes, I know it's used to treat disease worldwide, but people usually get—and governments require—the anti-zombie antibiotic afterward."

"Dummies!"

I chuckled. Diane had no understanding of anyone who had the least fear of zombies.

We sat quietly in the darkness for an hour, gaining strength and healing.

"I know they're sending the zombie animals to attack, but I'd like to get out and greet them." Diane cared for all the zombie corgis, bulls, and turkeys that we kept on board the ship.

"I'm feeling pretty good. Let's see if I can make a dent in that door." I went to the door and felt carefully around the edges. There were no gaps, but the door wriggled slightly against the steel rods holding it closed.

"Hmmm. I might as well attack the sides of the container as the door. I don't want to bang against it, but that's the only way to fatigue the metal and bust out of here. What's to stop them from coming and firing another fléchette rocket or two?"

"How about if we get out with one big bang?" Sharon said.

"How do we do that?"

"I've got two shaped explosive charges right here."

"And I've got two more," Lulu added.

"How? How did you smuggle them in?"

"Let's just say our figures had some additional padding," Lulu said, smiling in the dark.

"Oho! Your padded bras have C4 explosive!" Diane exclaimed. "I wish I had thought of that. I'll do that from now on!"

"You got it in one," Sharon admitted.

"You don't need any more padding," I said sotto voce.

Our bodyguards fixed the four shaped charges around the door, right behind the two steel rods holding the door closed. We retreated to the other end of the container and covered our ears as Lulu detonated them.

BANG! The pressure wave bounced off our end of the container and slammed into the back of the door, now containing four holes where the rods used to be. The door squealed on its hinges and opened.

"It worked!" Diane said.

"Let's go and hit them before they come here with the fléchette rockets," I said.

"Charge! I've got some Somali butt I want to kick!" Diane yelled.

Lulu and Sharon and I tried to keep up with her as she raced out of the container.

Immediately a guard raised a rocket launcher at us. Another opened fire from the opposite side. Diane and I knew this drill well.

Diane covered the ten feet to the guard with the rocket launcher in one quick bound and dove below it and rolled into his legs. Down he came, even before he fired.

I did the same in the opposite direction with the machine gunner. Before I hit him, a bolo took his feet out from under him and another tore away his gun.

Popping up from the ground, I looked at Sharon and Lulu. They smiled smugly.

"Bra bolos again?" I asked. Strategically weighted bras with steel wire were one of our bodyguards' favorite weapons.

"Sure. We had to get our bras off to get our shaped charges anyway," Lulu said.

We tied up the guards using their bras and went outside.

The garage opened from the foundation of a house built like a fortress. Lights came on in the house and guns appeared at the windows.

"Where do you think Ogala is?" I asked.

"I don't know, but I know those guys are about to start shooting, and I don't want that! Let's take them out!" Diane jumped to a second-story window, and I followed her with our bodyguards.

The poor gunner there didn't know what hit him as four zombies jumped through the window, took his gun, and tied him up, using zip ties from his own pockets.

Sharon asked him in Arabic, "Where is Omar Ogala?"

"Top floor," he said, shaking in fear, his eyes bulging out.

We ran up the stairs, pausing to overcome gunners. The top room had a guard with a fléchette launcher.

"Oh no you don't!" Diane yelled as she rocketed toward him. This time, instead of rolling into his feet, she jumped to the ceiling, flipped around, and pushed off, landing on top of him. A 150-pound woman hitting on his head knocked him out as well as a prizefighter's punch.

I found the door locked, but with a little persuasion with my sausage-sized fingers, I ripped the bolt through the doorframe.

"They don't make them like they used to," I said.

Lulu and Sharon raced ahead of us.

"Gone," Lulu said, disgusted.

Looking out the window into the black night, Sharon said, "There's a guy racing for a pickup truck."

We removed our contact lenses so we could see him clearly in the dark.

"I think that's Ogala. It looks like him. He's taller and heavier than the other Somalians," I said.

"He won't get away from me!" Diane shouted as she jumped out of the fourth-story window.

Sighing, I followed her. I loved Diane dearly, but she always acted first and thought later. Maybe that was why we got along so well. I always thought first.

Lulu and Sharon hurtled down with me.

I didn't know if we could catch Ogala in the pickup truck. We zombies could run twice as fast as a normal human, up to forty miles per hour for a time. The truck was already spraying dirt and gravel as we chased it.

Then I heard a helicopter. The ship sent the V-22 Osprey and the zombie animals as soon as the ransom call came. Ogala might get away from human zombies, but zombie animals? Never.

The pilot was on the ball. He saw us chasing the skidding truck, and he landed on the road in front of it. The truck veered wildly into the desert. I wondered how rough the desert was, considering the road required a four-wheel-drive truck.

Diane and the other women headed directly for the V-22. The back cargo doors opened, and zombie bulls, corgis, and turkeys piled out.

"OK, everyone, listen up! I'll take Whip and catch Ogala. You take your bulls, the corgis, and the turkeys and subdue everyone in this base," Diane said.

"You should take one of us along as backup," Sharon said.

"No, you stay behind and interrogate the prisoners. I can handle one crime boss myself." She and Whip sprinted after Ogala.

Looking at Lulu and Sharon, I said, "I'll take half the animals and go to the left around the main base. You go the other way. Try not to kill anyone unless it's absolutely necessary. You know how pro-life we are."

The zombie animals all obeyed human zombies, but not much else. They could follow simple commands: "This way," "Stop," "Left," "Right." The corgis were the most obedient, the turkeys the least. They knew not to eat people without permission—barely. The bulls followed heel and leg direction like horses—eventually.

The corgis and bulls raced around the compound with us. The zombie turkeys milled outside the walls, eating anyone who sought to flee. As we caught people, I directed them to lay down on the ground and I tied them up with the zip ties I had picked up in the garage. I encountered steady gunfire, but after it proved completely ineffective against us zombies, people just started running. I pursued.

* * *

Now what? Omar Ogala wondered as the truck jounced across the dark desert. He could see by the moon he was headed east toward Hobyo, so he knew he paralleled the road. He'd go a lot faster if he could go by road, but a huge ravine kept him from cutting back to it.

At least he'd lost those crazy zombies. He knew they'd dezombified; he'd checked himself. Using his home's remote security cameras, he'd seen the cargo container door blown open by explosives. Where had they gotten those? He'd been prepared for zombie speed and strength, but not for smuggled explosives.

His error. He'd have to learn from it. Ah! The ravine's ending. Now he'd cut over— "What?" he shouted.

Something large almost hit the back of his truck! What was it?

Looking in his rearview mirror, lit by the lurid glare of his taillights, he saw a red figure on a huge red horse. It was the second horseman of the apocalypse, War! He wasn't a Christian, but his childhood teaching in the Christian school flashed back to him.

Stunned, he watched the red figure leap from the horse, nearly ten meters, and land in the bed of his truck. Now closer, he recognized him—or her. Diane Newby, the zombie leader!

Immediately he put his truck into a tight spin in the loose sand of the desert. He saw Newby fly to the side and flip over the bed wall. One hand clung to the wall.

He kept spinning, trying to throw her off. CLANG! The giant horse—he now saw it was a bull—crashed into the side of his truck and flipped it over!

It skidded to rest upside down. He wriggled loose from his harness and grabbed the fléchette launcher in the rack behind him. The door was jammed. He rolled the window down and stared into the red eyes of Diane Newby.

"Omar Ogala, I presume?" She grinned wickedly, took his fléchette launcher, and hurled it far into the desert. A mammoth bull snorted behind her.

He knew quite a bit of English, which he hid from his subordinates. "Let's cut a deal. You let me go, and you and your friends can go too."

She smirked. "We're already gone. So is your base. And now you'll go." She grabbed his shirt and belt and put him on the bull as easily as if he were a child and not someone who massed fifty kilos more than her.

The bull snorted angrily as they rode away.

It was a ride from hell. With every wild bound of the galloping bull, Ogala flew into the air, in danger of crashing into the desert at more than a hundred kilometers per hour. Diane's single small hand on his wide belt pulled his 150 kilos onto the bull's broad back. Her other hand hung on to the bull's harness. Then he would fly off again with the next bound.

At the apex of one of his flights, he saw an animal dart next to them. A lion? No, a cheetah! It paced the bull for a while and then fell behind. Maybe he underestimated their speed.

He was so relieved to get off that bull that he meekly answered the blond zombie who began questioning him when he was released into captivity in his own compound.

* * *

Lulu, Sharon, and I herded our prisoners into the compound. The zombie turkeys, while crummy at following orders, made great guards. You showed them their territory and then they ate everything that came within it.

Diane galloped back with Ogala, riding full speed on Whip. The whites of Ogala's eyes stood out against his dark face. Diane had him sit in front of her. She held on with one hand to the Kevlar harness that served as a saddle, and with the other, Ogala's belt in the back of his britches.

Diane rode through the ring of turkeys, then picked up Ogala and dropped him in the middle of his followers.

"What have you found out from the prisoners?" Diane asked Sharon.

"They're a combination of starving farmers and fishermen, along with some professional military men. Ogala's been here for two years, getting them organized. He seems pretty good at that."

"We'll turn Ogala over to the NSA and let them figure out what to do with him," Diane said. "What about all these people and their weapons? If we leave, they'll just go back to piracy. They seem to need the weapons to keep their families alive."

"I've got an idea," I said.

"What's that, George?"

"How about we subsidize them to *not* commit piracy? We can send them some money monthly from SPEwZ Inc., which will continue as long as there is no piracy. They can still patrol their territorial waters and prosecute dumpers and foreign fishermen."

SPEwZ Inc. was the business arm of our zombie charity, Society Promoting Equality with Zombies. The nonprofit portion helped zombies fight for equal rights and become acclimated to life as a zombie. The for-profit portion, which I had set up, bought zombie blood and then resold it for medical cures. The zombie bacteria (E. coli Homo Zapiens, or ECHZ) could conquer any disease or injury known to man.

"Great! Let's do it!" She paused. "Sharon, what is Ogala going on about?"

We could hear him yelling in Arabic in the background.

"He's ranting about how this is a US invasion and how he'll lead his people to throw us back into the sea," Sharon said.

"OK, we'll deal with Mr. Ogala! Please translate for me."

Diane rode into the midst of the prisoners on her bull, Whip. She stood easily on its broad back and spoke.

"First of all, we're not part of the US government policy. We have permission from the president to go into countries like Somalia and get criminals like Mr. Ogala. He's got a record of corruption and crime a mile long before he ever came here.

"But I do admit, he's done some good here. He's gotten some money and food flowing into your economy. Anything that stops starvation does some good.

"We know about your problems with foreign fishermen and dumpers. They're illegal in your waters, and you should be able to patrol them, just as you were doing.

"To aid you, we're leaving our ship's boat to help you patrol. It's faster than your craft and has radar too.

"We'll make a deal with you. This is a deal between SPEwZ Inc. and your area of Somalia under your control. We'll subsidize the cost of your boat and pay you to patrol your own waters. You still get to keep any ships violating international law in your waters.

"We just ask you to stop pirating other ships and to capture any other pirates you find. And don't go outside your territorial waters. Deal?"

"We'll need time to think it over," Ali said. He'd emerged as the spokesman for the Somalis, with Ogala unseated.

"Of course. We'll stay until you decide, and we'll train you how to operate our ship's boat."

Turning to Omar Ogala, Diane said, "Mr. Ogala, we'd like to talk to you. Come with us."

Back at the ship, Sam and Lisa Melvin reported on the successful defeat of Somali pirates by the *Resolute Too* assault team. Sam wrote daily blog reports.

The ship's helicopter flew Ogala to an Egyptian prison, where he was interrogated by US agents and Egyptian officials as well.

* * *

The brilliant Mediterranean sun shone upon the azure bay around the Greek island of Kristos. Small fishing boats dotted the bay, leaving the docks and going out for the evening's fishing. From the bay, the island rose swiftly to cliffs surrounding and protecting it from fierce winter storms. Atop the highest cliff stood a white villa made of local marble. Hundreds of years old, it had seen Napoleon, Mussolini, and Hitler come and go as rulers of the Mediterranean.

Inside the villa's courtyard, shaded from the sun under a striped awning, I studied a screen covering the wall. The screen showed a large ship departing from a desert port. Crowds cheered and waved goodbye as it pulled away.

I grimaced.

I sourly noted the flag flying from the white yacht: a Jolly Rogers with bright-red eyes and cat's-eye glasses. *Crap*, I thought.

If I didn't swear out loud, it didn't count. Although I was free from any morality left over from St. Maria, my parochial school from over a century ago, I still felt guilty if I swore. The guilt continued, even though I had obliterated my old identity when I'd adopted my current name, John Smith.

I gritted my teeth as the source of my anger steadily increased in speed as it sailed from Hobyo, trailed by the drone sending me the video. I was glad I'd made my drones look like seagulls. They'd never spot them.

But I was avoiding the issue. These zombies were a pain in the butt. I didn't want to make a premature move and fail, but I couldn't have them capturing my clones like that. Sure, I'd get Omar free, but he'd have to have a completely new character re-creation and setup as a dictator somewhere else. They'd ruined my Somali operation just as I was poised to take over the whole country.

Where did Omar go wrong? He did nothing wrong. He did just as I asked him and had taken control of the shipping around the country and won the hearts of the populace.

So where did I go wrong? First, I erred by not tracking the zombie pirate ship. I knew Trump commissioned them as privateers, but I didn't expect they would attack me, John Smith. Nobody knew I controlled most of the world. I swear, these zombie pirates would give me more gray hair. They'd ruin my salt-and-pepper pompadour!

The US intelligence was better than I'd thought. I knew the zombies had worked with the US intelligence and military to overthrow my US and European clone, Vik Staskas. I hated to lose a clone. They were my family. Now I'd lost two. I'd assume they would attack my other bases, and soon.

What were the next closest bases? Egypt, Syria, Turkey, Crimea. I'd prepare something for them before they even got to Egypt. I checked my live map of the ship's direction. Yes. They were headed toward the Suez Canal.

What did I have that would affect zombies? Suitcase nukes? They were dangerous. If anyone tied them back to me, I might get the full force of the US military, not some souped-up paranormal Batmen. Ricin? Botulism? Mustard gas? I could make those look like some terrorist group, but I didn't think those would work on zombies.

That only left my latest bioweapon I'd designed to neutralize zombies. I hadn't fully tested it yet. I laughed. Nor had it passed FDA regulations. But that hadn't stopped me before. It was worth a try. If it worked, it'd be wonderful and I'd clear the world of zombies. If it failed, they wouldn't be able to trace it to me and I'd learn.

I reviewed my delivery methods and how to send the germs to the four bases in the zombies' reach. Afterward, I planned to distribute it throughout Europe, the States, and then Asia.

I sighed with contentment. I had a plan but worried it would fail. And if it failed, I had to see how it failed to improve it. I foresaw only stress in my future until I wiped zombies from the earth.

Chapter 3

Butt

Crimea

The late-spring Egyptian sun blazed down on the *Resolute Too* as it sailed through the Suez Canal. Lulu Gutierrez sunned on the pool deck. She'd tanned there when she was Sid Boffin's bodyguard, and she still loved it. Having grown up in Acapulco, she craved the hot sun.

Despite her fair skin, Sharon Wyndham sunned next to her. Her zombie bacteria repaired any sun damage as it occurred. She didn't get the killer tan Lulu had, but she liked the golden color the sun imparted.

"This is the life, isn't it Lulu?" Sharon spoke Spanish, Lulu's native tongue, one of the eleven languages she spoke. That was how they'd become friends in the beginning, on Sid's yacht.

"Sure is. You'd hardly know we're now on the side of the law instead of a worldwide criminal."

"We have to dodge bullets either way!"

"Or catch them," Lulu responded.

"Now with Sid, we just thought he was a billionaire."

"But the clue phone began to ring when he taught us how to use his antiaircraft missiles."

"Also, why would he need a hundred katana-wielding bodyguards?"

"Yeah, that was pretty suspicious. But we had it so good. I just looked the other way."

"Which we could do until the US Marines landed."

"And Diane and George."

"I didn't feel right fighting the marines, let alone a middle-aged couple—even if they were zombies. I just did it because I didn't know how to get out," Sharon said.

"Diane saved us. She rescued us from the sharks and then from Sid."

"What a slimeball he was! He put bombs in each of us to cover his escape."

"None of the other zombie guards escaped. He blew up a hundred loyal guards!"

"It's kind of just. We went over to Diane after she saved our lives and helped her stay alive. Then she led us to the one place where the detonation signal couldn't reach us: Sid's private deck."

"Did you get your internal bomb removed like I did, Sharon?"

"Of course. Surgery as a zombie is a breeze when you don't need anesthesia or sutures. I did it as an outpatient. The cardiologist at the Cleveland Clinic said he'd never done open-heart surgery as an outpatient operation before."

"That Sid! I wish he weren't dead, so I could kill him again! Imagine placing C4 high explosive in our chests, next to our hearts!"

"Yes, we had enough to destroy a whole room. He was the most paranoid man I've ever met."

"So when do we get through the Suez Canal?"

"We can't go through at full speed. It'll take us twelve hours, and that's expedited. We should be out in a couple hours."

Sharon chuckled. "You should have heard Diane yelling at Captain Dmitri Koumondoros to go faster. When he explained there was a strict speed limit in the canal,

Diane fetched me and used me to explain to the Egyptian authorities we *had* to go faster because of a life-and-death emergency. I don't know if the canal official expedited us because he believed her or because he wanted to get rid of her!"

Sharon paused, then added, "Diane was right: this is a life-and-death emergency. Every hour we delay could lead to another slave's death."

"So we've got to get to Crimea as quickly as possible. I'm with Diane. I feel a special urge to take out those slavers. Human trafficking and slavery is the worst crime I can imagine!" Lulu sat up in the lounge chair, stirred by anger.

"I'm known as cool and calm, but that makes my blood boil too."

"I've heard Sevastopol and Crimea are very beautiful. I'd like to actually be a tourist there, rather than just play one to fool the authorities. How sad that it's the home of slave distribution!"

"You know what General Figeroa said in this morning's conference. We'll have to be very careful and clever. We'll have both the Russian government watching us and the criminal slave gang. I wish we knew more."

"We'll have to watch it with Diane too. Once the zombie corgis sniff and find the slavers, she's going to charge in, no matter the odds."

"That's her style: charge first and ask questions later."

"Whew! These flies!" Lulu caught one in midair and added it the pile next to her. "That's forty-two for me!"

"I've got you beat," Sharon said. "I've got forty-three."

"Enough of these flies! I'm hungry! Let's see what's left at the buffet table!"

"One nice thing about being a zombie, you can eat all you want and never get fat!"

They headed up the stairs to the dining room.

After a three-thousand-calorie snack at the buffet bar, they found Diane arguing with Captain Koumondoros on the bridge of the ship.

"No, Captain K," Diane said, using her shorthand for his name. "I want *full speed* out of this ship just as soon as we clear the canal."

"But, Mrs. Newby," Dmitri Koumondoros protested. "We can't go faster until we're out of control of the canal authority and then the Egyptian coast guard." His slightly accented English sounded pained.

"OK, I'll give in. We have to keep the law. But as soon as we're in the Mediterranean, we'll go to max power!"

"Our top speed is just over twenty-seven knots. That's over thirty-one miles per hour. That's under optimal conditions like we had in our shakedown cruise in the Caribbean. With adverse winds and waves, we'll make less than that. Do you know how rough that'll be on the ship?"

"Not as rough as riding a zombie bull at eighty miles per hour while chasing a gang lord!"

"But most of the crew are not zombies!"

"The crew are professional sailors *you* selected. Are you saying they'll be throwing up?"

"No, they all have their sea legs. But the shaking would go on for two days at that speed! It's over eleven hundred nautical miles to Sevastopol, and even at twenty-seven knots, we'll need forty-eight hours. I can't guarantee their alertness or safe sailing."

"Any sailors who can't take it can get off by our V-22."

The captain threw up his hands in exasperation.

"Diane, maybe, for safety's sake, you should let the crew get some sleep," Sharon put in.

"I'm sure they'll be able to sleep once they get tired. Zombies don't need much sleep, but when we're tired, we sleep like the dead!" She laughed.

Zombie jokes arose spontaneously around the Newbys.

After she stopped laughing, Diane said, "Captain, I'm a reasonable woman—at times. We'll start at twenty-seven knots, maximum power. If the first shift of the crew can't sleep, we can slow the ship down—after the first night. How's that sound?"

"Even if the crew sleeps, you may harm the ship. The engines aren't designed for two days of maximum power."

"Oh? What's the worst that could happen?"

"The engines could overheat and seize up."

"We'd fly out then by the V-22 while you repair them. No, Captain, I won't stop or slow to save these slaves, not even for a billion-dollar ship. That's final!"

Captain Dmitri Koumondoros nodded.

"Hey, Lulu, Sharon, let's get General Figeroa on the video conference before we hit the Mediterranean. I want to let him know our schedule and see if he discovered anything else about the slavers. And I want Sam and Lisa in on the convo too."

"It's four p.m. Egyptian time," Lulu said. "That's midnight Eastern Standard, one p.m. on Daylight time. Should we wake him?"

"Oh, he'll be awake. He said he'll live and work in our time zone."

"It'll take about half an hour for an unscheduled call like this."

"I'll get the rest of our team together. See you in a half an hour!" Diane dashed out of the room.

* * *

The six zombies gathered around the video screen table again and called the general's headquarters at the NSA. The NSA seal appeared.

Then the seal dissolved to reveal General Figeroa sitting behind his desk. His trim light-brown hair topped a calm face with a thin nose and lips. Even over the video link, his bright-blue eyes were striking.

"Good evening to you all. This is a little earlier than our regular call. What do you have for me?"

"It'll take us about two days to get to Crimea, General," Diane began. "That's going at maximum speed, which our captain tells me is a little risky. But I can't bear to leave those enslaved any longer than necessary. What further information do you have for us?"

"Nothing more than the slaves are transshipped in the warehouse district of Sevastopol. We have tracked the shipments of slaves from refugee camps and ships to that district, and then they disappear. Not only slaves, but entire trucks vanish. We'll have to rely on the zombie corgis to sniff them out."

"They're good at tracking, but what scent do we use?" Diane asked.

"Our agent has some of the slaves' clothing. She'll meet you when you dock at Sevastopol."

"Do you know how many slaves we're talking about?" I asked.

"Hundreds come in from Africa, the Middle East, Europe, and Asia, and then they are sold to the highest bidders and shipped around the world."

"What kind of security will we have to overcome?" I continued.

"I assume it'll be at least what you saw at Haradhere, possibly more."

"General, the boss in Haradhere knew we were zombies and hit us with saltwater fléchettes. Do you think we'll face that here?" Sharon asked.

"I'd plan for it. Wear your Kevlar armor."

"We'll be conspicuous in Kevlar armor," I said.

"We can just wear loose sweat suits like normal American tourists, George," Diane countered.

"We'll look overweight too. I guess that's a typical American tourist."

"My BMI is twenty-six and a half, so I am overweight. It's my cross to bear." Diane sighed.

"Nope, you're not overweight, honey," I said. "That's muscle weight. The BMI tables are not designed for zombies with our denser tissues and higher muscle percentage."

"You always make me feel better, George," Diane said, batting her eyelashes at me.

"I hate to interrupt this marital bliss," General Figeroa said, "but let's go over your cover stories again.

"Diane and George, you'll just be American tourists on vacation in Crimea with your four pet corgis. Lulu and Sharon, you'll be their dog trainer and translator, respectively. Sam and Lisa, you'll just be yourselves, ace reporters from the *Midley Beacon* looking for zombie stories while you're on vacation."

"Be myself? That I can handle," Sam said.

"Work while on vacation? I always do that! This'll be a cinch," Lisa said.

"I get along with the zombie corgis, but not as well as Diane," Lulu said.

"If they give you any trouble, Lulu, kick them into a wall. That'll get them to submit. It did for me!" Diane said.

"My Russian is good," Sharon said, "but I'll have to brush up on my Ukrainian dialect. I'll do that over the next two days."

"I'll see what I can get out of our personnel in Sevastopol. They're watching the docks and airports carefully, but they can't track every truck or shipping container that goes out of there."

"They put slaves in shipping containers?" Diane gasped.

"They do. Hundreds of slaves are rescued from such every year in Europe alone. Sam and Lisa, you didn't show any identifying shots of the ship; thanks for that. Continue to be careful. We're not censoring your reports—yet. Don't make us do so."

"You know how I hate to be censored, General. I know where the line is," Lisa assured.

"That covers it for now. Listen to your captain. He's a professional sailor. You're professional privateers. Paranormal privateers. Now let's get to work! Figeroa, out."

* * *

After two days of bouncing over the Mediterranean like a truck over rumble strips, the *Resolute Too* slowed and smoothed as it went through the Bosporus strait. Soon we will dock in Sevastopol.

I took advantage of the relative calm and updated my scrapbook. I couldn't add my Egyptian souvenirs while we lurched like an amusement-park ride. I couldn't get the smooth, symmetrical appearance I wanted for each page.

I had a date pit from a bunch of fresh dates brought on board on our Suez journey, and an Egyptian lotus flower, the flower of Egypt. I'd bought some for Diane. After they'd died, I pressed one in a book inside of plastic sheets. It would be the centerpiece of my page. I added some

Egyptian coins and stamps around it. I also had some of those infernal flies that bugged us all along the Suez. Those would symbolize our hardships as well.

Overcome with emotion, unusually so for me, I sniffed. Hmmm. Was I coming down with a cold? I hadn't been sick since becoming a zombie three years ago. Decapitated, dismembered, disjointed, yes. Sick, no. Perhaps some local bug could overcome the zombie bacteria? That was the only explanation.

Diane entered our room. "George, are you getting sick too? Lulu and Sharon both have colds."

"Yeah, I think so. It must be some local bug able to resist our zombie bacteria."

"Weird. Well, I'm hale as ever!" She sneezed.

"Really?"

"Something got up my nose," she said, sniffing.

"Maybe you're coming down with it too."

"Maybe. Sam and Lisa are sniffling too," she admitted.

"How about the non-zombie folk?"

"No, they don't seem to be sick."

"Well, it won't slow us up. We're back up to speed now that we've cleared Istanbul. We'll be in Sevastopol in about twelve hours. I worked plenty of twelve-hour days with a cold when I wasn't a zombie."

"And I've done housework and taken care of the kids when I was sicker than this."

"So we'll be fine."

* * *

A weary and ragged figure appeared on my video screen. His normally massive physique sagged. His face reflected discouragement on its brown features.

"Omar," I said.

"Hi, Grandpa," he said without his usual energy.

"Grandpa" was how all my clones addressed me. They knew me as distantly but vaguely related. I helped them establish and grow their crime empires. They didn't see how I tapped their wealth and knowledge for my own purposes.

"Thanks for getting me out."

The zombies had used their V-22 to fly Omar Ogala from Haradhere to an Egyptian prison. He was wanted there, as well as numerous other places around the world.

It was a big step down for him. The Egyptian prison was a hellhole, and that was before they began beating him. They hadn't started the official torture yet when I rescued him. I used Vik Staskas's cyborg animal technology in my crime empire for years, improving it in many ways. Still, I couldn't beat capuchin monkeys and black mambas as a means of rescuing Omar. I killed half a dozen guards before I found one who was willing to let Omar out to save his life. I killed him after freeing Omar, of course.

"I'm sorry I failed," Omar said, to himself as much as to me.

"Now, let's take this painful lesson and use it to make you better," I soothed him. He was one of my more recent clones, barely thirty years old. He still had the vast potential all of them had, my own abilities and talents.

"I didn't anticipate the zombies would have plastic explosives."

"Yes. Why didn't you strip-search them first?"

"I was so nervous about their abilities, I wanted them enclosed in steel before I did anything. Then I shot them with salt water. I thought I was good for hours yet."

"If you had strip-searched them immediately after shooting them, you would have found their explosives and their zombie blood capsules, as well as their miniaturized headsets."

"What? What zombie blood capsules? What miniaturized headsets?" he asked, startled.

Good. That was his first sign of animation and interest. "Here's your first fail—lesson." I reached to my bookshelf behind me and brought out Andy Zach's book *My Undead Mother-in-law*. "You need to know your enemy. I read Andy Zach's book as soon as it came out to learn how Sid Boffin failed, from the enemies' point of view. The zombies always carry ampoules of zombie blood with them in case they lose their zombiism. Also, although the book was vetted by military censors, certain processes slipped through. One of them was the use of wireless headset communicators so they could stay in touch with each other and their headquarters."

"Oh. My. Bad." He switched from Arabic to English to use the American cliché. Like me, Omar was multilingual, and with an eidetic memory.

"Yes. Learn, and don't repeat your errors. Underestimating the zombies cost Sid Boffin his life, as I reviewed with you six months ago. I can help you in dealing with them." I kept Vik's name secret.

"I wish we could just get rid of zombies for good!"

I permitted myself a grin. "I agree. I have developed a bioweapon to kill the zombie bacteria."

"Great! When will they die?" Omar said with his normal energy and animation.

"I'm deploying it now, as we speak." I like giving out information to my clones in dribs and drabs so they learn to depend on me. It wasn't easy for them to depend on another, nor for me. I didn't even tell them I was their clone father. I let them think I was their grandfather.

"I wish it had been out when they attacked me!"

"It's not easy to deploy. For that reason, I wanted to delay it even more so we could launch it worldwide simultaneously. Your capture forced me to move faster than I was ready. I'm worried about them developing countermeasures to my bioweapon."

"Countermeasures? How can they stop an anti-zombie disease?"

"Like any other disease, they can develop a vaccine."

"Who would care enough to preserve zombies?"

"The United States. They feel everyone has the same rights, even zombies."

"That's crazy. Obviously, the more money and power you have, the more rights you have." Omar shook his head in disbelief.

Good. His spirits seemed to bounce back, enough to argue. "You and I know that, but hundreds of millions of people disagree. One advantage of moving more swiftly than I planned is I'll catch the Newbys off guard, without their zombie powers."

"Do you know where they're going next?"

"It looks like our slave center in Crimea, but I'm not sure yet. They might veer to Bulgaria, where we also have slave factories.

"Now, let's plan where you should go next. Do you want to stay in Africa or go to another part of the world? I can also change your race to anything you'd like."

"Where else could I go? I know and love Africa. I've always wanted to take over South Africa."

"How about Zimbabwe first, then South Africa? My old puppet Robert Mugabe is out."

"Great!"

* * *

Once we docked in Sevastopol, we met General Figeroa's agent. She appeared as a girl selling flowers to the sailors and tourists as they debarked. When she saw us, she said in Ukrainian, "Oh, visitors from the United States! Welcome to Sevastopol! I have a special gift for you!" She took off her hat, covered in colorful flowers, and gave it to us.

"We couldn't take your hat!" exclaimed Diane, with Sharon translating for her.

"I insist! It may be useful." That was the key phrase the general had told us to look for.

Diane and I looked at each other. "We're extremely grateful," she said. That was our code response.

"Use it well!" And she waved and left the dock.

"Sharon, are you sure that was the general's agent?" Diane asked.

"Yes. She spoke Ukrainian, which is slightly different than Russian. Russian is nearly universally spoken in the Crimean peninsula. That was one of the signs."

We went back on board and examined the hat carefully. Several squares of old, dirty cloths were tacked onto the inside of the crown, like padding. We held the clothes to our corgis' noses, to get the scent. Then we, Lulu and Sharon, and Sam and Lisa each walked four zombie corgis through the port district, searching for slavers.

We split the several square miles of the port into three areas and divided up. Sam and Lisa took the eastern third, by the Southern Bay, jutting south from the Bay of

Sevastopol. Diane and I took the middle third, and Lulu and Sharon took the western third. We would call on our communication headsets if we found anything.

Sharon could also provide translation help, if necessary. All of us had become proficient using the translation app while in Somalia. We switched it to translate Russian.

Diane and I walked briskly down the main thoroughfare, American tourists walking their dogs. After picking up the scent, all four pulled at their leashes with their noses to the ground. I held them, and even with my zombie strength and two hundred and fifty pounds of muscle, four forty-pound zombie-strong corgis put a good strain on my arm.

People gave us wide berth, although we'd disguised our zombie eyes with contact lenses. Even the corgis had dark-brown contact lenses. Boy, were those a pain to put in!

We cut down the first narrow alley between buildings. A smiling man came up and spoke. I consulted my phone app. "Would you like to buy some Russian treasures? I've got great deals!" it translated.

"No thanks," I said.

"I insist!" he insisted.

Two men attacked us from behind. One hit me over the head with a club, and the other held Diane's arms. Meanwhile, the smiling man, still grinning, pulled out a gun and pointed it at us.

I shrugged off the blow and held my assailant by his shirt with one hand while holding the snarling corgis with the other. Diane flipped the man over her back, and he lay stunned on the ground.

"You'd better get away now, or these corgis will kill you!" Diane yelled. The phone grated out the translation.

The man laughed and shot one of the corgis. "You're next if you don't empty your pockets of all your money and jewels." His words came through the app translation.

"You beast!" Diane screamed and leapt at him.

He shot her, but it just grazed her side while she ripped the gun from him. The corgi he'd shot bounced up from the ground and charged with its fellows, surrounding him and

Diane, growling like they wanted to tear off his head—which they probably did.

After knocking him down, Diane picked him up and pressed him against the brick alley wall. "Don't you dare hurt my corgis! Or I'll let them get you!"

The slavering dogs ripped off one of his shoes and chewed and ate it before his eyes, fighting over the shoe leather.

His eyes bulged white. I picked up his pistol, while the other two muggers ran away.

"I'll never mug another person!" he screamed. "Save me from those dogs!"

They'd eaten his other shoe and one of his socks.

"Sit. Stay," Diane commanded the corgis.

They sat, growling at the man. She let him go. He ran faster than the other two.

"More proof that crime doesn't pay," Diane said.

"Uh-oh."

"What, George?"

"I've lost some of my zombie strength. I can't crush or bend this pistol." I sneezed.

"It must be the cold is affecting our zombiism! I could barely pick up that man."

"Should we abort the mission?"

"No way! The corgis aren't affected. Let's check with the others."

She spoke into her headset. "Sharon? Lulu? Have you noticed any loss of your zombie strength?"

"Yes," Sharon said. "Some guys harassed us, and we had to beat them up when they attacked us. But we weren't much stronger than before we became zombies. But we haven't forgotten our martial arts training."

"Let me check with Sam and Lisa."

"Diane! I was just going to call you! We found the slaves!" Lisa said.

"Great! We'll be right there. We do have a problem. We seem to have lost some of our zombie strength."

"Uh-oh." Lisa echoed me.

"We'll talk it over when we get there. Meet you there, Lulu and Sharon. Diane, out."

We jogged over to the GPS location indicated by Sam's and Lisa's phones. We weren't as fast, nor did we have the endurance we usually had.

We met Sam and Lisa outside a large, dirty building not far from the South Bay. Their corgis barked furiously at the structure.

"Quiet!" Diane barked.

They ceased their barking but still whined and growled.

I heard the sound of machinery inside.

Then Lulu and Sharon arrived, running with their corgis.

"Here's the deal, team," Diane began. "We seem to have lost our zombie strength, and worse, our regenerative powers." She pulled up her shirt to show an ugly red scrape along her waist where the bullet had grazed her. That kind of flea bite would usually heal within a minute.

"We think it's connected to the colds we've all gotten," I put in. "We think it's a bug we picked up in Egypt."

"I'm definitely going to still attack and free those slaves," Diane stated. "Who's with me?"

"I am!" Lulu yelled. "I hate slavers as much as you do."

"Me too," Sharon added. "I owe you my life, and my life is yours."

"And I'm with you to death—and beyond, honey," I added.

"Um," Lisa said. "Could Sam and I serve as backup? In our last fight, on the yacht, we weren't very effective, even as zombies. We'll record the attack and document it all. If you get into trouble, we'll try to provide a distraction."

"Of course, Lisa," Diane said. "We know you and Sam are journalists, not fighters like we are."

"What's our plan of attack, given we've lost our zombie powers?" Lulu asked.

"First, I want us to go around this whole block and see how large it is and observe all the entrances," I said. "Then we pick the best way in. The corgis should lead the way. They won't be killed by gunfire, but they'll take out any shooters."

I added grimly, "Maybe we'll get to the shooters before they eat them."

"I hope not!" Lulu said.

"I won't shed a tear at that 'failure,'" Sharon said.

"We probably should try to save their lives, if only to stand trial," Diane put in, as if she was trying to convince herself.

I knew her true feelings.

"OK, that's our plan. Let's go!" she instructed.

When we finished circling the block, Diane said, "I counted twenty doors, but no knobs or even locks. If we still had our zombie strength, I'd just bash one open. Anyone got any ideas?"

"It's second-story work," Lulu said. "I was a rock climber and cliff diver in Acapulco before I became a bodyguard. It'll be a cinch to get to the second floor, break a window, and let you guys in—with the corgis."

"What's the best spot for you?" Diane asked.

"Let's go a little further along this side. I remember some smaller windows on the second floor."

Lulu led us to the spot. She pointed to small, dirty windows about fifteen feet from the ground. A blank locked door was below them. There were no obvious handholds in the concrete, but she made a beeline for a drainpipe about fifty feet away.

She put on her Kevlar gloves and shinnied up the drain pipe like a monkey. Then she pulled herself to the window ledge. Balancing, she sidled from one ledge to the next until she stopped by the small window. She punched it with her gloved hand, picked out the rest of the glass, and squeezed inside.

"It's pretty dark in here," Lulu said over the communicator. "This is a factory, and I'm on a staircase landing. I'm coming down to let you in."

The door opened slowly inward. "Good, no squeaks or alarms," Lulu said.

We entered, the corgis pulling for all their worth, feet and nails scraping on the concrete floor. The smell of hot oil and chemicals penetrated our clogged noses.

"Phew! This is no garden site," Diane said. "The corgis led us this far. Let's follow their lead."

The twelve zombie dogs went down a major aisle in the factory. A hundred yards away, we saw some people going back and forth, working on an assembly line. It seemed to be some sort of plastics factory.

The noise increased as we approached the workers. The line made bright plastic toys, and the workers took them off and boxed them. They didn't hear us approach over the noise of the machinery. They were gaunt, apparently with starvation. Manacles weighted their ankles.

They worked like machines: swiftly, efficiently, without ceasing. Three in front of us, then another three on the next line, and so on into the distance. Slave labor.

When they saw us approach, they turned and stared with open mouths. Our mouths gaped back. Their eyes were red. They were zombies!

The corgis ran up to them, wagging their tailless bottoms for all they were worth. They knew zombies when they smelled them. This was what they'd been seeking.

"Oh my goodness!" Diane exclaimed. "Let's free them, George!"

I bent and examined their manacles while Sharon talked with them in Russian. Even with zombie strength, I wouldn't have been able to break the welded circlet. It was designed to hold zombies. The chain was the weak link. Going down the machinery line, I found a tooling cabinet containing a hammer and a chisel. That'd do the job!

Pounding the chisel into a link, I busted it. Turning to the next chain, I broke that too. I freed the other zombies as well.

"They're extremely grateful," Sharon translated for us, "but also very frightened. There's a guard on the catwalk overhead who'll shoot any escapees. They're not afraid of death. They're afraid of more slavery. As zombies, they've been working seven days a week, twenty hours a day, with one meal a day, for over a year. Others are enslaved on the second floor."

"I'll take out the guard!" Lulu climbed the nearest thirty-foot I-beam support to the catwalk. She hunched down in a low profile, then headed stealthily at right angles to the assembly lines.

About a hundred feet away, I saw her climb up the catwalk support to the ceiling. She went hand over hand along a girder parallel to the catwalk and then dropped back down. I heard a yelp and a single shot. Then Lulu, holding a submachine gun, frog-marched the guard to the nearest ladder.

Diane let the corgis loose, and they surrounded the base of the ladder. They leapt like salmon going up a waterfall, trying to reach the bad man on the ladder. He screamed in terror.

Diane reached them and took their leashes in hand. She glared at him and spoke through Sharon.

"Give me one reason we shouldn't throw you to the dogs."

The man spoke wildly in Russian. Sharon translated.

"I'll tell you anything! Just don't let those dogs eat me!"

"How many guards are there?"

"Three on this floor, two on the second floor, and one in the shipping center below."

"You will lead us to each one, and maybe you'll live."

"Anything you say!"

With his help, we captured and held the other two guards. We gave tools to the freed prisoners, and they unchained their fellow prisoners. They numbered almost a hundred on the huge factory floor.

The guards showed us where the food was stored, and we fed the prisoners. We then went to the second floor.

That was worse. The slaves weren't zombies, but sex slaves. We freed another hundred and nabbed the guards.

"Where's the boss?"

"She's downstairs in the shipping room."

We tied the guards' hands with wire behind their backs and put wire nooses around their necks. We hooked them all together with wire, like a line of slaves. The zombie corgis scared them all. I didn't think they'd try to escape.

We descended the stairs to a barren corridor, armed with the guards' weapons. The sentry in the hallway saw us coming and sprayed the corridor with machine gun fire. We let the corgis loose. He winged a few, but they kept coming. When we reached him, only bones were left.

In the shipping room, we found and smelled the worst of all. Hundreds of cargo containers lined a warehouse, each filled with slaves. Many were sick and starving, with no sanitation. We put the guards to work cleaning up. Sam and Lisa came in at our call and opened the containers and fed the slaves, while Lulu, Sharon, Diane, and I raced ahead to the boss's office.

We found a brightly lit, luxuriously furnished room with screens showing views of the factory—and empty. The only place she could have gone was down a dank, square tunnel located behind the office. It spread large enough to hold one truck. Diane let the corgis loose, and they raced ahead.

"Who let the dogs out?" Diane sang.

"Woof! Woof! Woof!" Lulu chimed in.

"Who let the dogs out?" Diane repeated.

"Woof, woof, woof," I barked.

The sound of barking dogs echoed up the tunnel as we ran behind them. Then machine gun fire. Then silence.

The tunnel led downward to the docks along the west side of South Bay. We arrived to see a speedboat racing away, then rise up on hydrofoils and increase in speed. The corgis stopped barking, sat down, and looked at us, panting and licking rapidly healing bullet holes.

"Sharon, can you call the Russian port authority and get that boat stopped?"

"Sure." She'd preloaded necessary numbers into her international phone. She talked a long time and finally disconnected.

"What's the word?" Diane asked impatiently.

"Not good. They didn't believe me about the slavery operation. They knew about the hydrofoil, but that is owned by a prominent local citizen. I gave them this location, and they're sending the police over."

"Let's go meet them," Diane said.

"Maybe we shouldn't," I said.

"What? Why not?"

"How will we keep our cover as American tourists? If they find out we're working with the US government, it'll cause an international incident."

"Now how can we tie this up neatly and keep these slaves free?"

"We're supposed to be here as investigative reporters, reporting on Russian zombies," Sam said. "We have a perfectly good reason to be here. And it was our corgis who found this place."

"Just leave Sharon here as our translator," Lisa added. "You guys hightail it back to the yacht."

"You're right," Diane said. "But what about the slaves? I want to make sure they're all OK and treated well."

"We have the SPEwZ and *Midley Beacon* bank accounts. We can help them," Sam said.

"Also, the Russian government doesn't want to be known as supporting slavery. They've come down hard on other slavery operations—when they're pointed out. They've come under international sanctions for not doing more against slavery. They want to clear their name and ease the sanctions. Crushing this slavery operation would be a diplomatic and propaganda coup for them," Lulu added.

"Sounds good! George, let's get out of here before the police come. C'mon, Lulu. We'll meet you three back on the yacht."

We hustled out of the slave factory with the corgis. The police sirens wailed in the distance. The corgis howled in chorus with the sirens.

* * *

Later, on the yacht, Sam, Lisa, and Sharon debriefed us on what happened after the police showed up.

"The police were madder than wet cats when they realized this really was a zombie slave factory and we were Western media journalists," Lisa said, sounding satisfied.

"Did they cause trouble for you?" I asked.

"Not after they understood we'd give them all the credit for shutting down the operation and freeing the zombie slaves," Sam said.

"Did you offer to help the slaves get reestablished?"

"No, the Russian government wouldn't allow it. After they gave all of them the anti-zombie antibiotic, they promised to give them state-funded apartments and jobs," Sharon said.

"Didn't any want to leave Russia?"

"No, they were all Russian. The non-Russian slaves were transshipped elsewhere," Sharon said. "Also, none of them wanted to remain zombies."

"Why not?" Diane asked, startled.

"The slaves associated their zombie state with slavery and torture. They wanted to be free of that forever."

"I guess we can forget about establishing a branch of SPEwZ here in Russia!" Diane said.

"In Crimea, at least," I added.

"In any event"—Lisa jumped back in—"Sam and I finished our reports and videos of the events and turned them into the Russian authorities. They're going to censor them, I'm sure." Lisa hated censorship. "But we've got the last laugh."

"How's that?" I asked.

"Although they took our memory chips from our cameras and deleted the files from our computer drives, we'd already uploaded the stories and video to the *Midley Beacon*! Won't they be surprised to see the *unedited* stories there and on YouTube!"

We laughed at her snarky announcement.

"I can hardly wait to report to General Figeroa!" Diane exclaimed.

"Why don't we? I'm sure he'll want to know right away," I said.

"It's three a.m., George! He said he'd be on our time, and he's not a zombie. He needs his sleep!" Diane protested.

She was always concerned about others.

"I'm sure he has second- and third-shift support," I said.

"I suppose it can't hurt to try. Let's fire up the video conference!"

Colonel Nguyen answered, one of General Figeroa's subordinates.

"Good evening, Newbys, Melvins, Lulu, and Sharon," he answered in his calm tenor.

"Have we got the news for you!"

"Yes, I just finished reading Sam and Lisa's reports, and I expected you to call."

"I didn't send it to you!" Lisa said.

"We monitor the *Midley Beacon* and your YouTube channel."

"By 'monitor,' you mean spy?" Lisa growled.

"Those are public channels," the colonel replied, unruffled by her accusing tone.

"Do you know where our next assignment is?" I asked.

"We've received an urgent communication from MI6 of the United Kingdom. They have uncovered a terrorist plot to attack downtown London."

"That would be terrible!" Sam said.

"Doesn't the UK have a strict policy against zombies? We entered as undeclared zombies when we went against Sid Boffin's Loch Lomond base," Lisa said.

"Yes," Colonel Nyguyen replied. "General MacGregor well remembers your work there. He spoke of how you risked your lives to defeat Sid Boffin and destroy his base. He strongly recommended Her Majesty's government enlist you again against this threat." The colonel's lips twitched upward on one side. "He must have been effective. We have a personal request from the prime minister for you, and a promise of diplomatic immunity. But they still prefer you to go as undeclared zombies."

"That makes my blood boil!" Diane raised her voice.

Uh-oh. I'd better defuse her. "Diane, zombies are a politically sensitive issue in Britain. The Tories and Labor are each divided on the subject. The people themselves are fairly pro-zombie. If we are successful at getting these terrorists, perhaps that'll push the politicians over the edge. Look at how long it took to get zombie rights in the US."

"You're exactly right, George," Colonel Nguyen said. "I believe the prime minister and the Queen are pro-zombie but can't say so openly. The Queen, because she's officially politically neutral. The prime minister, because half his party is pro-zombie and half is anti-zombie."

"They just want to defend their knee-jerk prejudicial laws against zombies!" Diane fumed.

"The whole world reacted that way against zombies when they first appeared in the US," I pointed out. "People fear what they don't know and understand."

"OK." Diane took a deep breath. "We'll go as normal tourists again."

I knew Diane would see reason eventually. That had been my modus operandi throughout our marriage.

"Now, we're very concerned about your loss of zombiism," Colonel Nguyen said.

"Our cold symptoms have gone away, but our zombiism hasn't returned. We reinfected ourselves and restored our zombiism, but then lost it again." Diane gestured toward her green, non-zombie eyes.

"That looks like an ongoing disease," he commented. "While you're sailing toward Britain, I'll send an F-35 to land on the *Resolute Too* to collect blood samples. We'll diagnose the problem through the CDC and seek a solution."

"When do we need to be in Britain? Do you have any time estimates on this terrorist attack?" Lisa asked.

"No, we've just picked up rumblings on terrorist internet boards of some sort of mass attack. They don't seem ready to move yet. Prepare bugout bags in case we need to fly you immediately to London."

"We've already got them," Lisa said. "That's been our habit for the past three years."

"Great. The F-35 will land on your deck tomorrow morning after you pass through the Bosporus."

We adjourned and went to our cabins.

I settled down with my scrapbook. I had a link from a slave chain, a label from a jar of caviar, a Sevastopol tourist pamphlet, as well as pictures from our attack on the slave factory. I decorated the edge with thin slices of bullets I'd collected off my Kevlar armor and the zombie corgis.

Diane had a new craft project. She was embroidering a black Kevlar sheet with our skull and crossbones Jolly Rogers with the cat's-eye glasses.

Chapter 4

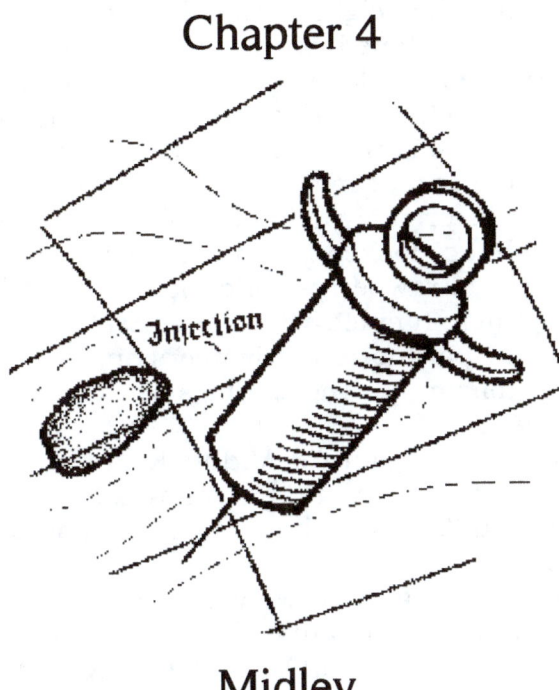

Injection

Midley

Sam and Lisa's reports from Sevastopol hit the *Midley Beacon* office like a bomb. Our website hits spiked into the millions once again.

Now that our editor and founder, Lisa, and her husband, associate editor, Sam, were sailing around the world on their privateer yacht, she'd assigned Charlie Gomez and me, Lashon Miller, as associate editors in her absence. We had to hold the fort in the chaos that was the worldwide zombie news hub, the *Midley Beacon*.

My husband, Rulon Miller, wasn't at all happy about having me away from him two days a week, let alone three. He ran his booming business of manufacturing turkey callers in south Chicago and wanted me to stay home with him.

I hated to leave him. But I loved the excitement of the newsroom and editing stories and seeing them develop. But every time I was away, especially at night, I missed Rulon, even his full, ugly beard.

And even in worldly south Chicago, Rulon and I turned heads. Me, the overweight former basketball player from Gary, Indiana, matched with my bearded, gun-loving, redneck entrepreneur clad in camo. I loved the contrasts in our marriage: black and white, ghetto and redneck.

"Lashon!" Julio Pinkas, our new intern, interrupted my reverie, calling in at my office door. "Did you know zombiism is mysteriously dying out all over Europe?"

His boyish face looked much younger than his twenty-one years. His strawberry-blond hair and smooth pink cheeks didn't help him look his age either.

"I knew our paranormal privateers on the *Resolute Too* lost their zombiism. Are the zombies in Europe also losing it?"

"Yes, and throughout the Middle East too."

"I didn't think there were that many zombies in Europe, let alone the Middle East. I thought a fatwa had been issued against zombies?"

"You're right. That was two years ago. That didn't stop many of the Saudi royal family from getting the treatment and hiding it. Any wealthy people anywhere got the treatment whenever they needed a cure. The same thing happened in Europe."

"This is a good story! Write up how the loss of zombiism is affecting society in Europe and the Middle East."

"I've already done it," Julio said with a self-satisfied smile. "It's in your inbox. That's why I came in here, to get your feedback."

"Let me check it out. I'm not the editor that Lisa is, but I know how to write a story that grabs a reader." She opened her email and clicked on the file.

"You start out well, describing how Europe uses zombie blood for medical cures and then removes zombiism to 'protect society.' Wow! Half the zombie-treated people remain zombies? I had no idea! That's against EU law! Great stat! Let me check your sources. You have an anonymous YouGov poll plus an in-person survey by *Die Bild* Good."

"What else do you have? Man! The loss of zombiism will more than double EU medical costs? People are protesting in the streets to get the government to restore their zombie condition? This'll play big in Europe. Great work, Julio! I'll lead off our European edition with this. I don't think any European news source has this."

"Nope. I checked. What about our US edition?"

"I'll put it on our international news section."

"Not a headline?"

"Nope. The US audience doesn't care about international news."

"Oh." Despite his success, he seemed deflated.

"This is great stuff, Julio! We can't help that the US public doesn't care."

"They'll care if it comes here."

"That's right. That's your next assignment. Find out what the US is doing about this."

He brightened like a puppy with a toy. "I'm on it!" He ran out my office.

What if this disease came here? I got an idea.

I called Don Newby, an advisor at SPEwZ Inc. on IT security. He also served as a conduit to and from SPEwZ to his parents, George and Diane, the CFO and CEO, respectively. This way he learned the family business by relaying their instructions to SPEwZ employees.

"Hi, Don."

"Hi, Lashon. Is this important? I'm in the middle of trying to solve some security problems."

"Yeah, it's pretty important. Your mom and dad lost their zombiism, possibly permanently."

"Oh! Is that the result of that cold they had? I thought that was pretty weird. I've never had a cold since I've become a zombie."

"Yeah. It seems to be a general disease against zombiism. I have an idea. Can you create a Kickstarter campaign to fund research for the disease?"

"Good idea! Sure, I'll get one started this afternoon."

"Send me the link as soon as you do, and I'll advertise it on the *Midley Beacon*."

"Will do!"

Let's see. I'll offer a hundred thousand of the *Midley Beacon's* money, plus a share of the profits from any cure. I guess we'll split fifty-fifty. Lisa would kill me if we didn't get at least 50 percent of any profits."

I sent the details to Lisa in an email, and she immediately called me.

"Hi, Lisa. I guess you got my email."

"Good work, Lashon! Quick thinking on your part."

"Thanks. How about the money I offered and the profit sharing?"

"Change the wording so we'll offer either a hundred thousand dollars or 50 percent profit."

"What will determine which we go with?"

"Whichever leaves us with more money."

"What about SPEwZ? They're the ones sponsoring the campaign."

"OK, let's offer a 'portion of the profits' up to a hundred thousand. We'll split fifty-fifty with SPEwZ since they're behind it and we're advertising. Now I can finally relax and get some sleep."

"What time is it there?"

"Eleven p.m. I've been awake since yesterday. I'm no longer zombie, and I'm getting tired."

"Get rest, Lisa. I've got your back!"

"Thanks, Lashon! Good night."

Later that afternoon Julio entered my office again.

"My report on the research into the mysterious zombie bacteria disease is in your inbox, Lashon."

"Great, Julio! Stay here while I skim through it. Lessee. The military got their blood samples and flew it to their medical base in Germany. They analyzed the blood and shared their data with the Mayo Clinic and the Cleveland Clinic, as well as the CDC. You got all that from Colonel Nguyen, the NSA spokesman.

"All three research facilities just started analyzing the blood data. Hmm...a doctor in the Cleveland Clinic *thinks* it is a bacteriophage? Um, that's a bacteria-eating virus?"

"Yes. I'm learning a lot as a *Midley Beacon* intern!"

"I've been here three and a half years and I'm *still* learning! How do you finish? You checked other virus experts, and they agree.

"This is great stuff! Now, you'll make the headline of our US edition *tonight*!"

"Woo-hoo! My mom and dad wanted me to succeed in journalism!"

"You've done it! Now, follow up the story. What's the ongoing impact in Europe? Where did this virus come from? Who is being affected? Get some human-interest stories."

"Is this the life of a reporter? One story leads to the next?"

"You've got it!"

Julio made me so happy I left the office a little early. I wanted to see Rulon again!

The next day, I entered my home office bright and early. I loved working from home! Three new stories waited in my inbox.

The first one, by our correspondents from Europe, described the protests across Europe. The photos showed the protest signs: *Zombie blood is a worker's right! Stop the zombie disease! Save the Zombies!* French citizens had gone on a countrywide strike to protest the medical disruption. The EU and UK parliaments were debating the issue. The EU said it was a serious problem and assigned committees to look into solutions.

The UK Commons and House of Lords agreed the problem must be solved, but disagreed on the solution. The Lords wanted to create incentives for private enterprise, and the Commons wanted to increase taxes on the wealthy to fund a new government department. They didn't seem likely to reach consensus before our paranormal privateers reached England.

The second article, also from Europe, dealt with human-interest stories of people dying of cancer while awaiting the zombie blood treatment, but hindered by the destruction of the zombie bacteria throughout Europe. Those with money flew to the US, which had not yet been hit by the disease. There were also hints of people smuggling the blood in as "nutritional supplements." I quickly messaged Julio to follow up on these rumors and get some concrete examples.

The third story dealt with the latest research on the virus. The Mayo Clinic tests suggested it might respond to a vaccine. The Cleveland Clinic DNA sequenced it and felt the virus was an artificial construct *designed* to kill the zombie virus. Both findings were confirmed by the CDC.

I called Julio on Skype.

"Hi, Lashon! Which story are you calling about?"

"Your last one. Drop everything and check with the military about the source of the virus. Also get in touch with the paranormal privateers and find out exactly when and where they got their colds. If we can get the origin of this virus, that'll be humongous!"

"Charlie Gomez told me to work on the vaccine angle."

"He's right—that's important too. Let's conference him in." I called Charlie and added him.

"Hi, Lashon! This is a big, exciting story, isn't it?" Charlie said.

"You bet! You've got Julio working the vaccine story?"

"Yes. Both the Mayo and the Cleveland Clinics are confident they can develop vaccines, but they want the federal government to fund them. Congress is debating an emergency measure today."

"I wonder how the SPEwZ Kickstarter campaign is going."

"That's the one you gave free advertising? Let me check the latest analytics. Whoa! We're at ten million dollars and climbing!"

"Great! Give five million to both clinics and tell them more will come. Whoever gets the cure first gets the profits!"

"Good old competition!"

"But in the meantime, who can we put on the origin of the anti-ECHZ virus? Julio found out it was probably artificially engineered specifically to take out zombies' E. coli Homo Zapiens bacteria!"

"We hired a new Egyptian correspondent, Mariam al-Senadi. I'll get her on the story."

"Thanks, Charlie! I can't keep up with all our new employees!"

"Neither can I. I don't know how Lisa does it, but she keeps hiring new people all the time. I have to call our HR manager to find who's on location closest to each new lead."

The rest of the day flew by. The markets crashed in Europe, and the UK because of the zombie blood crisis. Increased medical costs without zombie cures endangered all economies with defaulting on their national debts.

This prompted the EU to move even faster. They voted to fund the committees to develop a solution.

In the UK, people dressed up as zombies, complete with red eye contacts, and carried *Save the Zombies* signs around Parliament and 10 Downing Street. Lloyds of London faced possible collapse because of the numerous claims it faced if the zombie blood supply failed.

Before I knew it, Rulon was coming in the door from the turkey-calling factory we owned.

"I'm home, Lashon!"

Forgetting my work, I ran to kiss him. "I'm home too!"

The next day I actually looked forward to my three-hour drive to Midley. I knew it sounded silly, but being there in person made me feel more like I was in the middle of all the excitement.

In the early morning hours, I scanned for all the new reports for zombie blood news. Most repeated what we'd reported the day before. Then came a breaking story on NPR: the Cleveland Clinic announced they had a vaccine they were ready to test!

Oh no! Who scooped us on that? Usually, NPR picked up its news from other news services. Then the newscaster said, "This story came from the *Midley Beacon* reporter Julio Pinkas." Yay Julio!

As soon as Julio walked into the Midley office that morning, I gave him a hug. "Julio! You scooped the whole nation on the Cleveland Clinic story!"

Big-eyed, he looked up at me. I was six inches taller and a hundred pounds heavier than Julio. Abashed, I realized the hug was unprofessional and probably bordered on sexual harassment. Lisa wouldn't do that. Well, maybe with Sam.

"Sorry. I was just so darned grateful when I heard your name mentioned on NPR this morning!"

"Uh, that's OK. You aren't a zombie, are you? That was a pretty powerful hug!"

"No, I'm just big! I grew to this height by the time I was fourteen. The weight came more gradually."

"Hold back the hugs while I tell you the rest of the story. The air force took the vaccine from the Cleveland Clinic and flew it to the paranormal privateers last night!"

"Do you have that story written up?"

"In your inbox!"

"Of course! While I read it, you call the paranormal privateers and see if they've gotten it yet."

After I read Julio's story about the F-35's supersonic flight from Cleveland to the *Resolute Too*, complete with midair refueling, I scurried out to his desk.

"Any word from the *Resolute Too*?"

"Yes. They tried the vaccine and reinfected themselves this morning, which was last night."

"Success?"

"Complete!"

"Hurray! Let's make this a big banner headline! Isn't this record time for a vaccine?"

"Yes. SPEwZ already has major pharmaceutical companies bidding for it! I checked with Don Newby last night before I went to bed."

"There's your next assignment! Find out about the bidding, who wins, and for how much money!"

"I'm on it like white on rice!"

I read a fascinating story about the origin of the virus from Mariam el-Senadi. The zombies fell sick after going through Egypt's Suez Canal. They remembered only the unusually numerous and aggressive flies. George Newby had saved one in his scrapbook and donated it to the CDC. They found the anti-ECHZ virus all over the fly's feet! The world's medical authorities captured flies all over the Middle East and Europe and found 10 to 90 percent of them coated with the virus. Outstanding! I sent her a note of thanks and forwarded it to our copyeditor for publication.

European journalist Francois Piccard wrote a story about the spike in EU suicides, both from people facing incurable terminal illnesses and from financiers who lost all their investments. I put both stories on our European page, below Mariam's story about the virus origins. I also put the leads at the bottom of the US page. Even the insular US audience would be interested in suicides and the costs of no zombie blood.

"If it bleeds, it leads!"

Which gave me another idea. I wrote an editorial about the effects of the loss of zombie blood in Europe and linked to these stories. I closed with an appeal to support the vaccine research Kickstarter campaign and linked to that. I directed our webmaster to put the Kickstarter ad on the editorial page too.

After lunch, I scanned new stories. The Kickstarter campaign had three avenues for zombie vaccine distribution. First, Amazon sold it, with free shipping. Second, SPEwZ sold it at the same cost, also with free shipping. Third, the government packaged it with the DPT (diphtheria, pertussis, and tetanus) shot given to all children. The shot was renamed to DPTHZ—DPT plus Homo Zapiens, the zombie subspecies. Maggie Newby of SPEwZ appeared on nationwide talk shows and advertisements stating that the zombie vaccine did not cause autism in any of these forms.

The Mayo Clinic and the Cleveland Clinic both recommended everyone get the DPTHZ shots or just the HZ shots. Those without the zombie condition would be protected against the anti-zombie virus in case they ever needed a zombie blood treatment cure. SPEwZ, after using the Kickstarter funds to jump-start the production processes at multiple pharmaceutical manufacturers, allowed them to bid on and sell the vaccine doses. SPEwZ sold the doses at the lowest possible prices, keeping the costs down for everyone.

I couldn't believe it! It was already time to go home to Rulon! I hummed happily as I walked to my car.

* * *

In Tattersalls, a London pub, David Leicester looked up from his half-finished pint of Guinness as a new guy came in. Leastways, he thought the man was new; he looked familiar. The new pubber had a square, muscular build, like a serviceman, but gray hair like David, and light-blue eyes rather than David's gray. The bloke gave him a big smile like he knew him. Then David recognized the guy.

"Paul! Is that you, Paul Huddersfield? I guess your time in the colonies agreed with you!"

Paul had gone to the US to get a special cancer treatment. Although the UK's PHS, Public Health Service, provided service free, the waiting lists for treatment were long, sometimes too long for life.

But Paul looked far better than just healthy. As far as David could tell, flat muscle replaced his beer belly. Further, his face looked less wrinkled and less worried than the last time David had seen him. If it weren't for the gray hair, David would think he was seeing Paul like he knew him in the SAS at forty, twenty-five years ago.

"Let me buy you a pint!"

"I'll never say no to that!" Paul's voice was younger too, stronger, more vigorous than it had been in years.

"So tell me all about the States! I can see the cancer treatment was successful."

"I had a fine time there. They're great people, but I missed my fish and chips and good beer. And my old buds."

"Did they put you on some kind of exercise program? You look brilliant!"

"Thanks, David. You can say that. I got a secret for you." He lowered his voice to a conspiratorial whisper, although no one was within three meters of them at the bar. "I'm a zombie!"

David just stared.

"Yeah, I know I'm illegal. Look at me orbs."

Squinting, David saw the faint line of contact lenses.

"So how does *that*"—David avoided the z word—"make you look twenty years younger? Hell, you look thirty years younger, except for the hair!"

"I feel like I'm twenty years old, full of energy, ready to tackle the world. I'm hungry all the time, and I can eat anything—and drink anything. And my cholesterol went down. In fact, the only drawback I've found is that I *can't* get drunk."

"But what about the anti-zombie law?"

"Shhh! I'm here as an undeclared 'zebra.' Here comes Andy."

Andrew Brown, the third member of their old SAS squad, walked to the bar. "Paul! I hardly recognized you! You look smashing!" Andy looked like a wiry Gollum, short, bald, and skinny,

"I feel smashing too! I'm a 'zebra'!" Paul laughed.

"Right."

"Uh, Andy, 'zebra' is code for," David whispered, "zombie."

"Oh! I think I need a pint of lager!"

Overhearing Andy, Christopher Stewart, the last member of their retired SAS squad, called out, "Get a pint for me too!" as he walked up and sat with them at their table. He was tall and refrigerator shaped and wore a kilt over his hairy legs. The stool creaked as he sat.

"Big news, Christopher," Andy said. "Paul's become a zebra."

"Make that two pints!"

They explained about Paul's new illegal status.

"Make that three pints!"

"I'll have three with you!" Paul laughed.

"We'll make that an even dozen then!" Andy called out.

"Just bring the keg over here!" David cried.

Pint after pint went down the hatch as the old friends shared stories and marveled at Paul.

"So you can drink all night and never get drunk?" Christopher asked sometime later.

"Sorry to say, yes."

"And your beer belly just disappears?" Andy queried, looking at his paunch.

"Right. It took about a month after I became a zebra."

"And all your old aches and injuries are gone, right?" David followed up.

"Right, just like I told you five minutes ago."

"Hell," Stewart exclaimed, "why don't we all become bloody zebras?"

"I'm in!" Andy said.

"Me too," David said.

"You've come to the right man, boys." Paul pulled out three EpiPens from his coat pocket. "One for each of you, guaranteed to make you into zebras! All I ask is free beer for the rest of my life."

"Deal." David agreed. "One, two, ready, go!"

They all jammed the EpiPens into their legs, through their pants—except for Christopher. He pulled up his kilt.

"How long does it take?" Andy asked.

"Not long," Paul said. "Maybe half an hour."

"Might as well keep drinking. I've got a good buzz. I want to enjoy it as long as I can!"

The next week, after buying contact lenses to hide their now red eyes, they met again to plan their new lives as zebras.

As they sat around with their pints, Paul said, "We're in trouble. Did you read the *Mirror* this morning?"

"No," Andy said.

"There's a new disease that attacks only zebras and removes their zebraness."

"Uh-oh. Looks like I'll never get rid of this beer belly," Christopher moaned.

"At least it's down a bit, like mine," David said. He sneezed. "Sorry. I've got a bit of a cold."

"Oh no! That's how it starts!" Paul cried. "The anti-zebra disease, I mean."

"What can we do?" David asked.

"Have you guys ever heard of the *Midley Beacon*?"

"No," Andy said.

"Um, maybe. They're a US paper or website, aren't they?" David said.

"Yeah, they're the zombie news site," Christopher said.

"That's them. They have an ad for a vaccine against this zebra disease."

"What's it cost?" Andy said.

"About a hundred quid online, on Amazon UK. Free shipping too," Paul said.

"I just started a job, so I've got the money," Christopher said. "If you blokes need some help, I'll chip in."

"Decent of you, Christopher. I've got the quid I need," Paul said.

"I'm good. No quid pro quo necessary," David said.

"I've got enough too. Are we in this together? We'll all keep being zebras?" Andy asked.

"All for one and one for all. We're zebras in a bloody zoo!" Paul finished.

"That leaves the next big question," Andy said.

"What's that?" Christopher asked.

"Should we get next-day shipping?"

"Hell yes! I'm not going a day without being able to drink my pints of beer and lose weight!" Christopher almost shouted.

"Once more, all for one and one for all! Let's get a round of beer for the zebras!" Paul said.

Chapter 5

London

"Greetings, paranormal privateers," General Figeroa said to us in our last planning session before London. "Here is the latest intelligence on the London terrorists."

"We're picking up more buzz on the internet about their operations. They plan an attack in downtown London sometime in the near future. There is also chatter about an attack on the royal family."

"Oh no!" Diane exclaimed. "I love the Queen!"

"It's pretty vague. It might be her or her children or grandchildren."

"You've just doubled my motivation!"

"Any luck on finding the terrorists' headquarters?" I asked.

"No. But we've analyzed the messages, and they all seem to originate around a couple of dozen blocks of London. I'm displaying the search area for you on the screen.

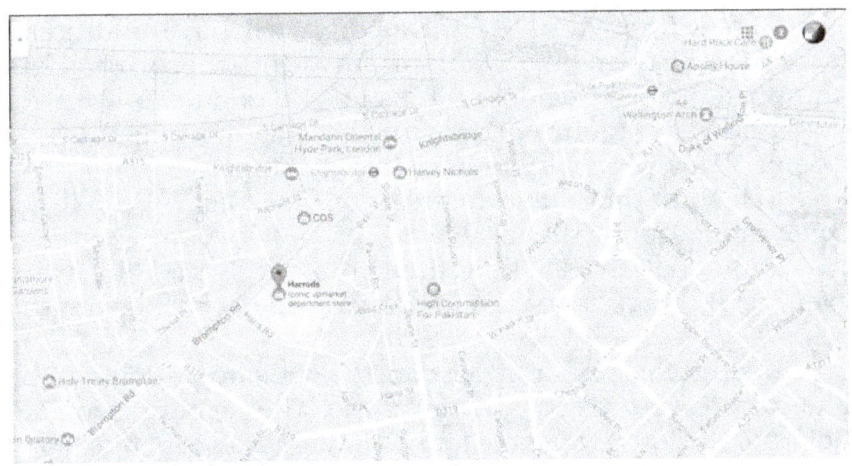

"Oh! Harrods is in the search area! Can we go shopping?" Diane asked.

"If the bloodhounds lead you there." The corners of the general's mouth twitched.

"That's a lot of city to search. And what are we searching for?" I asked.

"These terrorists don't exactly wear name tags. The best we can do is search for their favorite explosives."

"Do you have samples of explosives for our corgis to learn?" Diane asked.

"Better yet, Scotland Yard has trained bloodhounds to sniff out C-4 and other explosives. You can go as American tourists again, walking your dogs. We'll put service vests on them. And you can be blind, deaf, or disabled and go into any building with them. Even Harrods."

"Ooo!" Diane called out. "I want to drive an electric wheelchair! They're so cool. I want one of the two-wheeled ones that goes up and down stairs!"

"I'll be blind," Lulu said. "I'll put my katana in a cane. And I already have sunglasses."

"I'll be a deaf-mute. I'm already good at being mute," I said.

"I'll be different, a narcoleptic with an alert dog," Sharon said.

"Can we just be ourselves?" Lisa asked. "We won't follow you around, but we'll come in afterward and report on the action."

"That's fine," the general said. "We'll have additional forces for backup. We want to surround these terrorists and prevent any suicidal attacks on the populace."

"Can we mix our corgis with the bloodhounds?" Diane asked. "They were very helpful in Sevastopol."

"Yes, but they have to wear service vests too. I'll get some made up for them."

"Don't bother! I'll knit them tonight. I do that every evening to relax. Just let me know the wording on the vests."

"Keep them under strict control. This operation will be like when you freed Dayton from the cyborg animals holding the city ransom—only harder. London has forty times the population of Dayton and is more densely populated."

"The terrorists are willing to die to achieve their goals. But their goals are not merely money. Rather, they use terror to force Britain to conform to their cultural and foreign-policy goals. They use high explosives laced with shrapnel and suicide trucks."

"I want to see one of those suicide trucks try to get my pet bull, Whip," Diane said.

"Let's hold the zombie bulls in reserve, in case we need them. I don't really want them wandering through London," General Figeroa said.

"They're perfectly obedient! To me, at least. But they do take up a lot of room, and they do make messes."

"We can't really plan further until we find exactly where the terrorists are. We'll have our reserve forces in the area and then move to the terrorists. Figeroa, out."

"I really like this traveling and adventure," Diane said. "I've never been to London before."

"Join the paranormal privateers," Sam said. "See the world. Meet strange new people."

"And kill them," Lisa finished.

That evening, I pasted my pictures of Gibraltar, Dover, and the mouth of the Thames in my scrapbook, along with photocopies of my passport, all around the vaccine syringe. Daily scrapbooking was like journaling, only with the daily souvenirs of life.

Diane busily knitted her corgi service animal sweaters. She'd been a fast knitter before she became a zombie. Now her needles clicked like castanets while the knitted material appeared smooth, as if coming off a conveyor line.

I looked at her completed sweaters. "SERVICE DOG NARCOLEPSY ALERT DO NOT PET OR APPROACH HANDLER" said one bright-red vest. "SERVICE DOG IMPAIRED VISION DO NOT PET OR SEPARATE DOG AND HANDLER" a blue one proclaimed.

"I'm doing yours now, George," Diane said. She finished the lettering as I watched: "SERVICE DOG HEARING IMPAIRED DO NOT PET OR SEPARATE DOG AND HANDLER."

"I thought of adding 'may cause amputation in case of petting,' but it was too long. Here is the vest."

"I'd better practice being deaf and mute."

"As long as you keep kissing me, I don't mind if you're mute!"

I practiced.

* * *

Scotland Yard met us the next morning when we docked in the port of London. We divided into three groups to cover the area.

Diane had picked up the special two-wheel wheelchair, iBot, and loved tooling along at six miles per hour. I had no trouble keeping up with her, even as a deaf-mute. If people talked to me, I just handed them my deaf-mute card. The dogs, our two corgis, and two bloodhounds, also in service-dog vests, seemed to love trotting with us.

A yell came over our headsets. It was the Scotland Yard crew, Jerry and Ben, both screaming.

"We've found them! The terrorists! They're on the second floor of Harrods, in the tableware section!" Jerry said.

"We can't get any closer! They've got Tasers!" Ben said.

"The hounds found C-4 in Crock-Pots. When the sales clerks saw us, they shot Tasers at us!" Jerry continued.

"We would have been fried, but our Kevlar vests stopped them," Ben added.

"Now they've surrounded us in the ladies WC, taking shots at us," Jerry interjected.

"We're not far away!" Lulu said. "We'll be right there!"

"George, we're over a mile away, but we're close to our truck, er, lorry holding the bulls and more corgis."

I nodded. We decided killer turkeys and the crowds of London were not a good combination.

Diane jumped out of her wheelchair. "I'm breaking cover! Let's go, George!"

We ran to the truck, about two blocks away.

"Let me drive, Diane," I said.

"Of course. Left-hand driving scares me!"

Left-hand driving just required flipping all my US habits around. Look right first, then left. Keep left. I nosed the lorry into traffic. We drove into the traffic circle off Grosvenor.

"Look for Brompton exit," I said.

We went around the circle. No Brompton.

"Let's try Chesham," Diane suggested.

"We just passed it," I said.

"What about Wilton?"

"You mean that last exit? We can't go back to it now."

"Here comes Belgrave again."

"Let's pull off." I consulted the map on my phone. A pop-up appeared. "Directions disabled by order of the City of London. Please consult an official London cabby," I read aloud, incredulous.

The bulls bawled in the lorry. "There's a taxi stand over there." I pointed.

"I'm on it!" Diane leapt out of the lorry, ran across the busy traffic circle, amid honking cars, and talked with the cabby. She gave him some money and ran back.

"He'll lead us to Harrods!"

I followed him out of the traffic circle. Then I heard in the headset, "Yow!"

"Ay caramba!" Lulu said

"What happened, Lulu?"

"Sharon caught a Taser in the face. She's down! It's way more electricity than a regular Taser. It can stop a zombie!"

"How are you Scotland Yard guys, Jerry and Ben?" I asked.

"We're fine!" Jerry answered.

"After Lulu and Sharon attacked, the clerks left us," Ben added.

"Then we slipped down to the first floor," Jerry said.

"That's the second floor in US terms," Lulu said.

"So if the tableware is on the second floor, that's the third?" I asked.

"Yes," Lulu said.

"What's your situation, Lulu?" I asked.

"I'm using a cutting board as a shield. When the Taser hits it, I cut the wires with my katana."

"Are they going to rush you? Where are you?"

"I don't think so. One tried sneaking past me, and I bowled him down by throwing a mixer at him. I'm guarding the exit to the dinnerware room. They can't leave past me, but I can't advance. I can't leave Sharon anyway. How long until you get here?"

"We'll be there in a couple of minutes."

"We'll need about ten more minutes," said General MacGregor, who was in charge of the backup forces.

"Good! Double backup! Lulu, hang on. We're bringing in the heavies!" Diane said.

"What do you mean?" MacGregor asked.

"Let's see if Tasers can stop zombie bulls!" Diane yelled.

"No! You can't take bulls into Harrods!"

"You shouldn't have Tasers or C-4 explosives in Crock-Pots in Harrods either!"

"It's the appropriate response, General." I tried to calm him.

"Like hell it is! You wait until our backup forces get there!" General MacGregor was losing it. I'd never heard him yell like that.

"There's no way in hell I'll leave my friends in danger, General!" Diane yelled back.

I'd never heard Diane swear like that.

"You hold off until we get there! That's an order!"

Diane snatched off her headset as we pulled up to Harrods entrance on Basil Street. "Tell the general I lost my headset!" she shouted as she ran to open the lorry.

"Diane's having a communicator problem right now," I told the general.

"What kind of problem?" he barked.

"It seems to have fallen off her head."

"Arrgh! Tell her I order her to not enter Harrods with her zombie bulls!"

"Will do, sir," I said, knowing the orders would not affect her.

Diane, already astride her bull, Whip, led three others on Kevlar reins. "Here's your bull, Durham, George. I also have Lulu's bull, Toro, and Sharon's, Wallstreet."

"Can't have too many, I suppose. General MacGregor orders you to not enter Harrods with the bulls, by the way."

"Bull! He's got to work through my superior officer, General Figeroa! I know my chain of command!"

"Why don't you tell him that?" I held out her headset to her.

"I'd better not. He might get him to issue the order! It's better to get forgiveness than ask permission! Let's go!"

On Durham, I followed her and the other bulls through the sliding electric doors of the Basil Street Entrance.

"Uh-oh." Diane perched on her one-ton bull, looking at the narrow, winding stairway to the next floor. "We'd better take the escalator."

The store had been evacuated by this time. Each bull followed Diane up the escalator, brushing the handholds on each side with their huge chests.

Up one floor, two, then three. The moving stairs didn't faze the bulls, who negotiated them as nimbly as gymnasts.

We left the escalator on the third floor and raced through the luggage department. The bulls' horns snagged fine luxury calfskin bags. Festooned by fashion, we raced down a broad hall across the store toward the housewares department. We thundered through the Halcyon Gallery, the exhibit hall where Harrods displayed artworks. Expensive paintings rattled on walls as we rumbled past them, the bulls' rush randomly depositing expensive leather goods everywhere.

We saw Lulu and Sharon crouching outside a doorway labeled *Entertaining at Home.* Lightning bolts flashed through the archway.

Whoa! I thought. That was no Taser. That was artificial lightning! It was entertaining, I supposed.

"I've brought your bulls! Jump on!" Diane yelled. She charged directly into the lightning.

Her sheer audacity saved her. The giant Taser's first shot missed her, singeing the bull's tail off. The pain drove the bull into an all-out sprint. The terrorists behind the Taser saw the two-thousand-pound bull ten feet from them and dove aside. The bull lowered his head and smashed the Taser with an explosion of sparks.

Diane put the bull into an emergency four-footed stop. He skidded, tearing up the carpeting with his hooves and knocking aside heavy, expensive Italian furniture, like Styrofoam blocks. Diane wrenched Whip's head and body around to get back to the terrorists, but I picked up one by the nape of his neck and Lulu picked up the other.

"Where is your boss?" Diane asked.

He spoke something unintelligible in Arabic.

"That's not really credible, that you worked as a clerk in Harrods and don't speak English." I shook him. I intended to shake until he changed to English.

Then Sharon said something in Arabic.

"I'll talk! I'll talk! Don't turn me into a zombie!" he screamed, hanging from my hand.

"Our boss is defending his position in the Cook Shop, the next room over!" squealed the other one, held aloft by one of Lulu's arms. Her other arm held her razor-sharp katana at his throat.

"We know where he is now. Follow me!" Diane reared her snorting bull and charged into the next room.

We followed while Lulu tied up the terrorists using zip ties.

The next room held beautiful displays of fine china in glass cases. There were also complete dining room settings of Wedgewood china and crystal. Unfortunately, the interior designers had not planned for four one-ton bulls charging through the store.

The bulls made the aisles of china accommodate their long horns by swinging their heads back and forth. The glass cases and their precious contents flew backward like KOed fighters. Glass and china alike dissolved into fragments, covering the floor in a random mosaic.

The heavy hardwood dining tables had no greater luck against the rampaging bulls' torsos. Tables and chairs flipped over like cardboard. Oak and cherry splinters joined the glass puzzle pieces on the floor. Champagne flutes flew high into the air like little glass rockets. Sadly, they had no reentry vehicle. Vintage china plates soared like flying saucers and then landed and split into broken wedges like pie pieces.

People's lives are more important than a few thousand dollars of dishes and furniture, I thought as Durham ran over the luxurious rubble.

Then a Crock-Pot zoomed at Diane and Whip from the far wall of the room. It exploded into fragments, shredding Diane and the bull. Covered in blood and stunned, Diane managed to shout at the assailant, "Now you've done it! Now, you've got me REALLY mad!"

Shaking their heads and spraying blood like two sprinklers, Diane and Whip charged down an aisle of Aga ovens toward their attacker. With a stupendous flash of light and heat, one of the large ovens exploded. The concussion knocked me off Durham, hurling us both back into the broken dining merchandise. I had a midair glimpse of seeing Sharon and Wallstreet flying through the air next to me in an oddly graceful ballet. Then everything went black.

* * *

"Hey, look at that!" Paul Huddersfield pointed at the emergency alert on the telly in Tattersalls Tavern.

The four former SAS buddies gathered at the tavern daily. Now that they all were zombies, they drank daily and worked nights, catching a few hours of sleep each morning. Working the night shift while still collecting their pensions made them all comfortable.

"There's some kind of terrorist attack at Harrods!" Christopher said.

"That's only a few blocks away," Andy said.

"My missus just started shopping there now that we have a few more pounds," David said. "Wait! She just texted me! She was in the tea room when the explosions started! She's safe though." David read a series of text messages.

On the telly, the police cordoned off the Harrods block as the last few people ran from the building. Then a lorry pulled up and four bulls got out. A big bloke and a woman rode the bulls into Harrods.

"I can't believe what I'm seeing!" Andy said.

"I can," Paul said.

"What do you mean?" David asked.

"I was in the States for months. That's the undead mother-in-law, Diane Newby, and her husband, George. They fight zombie animals and criminals, and I guess terrorists too."

"We used to fight terrorists. Remember that operation in Libya?" Andy said.

"Yeah, and on the Falkland Islands too," Christopher added.

"Plus dozens of others. We were a good team," David said.

"You know, we could still do it, now that we're all zombies," Paul stated, thinking out loud.

"What do you mean, Paul?" David asked.

"I think we can take out those terrorists right now."

"I guess we're as quick and strong as ever," Andy said.

"Quicker and stronger. At least I am," Christopher said. "I joined a rugby club, and I'm really walloping those losers."

"Isn't that kind of unfair?" David asked.

"Not if they don't find out. And unfair is what you want if you want to win."

"I'd like to work an operation without worrying about being shot," Andy said.

"We wouldn't need body armor," David said.

"Not that we have any. But I've got my old MP5 submachine gun in the glove box," Paul said.

"S'funny you mention that. I've got my MAC 10 submachine gun in my car's bonnet," Christopher said, looking at Paul.

"You wouldn't ever imagine it, but I have my L119 carbine in the bonnet of my old buggy," David said, his eyes shining with excitement.

"Might as well make us four of a kind," Andy added. "I've got a bonnet with a Remington 870 sawed-off shotgun." He paused. "And some R.I.P. rounds."

They all nodded. R.I.P. rounds were perfect for hostage situations. They could penetrate a door or wall and fill a room with tear gas, incapacitating terrorists without killing hostages.

"You know, all these weapons are illegal," Paul commented, as if he were discussing the weather.

"Not if no one finds out," Christopher countered.

"So let's plan our entrance and exit." Paul segued the four bar buddies into a normal SAS team-planning session.

The latest news reports put the terrorists on the third floor. They finished their planning when the live telly showed an enormous explosion blowing out windows on the third floor of Harrods.

"Let's go!" Andy urged.

Five minutes later they were at the Knightsbridge station.

They entered the station and ran underground to Harrods. David knew the route through maintenance tunnels, where he worked for the Underground.

The maintenance tunnel let them out in the subbasement of Harrods. They ran up the still-operating escalators to the third floor. They were not the least tired. Bull dung splattered over the last three floors.

"I scent that we're on the right trail!" Christopher said.

"Right," David said as they raced through the third floor. "I also smell high explosive C-4, unless I miss my guess."

"Ah yes! The smell never leaves you," Paul said. "This is where we split up."

Three of them marched to the three sides of the store and checked the stairs and elevators for terrorists. David tracked the terrorists down to nail them with his R.I.P. shell. The others would get any that slipped away.

David ran swiftly but stealthily along the wide halls of Harrods. He peeked around each intersecting corridor using a small mirror below his gun muzzle. He listened carefully as he ran. That was how he heard someone running down the stairwell at the end of the cross hall after the Halcyon Gallery.

No one was in sight. He sprinted to the steps. In the stairwell, he heard the person a floor below him. He slid down the spiral banister, trying to peer down and ahead.

He saw a running figure, and the person spied him, stopped, and snapped off a quick shot with a pistol. It slammed into his chest like a punch, knocking him off the banister and onto the stair.

"Good shot," he said to himself, even as the stab of pain faded. "Too bad for you I'm a zombie! Don't bring a pistol to a shotgun fight."

He shot the figure down a floor and a half. He aimed more by sound than by sight. The R.I.P. shell didn't need to hit the person. Hitting the floor, a cloud of tear gas instantly filled the stairwell. Helpless coughing replaced running.

"Gotcha!" David said as he hauled the figure up by his hoodie.

"Is that you, David?" Paul called, running from the third floor.

"You bet! I got his ugly ass!"

"Good job!" Christopher added, running behind Paul.

"I'll buy you a pint for that!" Andy yelled, bringing up the rear.

They put on their portable gas masks, but they didn't need them. Their zombie bodies shrugged off the irritating gas and healed instantly.

"This was the only one I found," David said.

"I found two tied up in Entertaining at Home. They claimed to be hostages, and they had store clerk uniforms, but one of the zombie women met me and told me they were terrorists," Andy said.

"So there were survivors from the blast?" Paul asked.

"At least three of them survived. They didn't know where Diane's body was. She was the one right next to the explosion."

"Ouch!" Christopher winced. "I saw the damage from that, and I was coming from the other direction!"

"Let's see who we've got here." Paul picked up the coughing figure and tore off the face mask and hood.

A skinny, bearded youth's face wept and coughed.

"Let's go back to the third floor and interrogate this bastard."

They ran up the stairs, carrying the coughing youth. Before they arrived, the youth tried to talk. "S-Stop! Y-You gotta stop!"

"My! Isn't he the talkative one!" Christopher said. "Who are you? What's your name?"

"D-Doesn't matter! The whole store will blow in five minutes!"

"Oh-ho! No torture is necessary! Too bad," Paul said with an evil grin. "So where's the bomb?"

"All through the store! The whole block is wired with C-4!"

* * *

I groggily rose to my feet. Durham snored nearby beneath a pile of Aga ovens and shattered shelves. The air reeked of smoke. Somewhere, a fire crackled merrily.

Once again, my shredded Kevlar armor showed many holes with pink skin. One hole slowly ejected a steel shard as my body healed.

Diane. Where was Diane? She had been ahead of me, closer to the explosion. I staggered forward, shambling like a zombie. Then I jogged, my panic growing.

All the room's furnishings had been swept in a circle by the blast and heaped up against the walls. The windows gaped empty, letting the smoke escape. *Where do I start?* I thought as I surveyed the mounds of appliances and furniture around the room.

Just begin. I trotted to the nearest mound and pulled it apart. Nothing but Crock-Pots, cooking utensils, and wrecked display cases.

Next heap had a smashed computer and stainless steel refrigerators, now suitable for scrap. Next to that lay broken furniture, chairs, and tables.

What's this? A large trail of blood led under another pile of stoves and microwaves. I tore it apart and found a bull. Or part of it. The barrel-like torso of a bull, squished against the wall, oozed blood in a widening pool.

That could only be Whip. The biggest piece of him was too small to regenerate. Oddly, I mourned. Diane and he had seen many adventures together.

"Arf!" A zombie corgi pulled and gnawed at the bull and looked at me, expecting me to do something.

"Too big for you to bite, little fellow?" I easily moved the carcass away from the wall. It only weighed a quarter of a ton. I felt better, but I had a hole in my heart only Diane could fill.

The corgi, rather than eating the side of raw beef, ran to the corner between the wall and the floor and whined. An unrecognizable bloody mass lay there. Then I saw the mashed cat's-eye glasses.

"*Diane!*" ripped out of my throat.

I cradled what was left of Diane in my arms. Like the bull, all that was left was the torso.

Some guys in camo gear found me rocking her remains in my arms and crying.

"Sorry, old man. A friend of yours?"

"My wife," I sobbed.

"Um, wrap her up and get out of the store. It's going to blow in a few minutes."

"OK." I took off my torn armor and wrapped Diane in it. Then his words registered. I'd better hurry. Carrying the last bits of Diane, I ran to the open window and jumped out.

* * *

David peered into the timing mechanism of the bomb while standing on the toilet. The terrorist leader, Syd Smith, led them to it, in the tank of a WC (water closet), all the while screaming they couldn't stop it and he was going to die.

"This is well wired. If I cut the power here"—he gestured to a wire—"it blows up."

"Can you stop the clock?" Paul asked.

"Hmmm. It's electronic, not mechanical, so that makes it harder. Let's see if I can isolate it."

"How much time is left?"

"Oh, about three minutes."

"What else can we try? Christopher and Andy are clearing the building now. Here they are."

"All clear," Christopher said.

"We found three zombies from the US. They're the ones that found and charged the terrorists," Andy said. "We also found the remains of a bull and their leader, Diane Newby."

"That's tough," Paul said.

"Yeah, her husband George took it hard. He jumped off the third floor holding her body," Christopher said.

"That makes it only two survivors then?"

"Nah. He landed fine. He cracked the concrete of the sidewalk though. What's the word? How much time do we got?"

"Two minutes," Paul said, eyeing the digital timer. "Should we split now, David?"

"I almost have this... Shit!"

"That's never good to hear with a bomb!"

"We're down to a minute, but I couldn't short out the circuit."

"Short the circuit?" Christopher said.

"Yeah, I need more voltage."

"Hell, I can solve that!" He grabbed the roll of wire David brought with him for his explosives and yelled as he ran out, "Place that where you need to!"

"You guys better go," David said.

"We're in this together," Paul said.

"Anyway, we're zombies!" Andy said. "Although, I saw my first dead zombie after that other explosion."

"What's Christopher going to do?" Paul wondered.

"Whatever it is, he's got ten seconds," David said.

"Maybe the giant—" Andy began.

ZAP!

Sparks flew from the wire as it vaporized from the massive pulse of electricity. The clock circuitry fused solid by thousands of volts of electricity. David's hands flew away from the bomb's timing mechanism, convulsed by the charge.

"You OK, David?" Paul asked.

"Uh, yeah?" David stared at his blackened hands as the skin peeled off, revealing new skin below.

"Are you guys alive?" Christopher yelled as he ran into the room.

"Brilliant, Chris!" Andy said. "What'd you do?"

"I hotwired the Taser's power into David's wire."

"Good job, Chris," Paul said.

Soldiers peered in at them from the door. "Hold it right there. Drop your arms."

MacGregor's backup forces had arrived.

"Hey, we're undercover SAS forces. We've got one more terrorist here." Paul pointed to a gibbering, weeping, bearded youth next to them, tied with wire. "I hope you enjoy interrogating him."

"Come with us. I'm sure General MacGregor will want to talk with you."

"OK. Guys, let's go."

Their impromptu SAS team fascinated General MacGregor. "So you guys paved the way for the Falkland Island invasion? I was in the initial landing force," he said.

"Yup. And now we led the assault on Harrods," Paul said.

"I heard you got another one of those terrorists. We've been questioning the first two, and they've been singing loud and long. We're taking them through Harrods floor by floor, clearing out all the explosives."

"Yeah, here he is. Don't get too close. He stinks. He says his name is Syd Smith."

The terrorist had replaced his fright with sullen silence.

"I smell what you mean. He'll get plenty clean once we waterboard him."

"Isn't that illegal?"

"Oh, I misspoke. We'd never do anything illegal to a murderous criminal. Maybe we'll turn them over to the paranormal privateers. They're not so bound to keep the law as we are."

The terrorist leader's eyes widened and lips tightened.

"Take him to Scotland Yard. They've got the best terrorist interrogation unit." After Syd Smith was hauled away, General MacGregor said, "I've got to see the paranormal privateers from the US and give my condolences about Diane's death. I worked with them. They were crazy, especially Diane, but fearless, and they got the job done."

General MacGregor found the zombies huddled around their lorry. Three bulls were in a pen, and a pack of corgis on leashes yipped around them.

George looked up as MacGregor approached. George's square, massive face was grim.

"George, my deepest condolences for your loss."

"Thank you, General MacGregor, but all is not lost yet."

"What do you mean?"

"Diane's body is slowly regenerating."

"That's spiffy! How long do you think it'll take? I remember when you and Diane were crushed in the collapse of the criminal headquarters in Loch Lomond. It took you three or four hours to regain consciousness."

"Diane's a lot worse off than that. We merely broke all our bones and internal organs then. She's lost all her limbs and her head and parts of her torso. She's barely got enough body mass to regenerate at all. She's recuperating very, very slowly." He sighed. "We have no experience with this level of injury. It might take weeks, or months, or fail altogether."

"Is there anything I can do to help?"

"If only we can get some calories into her. Her heart and lungs are working, and her skin has closed up, but the zombie bacteria need calories to grow. It's just cannibalizing her other tissues now, and she needs everything she's got!"

"Would an IV feed of glucose help?"

"I think it might!" Hope brightened George's voice.

"I'll send a medic over."

* * *

Syd Smith arrived in a police wagon at Scotland Yard, wearing a hood that blinded him. Soldiers led him through a maze of halls and corridors and then down an elevator to a windowless room, where the hood was removed. Then they cut off his clothing while leaving him in cuffs.

"Hey! My privacy is being violated!" he protested.

"That's not all that will be violated. Look at that!" exclaimed the male sergeant removing the clothing.

"So. That's your first lie, 'Syd.' What's your real name?" asked a plainclothes inspector.

"Synthia, with an 'S,'" she said proudly, now standing tall and naked and not cowering.

"So what's up with the stink? You have to bathe before we can talk."

"That's my defense against my fellow Muslims, to keep them from finding out I'm female. They're all misogynists, and if I stank, they kept away from me."

Even her voice sounded different, sure and confident.

"Walk under the shower. The sergeant will wash you."

A grim-faced female did the task efficiently and ruthlessly.

As the sergeant toweled her off and then dressed her in a one-piece orange smock and pants, the inspector chatted with her. "Now you said 'fellow Muslims.' Are you Muslim? Don't you agree with the treatment of women by Muslims?"

She barked a laugh. "My opinions don't matter. My religion doesn't matter. All that matters is the mission."

"What's the mission?"

She looked him straight in the eye and said with complete sincerity, "The total subjugation of Great Britain."

* * *

"She's a cool character, isn't she, Sergeant Calloway?"

Ann Calloway looked into the blue-green eyes of her boss, Inspector Mark Greenstreet. She thought before answering. She always thought, all the time, much more than she spoke.

"She's a remarkably different person than she was as a man. That makes me wonder if this personality also is fake."

"I guess we'd better assume so. I think I'll start off the interrogation trying to find out her other contacts, especially her superiors."

"I heard General MacGregor threatened to turn her over to the paranormal privateers."

"Yes, I've never contradicted that. I'll hint that'll be a possibility. I don't know what they did with the first two terrorists, but I've never had such cooperation."

"Why don't we cut to the chase and do that with her? Better yet, find out how they get such cooperation?"

"Good idea. Go to them tomorrow and find out. I'll do what I can. I have to do my job anyway. And in this case"—Mark's normally cheerful appearance turned grim—"I'm *really* looking forward to the interrogation."

* * *

I examined my cell methodically. A drainpipe, two inches in diameter. A toilet. A hard bed. A steel door with hinges on the outside. I'd probably need to escape from somewhere other than this cell. Once they established a routine with my interrogation, I'd look for escape routes.

I chuckled to myself. Synthia Smith was my true name, in the sense it matched my birth certificate and other current identification. Before Synthia Smith, I was Rachel Rathbone, and before that Quinella Quincy, and so on, through the alphabet. My earliest memory was a toddler named Betty Botter. I had to be cute and pick pockets. Who knew what my original name was? Changing identities was standard procedure for me with each new assignment.

This had been my most challenging operation, and I'd *almost* pulled it off. Those damn zombies! Had I blown up Harrods, the demands for billions in exchange for each national landmark's safety would have been credible.

They had no idea of the bigger picture—and they wouldn't get it. My terrorist cover story was completely true, but neither the terrorists nor Scotland Yard knew they were merely a means to an end. I gave them the truth: total subjugation of the United Kingdom was a reasonable goal for one like me, a child of the world's greatest criminal.

I knew more about Papa Smith, my ostensible grandfather, than any of my siblings. I think I actually touched his feelings as a loving granddaughter, and I think he shared more with me than with any of his other crime-lord grandchildren. Of course, he might be manipulating me, just as I tried to manipulate him. That was the most reasonable assumption, especially if we were actually related.

Regardless, I felt fond of him. When I overthrew him and took over his crime empire, I thought I'd keep him alive. I enjoyed our talks via our secured video line. When he'd shared Sid Boffin's failure with me, I clapped in delight as he praised me for staying in touch with him. I think that was genuine emotion and not an act. It was hard to tell sometimes.

A motion on the floor caught my eye as I sat on the bed. A cockroach crawled up the drain and onto the floor. Surprising. Usually, Britain kept their prisons pest free. Then another. Then a dozen more. Then hundreds.

This was not normal cockroach behavior. They did not come into the light in hordes. I sat cross-legged on the bed and watched the swarm with fascination. They climbed the door, walked its steel perimeter, and went back down the drain as others came up.

Curious, I nabbed one using my lightning reflexes. Examining it, I saw a metal dot under its thorax and a narrow tube attached to its abdomen. A pungent, acidic smell came from the tube. I looked back to the door. The acid ate a narrow trench in the door's perimeter, right where the cockroaches still marched. Near the ceiling light, I saw mist curl away from the door.

Modified and controlled cockroaches—like Sid Boffin's cyborg-controlled animals. I'd read his PhD paper as well as the *Midley Beacon*'s declassified reports on his battles with the zombies. Since Sid was dead at the bottom of the Gulf of Mexico, this could only be one of my siblings or Papa Smith trying to rescue me.

Using my perfect memory of the twists and turns when they'd led me here hooded, counting my steps, and remembering the doors, I was confident I could retrace the route.

The last of the cockroaches marched around the door, leaving its trail of acid. They etched the door perhaps a centimeter deep. Couldn't be much left.

I knocked on the door. Yes, it felt like a centimeter thick, and it echoed like it was almost cut through. Then someone knocked back, much harder.

"I'm here!" I called. I assumed this was my rescuer.

"Step back," grated a curious, tinny voice, like it was coming through a small radio.

I stepped away.

CLUMP! CLUMP! Two metallic thunks hit the other side of the door. Then, SKREERK! The door tore off like the lid of a tin of meat.

I didn't expect what I saw. A male silverback gorilla filled the doorway and the whole hallway beyond. Thick armor covered his body. Casually, he placed the door scrap against the hall.

"Follow me," he said.

We didn't return the way I'd come. Rather, we went to the guards' office. Two men lay on the floor, dead. Beyond the office was a hall leading to the bathroom and a utility closet and an elevator. We went into the utility closet, in which the back wall swung away into a tunnel.

"Go there." The gorilla pointed.

I followed the tunnel, observing the LED lighting and concrete wall. This kind of long-range planning was exactly what Papa Smith had taught us.

Before I came to the end, a quarter of a mile away, I heard the heavy padding of the cyborg gorilla following me. The tunnel dead-ended in a concrete room without doors or windows. The gorilla dragged in the two guards' bodies. A black mamba followed, its metallic cyborg controller shining on its head like a silvery yarmulke. Now I knew the cause of the guards' deaths.

"Allow me," the gorilla said. He pushed the base of the wall, and it ground upward on a hidden hinge above the ceiling. I dashed through the opening.

A rather prosaic car park greeted me. A hackney cab waited, motor running.

"You're polite, aren't you?" I felt giddy at the prospect of freedom, so I bantered with whoever controlled the gorilla.

"You're my guest," the tinny voice replied. It emitted from the scalp, not the mouth of the gorilla.

He dumped the bodies of the guards in a nearby dumpster. We entered the hackney.

The gorilla filled the backseat, while I faced him.

"A little privacy for you," said the cabby.

Window shades descended, hiding us.

"Where to, guv'nor?"

I suspected the accent was a put-on. It was too cliché.

"Grosvenor House," the gorilla said.

Grosvenor House was a nearby luxury hotel. It didn't seem quite the place to take a five-hundred-pound silverback gorilla, nor an escapee from Scotland Yard, but everything else about this escape had been flawless. I was sure Papa Smith had a plan.

"Here are your clothes." His apishly long arm reached to the front luggage area and pulled out a Louis Vuitton leather backpack. I looked inside. A chic black silk dress, black stiletto heels, with matching bra, panties, and hose fit neatly inside. A tiny black clasp purse lay at the bottom. Thoughtfully, someone had packed wipes as well as a comb, a brush, and makeup.

"Change before we get there," grated the gorilla's mechanical voice.

I ripped off the orange jumpsuit and popped on the clothing quickly. They fit perfectly. The gorilla held up a hand mirror while I finished my toilette and applied my makeup.

The purse held a credit card made out to "Tallulah Talent," a thousand pounds of cash, and a room key. Suite 1.

So. This assignment ended and the next began.

We arrived at the hotel. The gorilla stayed in the cab. The cabby took my backpack and handed it to the doorman. I walked confidently to the elevator to suite 1.

I entered the opulence of a penthouse. What a break from being filthy and hanging around with terrorists! A beautiful view of Hyde Park and delicious smells greeted me.

I hadn't realized how hungry I was. A gourmet meal with fine wine lay on the dining room table.

After eating, the large television screen flashed on. Papa Smith beamed at me, his salt-and-pepper pompadour gleaming in the bright sunlight somewhere. I wondered where he was.

"Greetings, Tallulah! Are you feeling better?"

"Quite. Thank you for rescuing me, Papa." I kept my enthusiasm down, so as not to seem fake, but amped up my earnestness.

"First of all, the failure of your mission is entirely my fault, not yours."

That was good. I knew Papa dealt patiently with failures, using them as teaching exercises. But repeated failures—and betrayal—led to death.

"Thank you, Papa."

"Reviewing what went wrong, the zombies showed up. But not the zombies we worried about. You dealt with them quite effectively. Diane Newby is dead. Again. Probably." He sighed. "That's the problem with zombies. They don't stay dead.

"No, our problem was a group of undeclared illegal zombies, former SAS members, as far as I can tell. I didn't know anything about them until they showed up in Harrods. They stopped your bomb and they nabbed you with tear gas.

"That's the first thing we can do—get you a portable gas mask as a part of your standard kit. Your purse's interior lining comes out and becomes one."

"Ah. That would have helped."

"Nice shot of your shooter, by the way. Had he not been a zombie, he would have died."

"I thought he was dead."

"Naturally. In a world with zombies, we must expand our thinking, me quite as much as you."

"Isn't that the nature of life? We're always learning new things."

"Indeed yes. I will address the zombie problem—again. They've developed a vaccine against my anti-zombie virus. Meanwhile, here's your new assignment."

I listened while gazing on Papa Smith's face and analyzing the background. Definitely south of England, probably the Mediterranean. Or maybe that was what he wanted me to think. Then the import of the new assignment dawned on me. This was a golden opportunity.

* * *

General Figeroa rubbed his hands over his eyes. Then he took out his bottle of ibuprofen. *I should buy stock in this company, with all the headaches I get*, he thought. But the headaches came with the job.

He'd known what was coming when he'd taken his boss's old job, assistant to the NSA head Junia Lyndhurst. It had nothing to do with the fact she was a zombie. He worked frequently with zombies, first with Sam and Lisa Melvin during the zombie turkey apocalypse and then with the Newbys fighting Sid Boffin.

No, his problems were far worse than zombies: politics! *Everything* he did had political ramifications, and even when he did everything perfectly, another politician might do something that changed all the political rules. He much preferred strategizing against a hundred thousand carnivorous turkeys!

Then there were his operatives. Although his title was assistant for special operations, what was really meant was he was in charge of all the zombie agents in the NSA. That included the six paranormal privateers on the *Resolute Too.* He loved their bravery, their patriotism, their creativity. In many ways, they were ideal American citizens and agents. But that was the issue: they weren't exactly agents—they were private citizens hired to do the worst and most difficult jobs the US couldn't or wouldn't do with the military.

They'd done a flawless job with the Somalian pirates, wiping out their boss and changing them into a peaceable Somalian coast guard. They followed that success with their coup against human trafficking. The State Department was still milking the political capital that generated with the US public and the Russian government.

But now, Harrods. It wasn't merely they'd ridden their zombie bulls through the country's premier luxury store and then blew up the cookware department. Those little peccadillos were easily covered by saving the entire block from destruction by the terrorists.

No, it was the fact that zombies had snuck into England against the law and caused death and destruction. Anti-zombie protest groups marched in Hyde Park. Her Majesty's government, staunchly defending the zombies, was threatened with overthrow by the opposition.

Were these anti-zombie groups the source of the anti-zombie bacteriophage? Or was it one of the Islamic imams who had issued fatwas against zombies? Or perhaps some of the US churches that proclaimed them spawn of Satan and a sign of the end times? Even some of the voodoo religions in the Caribbean were adamantly against zombies Perhaps Sid Boffin come back from the dead? Or maybe he never died at all and had faked his death for the third time? No body had ever been found after his sub had sunk in the gulf.

The anti-zombie bacteriophage had to come from *somewhere*. The US medical centers all agreed it was man made, like the original GMO corn that caused the zombie turkey plague. Just knowing there was a sophisticated bio lab out there with hostile intent toward zombies—and by proxy, the US—made his blood run cold. They could reintroduce the Spanish flu and make it drug resistant! They could do the same with the bubonic plague. And his job was to find them. No wonder he had daily headaches.

"Ramon?"

His boss peeked in his door. Concern lined her pleasant face. Immaculately dressed, as always, she looked quite as good as Condelezza Rice had in the NSA role, and she was equally popular with the public.

Her eyes glowed red. She had gotten the zombie blood treatment to combat fatal lymphoma. Like the Newbys, she enjoyed her zombie energy and wellness. Not only did she refuse the zombie antibiotic, but she even refused to wear the contact lenses most zombies used to hide their red eyes.

"I can't hide I'm black, and I don't want to. I'm not going to hide my zombiism either," she'd said.

"Any progress?" she asked.

He knew what she wanted. The same thing he did: the source of the bacteriophage.

"Only headaches. Want one?"

"No thanks. I've already got one. What are your most promising leads?"

"I've filtered my threat list by who would have the biological capability and who would use it against zombies. We have several hostile governments, one of which is Russia. I'm thinking of taking them off the list because of the Crimean incident and our improved relations with them."

"Don't until we know for sure."

"I also have China and possibly North Korea."

"I wouldn't think the Norks would have the technology."

"They could have been given it or stolen it. And they are smart, even if we think Kim Jung-un is a nutcase."

"I can see why you're not in the State Department." She smiled. "Anyone else?"

"There's still a possibility that part of Sid Boffin's crime empire is intact. In fact, I'm almost sure of it, given the latest report from Scotland Yard."

"What report?"

"The lead terrorist the zombies captured, Synthia Smith, has disappeared from their maximum-security cell."

"Somehow, the cell door was etched with acid from the inside and then ripped from the doorframe, probably by magnets. The two guards on duty on that level have disappeared. The security cameras were all disabled on that level, also by acid."

"Any theories?"

"The guards are probably dead. This is similar to when Sid Boffin hijacked the cargo plane of zombie blood. The same MO could be used by someone else in the criminal network. What really scares me is that this hypothetical criminal also has cyborg animals."

"Do you think he might use them like Sid did, to steal and extort?"

"Worse. I fear he's using them and we don't know why or how or where!"

* * *

I said goodbye to Tallulah Talent and hummed with anticipation. She should easily be able to accomplish this plan. She was my most promising child: only twenty-two and close to becoming a regional crime lord. I was so proud of her.

She was also one of the few of my children I had not caught lying or plotting to overthrow me. That meant she was exceptionally good at acting and deception. I assumed all of them wanted to overthrow me; it's what I would do. And as my clones, they were like me, with their individual differences.

Having a hundred and twenty years of experience as a criminal counted for a lot, especially with an eidetic memory. I'd seen it all, and I'd conquered all. Except for the zombies.

My humming turned into a growl. I had another bioweapon at my disposal. I wouldn't err like I had in Europe, rushing its deployment. I'd hit the whole world at once and wipe out all vestiges of zombie disease in humans.

The CDC had discovered I used flies to deploy the bacteriophage. I'd use ants and beetles next time. There were plenty worldwide. Maybe some termites too? Why not? Bees? Sure! I'd put it on fleas too. Then to complete the assault, I'd place it in microbeads in all deodorants manufactured in the US and Europe. The zombies wouldn't escape this time!

I worried only about the time I needed. It'd take a month to deploy the new disease. What damage could the paranormal privateers do in that time? I shivered to think.

When I worried, which I did daily, I listed all my worries and then planned to deal with each one. This'd take some time this time.

Chapter 6

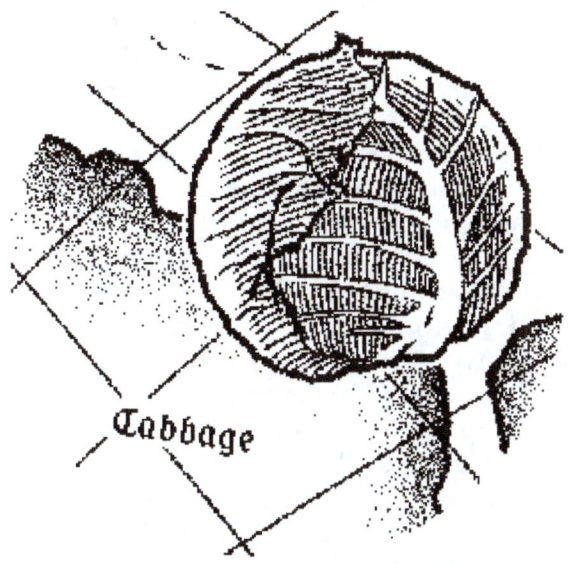

𝕮𝖆𝖇𝖇𝖆𝖌𝖊

Tumen River

I huddled by the bank of the Tumen River, watching, listening. I hadn't seen guards in half an hour, but that meant nothing. Their patrol patterns were erratic, and sometimes they'd stop undercover and have a smoke, watching for escapees. Like me.

Just yesterday I'd been a respected North Korean army sergeant, Kim Chi-un. Now I hid from my own army.

I hungered, but that was nothing. I had survived the famine of the nineties, when I'd almost died. I didn't know what my parents had done, but we'd received a kilogram of rice and survived. I know they did something, probably illegal, to live.

That was what had driven me into the Communist Party, spying on my classmates, reporting on my parents, joining the army as a teen. I never wanted to feel that kind of hunger again.

Now, a different hunger drove me to risk my life, betraying my homeland of North Korea. I thought nothing could be worse than the famine I'd suffered as a child. I was wrong.

Because of my good army record, I'd had the privilege of guarding Kim Jung-un when he'd traveled to my home, North Hamgyong Province. My military commanders disillusioned me by jockeying for political advantage, but I'd trusted the Great Successor to straighten things out.

There in the port Kimch'aek, I'd seen Kim Jung-un lose his temper at my fellow officer and friend, and have him shot—by me. I had to shoot him, or I would have been shot too. I did what I had to, to survive. He died quickly, thanks to me. But I also began dying that day.

My bullet tore out his heart. Now my heart had a hole it, and my soul bled out. I killed the last person I admired and respected. I wanted to quit the army right then, but my elderly parents would starve.

So I had continued my mindless service. Sometimes we'd harvested grain, sometimes we'd shoveled show, and sometimes we'd built walls or a road. The army was really governmental slave labor. I had no hope of advancement or desire to play the political game. All I'd wanted was out. But I'd been trapped between my desire to commit suicide and my duty to my parents.

This past year, my mother died of cancer, and then my father in grief had a heart attack. Good for them. They no longer suffered like I did.

I'd begun planning my suicide carefully so none of my remaining relatives would be blamed and killed or imprisoned. Then I'd met smuggler Park Sun.

We had sat together by happenstance at a tea shop.

"I see you're a soldier," he said. "I'm in the import-export business."

We both knew that meant he was a smuggler. That was illegal, and I was supposed to arrest him. If he was smuggling for my superior officer Lee Sung, I would be reprimanded or imprisoned. I had already been through that once, after reporting on a superior officer.

"That's very interesting," I said. "Would you know my commander, Lee Sung?"

"I might," he said. That meant yes. "Is there anything I could get for you?"

"Oh, I don't know. Do you have any chocolate?" I asked for something frivolous and hard to get, thinking it would put him off.

"I might," he said. "It would be a hundred won."

That was a day's wages, probably for a small bar.

"It must be very difficult to get such goods."

"Not for someone who knows how."

"If you know how, then do you know how to transport out of North Korea?" This had a double meaning. I might mean send out goods without government inspection. Or I might mean smuggle a person out.

"I might be able to manage. What goods do you have to transport?"

"Just one item, but it's rather large. About my size." I gestured the length of my body.

"That would be expensive to transport. A hundred thousand won."

When I didn't respond or show any expression, he added, "But I could get it done."

That was all my savings. I'd have to think about it. But for the first time in years, I had hope. "I'd like to talk again about this. When can we meet?"

"Tomorrow at this shop. Then I'll be gone for a month. The price may go up by then."

"Tomorrow then."

I had paid him the hundred thousand won that day. I sold my parents' house in Kimch'aek. I told the neighbors I had a new assignment. I told my officer I was taking a few days off.

That night, Park Sun introduced me to the person smuggler, Hwang. He was short and skinny with a narrow, pinched face.

Park paid him money, and Hwang said, "Follow me."

We walked a couple of miles outside the pitch-black city. We approached a donkey cart tied to a tree. Hwang drove it up the hill to a cave. There he stabled the donkey and again said, "Follow me."

We walked another couple miles along a dark mountain path to another cave. To my wonder, Hwang pointed to an old army car. "Get in," he said.

We drove through back trails all night to the border with the Tumen River. "Follow this path to the river. Watch carefully for guards. When there are no guards, cross the river." He sped away.

I started across the river twice, slipping back when I heard or saw a guard. I traveled upriver several kilometers to get away from one guard station and ran into another. I finally picked a spot right between two and started over, crouching as low as I could.

The hundred meters of cold, dirty water stank, but I was too afraid to care. I swam the deeper river channel, then waded again on the Chinese side. As I walked up the riverbed to the shore, my heart lifted. I was out! I was free! I—

I awoke on the ground. I didn't know why I was there. Distantly, across the river in North Korea, I heard laughter. I turned my head, dazed. Two guards pointed at me, laughing.

My legs didn't work. I crawled up the bank. CRACK! CRACK! Two shots whizzed by. I kept crawling.

More shots came. I crawled on. After some time I fainted.

I woke at evening. I was in a cart, jostling on a rough track. I heard two people speaking Chinese, which I could speak a little.

A woman with a round, wrinkled face looked down at me and said, "Are you OK?"

"I'm weak," I said first in Korean, and then I repeated it in Chinese. "I'm thirsty, and I can't move."

"Here. You drink." She spoke in Korean.

The water was delicious. I'd never been so thirsty. "Thanks." I didn't know what language I used, for I passed out.

I revived later that night in a small, one room house. I shivered with fever. "Oooh!" I moaned.

"You hot!" the woman said. She bathed my face in cool water and gave me a drink.

I still couldn't move my legs. I raised up on an elbow and looked around. A gold cross gleamed on the wall. I stared at it. Of course I knew about Christianity. It was one of the worst lies in the world, which I had been taught since childhood.

Everything else the Korean government had ever told me had been a lie. Maybe that was too. I lay back down, exhausted from just that little exertion.

The doctor's arrival startled me awake.

"He's got a terrible fever!" the woman said. "Can you give him something for it?"

"Let's see him. Oh, he's been shot! Why didn't you tell me?" the doctor asked in anger.

He could be imprisoned for helping North Korean refugees.

"He's a refugee, isn't he?"

"We did find him near the Tumen River," admitted the man who'd joined the woman and doctor in the room.

I guessed he was her husband.

"What does it matter?" the woman demanded. "He's sick! Cure him!"

"Nothing I can do. He's got a systemic infection from the gunshot. The bullet's in his spine, and the infection's probably in his spine. He'll die soon. And I'll get arrested if I'm caught with him. Goodbye." The doctor walked out the door.

"Let's pray," the man said to his wife.

They prayed.

"We don't even know his name!" her husband said after they were done.

"I got an idea," the wife said.

"What?"

"Remember that gift we got from the American missionary? The one who gave us our Bible?"

"Oh-ho! Yes, that's a good idea! Where is it?"

"I knew you'd lose it." She pulled up her necklace on which she wore her crucifix. Next to it was a small ampoule.

"When he left us, the missionary said this was his most precious gift he could give them. Use it when all other hope is lost."

"Hey, mister!"

She tried to ask my permission. I was scalding hot. I'd die soon. I couldn't talk.

"Well, here goes!" She plunged a sharp needle into my arm. I passed out.

* * *

"Greetings, paranormal privateers!" General Figeroa greeted us six zombies seated in the conference room. He now avoided the term *zombie*, which was considered insulting, demeaning, and bigoted by the politically correct elite in Washington, DC.

Diane and I and the other zombies still called ourselves zombies, of course.

Looking at the six pairs of red eyes around the table of the *Resolute Too* as it sailed down the Thames, he said, "Diane, it's good to see you're back to normal!"

"Yes, I feel great, but boy, that was something! That was worse than when the burning SPEwZ building fell on me!"

"First, congratulations on successfully neutralizing the terrorist cell in London. Besides the three you captured, we've found half a dozen others."

"I heard from Scotland Yard personnel that one of them escaped," I commented.

"That's supposed to be secret. 'Loose lips sink ships.' I can trust you six. Yes, Synthia Smith escaped, the ringleader of them all. This was not due to Scotland Yard's failing, but an outside organization sprung her. They left few clues, but the Yard found the guards' bodies in a dumpster nearby. Black mambas poisoned them."

"Sid Boffin! Oooh! I just know it!" Diane yelled.

"Possibly. Or someone from his organization with the same cyborg animals."

"Yes, he might have had a successor," I said.

"Or a boss," the general suggested.

"That fits with what Don said last night," I said. "After he read the *Midley Beacon*'s report of the battle of Harrods, he said it sounded like a video game and his mom got beaten by the boss of the Harrods level. If Synthia Smith has a higher up, he'd want to get her out to cover his own tracks."

"That's exactly what we thought in the NSA, George. Now, about your next assignment."

"Finally!" Lisa said. "I'm antsy to get our next story."

"Of course you can't let the cat out of the bag yet," the general said. "This next assignment is the most sensitive yet."

"Worse than London? They're still protesting zombies in Hyde Park," Sam said.

"Far worse. Those anti-zombie elements are just extremists. We have the full support of the Queen and prime minister. This next assignment will feature a hostile government that will literally go ballistic if they discover any of you within its borders. They have ICBMs, and they're not afraid to use them."

"Sounds good!" Lisa said.

"Or really bad," Sam said.

"Bad is good for news," Lisa said.

"But not for world peace," returned the general, trying to regain control of the conference. "Only you six will know your exact destination. You can let Captain Koumondoros know you're going to the Sea of Japan."

"That's on the other side of the world!" Lulu exclaimed.

"It'll take months to get there," Sharon said.

"Not if you go through the Northwest Passage," Figeroa said.

"Now that's cool," Sam said.

"That's global warming for you," Diane said.

"But what's our assignment once we get to the Sea of Japan?" I asked.

"We'll hold off on the exact location as long as we can. We still have some preparations to do before we give you the full reveal."

"Grrrr!" Lisa said. "Can't you ever tell us anything when we want to know it?"

"It's not that I don't trust you," General Figeroa said. "It's that I don't know what could go wrong between now and then. We'll tell you when you're in the Northwest Passage. This information is limited to me and the National Security head."

"How long will the Northwest Passage take?" Lisa asked.

"The best time is twenty-eight days. The *Resolute Too* can go faster."

"I had to drag Captain Koumondoros kicking and screaming to go faster," Diane said.

"Literally," Lisa added.

"Be careful of the icebergs. The southern channels are clear, but the northern ones may be clogged with ice. "

"We'll talk with Captain Koumondoros about this," I said.

"Just don't mention the final destination."

"We don't know it!" Lisa said with frustration.

"You know you have to get to the Sea of Japan. Don't even mention that to anyone. Just say you have to get to the Pacific Rim. I'm sending you the alternate routes now."

The map of Northwest Passage routes popped up on the screen.

"That'll be all for now. Figeroa, out."

They reviewed the map and the course with Captain Koumondoros.

"I'm excited to sail this route," he said. "I've always wanted to try it."

"Great!" Diane gushed. "We should have no more arguments about our ship's speed, right?"

"No arguments, but you'll be facing contrary winds in the North Atlantic. That'll slow our top speed. Then through the NWP, we'll be on iceberg watch. We have surface radar and sonar, but our speed must allow us time to maneuver. You don't want us to sink like the *Titanic*."

"No," Diane admitted. "We zombies would survive an iceberg, but we don't want anything to happen to the crew."

"Can we go at top speed if the sea is clear on satellite?" I asked.

"Yes, George, but this satellite picture was taken in the summer. Look at all the ice in the northern passages. I'd prefer to take the southern route."

"So it would be longer, but faster," I said.

"Yes, exactly."

"Whose side are you on, George?" Diane said. But her heart wasn't in it. "We'll see when we get there."

"How long until we get there?" Lisa asked.

"Let's take a quick estimate," the captain said as he entered the route into his computer.

"From London to Labrador, then to Lancaster Sound, and then the NWP starts. We'll go to Point Barrow and sail to the Pacific Rim. That totals twenty-six days at twenty knots. I assume you'll tell me where?" he asked.

"We don't know our final destination ourselves yet," I said. "We should find out by the time we're at the NWP."

"Let's go faster here in the Atlantic," Diane urged.

"We'll go as fast as possible, which is faster than I want to go," the captain said with a smile.

"I can't ask for more than that," Diane said.

* * *

I awoke not knowing where I was. The room was small, hot, and humid. It looked like a farmer's hut.

I stretched in a cramped, wrinkled bed. I was taller than usual for Korean men, and I barely fit.

It was damp with my sweat.

I felt great. There was something wrong with that, I thought. Why? Where was I? The last thing I remembered was...crossing the Tumen River! I had been shot! Thinking about it, I'd been shot multiple times. First in the waist and then my legs.

I checked for bullet wounds and scars. Nothing. I vaguely remembered someone finding me, an old woman with a round, wrinkled face, but nothing else.

I found a basin of water and my clothing, cleaned and folded—and mended. I fingered the neat patch on my shirt where I'd been shot. I washed, dressed, and then stepped outside.

"Oh, the sleeper awakes!" the old woman said. She sat on a stool, mending clothing with quick, sure jabs of her needle. She spoke good Korean, accented with Chinese.

"How long was I asleep?"

"Two days. We thought we were going to lose you, between the gunshot and the fever, but you pulled through."

"I feel wonderful! Thank you for saving my life! How can I repay you?"

"We'll think of something," she promised. "Did you see the water basin in the hut?"

"Yes, I washed up. Thanks again."

"But did you see your reflection?" she persisted.

"No, I don't usually look at myself."

"Men!" She put down her sewing. "Follow me and look at your face."

Mystified, I followed her back into the hut.

"Now look at your face," she repeated.

What was I to see? I studied my reflection carefully. I had some stubble on my chin; I'd have to shave. My brows were furrowed in concentration, and my eyes—my eyes!

My eyes shone bright red, like two coals, under my black brows!

"What's happened to my eyes?"

"My son, you've turned into a zombie," she said tenderly.

A zombie? I'd heard rumors of zombies in the US. That was just one of the many crazy reports we got from there. The national media assured us that no zombie would ever be permitted in North Korea. Now I was one.

"Can I be cured?" I asked, fearing the answer would be no.

"Yes, but the medicine is expensive. You can get the Chinese treatment or the US treatment from the black market. If you want to buy it, you'll have to earn the money. We have no money. I'm sorry."

"That's OK." I sat numbly on the bed. "I'll do whatever it takes."

"Good. We can use the help. What's your name, anyway?"

"Kim Chi-un."

"Huh. That's odd. Chi-un is not a usual Korean name. I know. I lived there as a little girl."

"Yes. I always have to explain. My father's name was Kim Ji-sung, a little like the Great Leader Kim Il-sung. When his son, Dear Leader Kim Jong-il, begot Great Successor Kim Jung-un, my parents decided to name me like him. Of course, I wasn't worthy to have the same name, so they made it unique." I didn't add that my parents loved kimchi.

"My name's Lee Mi-jin. I married Lee Hwang here in China many years ago, after my parents moved here during the Korean War."

"I'm glad to meet you, Lee Mi-jin. Where is your husband, Lee Hwang?"

"He drove our cart to the market. That's how we got you here."

"Thanks again! I might as well start working for you. What do you need done?"

"To start with, the pig pen needs mucking out."

I went to work. It was like my work in North Korea, only now I had hope.

* * *

"Greetings, paranormal privateers," General Figeroa said to us. "Today I can tell you your final destination."

"Finally!" Lisa and Diane said together.

"You two are like twin sisters," Sam commented.

"Separated at birth," Lisa said.

"United by the zombie bacteria," Diane added.

"Indeed," the general interrupted. "Your destination is North Korea."

A map blinked open on their screen.

"Specifically, we want to insert you up the Myonggan River." An arrow pointed to a small river on the east coast of North Korea.

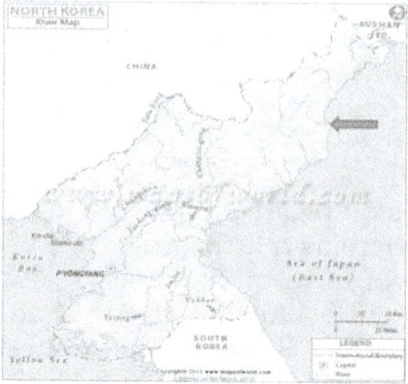

"Your mission, should you decide to accept it, is to penetrate their underground nuclear facility here." Another arrow pointed to a small triangle.

"Is that all?" Diane asked.

"No," the general said. "After you penetrate their nuclear facility, you will destroy the nuclear warheads. We'll train you on how to do that effectively. We'll send you diagrams of their warheads. After you complete that task, you will return down the Myonggan River and go back to the *Resolute Too*."

"Sounds exciting," Lulu commented.

"I'm sorry, but I don't know Korean, and my Chinese isn't very good," Sharon said.

"Yes, we know. We're sending a Korean translator for you. She can stay on the *Resolute Too* and translate through your headsets."

"Won't the North Koreans pick up the radio signals?" I asked.

"No," Figeroa answered. "We'll use the satellite cell phone signals for your international cell phones. They won't be able to tell the difference from normal cell phone traffic. We learned that trick from Sid Boffin."

"But why are we doing this?" Lisa asked.

"North Korea can now launch nuclear-tipped missiles. They just haven't joined the two together. We've uncovered a plan for them to do so and use them for nuclear blackmail of South Korea and Japan."

"That would be really, really bad," Sam said.

"Yes. There is also a substantial risk that once they demonstrate the nuke, they'll sell them to terrorists. We have no hope of conducting an official covert operation into North Korea. Our time window is too small."

"How small?" asked Lisa.

"North Korea has definite plans to launch a nuclear warhead at a Pacific island and explode it, as a demonstration, on the Fourth of July."

"That's less than a month away," I said in surprise.

"The nerve of them!" Diane said.

"That's their point. It's supposed to be a big provocation of the US and the world. This operation is more politically sensitive than anything else you've done. South Korea is fairly pacifist and seeks to accommodate—"

"You mean appease!" Lisa growled.

"Yes, in non-diplomatic language. To a lesser extent, Japan's foreign policy is the same. China and Russia would both react badly to a US operation in North Korea. But as privateers, you have plausible deniability. However, in the event you or any of the paranormal privateers be caught, killed, or captured, the secretary will disavow any knowledge of your actions."

"Have you been watching old episodes of *Mission Impossible*?" Sam asked.

"Yes, I've been binge watching. My wife bought me the complete set for my birthday."

"I can tell," Sam said.

"Will we face elements of the criminal outfit that we fought in Somalia, Crimea, and London?" I asked.

"No, we don't believe so. Due to North Korea's isolation and extreme totalitarian government, there is no organized crime there, just widespread smuggling and corruption." He paused. "Unless you consider their whole government organized crime. In any event, we believe you'll have a great advantage since no one in the whole country has experience with any kind of zombies, animal or human."

"And so they won't know how to fight us." Lulu sounded gleeful.

"Exactly."

"You mean, they're dumb enough to just shoot us with guns?" Diane asked.

"Yes."

"I can see why we're ideal for this operation and why you had us sail around the world," I said.

"General, we're at the decision point for taking the northern passage or the southern one by tomorrow. I'm pushing for the northern one since it's shorter," Diane said.

"General, do you have more details on the ice conditions in the NWP?" I asked.

"Here are our latest photos from our military satellites."

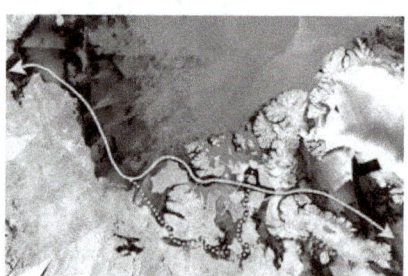

"Woo-hoo!" Sam whistled. "That's pretty clear!"

"Yahoo!" Diane yelled. "Wait until I show Captain Koumondoros."

"You can let him in on your destination. Just tell the rest of the crew you're going to the Sea of Japan. The Korean translator, Sergeant Jessica Rose, will fly in on an F-35 to your helicopter deck tomorrow. Make her feel welcome. Familiarize her with your communication equipment and procedures. I think you will like her."

"I'm so excited! I can hardly wait to meet her!" Diane said.

"You probably felt that way about the great white shark you killed," I commented, deadpan.

"Why yes," Diane said without irony. "I swam toward it as fast as I could. I wanted to get back to you, George. I knew you were in danger, fighting those zombie ninjas."

She referred to our defeat of Sid Boffin on this very yacht.

I couldn't think of a reply. "I love you." That was always a good thing to say.

"And I love you, George."

"On that amicable note, we'll adjourn. Figeroa, out."

* * *

Diane and I stood on the bridge of the *Resolute Too* with Captain Koumondoros the next day. We sailed at full speed. The wind was still, the sun blazed off distant icebergs, and the Arctic Ocean lay calm as a gigantic pond as we entered the northern passage next to Ellesmere Island.

"I have to admit, Diane," the captain said. "*The Resolute Too* rides very smoothly even at this speed. I believe the trimaran hull helps a lot. I'm more used to cargo vessels."

"Captain K, I have to admit that sailing full speed in a rough ocean is like going over speed bumps at seventy miles per hour," Diane said.

"Are you preparing for a career as a captain, Diane?" I ribbed her.

"No, I'm having too much fun as a paranormal privateer!" She laughed. "I suppose I could manage in a pinch."

"I'll keep my job, thank you. You take care of the landside, and I'll take care of the seaside," Koumondoros said. "Here comes the F-35."

An image swept across the radar screen.

The *Resolute Too* had military-grade radar and advanced software that identified the make, nationality, and pilot's name of each plane. We watched the airplane's icon merge with the ship. Looking upward, we saw the plane landing on the copter deck.

"Race you to the deck, George!" Diane took off like a deer.

I lumbered after her and followed Diane up the marble spiral staircase encircling the central atrium. I increased my speed from two steps at a time to five. Diane came into view, and I caught her on the fourth deck, where the ship's helicopter was stored.

We saw a flight-suited figure with a duffel bag jump off the F-35. Then the pilot hopped out.

A two-seater F-35? Who knew?

"Hi! You must be Jessica! I'm Diane."

"Hi, Diane," said a young woman of perhaps twenty-five, with curly brown hair and hazel eyes. "I'll be your Korean translator."

"Let's get you comfortable! George, we'll be in the dining room."

"Hi, I'm George Newby. Welcome to the *Resolute Too*," I said to the pilot.

"I'm Captain Charles Greenway," he replied.

"Let's get you some refreshments in the dining room. How far did you come?"

"Sorry. I can't say where I'm based."

Captain Greenway and Jessica chowed down on smoked salmon on toast with onions and goat cheese. Sam and Lisa had brought their gourmet cook, Dustin Fowler, from their *Midley Beacon* corporate jet, when the *Resolute Too* sailed.

"This is delicious!" Jessica exclaimed through a mouthful.

"Mmmph!" Captain Greenway agreed.

"Thank you so much!" Dustin said. "I'm used to feeding zombies with their enormous appetites, and they'll eat anything! I just can't tell if my meals are really good. I love getting feedback from non-zombies."

"Do you have any cabbage?" Jessica asked.

"Yes, we do. We have several dozen heads. I'm trying to figure out what to do with them. There's only so much you can do with coleslaw."

"I'd love to make some kimchi!"

"I've read about it, but I haven't made it. How many cabbages would you like?"

"How many fermenting jars do you have?"

"I don't know."

"Could you use a fifty-five-gallon plastic barrel? There's one in the ship's stores," I said.

"That's big, but it might work. Let's see: one cabbage for a three-gallon crock, two for five gallons, so twenty-two for the fifty-five-gallon drum. Can you spare twenty-two cabbages, Dustin?"

"Sure. I'll still have a dozen or so. That's enough coleslaw."

"Great. I love Korean cooking!"

"Wonderful! Maybe we can exchange recipes."

"Let's do it!"

After chowing down, Diane and I went back to the bridge. Based on the satellite photos we continued west past Somerset Island to the south and the Prince of Wales Island.

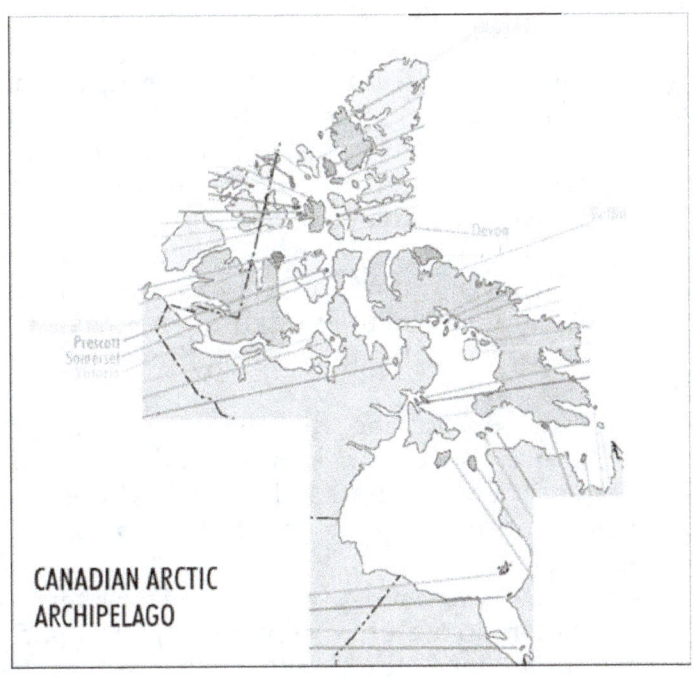

CANADIAN ARCTIC
ARCHIPELAGO

Standing next to Captain Koumondoros, we saw icebergs.

"Why are you slowing down, Captain?" Diane said.

"Icebergs. I want a half-mile clearance, and I'll be dodging them from here on out," he answered.

"Grrrr. I hate slowing! Full speed ahead, damn the icebergs!"

"Diane!" I chided. "But that is an accurate quote of Admiral Farragut at the battle of Mobile Bay, except for the iceberg part."

"Try hitting an iceberg," the captain replied. "That'll really slow you down."

"You're right, of course," she admitted.

"Diane, let's go to our cabin and let the captain guide the ship. I'm sure this is a high-stress situation for him."

"When will we hit the Prince of Wales Strait? That's where we decide again whether to go south."

"In about four hours."

"OK. I guess I can't do anything here. Sorry to add to your stress, Captain. I just want to go as fast as possible!"

"I think I know that by now," he said with a smile. "I was stressed at first, but I'm used to you by now, Diane. Your bark is worse than your bite!"

"Hah! I haven't tried biting anything. And I've already survived cyborg mambas. There's a bad bite!"

In our cabin, I updated my scrapbook. I added pictures of the icebergs, a puffin feather, and some bones from freshly caught fish that we ate yesterday.

Diane just stared out the port at the icebergs. "There are way more icebergs than showed in the satellite photo."

"The resolution isn't high enough to show them."

"But I thought with global warming this channel would be clear. It is summer."

"Yes, but the seasons lag. It's just June, still spring in the Arctic. Other crossings have taken place in August."

"The Arctic is colder than I thought. Where is global warming when you need it? I want to do something. I'll go help Jessica make kimchi."

"I'll stay here and surf the net." The ship stayed connected through a satellite receiver on the helipad.

"See you later!"

We got to Prince of Wales Strait and saw the icebergs nearly solid across the strait.

"Uh-oh," Diane said.

"I could hug the north coast of Victoria Island." Captain Koumondoros pointed to a gap between the island ahead and the icebergs. "But there's no guarantee it doesn't narrow. Then we'd have to reverse back to here and go south."

"Mmmm." Diane considered.

"Also, the distance around Victoria Island and then to Point Barrow on the Alaskan coast is just about the same."

"OK, let's take the southern route."

Around the pungent barrel of kimchi, frothy corgis sat and whined. Jessica trained them to sit, roll over, beg, and follow her with the fermented cabbage.

"Rather than carrying around a bowl, I wonder if I could dry this into dog biscuits?" she said.

Dustin, who was with her, said, "Sure. We have a dehydrator in the kitchen."

The dried kimchi tasted like spicy, salty potato chips. Diane loved it, but not as much as the zombie corgis. They became completely obedient to Jessica and followed her around the ship, like dogs.

Dustin and Jessica joined together for a Korean dinner. They served spicy barbecued beef with kimchi and rice and delighted everyone.

Jessica bristled with energy. She made kimchi, explored every nook of the ship, and played K-pop, Korean popular music, everywhere she went. Then she plugged her MP3 player into the ship's sound system and danced to it. She taught Diane, Lulu, Sharon, and Lisa the latest moves, as well as the "old-fashioned" (in her words) "Gangnam Style." Other crew members joined them until she had the whole crew dancing Gangnam Style—arm-flapping dance moves.

* * *

I expected to keep working for the Lees, but on Sunday, Mi-jin told me, "Today, Kim Chi-un, you don't work. We all rest."

"Oh. Can't I work anyway? I want to work off my debt to you and also buy the anti-zombie medicine." I said that, but I had doubt. I felt wonderful all the time. I never got tired, even after twenty hours of work. And I needed only a couple hours of sleep.

"Remember I told you we'd think of some way you can pay us back for the zombie blood treatment?"

"Yes."

"Here's what you can do. Rest today and come with us to church."

"OK, but that doesn't seem like much to me." I felt a little creepy about going to a Christian church after years of dire warnings in North Korea. I didn't want to tell the Lees. But now I wasn't in North Korea. "I thought my work for you was paying for that treatment too."

"No, we just need help because we're old and you're here. We want to share our church family with you. If you come with us once, we'll feel we're square."

"That seems like a very little thing to do."

"It's bigger than it seems. Although Christianity is legal in China, it's only legal for the state-run church, where they spy on the members and supervise the preaching. This is an unregistered church, which may be raided at any time. If we get raided, we can be imprisoned. But you'll be deported. Do you want to take that risk?"

"If you're willing to risk imprisonment, I'm willing to risk deportation," I said. "I'm willing to risk my life for you, for you saved my life. But why risk yours? Why do you take such a chance?"

"Our God, Jesus Christ, saved our lives as surely as we saved yours. You can understand that. He did that while we were still evil, yet He gave His life hoping we'd follow Him."

"Can't you worship in the state-run church?"

"Why did you leave North Korea?"

Startled by the abrupt change of topic, I paused. "Primarily because I felt I had no reason to live. All my family was dead, and my job was a dead end, with no meaning. I knew all the Korean government was fake and everything they said was a lie. I had to get away." I had never said it out loud to anyone before. I felt good sharing it.

Mi-jin nodded. "Yes. In the same way, the hope of Jesus is not mentioned in the state church. Rather, it's focused on supporting the government. It's a lie with no meaning. Do you see the similarity?"

"I never thought about religion that way." I laughed. "You make me even more curious to see this church. I have a guilty pleasure knowing I'm breaking one of Korea's iron rules."

"And China's. Don't forget that! We must be careful when we travel. We'll pack the cart with goods for market. If we're stopped, we'll say we're going to store them in the city—which we will. The church is near the storage area. We give our food to help the minister and the poor in the church."

"That's very good of you," I said with admiration.

"That's only what we're supposed to do. We're supposed to love other people as we love ourselves."

"That seems hard to me."

"It is at first but gets easier with time until it's second nature—then first nature. And finally, it's our only nature. That's why we helped you."

"If it's because of Christianity you helped me, then I need to learn about it."

We left early Sunday morning in the cart pulled by Lee's donkey. Soldiers inspected us once, and let us go. I pretended to be asleep, so I could hide my eyes.

The church was just a large house in the city. Maybe four dozen people crammed into the largest room. Everyone brought food, and we shared a meal. I assumed I wouldn't eat anything since I didn't bring anything, but they only laughed and said, "You're our guest!"

I thought the Lees were friendly, but they seemed subdued compared to some of the members. They treated me like I was their long-lost son. I felt awkward and undeserving.

The sermon dragged on and confused me. I tried to follow it, but all the new words—"redemption," "sanctification," "salvation, "Israel," "Trinity"—added to my confusion. Then these words cut through my haze: "For God so loved the world, that He gave His only begotten Son that whosoever believes in Him should not perish, but have everlasting life."

I heard nothing else the rest of the day. Those words echoed in my head and my heart. Was there actually a God? Did he really love me? Koreans worshipped Kim Jung-il, Kim Sun-il, and Kim Jong-un as gods, but I'd seen what they did. They weren't gods and didn't love. If God existed and He loved me, that would change everything. I'd be willing to die for Him. I was willing to die for the Lees. But He promised eternal life as well. That would be icing on the cake.

Someone called my name. "Kim! Kim Chi-un!"

"What?" I had no idea what he wanted. I had forgotten his name.

"Do you want to become a Christian?"

What an odd question! No one had ever asked me before. The question wasn't even legal in North Korea. Did I? Why not? If God existed, it was a great deal.

"Sure, I guess."

"Do you believe Jesus is the Son of God?"

Did I? The Lees were sure He was. I'd never felt such love from anyone, except my parents. All these church members loved me too. They'd welcomed me, red eyes, an illegal immigrant, a lowly pig worker, like a lost relative. And then there was my saved, zombie life. I should be dead.

The love that saved my life convinced me. "He must be if His followers are so full of love."

"Then you need to be baptized. Get dunked in this tub."

"I could use a bath!" I joked.

"We all *need* this bath, to be washed of sin. You must die to your old life."

"That's easy. I already did, practically, when I crossed the Tumen."

"Then you will be born anew in the Father, the Son, and the Holy Spirit."

There was that Trinity stuff again. I didn't understand it, but I trusted God.

I came out of the water rejoicing. I truly felt new! I was born again!

"I really don't understand very much," I admitted.

"We're here to teach you!"

And they began teaching me about God.

* * *

We conducted daily lessons about North Korea on the *Resolute Too.* We pored over the maps of the Myonggan River and that rugged coast. We studied the map of the nuclear facilities.

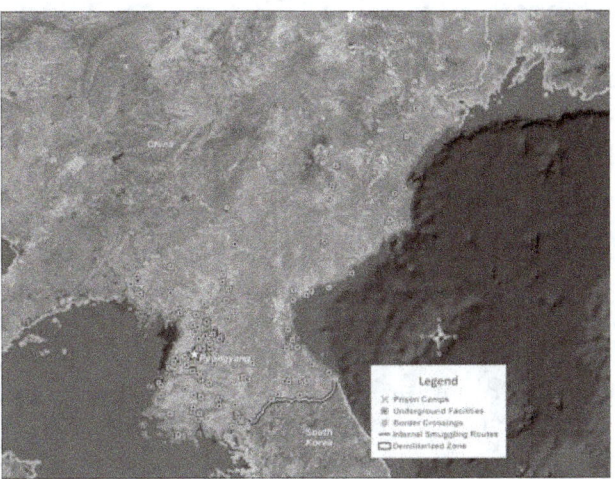

General Figeroa said, "The facility you'll attack is at the headwaters of the Myonggan, just outside Camp 16, one of the North Korean concentration camps." A map appeared on the screen in our conference room.

"Why do they have these camps? Who is in them?" Diane asked.

"Camp 16 has political prisoners. Hwaseong camp is a penal-labor colony in which detainees are imprisoned for life with no chance to be released. With an area of over two hundred square miles, it is the largest in Korea. In North Korea, a political prisoner means anyone who displeases the regime."

"Displeases?" Sam said. "How?"

"Just about anything. Failure to follow orders. Watching forbidden movies. Listening to forbidden music. Or radio. Or Christianity. Or anyone who is a relative of a displeasing person."

"Christianity is forbidden?" Diane gasped.

"Forbidden and illegal, as are all other religions. Citizens are to worship the Kims and no one else. Less is known about Camp 16 than the other camps, probably because it lies adjacent to the Mount Mantap nuclear test site and the Musudan-ri missile test site."

"Do you want us to hit the missile test site after we hit the nuclear site?" Diane sounded eager.

"No, it's just a test site," Figeroa said. "The actual missile factories and storage areas are elsewhere."

"How about this Camp 16? Since we'll be right there, we might as well free the inmates," Diane suggested.

"That's noble of you Diane, but more difficult than you think. I don't doubt you could overwhelm the guards and free them, but most of the residents are starving. They'd need food and help to escape. And there are twenty thousand of them.

"You need to escape the country yourself as soon as you're done. If you get out cleanly, then they won't be able to tie the destruction of their warheads to the US."

"I guess the most we can do is destroy those weapons so that no one else gets under their control. Maybe we can bring about a collapse of the regime."

"That's what we all want. Figeroa, out."

* * *

My whole life changed. I worked for the Lees with delight, knowing they'd saved me twice now. When I wasn't working, I was reading the Bible. A church member gave me a Korean Bible.

"Someone gave this to me when I became a Christian. Now you must give it to another new Christian when you have a chance," the man had said.

I was so overwhelmed, I couldn't even thank him. I only smiled like an idiot and kept nodding my head.

I looked forward to returning to church. I washed and dressed and prepared an hour before we had to leave. I greeted the members I met last week like my dearest friends—which they were. I had no other friends.

The church doors burst open, splintered by sledgehammers. "Everyone, lie down on the floor!" Soldiers at each door brandished submachine guns. Any one of them could kill us all in less than a minute, and there were four.

The congregation cowered on the ground. They cuffed my wrists tightly. Then the soldiers interrogated each of us. When they came to me, I copied what the others had said.

"What's your name?"

"Kim Chi-un."

"Are you a Christian?"

"Yes!" I felt proud to say it.

"Where do you live?"

"With the Lees on their farm."

"Do you know this is illegal?"

"Yes."

"You have an accent. Are you from Korea?" That was not a question they asked the others.

"Uh, yes." How could I deny it?

"Deport him," said an officer.

"You'll be back in Korea tonight," my interrogator told me.

That was the last I ever saw the Lees and the rest of that congregation.

They threw me bound in the back of a truck and drove to the border. There, I was placed in a pen with other Koreans who'd been rounded up. We were loaded in a North Korean truck and driven across the border. Had I known what I later learned, I would have fled then. But I didn't.

We traveled for several hours, up and down hills. We weren't fed and had no water, nor sanitation. We stopped in a village in the mountains and were marched to another pen. They stripped our clothing and gave us thin prison uniforms.

"Obey orders or you'll be shot," a guard ranted at us. "Don't try to escape, or you'll be shot. Don't talk about escape, or you'll be shot. Do your work, or you'll be shot." And so on.

"Now clean and wash the truck you came on," he said as he concluded. "Welcome to Camp 16." He laughed.

Chapter 7

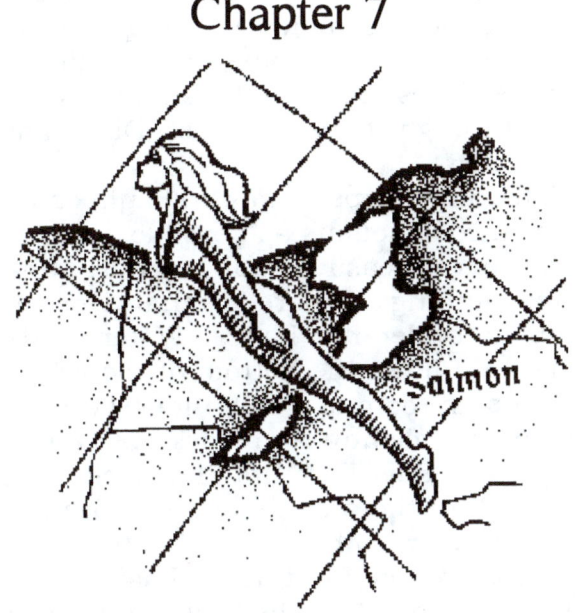

Salmon

Myonggan

After a week of sailing from Point Barrow, we arrived in the Sea of Japan just outside North Korean territorial waters. A submarine surfaced next to us. Diane, Lulu, Sharon, and I boarded.

We left at night inside the twelve-mile limit on a zodiac inflatable boat. We'd take it far as we could up the Myonggan and then go the rest of the twenty-mile journey on foot.

The river was narrow and shallow. After passing fishing piers, we were completely alone. Ten miles inland we came to rapids. We stowed the raft in the woods and hiked uphill along the river.

Up and up we went. Even with zombie strength and speed, we needed more than an hour to go uphill over rocks and water. As we struggled along, Diane munched on something in a bag.

"What do you have, Diane?"

"Dried kimchi chips. Want some?"

"Sure." The salty, spicy, crunchy chips hit the spot.

Finally we passed the source of the river to the plateau where the nuclear site sat. A ten-foot barbed-wire fence circled the complex, complete with guard towers and patrols between them. We scouted the facility's fence and determined the closest point to the storage building.

"Let's rip through the fence here!" Diane advised. "We can tear it open!"

"What if tearing it trips an alarm?" Lulu cautioned. "We want to be as inconspicuous as possible."

"I think we can easily climb over it," Sharon said. "This'll be like nothing compared to that river path."

"How about under it?" I said. Water eroded a gully under the fence. I lifted the bottom of the wire fence, and there was plenty of room to crawl under, even for me.

The night was cloudy and dark. Streetlights lit the fronts of the buildings, but not the backs. We skulked around the back of the storage building, but it was solid concrete. There was no other way in.

"So we knock on the front door," I said.

"Let me," Lulu said. "I'm the best at unarmed combat."

We didn't want to kill anyone unless absolutely necessary. She slipped along the wall into the light and walked quickly to the guard. He shouted something in Korean and aimed his machine gun at Lulu. She took it from him in a blink of an eye and knocked him out with one punch. We heard the crack of bone on bone fifty feet away.

After tying and gagging the guard, we entered, Lulu and me, then Diane and Sharon. A guard behind a glass window yelled when he saw us. I punched him through the window and knocked him out.

We heard no alarms or running feet. Diane crawled through the broken window and let us in through the locked door.

After securing the guard, we found building diagrams at the guards' station. Although Sharon was poor at Korean, she could read the building maps showing the bomb room.

We unlocked the doors to the bomb room from the guards' station. Everything seemed automated. We found no other guards as we walked stealthily to the lower floor.

Massive steel doors secured the bomb storage room. Even I had a hard time moving them. Inside, the bombs lay nestled in their cradles, like giant eggs of hell.

We counted them carefully. General Figeroa estimated that as many as fifty bombs might be here. The room could store forty, and we found thirty-one.

We divided the bombs among us. We each had a bag of tools to disassemble the bombs and destroy the carefully shaped lumps of uranium and plutonium inside.

What we were doing would be impossible for non-zombies. Within minutes the whole room had enough radioactivity to kill any normal person. As the radiation destroyed cells in our zombie bodies, our zombie bacteria regenerated tissue even faster.

"Don't stay any longer than you have to," General Figeroa urged in our coms. "We don't know how long even zombie bacteria can hold up to the radiation."

We needed no further encouragement, and we worked at zombie speed, even feverishly.

I actually felt hot, a steady body-wide glow. "Does anyone else feel hot?"

"You mean radioactive?" Lulu laughed.

"I mean like a fever."

"Yes, I've felt hot, but I thought it was just the hard work," Diane said. "There. I'm done. How about you, George?"

"Just finishing up," I said as I smashed the last globe of plutonium.

"Won't the Koreans have a fit!" Lulu chortled.

"You know, now that you mention it, I'm feeling hot too," Sharon said.

"I'm sweating! I never sweat!" Lulu said.

"Let's get out of here. That might be a side effect of the radiation."

The massive door swung shut with a clang and latched with a solid thunk. We heard Korean over the loudspeaker.

"Repeat that please," I said, holding my cell phone up to translate. Out came Korean.

"Intruders! Invaders! Imperialistic capitalistic scum!"

"That about covers it," Diane said with a laugh.

"You have ruined our bombs at the cost of your lives! You will never get out now! The radioactivity will kill you horribly soon."

"We have a surprise for you!" Diane crowed.

I looked at her. And I looked again. "Diane!" I shouted.

Startled, Diane stopped whatever comeback she planned. I never shouted. "What, George?"

"Your eyes! They've turned green! You've lost your zombie bacteria!"

"Oh no! You too! Your eyes are brown!"

"And so are yours, Lulu," Sharon said, aghast.

"And yours are blue, Sharon. Beautiful blue," Lulu said sadly.

"What happened to our zombie bacteria?" Diane cried.

"It could be the radiation killed it," I said.

"I thought we were sure it wouldn't kill it fast enough!"

"Or, it could be we've got *another* anti-zombie disease. This fever might be a symptom."

"I'm not going down without a fight!" Diane yelled. She charged the massive metal door, trying to tear through, to no avail.

"Ow! Look at my fingers!" she said. They were broken and bloody and not healing.

"Can we reach the ship?"

I tried my communicator. "Mine doesn't work."

We were cut off, probably when the door closed.

"I'm afraid," Sharon said. "Our zombie bacteria are dead. Our remaining cells are dying. The radiation is sterilizing us. If we die, it'll be like saline turkeys, which can't be resurrected. There will be no life left in cells, no intact DNA to resurrect."

"I think being cut off will trigger a rescue attempt," I said, trying to be positive.

"Sam and Lisa? With the zombie corgis?" Diane said with hope.

* * *

The first day in the prison camp, I was cuffed and beaten a dozen times and worked sixteen hours with just a cup of rice. The harsh voice had been right—just about every imaginable infraction would get you beaten or raped or shot. I saw all that my first day.

That was a week ago. With zombie energy, I could do my work, and I healed from beatings almost instantly, but I still was in a constant state of starvation.

Oddly, I was not as depressed as I had been in North Korea before I fled to China. I had hope God would do something. I prayed daily for help. I helped other prisoners with their work.

I even tried to tell one of them of Jesus. But he said, "Idiot! That'll get you shot quicker than anything! Don't you know that? Even talking to me can get you shot!"

"It's worth the risk to know Jesus! I escaped from Korea and almost died, but now I'm alive forever!"

"Shut up or I'll report you tonight in our confession circle!"

That was the first time I tried to share the gospel. I was discouraged. Later, one of the inmates collapsed as she was clearing rocks from a field. I finished her work and mine and gave her my food.

"Why are you doing this?" she whispered.

"Because of the love of Jesus," I said.

The next time I saw her, they were dragging her body off to be buried. I felt guilty. I hadn't done enough to help her.

I aided another person the next day clearing weeds. He looked at me suspiciously. "Why are you helping me?"

"Because Jesus loves me, so I love you."

"Shut up," he said.

I felt ready to give up. Then late that night, the guards came for me.

"We heard you've been talking about Jesus. Is that right?"

"Yes. Jesus loves me and you."

"Come with us." They cuffed me and led me to a field. There they uncuffed me and handed me a shovel.

"Dig a hole. Make it deep."

I quickly dug a two-meter-deep hole.

"Stay down there." Then they shot me in the head.

I awoke at night. I was buried under three or four other bodies. The zombie blood brought me back to life! As I climbed through the pile of bodies burying me, I saw one was the woman I had talked with the day before. I felt my head, where I had been shot. It was completely healed.

I had an idea. I grabbed a sharp stone from the ground and cut my wrist. My blood flowed. I rubbed it into her cuts. Then I did the same anointing with the four other bodies in the grave.

I waited. I knew it took me all night to recover when I was near death. How long would it take for these poor souls to recover from death? Would the zombie blood work? Would it work with my crude blood transfer?

I assessed the state of my life as I sat in the graveyard on a warm summer night amid the bleeding corpses and watched the stars above. I was alive. That was great, considering I'd been shot in the head. And in the back, as I'd crossed the Tumen River. I had survived because of zombie blood, which I'd been given. Now, I gave the same to these wretched prisoners.

I hungered, but that hardly mattered anymore. It wasn't as bad as the famine I remembered from my childhood. Somehow, my zombie body just kept going, like an automaton. The beatings and even shootings I received seemed like mosquito bites.

Beyond my physical state, I was strangely content. They'd already imprisoned and beaten and shot me; what more could they do? God was with me, even here. I felt sure of it. I felt a rightness to where I was and what I was doing. I sighed in contentment.

As if in response, a corpse also sighed, a tall, lanky man who'd been on top of the heap. I knew, from brutal experience, corpses often made sounds after death. Curiously, I pressed my fingers to his neck. A faint pulse beat there.

Excitement bubbled up into joy. I checked the other corpses. All had faint pulses. It worked! They were alive!

As the sun rose, they awoke to life, one by one. To each, I explained my history as a zombie, my conversion to Christianity, and how I saved their lives. Each wanted to follow Christ. We went as a group to the river, and I baptized them as I had been baptized.

We went back to our barracks and told our stories of life and death and life again.

By the end of the day, we'd all been shot again. This time we recovered more quickly, even before they dragged our bodies to the graveyard. We pretended to be dead. We all gathered there at night and shared our blood with the dozens of dead bodies there. The next morning more than thirty were baptized by the river.

The morning after that we baptized more than a hundred. The guards became frantic. Despite the fact we continued to work peaceably and followed all the rules, they shot us on sight and unprovoked. Then we got back up in five minutes or less. They would shoot us again. And again. Then they ran out of bullets and fled.

First, there were only a few guard desertions. As the rumors flew through the camp, more guards just disappeared. By the end of the week, all the guards and administrative people had fled. All that was left were perhaps a thousand zombies, all raised from the dead, and nineteen thousand other prisoners, awaiting orders.

We broke into the food warehouse and the medical stores. We zombies treated the sick and fed the hungry.

In a warehouse, I rejoiced to find my old clothing stored with other prisoners' items, even my shoes. Then as we rummaged through the commandant's office, I discovered, with a shock, my Bible in his desk drawer. Was he a secret Christian? Or on his way to conversion? I didn't know. I also found a pocketknife. That would be much easier to use than a sharp stone.

I knew eventually the army would come here, so I collected all the zombies and prepared to leave.

The girl I first helped, named Park Ji Su, had stuck by my side since her resurrection. She said, "You gave me your life. Now I will give you mine."

I jumped when I heard her echo my words to the Lees.

Then she said, "Chi-un, we should go to the nuclear site. There may be prisoners there."

"Nuclear site? What nuclear site?"

"It's just a few kilometers away. Sometimes prisoners go there to dig out tunnels after underground nuclear explosions."

We gathered the whole camp, and I made an announcement. "We zombies will go to the nuclear site and free any prisoners we find there. There may be shooting, so the rest of you shouldn't come.

"I offer these choices for you. First, you can stay here and eat the food stores until they're gone. The danger is the army will likely come here soon.

"Second, you can make your way home from here. I know the human smuggling routes go through these mountains. Kimch'aek is about a hundred kilometers from here, and you can find help.

"Third, you can follow your way to China's border, like I did. We zombies can distract the guards so you can cross safely."

"Fourth, and in my opinion, the worst option, you can follow me. I'm not sure what I'll do after I free the prisoners. You zombies can choose too."

The crowd murmured. The idea of freedom of choice, rather than following orders, was foreign in North Korea. I learned through my rebellion and fleeing the country. I learned even more in my weeks in China. I wanted to go back there and discover what had happened to the Lees.

Several zombies opted for each of the first three choices. Perhaps a thousand people stayed, mostly sick and elderly who couldn't travel. A quarter of the crowd walked toward Kimch'aek, planning to return to their homes. Half wanted to go to China. And the rest followed me, even toward the nuclear facility. The Chinese crowd followed them.

Now I was stunned. I'd never been a leader, only a follower. What was I to do with fifteen thousand people looking to me? I'd do what I had to do.

"Onward to the nuclear facility!" I cried. I felt a surge of joy as I passed out of the gate of the camp and onto the road. I was free! We were free! I began singing a song I learned at the Chinese church. I had a good ear for music, and I loved to sing. This song captured my feelings exactly.

Onward, Christian soldiers, marching as to war,

With the cross of Jesus going on before.
Christ, the royal Master leads against the foe;
Forward into battle see His banners go!

I was surprised by dozens of prisoners joining in. I didn't know the song was so well known! The tune was a familiar one, used to sing the praises of Kim Jong-un, but the lyrics were Christian and, apparently, famous. There must be hundreds, no thousands of secret Christians right in the prison camp!

Thousands more joined in on the chorus, both zombies and non-zombies

Onward, Christian soldiers, marching as to war,
With the cross of Jesus going on before.

Singing, Ji Su led us to the nuclear facility. I kept the crowd back in the hills and directed the zombies to circle the fence. There seemed to be quite a hubbub in there. Troops surrounded one of the buildings, and I could hear shouting and see officers directing their soldiers here and there.

"What should we do?" I asked Ji Su.

"The mining entrance is beyond those buildings, but I don't see how we can get past the soldiers."

"But I do," said a new voice in the bushes behind us.

Out of the bushes came the strangest sight I'd ever seen.

* * *

"Oh no! We've lost connection with Diane and the zombies!" Lisa cried. She'd monitored communication from their headsets and video feed since they'd left while she'd prepared news stories and videos with Sam.

"Shouldn't you say, 'paranormal people'?" Sam kidded.

"Cut out that politically correct crap, Sam! This is no time for joking!"

"What can we do?" I asked. As the newest member of the paranormal privateers' crew, I hesitated to give suggestions.

"We're going to rescue them, Jessica," Lisa said grimly.

"Would the zombie corgis help?"

"They sure would!"

"I'll get them ready to go with you and Sam. I'll come too, to help with translations."

"I think we'll have to use the V-22 Osprey to carry us there," Sam said. "Let's tell the captain so we can get as close as possible."

"I've already done that," Lisa said. "The ship is speeding up already. He said he'd bring us as close as possible to the territorial waters."

"Let's load the corgis," I said.

"And Bull-oney and John Bull!" Lisa added.

"OK," Sam said, "but how will Jessica keep up with us and the corgis?"

"I've been preparing for this," I said. "I knew I might need to be with you zombies in North Korea, so we packed an inflatable hovercraft on the F-35."

"I didn't know F-35s could carry that much cargo," Sam exclaimed.

"It's not that big. It was just attached inside a cargo blister on the plane's belly. Oh, I probably shouldn't have told you! It's a military secret."

"Jessica, *we* are a military secret," Lisa said. "Our connections with the NSA, the air force, navy, army, and marines are all secret. That includes you, Sergeant Jessica Rose, US Army."

"I probably didn't break any regulations then."

"Probably not. But I will self-censor"—Lisa grimaced— "and not mention the F-35 or any storage blisters or modifications. Or even you."

"Sounds good!" I whistled for the corgis.

All one hundred came running at zombie speed, which was twice as fast as a corgi could normally run.

We ran up to the helipad, where the V-22 awaited. We'd taken it out of the storage deck when the Newbys and their bodyguards had left, just in case of trouble.

Sam and Lisa rode closely behind on their zombie bulls. We climbed the spiral staircase from the gymnasium/animal stable to the helipad. Rubber mats protected the marble stairs from hooves and dung.

Captain Koumondoros's voice sounded on our headsets. "Paranormal privateers! We're as close as we dare get to North Korea, about twenty miles from shore, near the Myonggan. Take off now. Godspeed!"

Sam and Lisa stored corgis in four panniers on their bulls, two on each side. The panniers had corgi-sized sleeves that held each securely and vertically. Twelve cute heads with red eyes looked out of each pannier. Four corgis would ride with me in my hovercraft, completing our corgi company of one hundred.

I'd inflated the hovercraft when the first party left and stored it in the V-22's cargo bay. I secured myself in the seat harness and clipped each corgi to it.

Each bull occupied a diagonal corner, to allow for even weight distribution. We attached their Kevlar harnesses to the sides of the bay. You couldn't fool around with one-ton zombie bulls on a VTOL aircraft.

"When we land, I'll leave first, then Sam by the cargo bay, and then Lisa." Now that a military operation was underway, I naturally took charge as the senior commanding officer. Although Sam and Lisa had experience in other battles, they weren't military.

"We'll proceed upriver until we get to the nuclear facility," I continued. "Then we'll pause and plan how to free our friends."

"Understood, Sergeant Rose!" Sam said, saluting.

Over my headset, I said, "Pilots, let's go!"

The *Resolute Too* was truly a mixed-service operation. The navy maintained its avionics and sonar and treated it as one of their ships. The marines piloted and maintained the V-22, as well as the ship's communications. The air force flew in secret cargo, like me. And I, the lowly Korean translator, came from the army. Of course, all the intelligence and overall direction came from the NSA. All the while its privateer status kept the US diplomatically isolated from its outrageous actions. I loved it!

With a roar of engines, we took off. We'd be on the beach at the Myonggan's mouth in ten minutes.

The engine noise was just starting to annoy me, when we slowed and landed. The rotors kept turning. I started the silent electric motor that powered the hovercraft. The cargo door came down.

And I was out! With a bellow and a snort, John Bull followed me, leaving a stinking pile of dung in his wake. Another clumping of hooves announced Lisa on Bull-oney.

As soon as Lisa left, the rotors revved to the max and the V-22 zoomed away. Few people lived in this part of North Korea, and it was late at night, so no one saw us.

"Hi-ho Bull-oney and away!" Lisa shouted as she reared and raced upstream, followed by Sam.

I revved up to max power and zoomed after them, following the shallow stream. My hovercraft could make sixty miles per hour, and with the calm conditions, I hit it.

I barely kept up with Sam and Lisa! I didn't know those bulls could run so fast! They raced along the bank, a longer and rougher route than the smooth water.

After a few miles, we both had to slow as the land and river climbed steeply into the mountain. I couldn't follow the stream, as it alternated between rapids and waterfalls. I wove back and forth, finding the best path for my hovercraft.

The bulls leapt upward looking like gigantic whales breaching the ocean.

The corgis yipped with excitement. That sounded like their bark of greeting for Diane. Could it be they smelled Diane along the streambed?

"Hey, Sam, Lisa! Let's stop a minute!"

"What's up?" Lisa asked.

"I think the corgis scented Diane's trail."

"Mine began yipping too."

"Mine too," Sam said. "Let's let them out, and they may lead us to Diane!"

"Can they manage on this steep terrain?" I knew they were fast and strong, but the biggest was no more than forty pounds and thirty inches long.

"You watch!" Lisa pulled the quick-release lanyard, and all forty-eight of her corgis flopped out of the panniers and harnesses like a load of freshly caught fish.

Sam followed her example, and I let my four loose.

All one hundred corgis ran pell-mell uphill, leaping and bounding four, five, six feet into the air, over rocks and bushes. They looked for all the world like salmon going upstream to spawn.

"We'd better move it!" Lisa shouted.

She followed the corgis, and so did I.

Or I tried. The steep terrain was the worst possible for a hovercraft. It could surmount obstacles up to four feet high and slopes up to forty-five degrees. But hopping boulders and going up steep slopes turned sixty miles per hour to no more than ten. The zombies pulled away.

I got to the crest of the hill and tried to catch up, as they went down one valley and up the next hill. No luck. Then, past the top of the next hill, I almost ran into them.

Sam and Lisa, atop their bulls, peered through some bushes. The corgis sat obediently behind them, although quivering and whimpering with eagerness. I joined them.

On the other side of the bushes, a couple of people looked through another set of bushes at the nuclear complex beyond. I heard them talking softly in Korean.

"What should we do?" a male voice asked the smaller figure next to him.

"The mining entrance is beyond those buildings, but I don't see how we can get past the soldiers," answered a young female voice.

These were apparently people who wanted to get into the nuclear facility. Maybe they had intelligence. Maybe this was just the opportunity we needed.

"But I do," I said in Korean, stepping through the bushes.

The corgis all crept up on their bellies, following me.

The couple spun around, and their mouths dropped open. Mine did too—their eyes shone zombie red!

Since they didn't speak, I did. "I see you're zombies. We're here to rescue our zombie friends who are trapped in this facility. I have two more zombie friends with me. Sam! Lisa! C'mon out!" I called in English.

"Oho! Some Korean zombies are here," Sam said.

"Are they are on our side?" Lisa asked suspiciously.

That was a good question.

The man said, "I am Kim Chi-un, and this is Park Ji Su. We too are here to rescue our friends in this facility, if we can. They are prisoners who dig out the nuclear tunnels. Perhaps we can work together."

"Definitely! Let me talk with my friends a minute."

"Sam, Lisa, good news! These are Kim Chi-un and Park Ji Su. They're apparently trying to figure out how to rescue their friends from this place. They want to work with us."

"Find out as much as you can from them about the situation," Lisa urged.

"Will do." I turned back to them. "Are your friends you want to rescue zombies? Are you by yourselves?"

"No," the man said. "Our friends in the mines are prisoners, and they aren't zombies. We're not by ourselves. We have about a thousand zombies surrounding the fence and another fifteen thousand former prisoners down the road, hiding in the woods. Do you have more zombies?"

Wow! With a thousand zombies this place would be easy to take! "No, there are just Sam and Lisa Melvin and our hundred zombie corgis." I laughed. "They're much more dangerous than they seem. With your resources, you can easily take over this facility."

"The fifteen thousand prisoners are barely alive. They can't help. We have a thousand zombies, but we're unarmed. There are several hundred soldiers down there!"

Apparently, they didn't understand their full zombie power. "How long have you been zombies?"

"I turned zombie about two weeks ago. The rest of them turned since then."

"Thanks to Kim Chi-un, we were all rescued from death!" Ji Su said. She sounded almost worshipful.

"That's wonderful Ji Su! Your zombies have more power than you realize. You'll be able to penetrate the fence without trouble, and the soldiers' bullets will not kill you."

"Yes, we began to realize that in the prison camp. After the first time I was shot, I revived and then shared my blood with others killed that day, including Ji Su. That's how we got a thousand zombies. Then when they ran out of bullets, the guards all deserted."

"Sensible of them! There's your strategy. You can force the soldiers to use up their bullets. You can also take away their guns. Finally, Sam and Lisa and the corgis and bulls"—I could hear them munching on the grass beyond the bushes—"can provide a distraction by a direct assault on the gate."

"You would do that for us?" Ji Su gasped.

"You just met us," Chi-un said.

"Sam and Lisa are experienced in zombie fighting, as are the bulls and corgis. You'll be amazed."

"We are. Ji Su, you pass the word along the perimeter to the east that the zombies are to go over the fence when we attack the gate. I'll go to the west. We'll meet back here. Then you can attack."

As I turned back to Sam and Lisa, Sam said, "You were talking a long time. What's up?"

"We have a plan. Chi-un and Ji Su have a thousand zombie friends who already surround the facility. They're going to go over the fence when we attack the main gate."

"Wow! Lisa and I haven't led an attack since we captured the *Resolute Too!*"

"Yeah, and we got decapitated, remember?" Lisa said. "Jessica, don't you think the zombie corgis should go on ahead? I know we can recover from being shot, but I'd just as soon not be shock troops!"

"I agree. They're small and hard to hit with gunfire, and they'll absorb the troops' attention. Although with them in front, we'll have some of the troops die. We're trying to keep casualties down, you know."

"I don't see any way around it," Lisa said.

"Maybe if Lisa and I attack either side of the gate, through the fence, we can call them to us before they go into a feeding frenzy," Sam suggested.

"Good idea," I said. "I have some kimchi treats with me. That always gets their attention. Here, each of you take a bag."

Ten minutes later, Chi-un and Ji Su returned.

"The message has spread around the perimeter," Chi-un said. "They'll go over the fence. Each group will go to the nearest building, looking for your friends and ours. We'll ignore the shooting, but take the guns away if we can."

"Good." I looked into his red eyes, under his dark brows and hollow cheeks. "You two must be starving. Here are some rations I brought." I gave them my MREs (meal ready to eat) military rations.

"Thank you so much!" Ji Su said.

"Yes, thank you indeed! You are very kind, but thousands of others are starving too."

"We'll help as we can." I turned to Sam and Lisa. "They have thousands of hungry zombies and people. What food can we spare from the ship?"

"We have lots of MREs in the hold," Lisa said.

"And we have tubs of oats there too," Sam added.

"Plus, we have my barrel of kimchi. We can have the V-22 bring the supplies when we leave." We planned to get out by the morning.

"The marines are monitoring our communication right now," Lisa said. "Three shifts of them listen to the audio and watch video feeds ever since the paranormal privateers left. Did you hear that, Paranormal Control?" She spoke seemingly into the air.

"Roger, Ms. Pulitzer," came a voice. "Ms. Pulitzer" was Pulitzer-winner Lisa's code name, self-chosen. Sam's was "Buckaroo Bonzai," and mine was "Kimchi Goddess."

"Are we ready, paranormal privateers?" I adopted General Figeroa's formal phrase.

"We're ready!" the Melvins chorused back.

I gestured toward the corgis and caught their attention. "Go fetch Diane!" I yelled and pointed toward the gate.

Diane's name electrified them. They knew *fetch* and they knew *Diane*, their favorite human. I thought they had been amazingly fast before. Now they raced like furry brown lightning bolts along the ground.

They reached the closed gate and scrambled over its ten-foot height. Soldiers inside finally noticed them. They had time to point their rifles and fire a few shots before a canine wave overwhelmed them.

I watched from my hovercraft. I knew my limitations. I would soon die in the confused crossfire of the melee. I directed the battle as well as I could from outside.

The first guards were already skeletons on the ground when the bulls hit the fence. The steel wire tore like string before the uncouth power of the zombie bulls, each two thousand pounds of eighty-mile-per-hour might hurtling through the night like freight trains.

I heard Sam and Lisa whistle and call off the corgis, who obediently followed them. The Melvins rode into the first building on their bulls, smashing through wooden doors. I followed their progress on my video-feed monitor and my headset. I heard shouts in Korean. "Save the commandant! Defend to the death!" yelled one officer, just before a bull trampled him.

I heard the sporadic *pop, pop* of bullets through my headset, as well as the steady crackling of gunfire throughout the complex. Chi-un and Ji Su had followed the bulls.

"Sam, Lisa, you seem to be in some kind of headquarters! See if you can capture an officer and find out where the Newbys and their bodyguards are."

"We're on it!" Lisa yelled.

I followed her and Sam's progress through the building, watching my split-screen monitor, each side showing their head-cam view. The two images jostled and jumped through the narrow corridors, smashing through walls and doors. It was a good thing I didn't get motion sickness!

Suddenly Lisa's headset monitor showed her jumping off the bull and onto a bemedaled man. "Gotcha! She picked him up bodily and held his stomach against Bull-oney's sharp horn. "Now talk! Where are Diane and George? The zombies?" she said uselessly in English.

"Put a headset on him!" I yelled.

"Will do!" Sam said. He took off his and put it on the Korean officer.

"Your life will be spared if you tell us where the zombies are who entered your facility. They entered the nuclear storage area," I said.

"Oh! Those intruders! They're in the storage building, underground."

"Where is that building?"

"Straight back behind this one! It's a low concrete building!"

"Lisa, give Sam back his headset. I got the place where our zombies are!"

"Great! Here you go, Sam," She jammed it on his head.

"Go out the back of this building and you'll see a low concrete building. The storage area is underground."

"You hear that, Sam? Let's go! What'll I do with this piece of shit?" She looked at the gibbering general held up by her arms, feet dangling, unintelligible in Korean or English.

"I'll take him," Kim Chi-un said, walking up behind Lisa, his arms full of confiscated weapons.

"Lisa!" I called. "Give him to Chi-un."

"OK. I sure don't want him." She held out the general at arm's length to Chi-un.

He dropped the weapons on the floor and took the man by the collar and gently set him to the floor, where he collapsed in a heap. Chi-un squatted next to him.

"Commandant, I'd like to know about the prisoners you use to dig out the tunnels after the nuclear explosions."

"Th-The-They are gone. We send them back to Camp 16 after we're done with them."

"Where are they housed?"

"N-N-Near the tunnels."

"Let's go and check and see if any are there." Chi-un pulled him gently but inexorably behind him.

Sam and Lisa rode away, and I didn't hear anymore.

The nuclear storage building's doors gaped open, torn from their hinges. Two skinny Korean zombies stood by.

"We opened the doors for you, American zombies! Thank you for visiting us!"

I translated for Sam and Lisa. Then I said, "I want to talk to them!"

Lisa put her headset on one. He looked like a teenaged boy.

"Hello, I'm the translator for these American zombies. Could you help us?"

"Oh yes. We'd do anything to help our friends."

"Good. See if you can find the control room for this facility. We think our friends are in here, and we want to find where they are."

"We know where the bombs are. The doors are locked though. The guards said it was deadly inside."

"Yes, we know that. Our friends are zombies and can survive. They probably can't get out. Can you open the doors?"

"Yes. I'll look for the control room, and Min Jun will run back to the storage room and let your American zombies in."

"Thank you!" Then in English, "Sam, Lisa, follow the young man. He'll guide you to Diane and George!"

"We're on our way!" Sam called. "Lisa, this guy will lead us there."

"Lemme get my headset back!" She grabbed it.

Down the stairs they went. They left the bulls behind since the stairs were too small. The corgis followed though, noses to the ground.

Min Jun led to the lowest level. He pushed a button beside a massive steel door. It slowly slid open.

"Sam and Lisa, don't stay there any longer than necessary! That's radioactive!"

"No sense in taking needless risks," Lisa said.

Inside the room, dozens of bombs had been dismantled and smashed. Our four friends lay on the floor by the door. Diane and George in each other's arms, and Lulu and Sharon as well.

"Oh no!" Lisa cried. She immediately dragged George and Diane out. Sam pulled out Lulu and Sharon.

"Close the door!" I shouted.

"Jessica!" Lisa wailed. "There's no pulse!"

Crap! *That sucks.*

"I won't believe they're dead yet. They're zombies!" Sam said stoutly. "There's dead, and then there's mostly dead."

"Sam! I can't believe you're quoting *The Princess Bride* at a time like this!" Lisa said.

"My favorite movie! It seems to fit. Let's bring them into the fresh air."

"Fine! Fresh, clean air is just what we need to revive a pair of corpses!" she grumbled as she carried Diane's body upstairs.

Min Jun dragged George's body up, and Sam followed carrying the two bodyguards.

"Revive the corpses!" Sam shouted. "That's it!"

"Yeah, that's what I said. How does fresh air help?" Lisa asked.

"Not the fresh air, but what about the zombie blood ampoules we have around our necks?"

"Sam, you're a genius! Why didn't I think of that? I even have one!"

"Don't leave home without it."

They brought the zombie corpses into the street and plunged the ampoules into them.

The fighting died down as the guards and administrators ran away into the night, abandoning their useless weapons. Several fleeing soldiers and officers screamed "Zombies! Run for your lives!" as they ran panic stricken past me. I could see their point. It was terrifying seeing hundreds of zombies with red eyes and ragged clothing coming toward you. I brought my hovercraft through the shattered fence so I could translate directly.

Kim Chi-un and Ji Su appeared about the same time I met Sam and Lisa in the street.

"We've freed the prisoners. The commandant led us to them. They weren't in the barracks, but they were locked in the tunnels," Chi-un said.

"We also brought the corpses back to life," Ji Su added.

"Including the guards shredded by the zombie corgis." Shaking his head, Chi-un continued, "That was the first time I actually saw bones and limbs grow back. It was like Ezekiel's valley of the dry bones."

"You know, we have a song about that Scripture," I said.

"What? The valley of the dry bones? I'd love to hear it!"

"Let's see if I can remember it. I learned it as a kid in church." I knew the chorus. Now to translate the black slave spiritual to Korean and see if I could fit it into the rhythm.

"Dem bones, dem bones, dem dry bones.
Dem bones, dem bones, dem dry bones.
Dem bones, dem bones, dem dry bones.
Now hear the word of the Lord."

"I like that!" Chi-un said.

"Me too," Ji Su chorused.

"I'll sing that at church. Let's practice," Chi-un said.

We began singing it again.

* * *

"We have a problem, Houston," Sam said.

"Actually, Sam," Lisa said pedantically, "the correct quote is, 'OK, Houston, we've had a problem here.'"

"Irregardless—"

"*Sam*! You know I hate that!"

He grinned. "Of course. I love making you yell! Our real problem is moving our zombie casualties to the ship. They're comatose and"—he touched George's neck—"still dead. Mostly dead."

"Now you're repeating yourself," she said.

"Yup. We've got to get out of here soon, or we'll cause an international incident. But our friends are dead to this point, and we can't leave without them."

"And the Korean army will come down on this place any minute."

"I'm sure you're right."

"Of course I am! So we do have a problem. Let's talk with Jessica and the Korean zombies. Hey, Jessica!" Lisa yelled to where Jessica was singing with the Korean zombies. "Cut your caterwauling and come over here!"

"You're in *Midley Beacon* editor mode," Sam said.

"It works."

Jessica approached, followed by Kim Chi-un. "Hi, Lisa. What's up?"

"Not our paranormal privateers. They haven't responded to our zombie blood treatment. I want to give them more zombie blood, and we're out."

"Oh! I don't have any," Jessica said with dismay.

Chi-un asked Jessica in Korean, "What's wrong?"

"Our friends are not responding to the zombie blood."

"We can fix that. We have live zombie blood. Ji Su, do you have your knife?"

"Yes."

"Let's give our most precious gift." Together they slashed their wrists and then slashed the wrists of George and Diane. They pressed their bleeding wounds into the cuts of the corpses. They repeated the process for Lulu's and Sharon's bodies.

"What are they doing?" Lisa asked in horror.

"They're sharing their zombie blood. This is how they made over a thousand zombies from the prison camp," Jessica answered.

"Wow," Sam said. "Lisa, that's a fabulous story we need to get out."

"You're right. Type it up on your cell phone and send it to Lashon."

"It'll have to go through military censors, you know."

"Yes. I. Know," Lisa grated.

After the two Korean zombie heroes completed their bloody anointing, they sat down next to the dead bodies.

"What are you doing?" Jessica asked them.

"We're waiting and praying. That's what we always do when we share our most precious gift."

"Why do you call it your 'most precious gift'?"

"That's what the Lees called it when they gave me their zombie blood capsule. It's appropriate since it's the gift of life."

"Sam and Lisa! You've got to hear this!" Jessica translated for the *Midley Beacon* couple.

"Sam? You got all that?" Lisa asked.

"It's in there!" Sam said, holding up his phone with the recording app.

"Now, how long will this resurrection take?" Lisa asked Jessica.

"From what they told me, anywhere from half an hour to four hours."

Sam touched George's neck. "He's got a pulse!"

"That's only fifteen minutes!"

Jessica translated for Chi-un. "He said that's not unusual. What varies is the time from the pulse to complete healing."

"We've got to pull out in two hours," Lisa said. "Can you take care of them in case they're not up?"

"We need to get away from here now too before the army comes," Chi-un said. "We could put them in one of the cars or trucks, but then we'd be tied to the road. We need to go cross country to escape."

"We can use my hovercraft," Jessica put in.

"Don't you need that yourself? And how will we fly it? None of us know how to use it," Chi-un said.

"I'll stay behind with it and fly it."

"Then how will you get out?" Concern tinged Chi-un's voice.

"I will get out with George and Diane, Lulu and Sharon. I guess we'll have a beach pickup like Sam and Lisa."

"What's our best way to sneak to the beach? We can't go along the Myonggan with them comatose," Chi-un said.

"We can go south to port Kimch'aek and head north or south to a deserted beach. The hard part will be staying undercover."

"What about your plan to go north to China?" Jessica asked.

"Ji Su can lead them. Everyone knows she's my deputy. I'll catch up with them after you're safe."

"Let's do it! I'll tell Sam and Lisa."

"Jessica," Lisa began, as soon as Jessica stopped talking. "Diane and crew show no sign of waking. We need to get out of here, pronto! Can we leave them with the NK zombies? Can you escape detection?"

"That's what we were planning. The Korean zombies will split up. Some have already gone south to Kimch'aek. The rest will go north to the Chinese border. Chi-un will escort us undercover with the hovercraft to Kimch'aek. Then we'll go to a deserted beach and get picked up."

"Sounds good!" Lisa said. "Sam, let's go."

Sam and Lisa rode their bulls down the Myonggan to the beach, the corgis leaping and bounding behind them like dolphins.

The marines monitoring their communication and location sent the V-22 Osprey to pick them up in the predawn darkness.

On the beach, they loaded the corgis into their sleeves in the panniers on the bulls. As they rode their bulls into the VTOL craft, Sam said, "So much has happened already! It's hard to believe it's only the next morning."

"We've got a lot to do yet. We've got many news stories and tons of video to get past the censors."

"I don't think anything will come out until everyone's out safely."

"You're right. This time, I have to agree with the censors. It's funny how your perspective changes when it's your friends' lives at stake."

Chapter 8

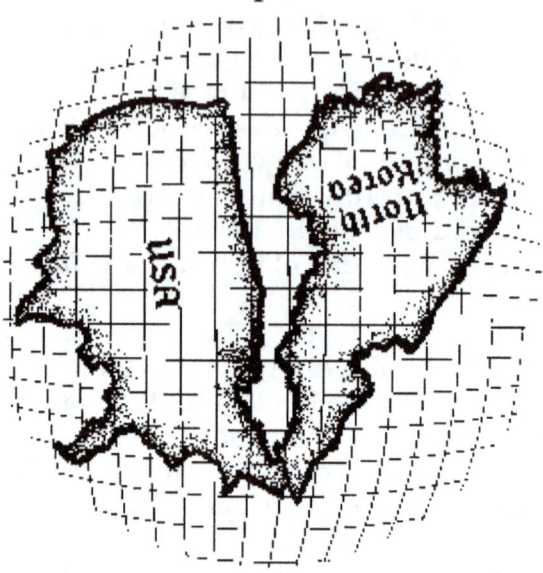

Kimch'aek

"**W**hew! I'm feeling hot!" Lisa said as she and Sam got off the V-22 onto the *Resolute Too*'s helipad after having left Jessica and the other zombies behind.

"That's not just now," Sam said.

"Sam! I'm talking about being overheated."

"Exactly! That's how I feel when I look at you."

"You're impossible!"

"Huh! I am hot too."

"Don't I know it!" Lisa said with a smile.

"It is hot outside here. Hey, it's July Fourth!"

"We've got to get our stories past the censors and into the *Midley Beacon*! I want to publish a special July Fourth edition about how the paranormal privateers destroyed the North Korean arsenal."

"Let's give General Figeroa a call," Sam said as he opened the door to the video conference room.

"OK, you call him. I'll go to our room for a quick shower. Maybe that'll cool me off."

The NSA logo dissolved into the General Figeroa. His blue eyes looked into Sam's.

"Sam!" he said. "Your eyes are brown, not red!"

"Uh-oh. Both Lisa and I felt hot, like a fever. It must be another attack on zombies."

"When did this start?"

"Just tonight, after we rescued Diane and company from the nuke site."

"Hmmm. That's in North Korea, where there aren't any zombies!"

"No, actually there are about a thousand of them among the North Korean prisoners who escaped."

"That info must be in the transcripts of your conversations. I followed your actions in North Korea, but I didn't have time to read all the transcripts. Great work! I'm dispatching another F-35 right now to take your blood samples."

"OK. Hi, Lisa! That was a fast shower!"

"Sam, I see you lost your zombiism too. I saw my reflection."

"I guess that proves you're not a vampire—or a zombie. So we're back to normal."

"As normal as we ever are. It's been an exciting year since we became zombies, but we really didn't improve our reporting through zombiism, so to hell with it!"

"That's what Kim Jung-un said about zombies," said General Figeroa.

"What?" Lisa said.

"Kim Jung-un's hopping mad about the destruction of his nuclear weapons and the escape of twenty thousand political prisoners. He blames the US, as usual, but he's also demonizing all zombies. They're to be shot on sight."

Sam and Lisa laughed.

"Yes, that's totally useless, I know. Even more so if the North Korean zombies get sick and lose their zombiism and red eyes. Then they'll be undetectable.

"The paranormal privateers knocked over a North Korean hornet's nest. We've had some intelligence reports of North Korean troops trying to capture prisoners and repulsed by zombies. The North Koreans say they're rounding up all escapees, but our satellite imagery shows Camp 16 is still empty. I think the North Koreans prioritized catching the escaped prisoners more than you paranormal privateers."

"We'll just have to be plain privateers from here on out," Sam said.

"I hope not," Figeroa said. "We should be able to solve this anti-zombie disease like we did the other one."

"How far has it spread?" Lisa asked.

"Much further than the previous one, worldwide. We're getting reports of zombies falling sick within the Americas, Asia, Africa, and Europe."

"I've gotta get in touch with my reporters at the *Midley Beacon* with this story," Lisa said.

"They're already on it, Lisa. I read your website before our conference. They're not quite up to my level of information, but they're close."

"Then that's even more reason I need to reach them! I've gotta keep ahead of the Feds!"

"You know, as privateers, you're Feds now! In any event, I'm sending you all back to the US for some rest and relaxation, until we get this zombie bug solved. The closest port for you is Seattle."

"It'll be nice to be back in the good old USA!" Sam said. "I will get a hamburger as soon as I get off! How long will it take?"

"That'll be up to you and your captain, how much you want to push it. At twenty-five knots, it'll take about eight days."

"Knowing Diane, she'll want to push it," Lisa said.

"I'll let you guys sort that out. I've got to get the CDC ready for your blood samples. The F-35 will arrive later today. Make sure you all have at least one sample, preferably two."

"Will do!" Sam said.

"That'll give us a chance to report on our Korean adventures and to catch up with the latest news," Lisa said.

"Then we're set. Figeroa, out."

* * *

Before the general faded from the video screen, Lisa said, "OK, Sam, we've got a *lot* to do. First, write up our stories. Next, clear them with the NSA censors. Third, check with Diane and the other zombies to see where they are."

"OK. What will you be doing?"

"I've gotta catch up with what's been happening. I'll conference right now with Lashon and Charlie." She dialed.

"Hi, Lashon."

"Hi, Lisa. This better be important! I was getting ready for bed."

"Yeah, it is. Sam and I have been out of contact for a day, and all the zombies here on the *Resolute Too* have lost their zombiism."

"Oh boy! So it's gotten you too? That just started today, across the US. We've filled the *Midley Beacon* with stories about it."

"I'll read those next. What have they found out so far?"

"Blood samples have been sent to the CDC, the Mayo Clinic, and the Cleveland Clinic. SPEwZ has had their biggest one-day sale ever as people everywhere bought zombie blood to renew their zombiism."

"We had trouble with zombie blood ampoules. They didn't resurrect George and Diane. We had to do a direct transfusion from Korean zombies."

"Direct transfusion, eh? That's a new one. But we have the same problem. The zombie blood works for a while. Then the fever comes back and the person dezombifies."

"Hi, Lisa," Charlie Gomez said.

"Hi, Charlie. I've got Lashon on the call too. We're talking about the loss of zombiism worldwide."

"Yeah, Lashon covered the US, and I got the rest of the world."

"Did you get Korea? We just ran into it here."

"Nope, but Japan lost its zombies, as did China and Russia, so I can't say I'm surprised."

"Did *all* this happen just yesterday?"

"Yes," Lashon said. "We made a timeline of the outbreaks. They started in Europe yesterday morning and spread across the world as people awoke."

"Now your assignment is to find out how this criminal network did that."

"The CDC and Cleveland Clinic are working on the infection vector."

"I expect you to beat them!"

"OK, Lisa!" Lashon said.

"Get going!" Lisa insisted. "I'll check back tomorrow on your progress." She cut the circuit.

* * *

After her image faded from their screens, Charlie Gomez said to Lashon Miller, "Uh, how do you propose we solve this mystery, *Senior* Associate Editor? I have no clue about where to start, let alone how to beat the CDC, the Mayo Clinic, and the Cleveland Clinic."

"Neither do I, Charlie," Lashon admitted. "But with Lisa, you agree to the assignment first and figure it out as you go."

"First, let's find out what those three institutions have done so far. I'll call our contacts at the Mayo Clinic and the CDC."

"That leaves me with the Cleveland Clinic," Charlie said.

"Let's meet tomorrow at Midley and discuss what we've learned."

* * *

"Ji Su, I want the other escapees to accept you as the leader in my absence."

"I do not feel worthy, Kim Chi-un. I am only seventeen and have no leadership skills."

"But you know the smuggler routes to China, and I *have* to go with these sick zombies to Kimch'aek. I never led anyone until we broke out. God will help you. I'll rejoin you as soon as I can."

We broke the crowd headed toward China into multiple groups, each led by zombies. They could protect them against any soldiers they met. Each group took a different smuggling route.

Those headed toward Kimch'aek, also led by zombies, spread across the wide Orangchon River valley. Jessica, I, the paranormal privateers, and zombie corgis traveled the road by night and hid by day.

We'd packed the hovercraft with George and two of the female zombies. It could barely hover with the weight, even at full power. We made our best time if it traveled along the highway. I carried one of the women on my back.

As morning dawned, the skirt of the craft dragged on the ground, slowing us more.

"Chi-un, we need to find a place to hide and camp. I have to recharge the batteries," Jessica said.

"Let's head toward the tree line." I pointed across a field to trees half a kilometer from the road.

Jessica hooked the corgis to the hovercraft and got out and pushed, while the corgis pulled it, still hovering, across the field. I trotted behind, carrying George.

She quickly arranged beds of leaves and pine branches beneath low brush and dragged the zombies undercover. She also hid the hovercraft, deflating it. Then she extended a pole into a treetop and opened a dish, which she pointed toward the sun. Shinnying back down the tree, she said, "There! I'm all set for the day. A day's sun should recharge the batteries for tonight. Oh, you've got a campfire going. You're fast!"

I felt like she'd given me a medal.

I had to give George, Diane, Lulu, and Sharon more transfusions of zombie blood. They did not wake, and their zombiism kept disappearing every two or three hours. I hadn't seen that before.

For hours, Jessica told stories about the four zombies' adventures and origins. I felt I was getting to know them through her. My zombie eyes didn't faze her, and she seemed hardy as a North Korean soldier.

"I'm surprised by how adept you are at camping and hiding undercover," I said.

"I *am* a US Army sergeant. We camp and hike all the time and keep fit with daily training. I'm not supposed to tell you my rank, but you're not a captor, but an ally."

I felt proud to be called her ally. Still, it seemed weird to be allied with an American soldier. But it was weird to be a zombie. And a North Korean Christian. And anyway, she was good looking.

I remember how her beauty awed me when I met her. First, by her exotic, fair, clear-skinned face outside the nuclear facility, then her magnificent curly hair when she took off her helmet. And those eyes... Not brown or blue or green, but a mixture she called hazel.

Even though I fought to not stare at her, constant close proximity made me more and more aware of her. I got used to her perfect face through constant conversation. Sometimes, what she was saying was so interesting, I forgot how gorgeous she was. Sometimes up to five minutes at a time.

I tried with all my might to keep my emotions in check. She had to leave and go back to the US Army. I had to stay and help my people, zombies, Christians, and all North Koreans.

Despite our looming separation, I felt happier than ever before. I'd led a whole prison camp to freedom! I'd led people to Christ! I'd helped my people. And I was traveling with the loveliest girl in the world.

Jessica seemed completely oblivious to her own beauty and her effect on me. She was casual about her modesty, not caring if I saw her in her underwear. She treated me like a friend, a buddy, a comrade. That was good enough for me. It was more than I dreamed of.

Jessica slept in the afternoon while I kept guard. I slipped away and caught some rabbits. It was easy for a zombie. I climbed a tree and then dropped on them from above, like a wildcat. I ate one raw. I learned to do that while in camp, eating animals raw for protein. I caught two more for us to share later.

Jessica awoke as the sun set over the western mountains. She took down her solar panel and inflated the hovercraft. Then she checked on the sick zombies.

"Oh, hi, Jessica," Diane said.

I listened to the conversation through her phone app.

"Hi, Diane. How are you feeling?"

"Weak as a baby. I feel like I had a bad bout of flu."

"You're not a zombie anymore."

"Yeah, George, me, Lulu, and Sharon noticed that after we were locked in the bomb chamber." She looked at her hands. "My hands and nails have healed. What time is it?"

"It's 8:30 the night after you struck the bomb site."

"So we've lost a whole day! What about our pickup?"

"They picked up Sam and Lisa—"

"Good!"

"And most of the corgis," Jessica added as one came up and licked Diane's face.

Another licked George's. His hands snatched the dog and held it at arm's length.

"None of that, you mongrel!"

"George! You're awake!" Diane said, her alto voice ringing with delight.

"Yeah. I was listening to you and Jessica talk when that mophead licked me."

"So you know we're still not zombies."

"Yeah. We stayed zombie long enough to heal, but the anti-zombie disease knocked out even our transfused zombie blood. And we missed our pickup. Where are we headed, Jessica?"

"To Kimch'aek. We'll go along the beach and find a deserted spot for another pickup."

"Sounds good. But," he said, his voice grim, "we may not be able to. I'm sure the whole North Korean army, navy, and air force are looking for you."

"I'd seen army convoys go up and down the road and several planes pass over before I crashed." Switching to Korean, Jessica said to me, "Were there many more convoys and planes while I slept?"

"Yes. I counted ten or twelve convoys in both directions. One group searched along the road with dogs, but they didn't follow us through the field."

"Maybe they weren't looking for our scent."

"I can't see how they'd know which prisoner to scent. Also, the hovercraft keeps your scent and the Newbys off the ground. I have my old clothes, which have been washed. Your group left nothing behind for them to use for tracking."

"Good. But what's not good is escaping by the beach. The V-22 won't be able to come in unobserved."

"I worried about that yesterday and thought of a plan."

"That's great, Chi-un! What is it?"

"I know some smugglers in Kimch'aek who smuggle with Russians and with the South. They have a fishing boat they use as cover. We may be able to get on their boat and get away."

"Wonderful!"

"It'll cost a lot."

"Perhaps they'll accept the hovercraft as a trade."

"They might!" I began to hope my idea might work.

Jessica talked to the four ex-zombies, as the phone app translated. All of them were weak. George and Diane told of how they'd lost their zombiism. This had happened before to them, but previously it had been like a cold. This time they had flu-like symptoms.

"Maybe it's something you picked up in North Korea," I suggested.

"No, they're pretty sure their old foe, Sid Boffin, or his crime network is behind it."

"It's dark now. Can they move with us?"

"Yes. If any of them gets tired, they can ride in the hovercraft."

* * *

Back on the *Resolute Too*, Lisa said to Sam, "I'm worried about this zombie bug. It's hitting worldwide, and millions of zombies are losing their healing powers and strength. How will the *Midley Beacon* continue its dominance of zombie news if zombies go away?"

"What will happen to the millions of sick and dying? Zombie blood treatment is the only hope for many of them," Sam said.

"Lashon and Charlie will give us updates tomorrow on any medical progress. Meanwhile, let's see how Jessica and our formerly paranormal privateers are doing."

Leaving the conference room, they went to the radio room. Lisa greeted the marine monitoring the communication. "Hi, Sergeant Kilroy, what's the latest on our injured privateers?"

"They're asleep," said Leroy Kilroy, a trim marine with brown hair and green eyes. He gestured toward the video monitor.

The screen showed someone walking through a lightly wooded area. They heard Korean spoken and then some laughter.

Lisa put on a communications headset. "Hi, Jessica, how's it going?"

"Hi, Lisa, it's good to hear from you! Glad you got back safely."

"Yes. General Figeroa said the whole country's in turmoil due to the twenty thousand escapees from the prison camp. They're more worried about them than about our task force."

"The twenty thousand prisoners are scattering everywhere," Jessica said. "Perhaps a quarter is headed through the smuggling trails to China. Everyone else is headed home, all over North Korea. Even the sick and injured we left at the camp have been healed by zombie blood and are headed to their hometowns."

"Hasn't anyone gotten sick yet, like Diane and George?"

"No, not yet."

"Hmmm. Maybe there's an incubation period. Or maybe the master hacker missed North Korea? Anyway, where are you and our favorite ex-zombies headed?"

"We're going to Kimch'aek. We're undercover, off the road about half a mile. We're taking a break. We walked all night."

"Sounds good. We're outside the territorial waters, about a hundred miles off the coast, but we can come closer."

"I'll tell you our plans once I know more."

"Great! Thanks for the update. See ya."

"Hey, Lisa," Sam said.

"What?"

"I'm calling Hank Williams and Betty Tuffield about how they're doing in this uproar."

"Good idea! We need a human-interest angle for our news. Facts alone are boring to readers."

Hank Williams and Betty Tuffield ran the Tom's Turkeys zombie turkey farm. They bred zombie turkeys for zombie sausages and zombie turkey wings. Both were highly popular and profitable for the couple ever since the turkey apocalypse four years ago. The zombie turkey wings especially were lucrative. They could cut off the turkey wings and they'd grow back in fifteen minutes, enabling them to harvest thousands of wings per hour. Then they could sell them at premium prices over chicken wings. Few turkey growers dared to mess with zombie turkey flocks.

Betty had lost her husband Tom to zombie turkeys, and Hank had lost his first wife, so the married couple had already faced and overcome the worst the turkeys could do.

"Hi, Betty! This is Sam Melvin," Sam said into his phone.

"Hi, Sam! You've surprised me. I never expected to hear from you and Lisa after the president awarded you the Presidential Medal of Freedom. Aren't you on that luxury yacht, sailing around the world?"

"Yes. But it's not just a pleasure trip. We're still running the *Midley Beacon*. Say, Betty, could we switch to video conference?" Sam had walked back to the conference room for that purpose while he called.

"Sure. I'm on my computer now. FaceTime or Skype?"

"Let's use Skype."

Soon Betty's square, auburn-topped face appeared on the five-foot wall screen. "Whoa, Sam! That's quite a conference room you've got! All I've got is this spare bedroom."

"It's the best your tax money or Sid Boffin's crime empire can buy! When the government refurbished his superyacht as a privateer, it had been trashed pretty badly in the battle. I'm not quite sure what's original equipment and what they've added."

"If it's our government, they have better taste than I'd expect. That's mahogany paneling or I'm a turkey!"

"Oh. I hadn't noticed."

"Men!"

"I didn't call about our furnishings, Betty. I was hoping to get a ground's-eye view of the new zombie disease sweeping the US and the world. Are you and Hank affected at all?"

"We sure are! As soon as the disease hit yesterday, we got a tremendous surge in orders. We had to work overtime to slaughter and grind up our turkeys for zombie turkey sausage. Apparently, lots of zombies thought they could get rezombified from our turkeys."

"Can they?"

"Not that I've seen! I taste each batch of zombie turkey sausage, and I haven't turned zombie! Anyway, we've sold out our turkeys. We only have our breeding stock left."

"Any of your turkeys get sick?"

"No. The disease seems only targeted at people. I talked with Heather Mallorn of Her Majesty's Kennels, which breeds the zombie corgis. No sick dogs there, nor are there any sick zombie bulls among those herds."

"That's some good news!"

"Betty!" Sam heard a voice in the background. "Who ya talking to?"

Betty's husband, Hank Williams, came into view, tall and lanky. "Oh hi, Sam! What's happened to your eyes? You're no longer zombie!"

"Those are contacts, Hank," Betty said confidently.

"Um, no, Betty. I came down with the disease, as did Lisa and all the other zombies here. We're all back to normal."

"How will you keep up your privateering work? I've followed your adventures around the world, and you need that zombie power," Hank asked.

"I'm not sure. We'll just have to wait while they work on a cure. Hey, I'm supposed to be interviewing you! What can you tell me about the effects of the zombie disease in the US?"

"Disaster, at least as far as zombie sports leagues are concerned," Hank said as he sat next to Betty in front of the monitor's camera.

"I hadn't thought of that!"

"Yes. All the zombie basketball, baseball, football, and tennis players lost their superstrength and speed. The television and internet networks are in a panic. The zombie leagues were their biggest income source."

"Can't they go play in the non-zombie leagues now?"

"Not really. The techniques and skills are different when you're twice as fast and strong and can't get injured. Most of the zombie players were retired from injuries or were never good enough in the first place to play in the major leagues. And anyway," Hank continued, "I've kind of lost my interest in regular sports. Once you see zombies play, the major leagues seem minor. I'm sure I'm not the only one."

"Wow," Sam said, typing furiously on his laptop. "Anything else going on?"

"There is the complete collapse of the medical system," Betty said.

"That only happened in Europe last time. How is the US coping?"

"Badly. There's widespread panic. That's why we're selling zombie sausage like hotcakes. It's a palliative, a zombie placebo for people. The political parties blame each other, although that's no change," Betty said.

"This affects the poor who can't afford non-zombie treatment. They went off government health insurance when the zombie blood cures came in. Most of the traditional healthcare system is still there, for people who didn't want zombie blood, but it's very much high-end healthcare," Betty said.

"That's not to mention obese people becoming fat again," Hank added. "Then the stock market crashed as soon as it opened today."

"Uh-oh. How much?"

"A thousand points in the first hour, two thousand in the second, and then the FTC suspended trading. They're considering suspending all trading for the duration of the zombie blood crisis. They call it the 'Zombie Crash.'"

"Who's being affected, besides stock traders?"

"Every retirement fund, of course," Hank said. "Everyone's lost a good portion of their savings."

"Wow. I go to North Korea, and all this happens! At least amputees don't lose their limbs again!"

"No, and people cured of cancer stay cured," Betty said.

"I'm after human-interest stories. It sounds like you guys aren't suffering enough to make it interesting," Sam said.

"Nope. Even the zombie turkeys are happily breeding and not being slaughtered—for the time being," Hank said.

"I'll call SPEwZ next to get their views since Diane and George are out of the loop for now. I'll let you go!"

"Goodbye, Sam!" Betty and Hank chorused.

Sam dialed Maggie Newby by video call. Her brown eyes and hair complemented her round, smiling face.

"I'm glad to see you looking so chipper, even though you lost your zombie powers."

"Yeah, well, I don't really use them—except for working twelve hours and partying ten. Now I work eight and party one or two hours, with Donnie."

"How's he holding up? I didn't even bother trying to call him. I know he doesn't answer his phone."

"Oh, he's fine. He's a little grumpy 'cause he can't play video games all night like he could when he was a zombie."

"Well, how's SPEwZ doing with the zombie blood infection?"

"Good and bad. Our sales are way up, but our supply has died. Everyone wants zombie blood while it lasts, but no one can donate it anymore. It works for a day or two, and then people get the anti-zombie disease and their zombie bacteria die off."

"That's horrible."

"In the short term, SPEwZ is having its greatest year ever. In the long term, we're sunk. Our stock crashed with the market. The investor community wants us to diversify from zombie medication. They're out for our blood!"

"How long can you last?"

"We have enough blood supplies for the next week. Then we have to close down."

"Will everyone be laid off?"

"Yes, even me. We'll shutter the warehouse and production facilities as well as the office and hope for the cure."

"Have you heard anything from the medical researchers?"

"Yes. We had a conversation with Dr. Marchanne Herbst of the Mayo Clinic. She's the one who originally analyzed our zombiism and identified E. coli Homo Zapiens as the cause. She says the ECHZ bacteria is being attacked by another bacteria."

"Wow. I've never heard of that before! But then, I never heard of a virus attacking a bacteria either until it attacked

ECHZ. Do you have anything more for me, on the cure or on SPEwZ, Maggie?"

"They think they've isolated the attacking bacteria, but they don't have a cure or any idea of where it's coming from. Sorry to be depressing, Sam."

"I'd better get on the phone with Dr. Herbst. Bye, Maggie."

Sam video-dialed Dr. Herbst's phone.

"Hello?" said a light soprano voice. Gray-and-brown hair in a pageboy cut framed her oval face on the video feed. She wore a bathrobe.

"Hello, Dr. Herbst. I'm Sam Melvin with the *Midley Beacon.* Could you answer a few questions about the anti-zombie bacteria?"

"I see our findings have made their way to the major media despite the blackout. That's fine with me. I never liked keeping our work secret."

"I'm glad to be called 'major media,' Dr. Herbst! Maggie Newby told me you discovered a bacteria was killing the zombie bacteria."

"It's absolutely fascinating how it works!" Excitement colored her voice. "We've learned more about ECHZ too."

"Tell me all about it!"

"As you know, ECHZ begins in the human gut and then moves from the small intestine to the bloodstream. From there it suffuses every tissue in the body, always present to reproduce damaged tissue by copying the local DNA."

"Uh, yeah. I kind of knew that."

"Its wide dispersion makes it very hard to eliminate by antibiotic or poison. We were shocked when a virus turned up specifically targeted for ECHZ."

"But that was bioengineered, right?"

"Absolutely. We still don't know who did that. We suspect this new bacteria is also bioengineered."

"Wow! That's really big news! Do you think it's the same guy?"

"Yes, or gal, as the case may be. We've found the bacteria on the feet of flies, beetles, ants, and other common insects, like we did with the virus. But there have to be multiple vectors for the infection."

"Why is that?"

"You folks on the *Resolute Too* got infected even though you didn't have flies in the Northwest Passage."

"Uh, we did. We had a gym full of bulls and bullsh—"

"Oh. There's still the puzzle of how everyone became infected at nearly the same time, worldwide. That wasn't controlled by flies."

"How could that happen?"

"It's like a timed-release capsule. I wonder..." She hummed tunelessly to herself while looking off into space. "Oh, Sam, you're still there. I don't have any more answers for you. Call tomorrow."

"OK. Thanks, Dr. Herbst! Bye."

"Bye."

* * *

We stayed off the road and went through farm fields and narrow wooded paths. Each of the paranormal privateers took turns resting on the hovercraft. With a lighter load, it had no trouble going over fields and ditches.

I chuckled at the term *paranormal privateers*. That was silly. It was good to laugh at something again.

We covered more distance that night and hid in the woods outside Kimch'aek before dawn.

"I'll go and contact the smuggler," I told Jessica.

"Here. Take my sunglasses. They might be looking for red eyes."

"I hadn't thought of that. In the prison camp, they just thought we had conjunctivitis."

"I'm sure the prison and nuclear officials told everyone about the zombies' eyes by now."

"Th-Thanks," I stammered, overwhelmed by her concern. I blew my nose and tried to get my emotions under control.

"I'd hate to have anything happen to you," she said softly, tenderly. It was almost like she loved me.

"I'd better go," I said brusquely, turning away before she could see the tears running down my face.

"Oh no you don't!" Jessica practically tackled me. "You don't get away without a goodbye hug, Mr. Kim!"

I trembled, feeling her warm body pressed against mine. I couldn't talk.

"Oh, you're crying! Why is that?" She studied my face. "You're sad to be going! You'll miss me, right?"

"Y-Yes" I managed to get out.

"In that case, let me kiss you!"

She thoroughly kissed me. Despite my zombie strength, I had to sit down on the ground or fall over.

It finally ended. I gasped for breath.

"Wow, that was something. Kim Chi-un, I think you like me. Am I right?"

"Yes."

"That's great! I like you too!" She helped me up. "Now that's a proper goodbye! See you soon, Chi-un dear!"

I walked toward Kimch'aek, but I felt like I was flying.

* * *

The fishing captain I knew had just docked and was unloading the night's catch.

"Here, let me help you!"

After we finished loading carts with ice for sale in the market, the captain said, "Thanks, stranger. I don't think I know you."

I looked into his leathery, weather-beaten face and shook his hand. He had an iron grip. "We met a month ago or so, through our mutual friend Park Sun. I'm Kim Chi-un. I'm sorry. I don't know yours."

"I'm Han Sung Min. Are you here on business of Park Sun?"

"More on business of my own."

"Oh? Let us go to my cabin for some privacy." We went belowdecks to a cramped cabin with two little portholes. He made us tea from his small electric kettle.

"Do you have something you need to transport?"

"Five somethings. Five people need to get out to sea to meet a boat."

"That's very, very dangerous. I assume you mean outside the territorial waters?"

"Yes. Thirty kilometers or so." I knew how close the *Resolute Too* was.

"You realize the navy is patrolling outside the limit and will board and inspect any fishing vessel?"

"Yes."

"To protect myself, if that happens, I'll put you in the ship's boat and cast you off. The boat costs ten thousand won. That must be paid before we sail. Then I'll want another hundred thousand won for the risk I'm taking. Do you still want to go through with this?"

"I don't have the cash, but I have a valuable item."

"No dickering! Cash or nothing."

"The item is an electrically powered hovercraft, solar charged. It's not available in Korea, North or South. It's US made and brand new."

"Interesting. These people, are they US citizens?"

"Yes."

"Do they have cash, US money?"

"Uh, I don't know. I'll check with them before I bring them here tonight."

"Tonight!? I'm fishing tonight. I only smuggle on the weekends."

"We can come along and help you fish."

"Hmmm. That might work."

"Oh, I just realized. They probably have money on their ship."

"Their ship's in danger of being sunk if it's out there tonight!"

"Not easily. It's big and well armed."

"Is it a military vessel?"

"Kind of. It's a privateer."

"A pirate?"

"I guess."

"I'm curious to see the hovercraft. This is insanely dangerous, but if we fish until midnight and take a break inside the territorial waters, I can have us drift outward. If everyone's in fisherman garb, we may be able to pull this off. But before they come, let me see your eyes."

Wondering how he'd react, I took off my sunglasses.

Looking at my eyes with wonder, he said, "I suspected this. I heard of an escape of dangerous prisoners with red eyes. I know prisoners aren't always dangerous. My mother and father were imprisoned."

"I was in prison a month before we escaped."

"How many escaped?"

"Almost twenty thousand, the whole camp."

"Woo-hoo!" He whistled. "No wonder the military is in a tizzy. These Americans, were they part of the rescue force?"

"Not exactly. They went to the nuclear site and got trapped there. We freed them."

"The story alone is worth the risk! You've got to promise to tell me the whole thing tonight, while we fish. I love seeing the government get such a big stick in their eye!" Sung Min gloated.

"I'll tell you all I can. Jessica can tell you more. She speaks Korean."

"An American who speaks Korean! Is she a spy?"

"No, just a translator. She'd be gone already, but four got sick and had to heal."

"Very curious! Here. Tell me the whole story, and I'll do what I can. Be here at nine p.m. tonight." We shook hands.

"That's a good grip you've got, Kim Chi-un. Very few can match me."

"That's part of the story." I smiled.

Hope filled my heart as I walked back to our camp, fifteen kilometers outside the city. It looked like we'd really get away! I was willing to die to get them out, but if the military boarded the ship, we were through. I was only one zombie.

My joy crashed. This would be the last time I saw Jessica. I tried to figure out some way we could stay together, but it was impossible. She was a sergeant in the US Army. I was an escaped prisoner. More than that, I promised Ji Su I'd return to help guide them over the Tumen. I had to keep my promise. My heart also yearned for the Lees, to find out what had happened to them after the police raid.

Then I saw Jessica smiling to see me—me! She ran up to me, hugged me, and my happiness was complete.

We rested until evening. Later, Jessica took the corgis and the hovercraft and cruised stealthily along the river to the port, while we walked through town to the dock.

"Hello, Han Sung Min, it's Mr. Kim and my friends."

"Hello." He studied the four Americans. "You're American all right. I think the clothing I got will fit you." He gestured toward a basket of used fishing clothing. "You can change in the cabin below."

Sung Min turned toward me. "You said there were five and a hovercraft. Where are they?"

"They should be hiding in the river." I leaned over the edge, looking out into the river. "Jessica!" I called softly.

"Louder! No one can hear that, not even over water. Jessica!" Sung Min said.

I laughed to hear her name with a strong Korean accent.

"Stop your yelling!" came a voice from the stern. "I've been here the whole time!"

I looked toward her voice and could barely see her. She wore her black armor and helmet. The black hovercraft blended into the dark water.

"So that's the hovercraft," Sung Min said. "And Jessica."

I gave her a hand over the gunwale.

She handed me a rope and then took another and said, "Help me haul this on board."

"Here, let me do that," Sung Min said.

We hauled it onto the deck. Jessica showed Sung Min how it collapsed and folded up into a surprisingly small package.

"Here. Stow it in our fish well. Even if we're boarded, once it's full of fish, no one will look beneath them. You speak Korean very well!"

"Thank you, Han Sung Min! That's why I'm here."

"If the government gets you, you'll be arrested as a spy. You might be held for ransom. We'll probably be shot."

"I already have been!" I said with a grin.

Once the privateers were dressed in fishing garb, complete with flat hats, we cast off. We had to dress George in an old blanket, pinned together. He was too big for any of the clothing.

George seemed to have some knowledge of fishing, as did Lulu, but the rest of us were beginners. But we all worked hard, and by midnight we had several netfuls of fish in the hold.

"Pretty good," Sung Min said. "This is almost as much as my regular crew gets. I had to pay them off tonight. They all know about my transportation trips.

"That's quite the story you told, Jessica and Chi-un. I can hardly believe they've had all those adventures. I look forward to seeing this yacht of yours."

Jessica studied her phone. "Based on my GPS, you're about ten kilometers from it now, northeast of here."

"I'd heard of phone GPS before, but I've never seen one," Sung Min said.

Jessica showed him hers. He sailed toward its location, but slowly, casually, like a fishing boat looking for another catch.

"We should pick them up in half an hour."

"They've already detected you on the radar," Diane announced, listening on her headset. "There are no ships around to the horizon, above or underwater. They're coming to you now. You're out of the territorial waters."

The privateers packed their armor and regular clothing in the basket. They wore their communication headsets hidden under their Korean fishing hats.

Jessica smiled, thrilling me. She spoke in English to Diane, then translated her words for me. "I won't tell Sung Min. Captain Han will be surprised!"

I grinned back. "He's eager to see the ship. He'll just see it sooner than—"

"What's *that?*" Sung Min shouted, pointing at a white shape on the horizon.

"That's the *Resolute Too!*" Jessica said proudly.

I could see it too, by moonlight. The white ship matched the white spray from the prow against the dark water as it sped toward us.

"It's huge! Gigantic! Enormous! I don't think the Korean navy has a ship that size!"

"What's he shouting about?" George asked.

"He's exclaiming about the size of the *Resolute Too*. He thinks it's bigger than any ship in the North Korean navy," Jessica explained.

"He's right. I checked on their navy while we were sailing here. Their largest ships are three frigates, about two hundred and fifty feet long, half the size of the *Resolute Too*. We also can go faster than any ship they have."

"Hah! I'll let him know that!"

The great white ship slowed, and we approached carefully. It turned its stern toward us, and I saw a boat dock between the twin hulls!

"You didn't tell me you had a boat dock!"

"Oh, it has a submarine dock too," Jessica said matter of factly.

The ship's boat cast off, and Jessica said, "They're telling us to dock in the ship."

"I've never docked inside a ship before," Sung Min admitted. "But the sea is calm, and I should be able to do it."

The dock proved to be bigger than it appeared, as was the entire ship. Jessica took me and Captain Han on a tour.

The size and luxury awed us. Then they treated us to a complete meal in a huge dining salon.

"Thanks for smuggling us out, Captain Han!" Diane said through her phone translator.

"It's kind of nice not having to translate for everyone," Jessica said through hers.

It was odd hearing her voice in English and then a feminine-sounding computer voice speaking Korean. It didn't translate as well as she did. I decided then, even if Jessica and I never saw each other again, I would learn English, somehow, someway.

The night flew by. Sung Min said, "We've got to be back by dawn. Thank you so much for giving me the hovercraft. There are thousands of ways I can use it."

Jessica returned to the table, carrying a binder of paper.

"Mr. Han, I've translated the hovercraft manual to Korean using our ship's computer and printed it out. You'll need this."

"Since we're giving gifts," Diane said, "I've got something for you, Mr. Han, for helping us." She handed him a handsome attaché case.

"Thank you very much. This case costs about a year's salary in Korea."

She laughed. "Open it up!"

It was filled with hundred-dollar bills!

"Oh my! Oh my!" he repeated over and over.

"Jessica told me you wanted some money for all the risk you took. Here's what we can spare from the ship's safe."

"Oh my! I could buy a new ship! Or retire! Or flee to the South. I can't thank you enough, Diane."

"You saved us at great risk. We thank you."

We all went below to the transom dock. The eastern horizon was lightening. Sung Min boarded after many hugs and tearful goodbyes. I dreaded what came next.

"I have to say goodbye, Jessica," I said, choking.

"I know," she said softly, tenderly.

"Could I have one more kiss?"

"Can you?" She leapt to my lips. This kiss was even better than the last one.

"That will hold me the rest of my life," I said as I stepped aboard.

"That's great!" She seemed surprisingly happy, looking at me from the dock.

Maybe she wouldn't miss me after all. Maybe she had another guy.

"But it doesn't have to!" She jumped into the boat.

"What are you doing?"

"Going with you!"

"But your army career?"

"I've been reassigned to the NSA. I've going to North Korea as a spy, per General Figeroa's orders."

"So you've become a spy?"

"For you. To be with you."

"So you're the spy who loved me?"

"True." And we kissed again.

* * *

I escaped the hot July sun burning the Mediterranean isle of Kristos under the awning of my favorite patio at my villa. It sat atop a ridge heading southward from the peak of the island and caught southerly, westerly, and easterly ocean breezes. I eased myself into my wicker recliner, took a sip of my piña colada, and flicked on my table-mounted screen with a wrist flip.

I loved my motion-sensor controlled computer. It was my window on the world and the window from my world.

My heart warmed at the thought of the two worlds becoming one. I would be a benevolent dictator. People wouldn't even know I controlled everything. They would still elect and choose their leaders. Over time, my family would control every government and every economy. There would be no more war unless it was necessary.

First, I read the news on my plague eliminating the zombies. I'd modeled it after the bubonic plague bacterium. There were two tricky parts to modifying the bacterium. First, I had to make it a bacteriophage, attacking the specific ECHZ bacterium. Second, I had to encapsulate it and time its release so I hit the whole world at once. I succeeded at both, of course.

Until now. I clenched my teeth as I read the news of the antibiotic and its success in the US. Naturally, they were sharing it with the world. I reflexively ordered a sample for my labs. *Let's see how it works so I can plan a counterattack.*

Or did I want to do that? This was their second effective counter to my biological warfare. Aside from being ineffective, did I also want to be boring? Did I want to fail three times? I thought not. The more I repeated myself, the more traceable I became.

I should be grateful to my enemies for teaching me new tricks and making me smarter. Also, there was the serendipity of having Kim Jong-un under better control after he lost his nukes and twenty thousand prisoners to zombies. He'd promoted my Korean clone, Su Ye Suel, after I gave her my anti-zombie spray. It only spread the existing infection faster, but what Kim Jong-un didn't know was to my advantage.

I often considered replacing Kim with Su, but she was perfectly positioned where she was as an assistant undersecretary. In the North Korean misogynistic society, Su was not considered a threat. If she became Kim's lover or replacement, a thousand crosshairs would focus on her.

How could I best use my new power in North Korea for my purposes? It already was a source of weapons and cheap labor and a destination for luxury goods for their oligarchy. I could now have it manufacture anti-zombie bioweaponry, even after the antibiotic had been developed.

For exorbitant prices I also could market the suitcase nukes I had in Russia. I sent these directions to Su.

Now, the least pleasant part of my cogitations: What could go wrong? There were twenty thousand prisoner escapees and at least a thousand former zombies. According to Ye Suel's intelligence sources, all of these were Christians. I didn't know what bothered me more, zombies or Christians. Both were unreasonable and unpredictable, willing to take insane risks to advance their causes. Both reproduced rapidly, spreading their contagion: one a bacterium and the other an ideology.

I remembered Vik Staskas failed due to zombies. Although my most successful clone, he consistently underestimated them. I wouldn't do that. I'd worry my way to the perfect solution to zombies, once and for all.

"I haven't failed. I've learned two ways that don't eliminate zombies," I said aloud.

"Do you want me to record that in your private journal, Master?" asked my AI secretary, Hera.

"Of course."

* * *

"Look at that jump!" Al yelled, pointing at the computer showing two telescope pictures taken a day apart.

A faint dot jumped visibly across the star field as the program overlaid the digital photos.

Al's friend Jacob shouted, "We've discovered a new asteroid!" Jacob had helped Al do the sky survey the last two nights from their home in the Sierra Nevadas in California. He also had bought the program that compared their digital photos between the two nights.

"Sure looks like it. Let's see: the comparison program says it's magnitude twelve, distance, four point three AU, speed—" He stopped.

"That can't be right," Jacob whispered.

"Right. It can't be. But it is. For this distance, four hundred million miles, and that apparent movement, it's fifty-four thousand miles per second. Thirty percent the speed of light."

"What travels that fast?"

"Nothing. Maybe some gas accelerated by a black hole, but nothing in our solar system."

"Do you think Dr. Linnehan will have an idea?"

Dr. Linnehan ran the local planetarium at their natural-history museum, a favorite spot for Al and Jacob to go with their astronomical questions. He also served as an advisor for their middle school astronomy club.

"Yeah, maybe. Let's get all the documentation on these photos, print them, and also store our data on this thumb drive. He'll want to look at this himself."

After gathering their data, they rode their bikes to Dr. Linnehan's office at the natural-history museum.

He smiled when he saw them.

"Aiden! Jacob, it's good to see you! What brings you here today?"

"Um, please call me Al, Dr. Linnehan. We think we've discovered a new asteroid, but there seems to be a problem with our data."

"Fantastic! That'll get you published by the American Association of Amateur Astronomers! Let's see what you got."

Dr. Linnehan loaded the data on his computer and ran the comparison program. "Whoa! That's an asteroid all right. So what's the problem?"

"Look at the speed," Al said.

"That can't be right."

"That's what we said," Jacob said.

"Let me double-check. One day apart, azimuth, declination—you're sure these settings are right?"

"Yup." Jacob nodded. "We oriented our scope's clock mechanism toward the North Star, as you taught us. We were doing a survey of the ecliptic since it's new moon and the sky is dark."

"Even if the program is off on the distance by a factor of four, it's still too fast. Definitely check again tonight."

"Will do!" Al said.

Jacob posted their results on their blog, Facebook, and the American Association of Amateur Astronomers asteroid web page. He could hardly wait for the night.

Several amateur astronomers around the world looked for the object at their coordinates and didn't find it. But they found it orbiting the earth, behind the International Space Station (ISS).

It was a disk, about eleven kilometers in diameter and two thick. The astronomical community turned all their telescopes upon it and viewed a clear view of a flying saucer.

Chapter 9

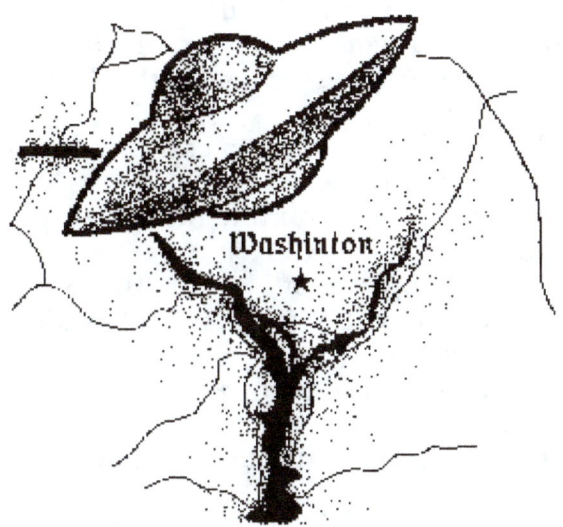

Washington DC.

The news of a flying saucer in orbit rocketed around the globe. People outside could see the clearly visible disk nearly seven miles across. It appeared three times the size of the moon, and the whole world saw it day and night.

Hundreds and thousands of official and unofficial radio and video messages bombarded the mystery craft. Markets plunged further than they had during the zombie crash. NASA and the world's space agencies and Space-X quickly collaborated to send a manned mission to the saucer.

But before the rocket got off the ground, the saucer sent a message to all the world's capitals in their respective languages. "We come in peace. We will land at your capitals tomorrow."

The world's markets shut down. Endless rounds of saucer news and speculation flooded the internet. Lisa Melvin fretted about the loss of traffic to the *Midley Beacon* site, although she wrote a saucer-based editorial—"Will the

Aliens Be Pro or Anti-Zombie?"—which gathered millions of hits.

"Sam, tomorrow may be the end of the *Midley Beacon*," she said from their office on the *Resolute Too,* docked in Seattle after their weeklong cruise across the Pacific.

"Why is that? People are still buying zombie sausage, flamethrowers, and zombie turkey traps. They're still reading our news stories from North Korea about the paranormal privateers."

"Yeah, but they don't seem to care whether the zombie disease gets cured or not."

"Wasn't there a bump on our hits when the antibiotic was announced?"

"A small bump, unnoticed in the saucer traffic. Somehow we've got to tie zombies, the saucer, and the *Midley Beacon* together."

"Can't we go to Washington, DC, to report on the saucer landing tomorrow?"

"Good idea, but that's not directly zombie related. I've got it!"

"What?"

"We rebrand the *Midley Beacon* as *the Zombie News Network*, ZNN! Then everything we report will be zombie related!"

"Uh, I know I'm not a college graduate like you are, but we aren't zombies anymore."

"It doesn't matter! People already associate the *Midley Beacon* with zombie news—this'll just make it official! I'm so excited! Sam. Arrange for our plane to pick us up and take us to Washington tonight!"

"OK."

While Sam called their pilot, Dan Cosana, Lisa hummed thoughtfully.

"You done yet, Sam? I've got another idea."

"All right. Dan will fly the plane here, and we can leave by eight. We'll get there at three a.m. Eastern time."

"Great! We'll be on the mall before our competition! Here's my idea: We can wear red contact lenses so people'll think we're still zombies! And all our reporters can do that too! Our slogan can be 'It takes a zombie to be fair.'"

"I don't know about that."

"I know they have red contact lenses! People have been wearing them for Halloween ever since human zombies first appeared!"

"Will this really help the *Midley Beacon*?"

"You mean ZNN? Now, don't you worry about this. Thinking isn't your strong suit. Trust me!"

"OK, Lisa. We've been together now eighteen years since high school, and you've never been wrong. Except for one thing."

"What's that?" Lisa said suspiciously.

"Flamethrowing around the crashed presidential helicopter."

"Oh. That. Yes, that was an oopsie. But it turned out all right in the end."

A pop-up window appeared on Lisa's computer screen. A tall, slender, handsome man in a silver lamé bodysuit materialized. He held up his hands beside his head, palms facing forward.

"Greetings, Earthlings! We come in peace! I am our race's representative to the United States. This broadcast is appearing on every computer and every broadcast and cable television network, as well as on all the radio stations in your nation. Our other representatives are addressing every other nation around the globe simultaneously, speaking in each language.

"Peace is our first and foremost message. We have no plans of conquest but only beneficial trade between our race and yours. We have no name for ourselves, but you may call us the *Old Ones*, for our civilization is much older than yours, millions of your years.

"Most of those years we've spent traveling. Our star went nova, and we transported our entire race in craft such as you see, throughout the galaxy. We have spent millennia looking for a suitable home. We have not yet found one, for we have no desire to take your planet from you.

"We do have an urgent need for supplies. For several hundred years, we've observed your planet from our orbit around Saturn. We've mined your solar system's asteroids and comets for many materials, yet there are some we still need from your planet.

"We know about your many wars and your suspicions of interstellar visitors from your movies, plays, and books. We've chosen human representatives from every nation and tongue, volunteers, and trained them to represent our race to yours.

"I myself am a native of Cincinnati, Ohio, named Micah Rigby. Born in 1990, I'm twenty-nine. The Old Ones contacted me about a year ago and offered me a vastly extended lifespan and limitless wealth for my services to them as their ambassador to the United States.

"They chose me because of my resemblance to Michael Renner, star of the movie *The Day the Earth Stood Still*. The Old Ones want a peaceful connotation to their first contact, and the character Klaatu was the most positive alien they found in your media. For the same reason, there will be no fearsome robot or policeman like Gort when I land in a saucer on the White House south lawn tomorrow. We thought Gort was too scary.

"I will meet with President Trump and whichever other representatives you wish to send. It will just be me and my saucer, unarmed, so there's no need for the military."

"Our agenda is open, and it's the same worldwide. In exchange for our advanced technology, we wish your permission to mine your ocean floors, deserts, and waste places for metals and elements we need. We will do nothing without your permission.

"We'll ask each nation for authorization to mine its continental shelves, deserts, and mountains. We will not harm the land, sea, or any life. In return, we'll help you extend your lifespans to thousands of years, like mine. We'll give you our computer technology, which will advance your computers to sentience. And if you wish, we'll arbitrate disputes between nations to bring peace in the various conflicts on your planet.

"I'm sure you'll have a busy day planning our meeting. I'll see you tomorrow on the White House lawn. We will broadcast my meeting with President Trump, and your representatives as well.

"All we, the Old Ones, do is transparent and above board. Goodbye for now!"

The pop-up window disappeared. Sam and Lisa turned to each other in wonder.

"Did you hear what I heard?" Lisa asked.

"I think so. I feel like I'm in a fifties science fiction movie."

"This is our golden opportunity, Sam!"

"How's that?"

"Here's the perfect chance to launch our new brand, ZNN! We've got a killer story—first contact with an alien race! Flying saucers! World peace! There are endless angles. Call all our reporters together for an online video conference. I don't care what time zone they're in! I want to speak to them all in one hour."

"That'll be tight, but if everyone cooperates, we can do that."

"While you do that, I'll take this alien broadcast and put it up on YouTube!"

"I didn't know you were recording it!"

"It's automatic! It's part of the surveillance software we got from Sid Boffin when he bugged our computers."

"I forgot about that."

"On your mark, get set, go!" Lisa turned abruptly from Sam and began typing furiously on her keyboard.

He stared at her, amazed. He knew she worked fast, but he'd never seen her fingers fly like this.

"Sam! It's been one minute! Get going!" Lisa said without looking up from her keyboard.

* * *

The *Resolute Too* conference room hosted the ZNN launch. Sam greeted each employee as they connected, while Lisa, using her phone, harangued those who hadn't called in. Finally, she began.

"My fellow coworkers in the world's premium *Zombie News Network*, this is the last time I'll address you as *Midley Beacon* employees. From now on, we're the *Zombie News Network*, ZNN. I had our logo redesigned by our graphic artist and sent it to you all. Our IT staff will begin updating all our web pages *now*. See you later, folks!" Lisa said as she stared at the startled IT employees until they signed off and went to work.

"The rest of you have your country-by-country news assignments. Here is the aliens' schedule for meeting each country's leader and your assignments: Julio Pinkas— Brasilia, Brazil, noon Brazil time, which is three hours ahead of Eastern. Lashon Miller—Ottawa, Canada, noon Eastern time. Charlie Gomez—Mexico City, noon Central time. Tokyo, Japan..." Lisa continued handing out assignments to various world capitals to ZNN's sixty-plus reporters and the ten editors.

"And that's all we can cover, except Washington, DC. Sam and I will fly there after this meeting. Don't forget to use 'ZNN' twenty-four seven. Get all your logos, stationery, and email templates changed by working with our IT staff. I'll be satisfied if you're updated by tomorrow," she concluded.

"Karen Mooney." Lisa addressed ZNN's HR director. "Please double our reporting and editing staff by next week."

"But—" Karen spluttered.

"And then in the following week, double it again. I know this is a tight timeframe. You can make it by hiring veteran reporters from other news agencies and news blogs and skipping the vetting process. Feel free to offer each whatever salary it takes. Our corporate goal is to have one reporter in each of the two hundred and four countries in the world within the month."

"What about North Korea? They completely restrict access to western reporters," Karen asked

"I've got just the person for you: Sergeant Jessica Rose, already in place and on the ground. You won't be able to hire her, but you can get exclusive interviews with her.

"All right, teammates. We've got a big challenge ahead of us. Let's get to work." Lisa cut the connection.

"Whew! You move fast, Lisa!"

"With breaking stories, we have to move at internet speed! The aliens' video already has ten million hits in less than an hour. ZNN's the first to post that. We're off to a great start."

* * *

Dan flew Lisa and Sam that night and arrived before dawn in Washington. It was a madhouse, packed with reporters, curious citizens, and protesters all seeking to get a glimpse of the flying saucer. To avoid the gridlocked traffic, Lisa hired a helicopter to drop them off near the mall. She and Sam had White House press passes to the south lawn press area adjacent to the saucer landing site.

"Badges?" asked the gruff guard.

"Here. Can we get these updated?" Lisa asked. "We've changed the name of our organization."

"Yeah, but I can't. You'll have to work with the White House press manager."

"I thought we left with plenty of time," Sam said, "but we're only a half an hour before the big landing."

"Hmmph?" Lisa said, focused on her phone.

"Lisa! Whatcha watching?"

"Oh, I'm watching *The Day the Earth Stood Still*. The aliens mentioned it, so I thought I should see what it was like. I see why they thought Gort would be frightening, although the special effects are crummy."

"That was made in 1951!"

"Special effects sucked then. But Michael Renner does look like the alien ambassador, Micah Rigby. I got an idea! Get an exclusive interview with him!"

"I'll try, but there's a big crowd."

"Too bad we're not zombies anymore. We could just fight our way to him."

"We could use the zombie corgis or turkeys! They still listen to us."

"That would clear everyone out! But they'd probably take a bite out of someone."

"Look up! Here it comes!"

Sam and Lisa craned their necks with thousands of others as the saucer descended to the cleared area on the lawn. A hundred feet across, of smooth, unbroken silvery metal, it looked more like a lens than a saucer, with a smooth convex curved top and bottom. It floated silently as a balloon and landed like a snowflake.

"Look! It's opening!" Sam said.

The edge of the saucer split, revealing a ramp to the interior. The alien ambassador Micah Rigby came out, holding both hands up in a gesture of peace. Tied to each of his wrists were silver strings, which pulled along two large red balloons. Hanging from the balloons were gaily wrapped packages.

"Greetings, Earthlings and my fellow Americans!" Micah Rigby spoke from the bottom of the ramp. Although he didn't have a microphone, Sam and Lisa clearly heard him from a hundred feet away.

"The Old Ones send along two gifts for President Trump. We learned from Klaatu, who got shot for bearing a gift. I suggested the balloons and wrapping to show the gifts are not dangerous."

"May I approach the president?"

"C'mon up, Ambassador Rigby!" boomed President Trump through the speakers.

Ambassador Rigby walked across the lawn and up the steps to the platform, balloons and presents bobbing merrily behind him.

"Here's the Old Ones' first gift for you." He unwrapped the pink-and-yellow-striped package. It looked like a small silver phone. Micah handed it to the president and gave the balloon to the Secret Service agent next to the president. "You can give the balloon to your daughter, Agent Smith."

Startled, the agent took the balloon.

"Mr. President, this is a voice-activated cell phone. Simply speak the person's name and you can see them and talk with them."

"That's like our cell phones."

"The Old Ones copied the normal cell phone voice interface. However, the person you call does *not* have to have a phone at all! If you wish, your image can be projected to them."

"Amazing!"

"Also, this phone is not limited by distance, nor can the signals be blocked. Finally, if you say 'Old Ones,' you can talk directly to them."

"OK. Old Ones."

Five translucent figures appeared near the president, all white haired and bearded. One white, one black, one Asian, one Native American, and one brown race that might have been Middle Eastern.

"Greetings, President Trump! How can we help you?"

"I wanted to see if you'd answer and what you looked like."

"To be honest," said the black one, "this is not how we look. These are merely our projected images. We use your races to show we are different to some extent, like your races are different. White hair and beards symbolize our age."

"What do you actually look like?" President Trump asked.

"We thought you might be curious," said the Asian figure.

"That's why we gave you the second gift," said the Middle Eastern one.

"Here it is, Mr. President," Micah said, handing him the larger orange-and-purple package.

The president unwrapped it and opened a sealed box. A cute furry caterpillar, with a head and face like a fox and long, furry pointed ears, quickly crawled out and up the president's arm to his shoulder. It moved with a rippling motion. Squirrel-sized, it sat on his shoulder, licked his face, and purred contentedly.

"That tickles! You're a cute little fellow, aren't you? What are they called?"

"There are no equivalent species on earth, but we thought you might like them. They're part of our ship's ecology," said the bearded white Old One. "You may call them anything you'd like, but we think they're most like the Tribbles from *Star Trek*."

"I can see that," the president said.

"Minus the uncontrolled reproduction in the *Star Trek* episode!" The black Old One laughed. "These Tribble-like creatures must go back to the saucer each day for food. There are certain proteins they need they cannot get from your biosphere. We withhold the amino acids they need for reproduction."

"They can eat harmful insects, flies, and mosquitoes, bed bugs, and cockroaches, but they cannot thrive or reproduce here," added the brown Old One.

"So do you look like caterpillars, foxes, or Tribbles?" President Trump asked.

"It's more of a metaphor than a literal appearance," said the Caucasian.

"We want you to think of us as cute, warm, and fuzzy," said the Asian.

"Will we ever get to see what you really look like?"

"It's not necessary," the five images answered in unison. "It has been pleasant talking with you, Mr. President. Our ambassador will discuss the trade arrangement we desire."

The images disappeared.

President Trump handed the Tribble, or whatever it was, to another Secret Service man.

"Shall we go into the White House, Ambassador Rigby?" the president asked.

"Wherever you wish! I can say we just wish to mine the magnesium nodules on the continental shelf and use some old, worn-out mines out west to extract minerals. In return, we offer limitless clean power, and more powerful computers, and an end to human disease and aging."

"That sounds like an offer I can't refuse! Of course, any treaty we sign must be approved by Congress."

"Of course. I remember my civics class from high school!"

They laughed and entered the White House.

"Sam, look!" Lisa whispered urgently. Her tablet showed the ambassador and the president sitting down at a table inside the White House.

"Who's broadcasting that?" Sam asked.

"The aliens! But I'm setting up ZNN to livecast it on YouTube and Facebook! We'll scoop the other news agencies!"

"I guess they don't copyright it."

"It's public domain!"

Lisa's livecast of the event gathered millions of viewers from Facebook and YouTube to the ZNN sites. Lisa delighted seeing the ZNN logo and headline replace *Midley Beacon*'s.

Sam collected reports from all over the world. In every nation, an attractive male or female of their race and nationality represented the Old Ones and gave cell phones and foxcats to the world leaders. (After much debate and lawsuits from the corporation owning the *Star Trek* rights, the US and the world settled on calling the new species "foxcats.")

The Old Ones virtually conversed with the world's leaders. Smaller countries rejoiced at getting equal treatment with larger countries. The Old Ones always offered and requested the same trade: high technology for mining rights to unused resources.

Poor countries eagerly agreed so they could help their economies. Rich countries wanted to alleviate their healthcare burdens without zombie blood. And everyone loved the idea of free, limitless power. All the world's countries agreed to the aliens' terms.

The UN debated whether to allow the aliens to mine the deep-sea bottom and Antarctica. Their automated mining vessels had already dug in the world's continental shelves, while the UN delegates hashed out who would benefit on the General Assembly floor.

The sole country still resisting the aliens was North Korea. Kim Jong-un insisted the aliens were a US-supported threat to North Korean existence. They sprayed antiaircraft gunfire at the saucer that landed in Pyongyang and the beautiful North Korean woman who walked out. An invisible force field deflected the projectiles from Ambassador Kang Ji-yeon as she coolly announced the Old Ones' trade offers.

Kim Jong-un directed a mass artillery assault on the saucer. The projectiles exploded all around the dome protecting the saucer and churned up the soccer field where they landed. The five Old Ones appeared, all Korean, and two appearing to look like Kim Jong-il and Kim Il-Sun, Kim Jong-un's father and grandfather. They urged peace, but Kim Jong-un called them "alien imposters" and threatened to nuke the saucer, regardless of the collateral damage to Pyongyang. Giving up, the saucer floated away.

After Sam finished writing up his stories and submitting them to their webmaster, he said, "Lisa, I'm going to hang around the White House and see if I can talk to Micah when he comes out."

"Good! I'm busy running analytics on our website and trying to sell more advertising. This story is gonna make us rich!"

"Lisa, we're already rich, aren't we?"

"Well, yeah, kind of, in a middle-class way. But this is our breakthrough to the big-time news! Megarich!"

"As long as I've got you, I'm rich."

"You sap! I love you! Now go get the story!"

Sam went to the South Portico of the White House, where a Secret Service agent stopped him.

"I'm sorry. You can't go any further," said a serious brunette woman in a navy suit.

"Could I wait here for Micah Rigby, the alien ambassador?"

"Let me check with Agent Smith," she replied.

"Agent Smith? He knows me! Tell him it's Sam Melvin of the *Midley Beacon,* er, ZNN, the *Zombie News Network.*"

"Hello, Agent Smith?" She spoke quietly into her headset. "I've got a reporter at the South Portico. He wants to interview the ambassador. He says you know him, a Sam Melvin... Very well."

"Agent Smith says you can wait here. He's busy right now, but sends you his regards."

"Thank you!"

In a half hour, Ambassador Rigby came out surrounded by Secret Service agents. From the door, Sam heard President Trump's voice saying, "Goodbye, Ambassador! This has been a huge, *huge* success!"

"Ambassador Rigby!" Sam shouted.

"Yes? How can I help you?"

"Could you answer a couple of questions?"

"Sure. Say, I think I recognize you! Aren't you the famous Sam Melvin of the *Midley Beacon?*"

"Yeah, but I'm nothing compared to you! It's ZNN, the Zombie News Network now."

"Whatever. What would you like to know?"

"Did you and the president agree to trade terms?"

"Yes, we've got an agreement in principle."

"How did you become the alien ambassador?"

"The aliens first contacted me through a pop-up ad on the internet. I tried to dismiss it, but couldn't. Once they convinced me they were real, they made me an offer I couldn't refuse."

"Then what?"

"They sent this saucer and picked me up. They made some biological changes to my body through nanobots, so I have perfect health and regeneration capabilities. Then they spent months training me to speak and represent them to the American people."

"Wow. Did you ever see what they looked like?"

"Nope. I spent most of the time around Saturn in the mothership, but never saw them, other than the projections you saw today."

"The mothership! What was *that* like?"

"I just saw a few hundred yards of it. They had a garden and forest for me to run in, a swimming pool, and exercise room. I enjoyed luxurious accommodations and gourmet food!"

"Sounds great! What's it feel like representing an alien species to your own countrymen?"

"Very odd at times. I've been well drilled in their way of looking at things, and it's quite different from our way. It's like I have double vision at times."

"What's so different about their way?"

"Everything is simple to them. They give what we want, and we give what they want. War and conflict? Give each side what they want. They have no concept of lying or deceit. They just think it's foolishness since the truth will always come out. You have to deal with the truth. They're very black and white on things."

"Do you mind if I broadcast this interview?"

"No. In fact, we're already broadcasting it, as we broadcast all my conversations on earth."

"Lisa's already rebroadcasted your transmissions. That's Lisa Melvin, my wife."

"I know her! Cincinnati narrowly escaped the cyborg animal attacks thanks to you two and the Newbys in Dayton." Micah stopped abruptly, as if he heard something. "I've gotta go, Sam. The Old Ones want me."

"See you later!"

Sam returned to Lisa, still pounding away on her laptop on the south lawn. She looked up.

"Hi, Sam! Good interview! I knew you would get to him. You're the firstest with the mostest! The interview's already posted on the ZNN website!"

"Thanks, Lisa!" Sam felt like he'd won a world championship whenever Lisa complimented him.

* * *

Six Months Previously

"Hi, Talana James, do you want to be rich and famous?"

I awoke. "Wha—" I started to say and then rolled over in my bed to where I heard the voice. A handsome black man, looking a little like Idris Elba, stood in my room by the door. "Who are you? What are you doing here?" I managed to get out. Then I noticed his shiny silvery outfit, rather like silver lamé.

"I'm your best friend. I can make you rich and famous and keep you young and beautiful forever!" A rich, smooth baritone poured out of him, like someone pouring a bottle of the finest whiskey.

"Sounds too good to be true! Are you my fairy godfather? Do you work magic? And what are you doing in my room anyway? I should call the police."

"Just hear me out. A year ago I was in your place, a struggling model trying to make ends meet, working as a waiter and bartender. Then a strange woman woke me up at night, just as I woke you. She made the same offer to me."

"What did you say?"

"I said, 'Prove it! I don't believe you!' Then she said, 'Come and see.' And so I say to you, Talana James, come with me and see."

"That's a great line! So how do I know you're not a rapist or murderer? What's to stop me from calling the police?"

"Try it. I've already suppressed cell phone signals."

"Why shouldn't I pull out my pistol from under my pillow?"

"Why don't you do that?"

"Uh, I'm just messin' with you. What's your name anyway?"

"Anthony Embry."

"OK, what have I got to lose but some sleep? Let me get dressed—privately!"

"Sure." He withdrew, silver bodysuit shimmering, into the hall.

I dressed as fast as I could. I just put on the dirty clothing I threw off before I collapsed into bed. Then I pocketed my switchblade and a large policeman's flashlight I kept for a club by my bed. *No sense in going unprotected.*

Anthony laughed softly when he saw me.

"What's so funny?"

"You're carrying the flashlight for protection?"

"Yeah. See this arm?" I brandished my thick bicep. "There's enough in here to knock you flat!"

"Just wait until you see what's outside before you start swinging."

Curious, I followed him to the roof of my Toronto apartment. On the roof rested a beautiful silver flying saucer.

Anthony turned to me. "Wanna go for a flight?"

"Are you an alien?"

"No." He laughed easily. "Just a gainfully employed ex-footballer and now ambassador-in-training for the Old Ones."

"Who are they?"

"An alien species who are preparing for their first contact with humanity by training human representatives."

"Like you?"

"Yes, and you, if you want the job."

"Are they going to eat us?"

"I don't know what they eat. I've never seen them, just their mothership, which is parked around Saturn."

"Saturn? We're going to Saturn?"

"That's where the training takes place."

"Whoa! What'll I tell my mom? I don't care about my boss."

"Your phone can work from there. Or from my saucer. The Old Ones have fantastic phone coverage."

"Do I get a saucer if I make ambassador?"

"Of course. And you've already 'made' it in the sense the Old Ones picked you to be their ambassador. They study us very carefully and pick us based on looks and personality."

"Personality, I've got. My looks are just average though. I can't make a living modeling."

"You will be able to after you're done training. Who do you think I look like?"

"Well, Idris Elba."

"Thanks! I was just a stocky, injured ex-arena football player when they picked me. They made me look more like Idris through body forming."

"So who do you think I look like?" I asked curiously.

"Beyoncé, of course. The blond hair and the creamy cocoa skin are perfect."

"C'mon, I'm twenty or thirty pounds heavier than Beyoncé—when she's pregnant!"

"I was forty pounds heavier when I began training. Now I'm stronger, healthier, and lighter. You will be too!"

"Lighter? Let's go then!"

* * *

My training consisted of a lot of memorization and speech practice. The Old Ones taught me how to speak. They ensured I knew my facts cold, about them and about Canada. They taught me to speak French as well as various regional accents. They enhanced my memory chemically after each lesson so I learned far faster than any human.

They injected me with nanobots to sculpt my body to look more like Beyoncé and let me work out in my own private park. I had a gorgeous view of Saturn's rings through a dome above my room.

I occasionally saw Anthony, but no one else. I could ask any question and an Old One would appear and answer it.

After about six months I asked, "When will I be sent back?"

A white-haired Asian woman appeared, slim and elegant in a shimmery turquoise dress. "You're almost completely trained. We'll be contacting earth in a few days."

"You've already enhanced me and trained me. I actually look like Beyoncé now! But what's to stop me from just picking up and leaving? Not that I would, of course."

"Of course. We value our ambassadors too much to lose you, so we'd have to pull you back. We can track you through the nanobots."

"I should have guessed that. What if I just refuse to work? What if I go on strike?"

"We can be very persuasive. Try it! Run a lap around the park."

"No." What would they do?

An ocular migraine struck me. My vision shimmered, and my head felt like I had two spikes through my eyes.

"OK, I'll go! How long will this go on?"

"Until you obey."

I ran faster than I ever had before. The migraine ended in a couple of steps, but I didn't want it to ever return. My new, slimmer body responded beautifully.

"OK. Lesson learned. I don't even need the memory drugs."

"You won't need them ever again! The nanobots are producing them within your body now. You'll remember everything you want to."

"How long will you need me as your ambassador?"

"Until we finish our mining for our supplies here."

"How long will that take?"

"At least five years, with complete worldwide cooperation."

* * *

Reports on the aliens' ambassadors poured into ZNN all day. In their hotel room, Sam read an email from Ottawa, Canada, from their editor, Lashon.

"The appearance of the Old Ones' ambassador Talana James shocked everyone. Imagine seeing Beyoncé in a gold lamé dress step out of a flying saucer on the quadrangle on Parliament Hill in Ottawa! Don't imagine. Watch this video!"

Sam played it again, as he'd done for dozens of previous stories.

"Hello, Canada!" Talana began after she bounced down the saucer's ramp, waving and carrying what appeared to be a silver briefcase. "I'm not really Beyoncé. I merely look like her. I'm model Talana James from Toronto. I represent the Old Ones, an ancient race that has observed the earth and mankind for hundreds of years. We've stopped in the solar system to mine essential metals and minerals, but we still need certain elements we can only get on the earth.

"We desperately need your help. We have traveled for thousands of years through the galaxy, looking for a suitable home, ever since we lost our original home due to a supernova.

"We're very cautious about how we approach mankind because you're so violent and warlike. We've decided to use human volunteers, like me, to show our good intentions. Rather like Canada's policy of 'peace, order, and good government' you've followed since your founding, we want peaceful, orderly, and good trade between us and mankind, Canada in particular.

"I'll proceed to the prime minister's office to discuss the details of trade, but to show our good faith, here are some gifts you may find useful."

Talana turned her briefcase sideways. Legs descended and the briefcase unfolded, revealing a cube and two glass vials, one golden, one scummy green. Disturbingly, the cube and vials were larger than the briefcase.

"Our first gift"—Talana picked up the cube, the size of a breadbox—"is a universal power source. Simply pour in water and out comes electricity. The unit produces electricity in the voltage and frequency you wish, controlled by these dials."

"Hey, Talana!" shouted Lashon Miller from the press box. The camera panned to her.

"Yes?"

"What's the catch? This is like those infinite energy scams you read on the internet."

"There's no scam! The unit works by splitting water into hydrogen and oxygen and fusing the hydrogen. Out comes oxygen and helium, which you may capture and use." She gestured to two tubes exiting the box. "Let me show you. My cell phone needs charging." She plugged the charger into an ordinary socket, and it began to charge.

"How long does it work on water? How much water? And how much power comes out?" Lashon asked.

"A cup is good for a year of phone charging. But you're not limited to that. See this power transmitter on this socket?" She plugged a black box into what appeared to be a two-hundred-and-twenty-volt socket. "This introduces our second gift." She called into the air, "Come here, Super Car!"

Zooming down the street came a sleek, bubble-roofed car. It stopped in front of the saucer and hovered.

"It's voice activated and powered wirelessly from this transmitter. It's autonomous, with the whole surface of the earth mapped into its computer. You can give it voice directions in any language, and it goes to the address or geolocation. It avoids collisions with people, objects, and other vehicles."

"How many cars can that thing power?" Lashon asked.

"Thousands. You see, this unit is big enough to power all of Ottawa."

"What?!" The crowd's roar of amazement drowned out Lashon's gasp.

"The Old Ones wanted to give you something practical you can use right now. Just use it to replace your existing power stations.

"The third gift is this." Talana held the crystal flask containing a golden liquid. "This solution of nanobots cures all human diseases, both infectious and genetic.

"It's not limited to the liter in this jar. Mix the nanobots into a solution of any living material, such as algae, and they'll reproduce, giving Canada an unlimited supply of this medicine." Talana poured some of the golden liquid into the scummy jar of slime. Before their eyes, the green viscous liquid turned golden and transparent. "Now you have two liters of this wonderful medical solution!

"I testify to this elixir's benefits, for I have taken it! It cured my genetic disposition toward sickle cell anemia and my case of scoliosis.

"Before I repeat myself in French and go see your prime minister, there's one more thing." Talana whistled.

Out of the trunk of the flying car came a flying skateboard.

"Here's something for the young and the young at heart!" Talana jumped on and zoomed around the crowd, just above their heads. She swerved like an expert surfboarder and returned to the base of the saucer ramp. With a flourish, she kicked the floating skateboard up and into her hands.

"The hoverboard comes with each flying car and is powered by broadcast power like the flying car. It too avoids collisions and can take you wherever you wish, on autonomous control. Or you can switch to manual and just play around! It's also programmed to keep you from falling off. I know—I've tried!"

Talana repeated her presentation in French and walked into the Office of the Prime Minister and Privy House.

After the video ended, Sam said, "Wow. I've been saying that a lot lately! No editing needed! I'll forward this to our webmaster for posting."

"I hope your stories are half as good as mine have been," Lisa said. "These aliens are earthshaking! This is bigger news than the zombie turkey apocalypse or even the paranormal privateers' adventures."

"How does a limitless power source sound?"

"I got that one too. They gave it to England. Their ambassador looked like Idris Elba!"

"Who?"

"Never mind! Did you get the universal cure-all?"

"Yup, they gave that with the endless power source and the flying car."

"That's the same as Mexico. Did Canada get the hoverboard too?"

"Yes. The Old Ones must have watched *Back to the Future II.*"

"I almost regret hiring those new reporters! There's more editing work than I can do!"

"Didn't you hire editors too?"

"Yeah, copyeditors. I need someone to sort the pepper from the fly specs!"

"You've got me and Lashon and Charlie."

"You're right. I'll have to call all the editors back from reporting and get them editing. Sam, arrange for us to fly to New York tonight."

"Why?"

"The alien ambassadors are *all* coming to the UN tomorrow!"

"How did you find out? I haven't heard anything about that."

"I have my ways. General Figeroa tipped me off by an encrypted text, and I also overheard a comment from Idris, I mean, the Old Ones' ambassador to England."

"All the ambassadors? That's over two hundred!"

"I'm not sure how they'll pack them into the General Assembly. I'm sure the aliens will think of something."

They did. The next day, hundreds of saucers landed on the UN Plaza and hovered over the East River. From each saucer came an ambassador riding a hoverboard. They streamed into the UN, past the guards, and above the crowd. Once in the General Assembly, they sat on their hoverboards above the UN delegates.

"Wow," Sam said, awed. "This is just like the *Star Wars* Republic's Senate!"

"You watch too many movies, Sam. Reality is much more interesting!"

After calling the General Session to order, President Miroslav Lajcák said, "According to the UN charter, this body may discuss any question relating to international peace and security and make recommendations on it. Accordingly, we are having a special session to discuss the new race that has contacted humanity. Their human representatives are here. Who will speak for them?"

"We will speak for ourselves." Five elderly figures appeared in front of the president.

"We will also translate to all your people, both here and in all the countries of the world. We will broadcast this session to all people around the world.

"We are the Old Ones. We survived our solar system's supernova and traveled here over many millions of years. Our race struggles to survive. Your planet has minerals and metals essential for our health.

"You too are struggling to survive. For thousands of years you have fought among yourselves, and billions have died through wars, disease, and poverty. Your survival is in the balance.

"We propose an equitable trade. We will solve your poverty, disease, and warfare problems through our superior technology. We will also teach you how to replicate it. In return, you will allow us to mine your unused oceans, deserts, and mountains. We will make little impact on your environment with our clean technology.

"With your cooperation, our efforts should be complete in five years and we will move on, looking for an inhabitable world. We will not take your world from you.

"We have negotiated agreements with a hundred individual countries and another hundred are underway. We desire one worldwide agreement through the UN to cover the international regions of the ocean floors and Antarctica.

"We will give each member and observing nation of the UN the unlimited power source, the medical cures, and the computing power we have demonstrated, in exchange for this permission.

"We have recruited and trained humans from every country to represent us. We, the more advanced race, must adapt to you. We're willing to serve you as a world peacemaker.

"Please come to an agreement today." The five figures vanished.

The General Assembly erupted into a noisy uproar. The president had to bang his gavel and bring the assembly back to order.

"Since time is of the essence, let us discuss this matter before lunch and have a voice vote on the necessary resolution afterward. The chair recognizes the delegate from Zimbabwe."

The morning's discussion mostly revolved around individual nations agreeing with the Old Ones' proposal. When questions came up, one of their ambassadors would answer. Sam and Lisa recorded the session, simulcast it on Facebook, YouTube, and the ZNN website, and wrote articles for ZNN.

By late evening, the General Assembly passed the resolution agreeing to the aliens' treaty unanimously.

* * *

I finished putting the final touches on my scrapbook page in our stateroom on the *Resolute Too*. I had the picture of the Old Ones in the General Assembly and the headline from ZNN announcing the UN's unanimous treaty agreement with them.

I sighed. ZNN was booming. Lisa's rebranding worked brilliantly. I wish I could say the same for SPEwZ.

The zombie blood industry had died. Everyone wanted the alien nanobot cures, which worked as well or better than zombie blood. The nanobots even cured zombiism in humans and animals. Diane and I had cut our SPEwZ workforce in half, and we might need to cut it in half again.

The only remaining customers for zombie blood were zombies like us, who wanted to remain zombies. But the number of zombies decreased daily, as zombies chose to "go normal." The zombie TV and internet shows were canceled or dying.

"Another internet phenomenon has hit its half-life," I murmured to myself.

"What did you say, George?" Diane asked.

"Internet half-life. The time it takes for an internet fad or meme to peak and then die back to half its popularity."

"Which internet phenomenon is that?"

"Zombies."

"I guess you've gotten more bad news about SPEwZ?"

"Yes. Our revenue decreases daily. People are canceling their zombie blood subscriptions and giving up on zombie blood and going to the aliens' nanobots for medical cures."

"We've been through downturns before. We just have to use our good old zombie perseverance!"

"If this goes on for another month, we'll have to close our warehouse and headquarters in Gary. That's our main cost. We still collect free zombie blood donations, and we can help poor, needy zombies through charity."

"It's not like we don't have enough money from our three years in the sun. We lost the warehouse once when Sid Boffin destroyed it. We can build it up again. Zombie blood is a proven cure-all. Who knows what side effects will come from these alien nanobots?"

* * *

A howling storm beat the ancient island's stones. White-capped ocean waves crashed along the shore, rocking the fishing boats tied there. Waves of rain moved visibly across the fishing village and up the slope to my white villa, now gray in the winter rain. It felt right, I thought as I watched it through the soundproof glass of my cupola tower. The storm mimicked my feelings, my uncertainty.

I stroked my pompadour as I thought. What was I going to do about the aliens? They dominated the world's commerce. Since they'd arrived six months ago, their nanobot cures had taken over the medical field. The world economy boomed and thrived with their limitless energy and advanced computer technologies, disrupting the computer, software, and energy industries.

The aliens cleanly and carefully mined the world's oceans and deserts. They shared half of what they mined with the country where they operated. They gathered and sold elements from the world's oceans and gave the profits to the UN.

Everything was just rosy, except for my crime empire. Corrupt and dysfunctional regimes, like North Korea and Somalia, were strengthened by the interstellar commerce. Kim Jong-un had given up his intransigence to the aliens and now cooperated with them instead of me. Somalia's central government strengthened and adhered together and lifted its people out of their grinding poverty.

The world didn't even want my drugs and sex slaves. The nanobots helped people get drug addictions under control: alcohol, heroin, cocaine, crack, and hashish. The new computer breakthroughs allowed people to manufacture sex robots that were indistinguishable from real people.

The only portion of my empire that was doing well were my worldwide gambling emporiums. With more disposable income, people gambled more than ever before. Perhaps I could milk that?

But I was just dodging the issue. The aliens dominated the world, not me. How could I take them over? I knew nothing about them. Their ambassadors freely gave interviews about all their experiences on the "mothership" where they trained. I analyzed every interview and created a map of the training portion of the ship.

The aliens' human representatives also gave free tours and rides in their saucers. The aliens had not revealed that technology, but scientists believed their engines actually warped the fabric of space-time to propel them.

I needed more information about them and their ships.

I smiled.

* * *

Secretary Unit: "Our reporting protocol: We verified our zettabyte communications channel between each of us. Then we checked into our conference. Unlike the humans, we do not schedule meetings. Any of us could initiate a meeting anytime when we all needed to know a new fact.

"We began reviewing the Intelligence Unit reports. We gathered all known human knowledge and history, from all internet material. We absorbed Analysis Unit's assessment of all possible outcome perturbations. We repeated the analysis more than necessary. If we were human, this would indicate surprise. The possible perturbations of our plans fluctuated far worse than expected, due to extreme human unpredictability.

"We repeatedly reviewed future scenarios because of the great quantity of contradictory information. Humans seem to use falsehoods against each other continuously.

We used human history to estimate probabilities of the myriad outcomes.

"As each of our units received new information, all our units adjusted their plans and goals and updated their reports. Thus, our meeting proceeded, as normal, in waves of updates and reviews, reflecting through us all.

"Finally our updating and estimation settled. We finished with each unit's final report, using our standard protocol.

"We have checked in with us.

"We conducted our review of new information. We the Diplomacy Unit, Analysis Unit, Resource Unit, Warfare Unit, Decision Unit, Secretary Unit."

Diplomacy Unit: "Our goal is maximum human cooperation. Assessment: Progress. Data: 69 percent of humanity is convinced of our beneficence, according to a weighted average of all their own polls and our own observations of 14,159 people. Our bioengineered foxcats appeal to people. These shipboard parasites give us good PR. This is an efficient use of our resources. Proposal: Examine the other 41,596 species on the ship for possible human use. Humans are convinced of our similarity with them psychologically, if not physically."

Analysis Unit: "Assessment: Maximum possible progress toward human cooperation: 80 percent. Twenty percent of humans will always reject us."

Secretary Unit: "We all noted this negative fact."

Analysis Unit: "Our estimated date to achieve our ultimate goal is three years. We have 99 percent confidence in successfully controlling all natural resources."

Resource Unit: "Assessment: Minimum loss of resources. Extraction of earth's resources—progress. Delivery of resources underway. We expect to increase volume 100 percent within three months, plus or minus one month. Acceptable results, within our project variables. We successfully added necessary elements with no losses."

Warfare Unit: "Minimal warfare to this point. Assessment: Success, no war yet. Future war probability: 99.9999 percent. Warfare outcome: victory 99.99 percent likely. Losses: Up to 10 percent of our resources. Human losses: 20 to 90 percent of world population, but no more than 1 to 2 percent of natural resources."

Decision Unit: "Diplomacy and Analysis Units will proceed to analyze ship species for use with humans. The Resource Unit benefits compared with the Warfare Unit loss risks are acceptable. Conclusion: Proceed as planned."

Secretary Unit: "After two hundred and sixty-two milliseconds, our meeting adjourned."

Chapter 10

Gary

I sighed with contentment as I filled out my scrapbook that evening. I taped in Jessica's and Kim Chi-un's newly arrived wedding invitation. They'd selected June 1, 2020, in Pyongyang, in the only government-permitted church in the country. Normally the church was for foreign visitors and selected non-Christian Koreans, to watch them. Since Jessica Rose was a US national, Kim Jung-un allowed them to marry there, probably for propaganda purposes.

The alien-spawned prosperity in North Korea absorbed the government's energy and attention, and their persecution of Christians and political dissidents ebbed.

Diane and I arrived back at Gary a month ago, after the *Resolute Too* docked in Seattle. SPEwZ and its employees needed us. I used a twisty tie to attach SPEwZ new blood capsule and EpiPen, updated with alien technology.

In our first employee meeting after we returned, Diane reassured our employees—"We'll scrimp and save and get by!"—with her normal optimism.

After the meeting, I told her, "Our cash flow must be balanced. We can cut salaries or cut personnel."

"We'll cut our salaries down to a dollar a year! We're independently wealthy."

"That helps, but we're still 10 percent short of our next payroll."

"So we'll cut everyone's salary 10 percent. We'll all bear the burden equally together!"

Her solution was simple but draconian. We lost several employees over it, but we made payroll that week.

Finally, SPEwZ was getting back on its zombie feet. We had a steady pool of a million or so zombie blood customers worldwide. Most of them were in hazardous work such as police or military, where zombie quick regeneration would save lives. The alien nanobots could regrow limbs, but not at the exponential rate of zombie bacteria, ECHZ. Also, nanobots could not revive corpses.

We played up these advantages in our advertising. I hired Ron Yardley of ZNN to develop our social media plan.

"For quick limb regrowth, there's nothing like zombie blood!" "When you're down and out, only zombie blood can give you new life!" were two of his tweets today. I already saw an uptick in our online sales.

Those new sales would have to cover our additional costs. We needed to provide a vaccine with each blood dose to prevent loss of zombiism through the diseases we encountered earlier this year. They were genetically engineered, but General Figeroa told us the NSA had made no progress in tracing their origins.

I pasted in a copy of Micah Rigby's signature on our contract with the aliens into my scrapbook. We leased out half our warehouse in Gary to the aliens for their automated factory. They would make medical nanobots for the US right here in Gary.

I clenched my teeth. That was like going to bed with the enemy. They were direct competition for zombie blood, but by working with them, we gained a portion of their profits. They also employed hundreds of truckers and warehouse workers supplying their factory with rare earth minerals and pure silicon for their microbe-sized nanobots.

Alien technology dominated the world's economy. Those who used it made stupendous profits and bought up firms that didn't move as quickly. The whole world depended on the new technology.

"What if they leave? How much would we lose?" I murmured.

"You're talking to yourself again, George," Diane said as she cross-stitched a wedding gift for Jessica and Kim Chi-un. "Who is this 'they'? The aliens?"

"Yes. If they leave, I wonder how much of their technology we could replicate? Would civilization collapse?"

"So that'd be an alien apocalypse? It'd be a relief from all the zombie apocalypse stuff I've heard."

* * *

The alien mining machine came out of its mile-deep tunnel and disgorged its load of rare earth elements into the waiting mining trucks in the Nevada desert. From each of its six sides, a tube extended to the truck beds. Billows of dust and dirt came from the truck beds as ore thundered in. This was the opportunity they waited for.

"Let's go! We've got about half an hour," urged their leader, Petra.

The eight conspirators ran from their van to the gaping wound in the earth. The hole only stretched about fifty feet across, hexagonal like the machine, with glass-smooth sides. The mining machine hovered a hundred feet overhead, towering hundreds of feet farther into the sky. Material poured into the six trucks. Each truck held four hundred tons, and the machine mined enough material to fill six different trucks with six different types of ore. The trucks carried their loads to an automated smelter several miles away.

Six of the team surrounded the hole, dragging their chains with them. They jackhammered massive pitons into the rocky ground and attached their chains. Then they handcuffed themselves to the pitons. Now the six chains crisscrossed the hole, blocking the mining machine from resuming its work.

Their other two coworkers were Karl and Petra. Karl ran the video camera, streaming its feed to the internet, while Petra chained herself to each of her team and began narrating.

"Greetings, fellow Earthlings! I am Petra Stronk of Gaia First, here on the frontlines of our battle for Mother Earth at the alien mining site.

"The aliens' machines have been raping our beloved Gaia for six months now, and we're putting a stop to it today—or die trying.

"As you can see," she continued as Karl panned the hole, the chains, the Gaia First volunteers, and the mining machine overhead, "we have totally blocked this machine from reentering the earth. This so-called 'alien sensitivity' to our earth is disrupting the earth's geology and crustal ecosystem. Already, earthquakes have increased around all Old Ones' mining sites worldwide, as the evil invaders suck out our resources and leave the earth an empty husk.

"This is beside the poisons they're injecting into our biosphere as trillions of these nanobots are manufactured and spread worldwide, carrying their deadly cargo of rare earth additives.

"The mining machine has begun its descent. In case I die with my comrades, I urge each of you to fight the aliens! Fight them on the beaches! Fight them in the fields! Fight them in the hills and mountains of our fair planet!"

"Goodbye, my love!" Petra shouted to her husband, Karl, as the machine touched the crossed chains, pulling on the pitons. Each piton was an inch in diameter and four feet long, driven into the rocky ground. The chains were high-test, case-hardened steel, each with a tensile strength of ten thousand pounds.

The chains pulled, stretched, bending the pitons. The Free Gaia group started shouting, "Hell no, aliens must go!"

Karl streamed the whole event online on Twitter, Facebook, Instagram, and YouTube.

The machine paused as if puzzled by the resistance. It elevated back to its hundred-foot height, amid the cheers and jeers of the eight protesters. Then, FLASH!

Instantaneously the six chains and the exposed pitons vaporized under the immense power of the machine's mining laser. The protesters fell silent, shocked by the sudden show of force.

Getting to her feet, Petra looked directly at the camera and spoke.

"Now you know, fellow Earthlings, inhabitants of Gaia. The aliens' machines are also weapons, and we are all beneath their threat. At any time we can be exterminated. Now you see the threat we have known. Now is the time for you to act.

"Each and every one of you viewers worldwide, go to your respective governments and break off the agreements with the aliens. Tell them to go away. They're not wanted here."

* * *

Sam watched the video until it repeated its loop, from their conference room in Midley, Illinois. They'd returned home after their visit to the UN. The *Resolute Too* remained docked in Seattle until the world situation settled down. *If that ever happened*, Sam thought.

"Wow. Lisa, guess what just happened?"

"Don't make me guess! And don't yell from the conference room!" Lisa yelled from her office.

"OK. Sorry." Sam walked to Lisa's corner office.

"I just saw a video of a Gaia First protest of the aliens' mining."

"That might make a good story. ZNN has several popular videos of the Gaia Firsters' protests. What happened?"

"They blocked a mining machine from reentering its tunnel with chains. Then the machine vaporized the chains with a laser!"

"Get on it! Publish the video first and then write a story."

"Will do!"

While Sam wrote his story, Lisa watched Lashon's recently delivered interview with Anthony Embry, alien ambassador to Great Britain.

"So, Anthony, what's with the lasers on the mining machines?"

"That's how they work. They vaporize the rock and ore, vacuum out the vapor, and distill the desired elements into the machine. Naturally, if there are impediments in front of the machine, they'll vaporize them."

"Including people?"

"Of course not! Notice that none of the protesters were injured, despite how close they were to the beams."

"You know, people worldwide are buzzing. Many are saying humanity should break off our agreement with the Old Ones because they're too dangerous."

"Take a deep breath and don't panic! There is a lot of power in each machine and factory on the earth for our industrial and mining work. The Old Ones have it all perfectly under control."

"But many politicians and protesters say you've broken your word to not harm the earth."

"What's the difference if you melt the ore in situ or in a blast furnace? Our mines are far safer than any human blast furnace. And you have thousands of deaths each year in mines and blast furnaces combined."

"What about those miners and steelworkers who will be out of work due to your automation?" Lashon asked.

"The world's economy has improved enough with the savings in medical and energy costs to easily support the unemployed until they get new jobs," Anthony said.

"That sounds good, but what guarantees the Old Ones won't use their lasers against us?"

"If we wanted to destroy mankind, we would have done it already. Trust me on this, Lashon. The Old Ones are as good as their word. They never lie."

"I guess that really says they're aliens! Thank you for the interview, Anthony Embry, Old Ones' ambassador to Great Britain. This is Lashon Miller signing off."

Lisa reviewed Sam's story when it arrived in her in-basket and added Lashon's video. "Expect another spike in our internet ratings, Sam!" Lisa shouted after she uploaded the completed story.

"Don't yell from your office!" Sam yelled from his office. He peeked around the corner with a big grin.

"Gotcha!"

* * *

I read the latest data from my spies, snug and warm by my marble fireplace in my villa, while I sipped my snifter of brandy. Gesturing at my tablet on my lap, I quickly scanned the latest maps from my spies. Nothing new. Apparently the aliens only had one section on their mothership for humans—and it was sealed from the rest of the ship.

That bothered me. I didn't like not knowing things, like what the aliens looked like or what their weaknesses were. I checked my map again. Eighty-five percent complete. The remaining 15 percent was unlikely to lead to a breakthrough, but I had to explore it, just in case.

I had a bigger worry though. Even if I knew all about the aliens and their ship and their technology, how could I get at them or control them? I studied their technology daily but learned nothing about their gravity-bending flight mechanism.

On the good side, the zombies seemed to be more off balance than I was. I was glad to get on top of them. But so what, if I was a menial cog under alien rulership? Plus, there were all these things they could do to eliminate my empire if they wanted to. I shivered.

Think outside the box. Two enemies, a greater and a lesser. What to do? I could co-op one or the other. If I joined with the aliens, they would give me near immortality. I already had that. Several of my clones tried to join the aliens as ambassadors, but none had been approved. This made me suspicious the aliens knew about my criminal empire.

My children did find out the aliens required an injection of their nanobots. I would never do that myself, due to the risk of them having a "kill switch" that could wipe me out with a signal. That didn't even touch the possibilities for control and torture. I could end up as an alien slave for all eternity!

Or I could join with the zombies and by extension, the US government. The resources of the US government plus mine plus the zombies might be enough to take over the aliens. But that meant I'd have to fake being good and actually follow the law for *dozens* of years. Ugh! It'd take at least five to ten years to defeat the aliens and then an equal time to safely betray the zombies and US government.

Alien slave, or faking being good? Both options were equally bad. I'd chew on that for a while. Maybe something else would occur. I'd review these options with my children for ideas. I could hint they'd get world rulership after our victory.

There. I had an action plan. I called my first clone from my encrypted landline.

* * *

Secretary Unit: "We have checked in with us."

Secretary Unit: "We conducted our review of new information. We the Diplomacy Unit, Analysis Unit, Resource Unit, Warfare Unit, Decision Unit, Secretary Unit."

Diplomacy Unit: "Assessment: Progress. Data: 85 percent of humanity is convinced of our beneficence, according to a weighted average of all their own polls and our own observations of 27,444 people. The remaining population worldwide continues resistance. Acceptable results."

Analysis Unit: "Assessment: We have maximum human cooperation. Maximum possible progress toward human cooperation: 85 percent. At least 15 percent of humanity will always reject us. The cause of this discrepancy and our earlier estimate of 20 percent is extreme human variability. At least 5 percent will flip between two or more opposite opinions."

Secretary Unit: "We all noted this negative fact."

Analysis Unit: "Our estimated date to achieve our ultimate goal is two years. We have 99 percent confidence in success through control of all natural resources."

Resource Unit: "Assessment: Minimum loss of resources. We have extraction success with no losses, but some inefficiency in paying and working with humans. We currently tap 10 percent of annual human production. We will increase to 50 percent within a year. These results are acceptable. We expect human inefficiency to be remedied by direct guidance."

Warfare Unit: "We have minimal warfare. We have no war yet. The probability of human-initiated war: 50 percent by small units within the year, 99 percent by countries within two years. Warfare outcome: Victory 99.99 percent likely. Losses: Up to 13 percent of our resources. Human losses: 25 to 95 percent of world population, no more than 2 to 3 percent of natural resources."

Decision Unit: "Our ultimate goal assessment: We have progress. Our economic domination is 89 percent. Our estimated goal asymptote is 95 percent, with 15 to 20 percent resistance remaining. The Resource Unit benefits compared with the Warfare Unit loss risks are acceptable risk, but the timeline is too slow. We have one year to our ultimate goal, total world domination, with 99 percent confidence. Conclusion: Accelerate our plan, destroy all resistance, correct disobedience through nanobots, and reward obedience."

Secretary Unit: "After three hundred and forty-five milliseconds, our meeting adjourned."

Chapter 11

Gulf of Mexico

It crawled. It staggered in cold darkness. It drifted and thrashed with its appendages aimlessly. It moved with the current. But mostly it suffered. It suffered continual agony. It breathed water through its mouth but was not satisfied, even when it occasionally ate something by accident. Plankton. Small fish. Jellyfish. It needed something passionately. It didn't know what. But it knew it had to keep struggling to get what it wanted. It had no other self-awareness but that burning need.

It moved blindly. It suffered every second, except the few occasions when it lapsed into unconsciousness. The pain returned more strongly when it awoke, sucking water madly, its pain increased twofold.

It did not think. It only sucked water and struggled to move, minute by minute, hour by hour, day by day. For weeks it struggled. Then it felt a change.

The current pulled stronger. It lifted its body all the way to the surface. And it found what it wanted.

GASP! Air! It had never felt so good. It gagged and vomited the remaining seawater from its stomach, along with its last meal of plankton. It had suffered anoxia for so long that the relief from the pain of constant suffocation alone almost satisfied.

LIGHT! Stars blazed above like arc lights, dazzling long-darkened vision.

LAND! It staggered through the surf, buffeted by waves but steadily moving upward toward shore.

A sharp pain tore its lower appendage. A shark jerked it underwater, seeking a quick meal. Rage flashed in its mind like a nuclear explosion. It would not suffocate again! Using its two upper appendages, it ripped the shark's jaws apart. In uncontrollable fury, it tore gobbets of flesh from the fish until it was a bloody cloud of floating meat. It gorged on the meat between gasps of air. It needed food as much as it needed air.

The pain in the bleeding appendage slowly subsided once it climbed out of the water.

But still, something was missing. Some deeper, stronger need than air. Some need that had been masked by the continual pain of the past months under water.

It, no, *I* was still muzzy headed, but I'd solve that soon, now that I was back where I belonged.

* * *

"It seems like we were just here," Sam commented as he and Lisa parked near the UN building on the East River in New York City.

"It was a year ago, if you can believe that. So much has changed since the aliens, er, Old Ones came."

"Lisa! That's a big change for you. I've never heard you be politically correct before."

"I know they like 'Old Ones' better, and we're going to be meeting their ambassadors here at the UN, so I thought I should get into the habit."

"Do you really think they report back everything they hear to the Old Ones? We've interviewed all two hundred of them, even the North Korean one."

"That's the way I'm betting! Here are our press passes," Lisa said as she showed them to the security guard.

"I didn't know you had mine," Sam said.

"I knew you'd forget," Lisa said.

"I guess I did."

Once again, Sam and Lisa live streamed the two hundred ambassadors arriving on their flying hoverboards in the UN General Assembly. Again, they floated above the UN delegates packed in the hall, seated on their boards.

Five figures materialized before the podium after the assembly had been called to order and the special agenda of the Old Ones' announcement introduced.

"Greetings, Earthlings! We come bearing good news for the whole planet. We have decided to end all wars for all time, using our power and technology."

The assembly erupted into thunderous applause.

"Furthermore, we will end all crime and violence. We will cause all murders, rapes, and robberies to cease."

Again the General Assembly applauded. It grew and grew until all members were standing.

The Old Ones waited until the applause ended and the delegates were seated again.

"Just as we recruited humans to represent us to your race, so we intend to use the UN to implement our world peace program. Our two hundred ambassadors will join your General Assembly. Then you will select twenty of them to sit on the Security Council."

Some General Assembly members murmured and cried out.

"We realize these changes require some updates to the UN charter, but do not fear. We have anticipated what changes are necessary and now supply all of you with the new charter proposal."

The ambassadors on their hoverboards flew to their countries' delegates and handed each a portfolio.

Lisa whispered to Sam, "Sam! I got a copy in my email!"

Sam glanced at his phone. "Me too!"

"I don't like their ability to penetrate our security effortlessly," Lisa grumbled.

"Normally, a change of this magnitude requires months or years to approve. Security Council changes are politically sensitive, with each member protecting their power and influence," said the Old Ones.

"Fortunately, today we will vote on these changes and implement them before this meeting is over."

The uproar grew like an approaching wave. When it peaked, the Old Ones' spokesperson, the Asian, made a swiping gesture, and absolute silence filled the hall. People's mouths were still moving, but no sound came out.

"Our technology makes controlling a large meeting like this much easier. Let's begin by adopting this amendment. We'll begin the voice vote. Afghanistan?"

The delegate from Afghanistan stood up defiantly, opened his mouth—and nothing came out. He put his hands to his head as if in great pain, and then weakly said "Yes" in Pashtun.

The process repeated through St. Lucia, when the Old One said, "Now we have the required two-thirds. Let's see if we can get unanimous consent!"

There was unanimous consent.

"Congratulations! You've done it. Amendments require the approval of the five permanent members of the Security Council. You'll be pleased to know we've already run these changes by them and they've approved them! You've created a new world order!"

Slowly, the whole assembly began clapping. They looked shocked, dazed, and confused, but they clapped mechanically, even enthusiastically standing to their feet.

"We will now, through our ambassadors, take steps to remove all poverty and crime from the earth. Our two hundred flying saucers are destroying weaponry around the world, without loss of life.

"We will begin our world health program through mandatory injections of nanobots in every person on earth, just as all of you have received. These will prevent disease and aging far better than the zombie blood treatments. The nanobots also eliminate zombiism, with all its bad side effects.

"One side effect of our nanobots is that they allow anyone to experience realistic virtual reality. This will enable new entertainment delights for your species. Any of your entertainment media—movies, television, video, or games—can be adapted to virtual reality for every member of the audience, worldwide and online."

Almost as an afterthought, the Old One said, "The nanobots also allow us to discipline any criminals before they commit a crime. We can cause sufficient pain to stop any criminal activity.

"That concludes our message and our meeting with you today." The Old Ones' images vanished.

"Sam! I knew the aliens were too good to be true! There's no pie in the sky and no free lunch! People won't stand for this! I won't stand for it!" Lisa said.

"You're right, but I'm not sure what we can do about it."

"I'm not getting that nanobot injection! In fact—" Lisa took an ampoule from around her neck and injected herself with zombie blood.

"I'm going zombie on their alien butts!"

"Me too!" Sam followed Lisa by injecting himself. They watched each other's eyes turn red.

"We've got our story. Let's get out of here. I've got an anti-alien editorial to write!"

* * *

Lisa finished her editorial on the flight back to Midley and published it immediately. While she did that, Sam called their medical researcher at the Mayo Clinic, Dr. Marchanne Herbst.

"Hello?" said a calm soprano voice through Sam's phone.

"Dr. Herbst, this is Sam Melvin. Did you watch the UN meeting today?"

"Yes, we all did. We had no choice. It popped up on our internet devices all through the clinic!"

"It appeared all over the world. The aliens seem to have complete control over our internet. I have an urgent question for you: Can you remove the alien nanobots from human blood?"

"I don't see why not. We've studied the nanobots since the aliens arrived, for FDA approval. They are larger than red blood cells, as big as white blood cells. Once blood is removed from the body, plasmapheresis through continuous centrifuging will separate the nanobots."

"Uh, how can you live without blood?"

"Only a cup or so is outside the body at any time. It's added back after separation. We use this to treat various blood diseases."

"Thanks. I think a lot of people will want this treatment soon, to get the alien nanobots out."

"Ah, due to their world dictatorship. I can see that. Interesting," she said. "I can see several ways to do this. I'll begin testing protocols for nanobot separation."

"Thanks, Dr. Herbst! You may be breaking our bondage from alien nanobot chains!"

"I never thought of it that way!"

"You'll be a heroine, Dr. Herbst."

"I've always thought of myself as a medical nerd."

"Keep your research quiet though. You don't want a visit from the aliens. That reminds me. I should call General Figeroa at the NSA. See you later!"

"Sam! The US military is fighting back!" Lisa said.

Sam looked at the wall monitor on their private plane.

"We interrupt for breaking news. The flying saucer used to bring Old Ones' ambassador Micah Rigby to Washington, DC, began attacking US military installations during the UN General Assembly meeting. US forces returned fire, but unsuccessfully. The saucer destroyed guns, rockets, and planes using a gamma-ray laser. We now have a statement from President Trump."

"In a day which shall live in infamy, in a heinous attack on the United States of America, the alien spaceship has destroyed US military equipment. I've authorized our military to use all necessary force to neutralize and destroy this craft.

"I urge all citizens to remain in their homes for the duration of our operations today. We will do whatever it takes to keep Americans safe.

"In the meantime, all government employees and any citizens who desire to be free of the alien-control nanobots in their bloodstream should come to any hospital to have them cleansed from their system."

"Way to go!" Lisa shouted. "Stick a nuke up their butts!"

At that moment, the US military shot a hypervelocity slug of tungsten at the alien saucer from one of the navy's secretly deployed electromagnetic rail guns. The slug penetrated the saucer and knocked it down.

Immediately the aliens' mothership vaporized the ship using a powerful gamma-ray laser. Then it proceeded to vaporize all the US Navy ships on earth. The aliens did the same to the other nations' military ships.

Fortunately, they didn't consider the *Resolute Too* a navy ship.

The alien ambassadors on duty at the UN received protests from every government with a military.

Again, the Old Ones appeared on the UN General Assembly floor.

"We have read all your protests, and we deeply regret the loss of life. However, we must defend our flying saucers. We removed the source of any such attacks. We will also warn you, if your attacks come from a civilian area, there will be collateral damage and needless civilian deaths. Simply permit us to destroy all your military equipment worldwide, and no one will get hurt."

The world's governments protested, but civilians worldwide rejoiced to see the end of warfare and crime.

The aliens gave free virtual reality (VR) helmets to all humans working for them and to any who received the nanobots. With them, people could experience movies, television, the internet, and sports as three-dimensional, tactile, olfactory, and taste sensations. As consumers enjoyed the Old Ones' virtual reality, their silvery VR helmets became popular worldwide. The streaming sensations ended before civilians had to go to work. The aliens made sure everyone worked daily, for their purposes, or no VR.

The world gravitated toward the new entertainment. Soon, the majority of mankind worked for the aliens, with varying degrees of enthusiasm. A stubborn remnant rebelled, including the world's zombies.

* * *

"Are we ready?" President Trump asked from inside his secure remote White House under Cheyenne Mountain in Wyoming.

"As ready as we'll ever be," said Junia Lyndhurst, the director of the NSA, her red eyes gleaming at the president. The director had gotten a zombie medical treatment four years ago before Sid Boffin ever showed up and before President Trump's election. She maintained her zombie condition and was vaccinated against the anti-zombie diseases afflicting the world. Even the aliens' promise of nanobots had not lured her away from her zombie health.

"You know, I feel a little like Princess Leia in *Star Wars*, talking to Obi-Wan Kenobi," the president remarked.

"How, Mr. President?"

Looking at her, he said, "You're our only hope, Junia Lyndhurst. You're our only hope. We took a gut punch when the damned aliens blew our military weaponry to smithereens. Then you got the brilliant idea of refitting a nuke from our subs onto one of our NASA space launch missiles, in place of our scheduled mission to Jupiter.

"What I really loved was how you placed the nuke into the shell of the satellite so that even the operational personnel didn't know about the change."

"I can't take full credit, by any means, Mr. President. My associate, General Figeroa, figured out how to implement it." Junia gestured toward the general standing beside her.

"Thank you, ma'am," General Figeroa said quietly. "But I, in turn, must give credit to my staff. They reprogrammed the software and hardware of the rocket so it would launch and fly by the alien mothership and then deploy the bomb straight toward it, using the upper stages of the rocket in a way quite outside the original design parameters."

"They also added a defensive system to each of the nuclear warheads to protect them from the aliens' laser."

"How many warheads does it carry? What's our chance it's going to do some damage?" the president asked.

"It carries seventy-two independently targeted warheads. Each has a half-megaton nuclear bomb on it. I'd say," continued the general with a smile that never reached his eyes, "they'll feel the thirty-six-megaton payload."

"It's launching in a minute," said the NSA head.

Director Lyndhurst, General Figeroa, and President Trump watched the launch together. The camera followed the rocket far into the atmosphere, and then it was lost to sight.

"How long until it separates?" the president asked.

"The booster stages have dropped away, and the second stage is underway. Less than fifteen minutes," Figeroa said. "I think we can switch to our secret feed." He pressed a button on the remote control.

A blue earth arced against a black sky in utter silence. The camera pointed directly forward, showing the nose cone of the rocket.

"Soon we'll see the alien ship rise above the horizon," the general said.

The president saw a white dot separate from the earth and slowly rise against the blackness. It grew and grew into a visible oblong. Then it became a tilted disk, growing rapidly.

"How close does the rocket come?" he asked.

"It's planned to get within ten miles, which is quite close. But due to an 'error,' we'll be about a mile and a half away when the warheads separate. The individual rockets on each warhead will steer them directly toward the mothership. They'll be within a hundred yards when they detonate," Figeroa said.

"How soon now?"

"Soon."

The disk swelled and grew in the camera like a giant Frisbee or pie plate. A bright flash and the whole nose cone exploded.

"Now the rear camera," Figeroa said. The camera showed a sparkling cloud headed toward the saucer. "That's the chaff to deflect the laser. You can't see the laser, but those sparkles—oh!"

The warheads detonated simultaneously into seventy-two baby suns, engulfing the mothership.

"We have successful detonation of all seventy-two warheads," said a voice from mission control.

"I expected something more dramatic," Junia said. "That looks like a regular nuke."

"No sound effects either," the president added.

"No, we didn't have the budget for that," Junia said. "Now what?" she asked as the glowing ball swirled and turned into a doughnut shape. In the hole of the glowing doughnut, they could see the circle of the earth—and the unharmed mothership.

"Uh-oh," Figeroa said.

"Does that mean they *took* it? Without harm?" President Trump said, incredulous.

"It sure looks that way, sir," Junia said, her mouth in a grim line. "What do you think happened, General?"

Looking into her red eyes with his blue ones, Figeroa noted the sudden formality. Their multibillion dollar project failed in front of the president.

"Without analysis of the telemetry feed we're getting from the rocket, I can't be sure. But based upon physics and the shape of that plasma, I'd say an intense magnetic field *bent* the explosion away from the mothership," he said.

"What worries me is what comes next," the general continued.

"What do you mean, General?" asked the director.

"How will they retaliate, where, and when?"

"Order evacuation of Cape Canaveral!" President Trump shouted.

"I'm on it, Mr. President!" Junia said.

"I think we're too late," Figeroa murmured.

"Why?" the president demanded.

"The mothership just left. I was watching it, and it flicked off screen."

"Which way did it go?"

"Here's the NORAD feed," Figeroa said.

The screen showed thousands of lights of orbiting satellites against the globe, like a Christmas tree. Only one moved—very quickly.

"Those are all the objects in space over North America," the general said. "And that is the mothership." He zoomed in on the display. Figeroa projected the state boundaries on the surface of the earth. The mothership stopped over Florida. Cape Canaveral.

"I just lost connection with the Cape!" Junia said.

"What happened?" the president demanded.

"They issued the evacuation order and were leaving the buildings when my contact's phone went out."

"It's moving again," Figeroa said in a quiet voice.

"Where?" the president asked.

"White Sands Air Force Base."

"Evacuate!"

"I'm calling now!" Junia said.

"It's too late," the general said sadly. "They're moving on to Upham, New Mexico. I believe they'll destroy every launch site in the US."

Stunned, the three stared as the glowing dot moved across the US, destroying the country's existing rocket facilities. Then it moved around the world, doing the same.

"Now what do we do?" President Trump asked, more in desperation than hope.

"The general and I will begin working on it now, Mr. President," Junia said quietly.

"There is one more resource we have," General Figeroa said.

"What?" President Trump asked.

"Zombies."

* * *

"Hello, Mr. President." Diane answered her red encrypted phone she used for secure communication and put down her knitting. "Yes, he's here. We're by ourselves. I'll put you on speakerphone." She activated her wireless speaker in their living room.

"Diane, George, I know you've been resting since this alien invasion, but now your nation needs you again," the president stated.

"Yes, sir! We zombies are always ready to serve!" Diane said.

I nodded.

"Great! This will be a huge risk, but I think you're up to it. We want you to board a flying saucer and take it to the mothership. Then you'll take it over or incapacitate it. After that, you'll fly back to the earth in the saucer."

"Yes, sir!" George and Diane said together.

"Which saucer, Mr. President? There's one in every world capital," I asked.

"We'll fly you to Washington, DC, aboard Air Force One. Vice President Pence will be in Gary to address the National Governors Association about the aliens. We'll slip you on the plane secretly. The aliens won't suspect zombies are coming to them. They'll be completely unprepared."

"Let's do it!" Diane cheered.

"How about our bodyguards, Lulu and Sharon?"

"They'll be part of the attack force. We'll give you full tactical armor and a schematic of the known layout of the mothership. We've gotten that from the interviews with the alien ambassadors."

"Sounds good to us, Mr. President! George and I will lay them low, and Lulu and Sharon will finish them off!"

"Mr. President, do we know how these saucers work?" I asked.

"Yes, we do. We've discussed their operation with the ambassadors, and we've been inside on tours. They are as simple as you can imagine. They work like elevators. There's a button for each world capital and the mothership. You simply press the button, and away you go, at 30 percent the speed of light. A child could operate one!"

"Seems straightforward. When do we leave?"

"As soon as you're ready, head for the Gary airport. The Secret Service will slip you on Air Force One. I believe you know Agent Smith?"

"Old blue eyes!" Diane said.

"That's it for now. Let me say, as your fellow American and commander-in-chief, how proud I am of you! I expect nothing but huge success!"

"Yes, sir!" we said.

* * *

Diane and I arrived with Lulu and Sharon in Washington, DC. Diane exclaimed, "George! It's Valentine's Day!"

"I can't think of who else I'd like to spend the day with, killing alien invaders," I said.

"It was exactly four years ago we had our first zombie dinner with the kids, Don and Maggie, Ron and Karen."

"That's when you tore off your first arm."

"Poor Donnie. I think I really shocked him. But he hasn't given me any trouble since then!"

"And nobody else has topped you since. Or before."

Agent Smith met us as we came off the airplane.

"Hello, Diane and George, Lulu and Sharon. It's good to see you again. I will escort you to the preparation center."

"What's the preparation center?" Diane asked.

"We can talk more in the car. The airport is not secure."

A stretch limo awaited them outside the terminal. "This is a secure limo. We can talk here," Agent Smith said.

"Where is the preparation center?" Sharon asked.

"And what is it?" Lulu asked.

"It is a secret base used for equipping the Secret Service. There you'll get your equipment."

"We wore our armor under our traveling clothes, and we checked our knives at the airport," I said.

"We have much better equipment for you. It's what the zombie Secret Service get."

"Oooh! I feel like James Bond!" Diane said.

"You look like a Bond girl," I said.

"George! There are no middle-aged Bond girls! And I want the gadgets, anyway."

"You get the gadgets—I get the girl," I said.

The limo stopped by the Lincoln Memorial. We got out and went inside. Once inside, other agents in dark suits handed each of us a broom. The agents then escorted the tourists inside the memorial out of the facility, saying, "Sorry, folks. The Lincoln Memorial is closed for half an hour. It's time for the Lincoln statue cleaning."

"Will people actually believe that?" Lulu asked.

"Sure," Agent Smith said. "It's our standard operating procedure. We wait here until the agents place rope lines at all the entrances. There we go."

"All entrances secure, Agent Smith. You and your guests may proceed," said a short, stocky dark-haired agent.

"Please stand in front of the statue," Agent Smith said.

We complied, facing the ten-foot-tall marble block on which the Lincoln statue rested. Smith jumped up and grabbed Lincoln's right foot. He did something with his hands, which couldn't be seen, and the marble slab on which we stood ponderously pivoted toward the statue. We could see a round two-foot diameter tunnel going down at a forty-five-degree angle under the statue.

"This is the secret entrance. Enter quickly and I'll close it behind you."

"Here goes!" Diane said, diving in. "Into Lincoln's basement!" Her voice echoed up the tunnel.

I followed, then Lulu and Sharon.

Quietly, the slab closed us in.

"That's remarkable," I said, squeezing along the dark tunnel. "The entryway is completely silent. They must use some hydraulic system."

We emerged from the tunnel, and the lights blinked on in a bare marble room.

A dark agent in a black suit and black sunglasses greeted them. "Welcome, paranormal privateers. I am the Equipper."

He took us to a room lined with equipment: guns, pistols, armor, knives, as well as hundreds of electronic gadgets. Diane was thrilled.

"Oooh, look at this little knife!" She held up a penknife. It flipped open like a switchblade, and then again.

"So the blade is twice as long as the handle," I said.

Then Diane flipped it, and the other side also opened into a six-inch blade, with the handle in the middle.

"This is cool," Diane said.

"It's yours," the Equipper said.

Adorned with the latest armor and more weaponry than we'd ever dreamed of, we were led by the Equipper through a long tunnel to a narrow spiral staircase. Checking an adjacent monitor, he said, "The coast is clear. Ambassador Micah Rigby is on his way to the saucer after meeting with the president. Follow him into the saucer, and you're on your way. God be with you," he added, sounding doubtful.

As I climbed the narrow spiral, I squeezed my body between the center steel post and the concrete walls. Diane, Lulu, and Sharon followed.

We emerged from a massive oak on the south lawn. The hidden door wrapped around the six-foot-diameter tree trunk. Ahead, through some bushes, we spied the saucer. I couldn't see where the aliens had repaired it after it had been shot down by the military. Ambassador Micah walked toward the ramp.

"Let's go!" Diane said, and she charged across the lawn.

Hearing them, Micah turned and said, "Hi! You must be tourists. You can schedule free rides and tours of the saucer at the White House. Sorry, but I can't take you on now."

"That's true," I said, coming up behind Diane. "You can't take us on." I grabbed Micah, picked him up like a baby, and entered the saucer. The others followed.

The ramp withdrew smoothly into the saucer, and it took off into the sky.

Inside, I put Micah down and said, "You just stay there. I don't want you to send any alarms."

"I won't. I'm sure the Old Ones won't mind you going to their mothership. We'll be there in a few minutes."

"That's hard to believe," Sharon said. "They don't mind us barging in, hijacking the saucer, and going aboard their ship?"

"No. They gave me very explicit instructions to never oppose anyone who wished for a ride, or even a visit to their ship."

"Did they tell you what they'd do when we get there?" Lulu asked.

"No."

"I guess we'll have to be prepared for anything!" Lulu said.

"Just like always! Zombies charge first, ask questions later!" Diane said.

"Here we are," Micah said.

"When we get out, remember the plan," Diane said. "We spread out in four directions, searching for a way out of the training area. Stay in contact through these." She touched her headset.

We lined up in front of the ramp. As soon as it came down, we charged out like soldiers at D-day.

Chapter 12

Earth Orbit

Diane ran forward. I ran to the right, Lulu to the left, and Sharon backward. Micah stayed behind. Each zombie sped to the farthest wall and examined it minutely for entrance into the rest of the mothership. They quickly confirmed the overall shape of the chamber.

Sharon called in first. "Slightly curved wall here, twenty meters from the saucer. There are no visible seams, and no vegetation or rocks. It appears to be the entrance to the outside of the ship. The wall is a hundred and eighty-six meters wide."

Lulu spoke next. "Straight wall leading away from the outside. It looks like it goes"—she paused as she climbed the shoulder of a rocky hill to nearly the ceiling—"about a half a kilometer into the ship. The laser range finder says"—she grabbed it from her breast pocket—"four hundred and fifty meters from where I am. And I'm a hundred and thirty-three meters from the outside wall."

"You're fast," I said. "I got to the right wall and measured the depth of the room the same, five hundred and eighty-three meters."

"And I'm just taking my good old time, enjoying the flowers and the trees!" Diane laughed. "I'm at the back wall. Like Sharon said, it is slightly curved, and it's a hundred and seventy-one meters wide."

"So we've got our walls. Let's look for secret entrances," I said.

The next half hour passed in silence, and then Sharon said, "I'm done. I've gone floor to ceiling, and it's bare metal."

"What's the ceiling look like, Sharon?" I asked.

"The wall curves smoothly into the ceiling, and then the blue lighting begins, which matches the sky."

"Have you been able to get behind the lighting?" I asked.

"Can't reach it. It starts at fifteen meters up and then arches another fifteen or twenty higher."

"Use the hill by my wall," Lulu said. "I looked at it, and it's only five meters or so above it. Also, the ceiling lighting curves down to just a meter above the hill. That last meter is a screen with some kind of 3-D projection of a horizon."

"On my way!" Reaching the top of the hill, Sharon grabbed her titanium tomahawk and whaled with all her zombie strength on the horizon projection screen and the blue lighting with the weighted head. She made no effect on either.

"I didn't make a dent in the screen or the lighting, but I blunted the pick!"

"I wonder if the ceiling and screens are made of diamond," I said.

"Diamonds are a girl's best friend!" Diane sang at the top of her voice.

"Why not?" Lulu said. "They have unlimited energy. They can make diamonds. Heck, we can make diamonds!"

"And carbon is one of the most abundant elements in the universe," I said.

"If it's diamond, we're not getting through it," Sharon said.

"I'm just about done with my wall," Lulu said.

"Me too," I said.

"And slowpoke me is bogged down—literally! I'm standing waist deep in a swamp with swans and ducks looking at me like I'm a duck," Diane said.

"We may have to dig down," I said. "But first let's help Diane. Her wall is the one most likely to have a secret entrance since it leads deeper into the saucer. I suspect there are ducts above the ceiling and drains and pipes below."

We tackled the wall with a will. Despite the thick forest, with trees reaching to the ceiling, and swamp with wildlife, our work confirmed our fears. There appeared to be no door out of the room, not even a pipe or circuit.

"Maybe we need a bigger hammer," Diane said.

"Break through the diamond?" I asked.

"Yeah, or this back wall. Let's try some of our shaped charges."

They each carried four of the palm-sized domed charges. I also carried a heavy-duty shaped charge.

They placed four of them in a square on the back wall.

"That'll do *something*," Diane said.

"Indeed," I said. "Why don't we stay behind this boulder, just in case, Diane?"

"Of course. I may be a zombie, but I'm not stupid."

We huddled as the charges detonated simultaneously. Eagerly we jumped out to see the results.

The charges did something. Four wads of molten metal glowed on the wall. The back blast stripped the vegetation in a five-meter cone away from the wall.

I pulled out my bowie knife and pried the glowing metal from the wall. A smooth, half-inch dent appeared underneath.

"Let me get out the heavy-duty one. It's like a Hellfire missile, only more effective," I said.

Then the five Old Ones appeared.

"No need to knock twice. We'll let you in. We want to meet you, paranormal privateers. We watched you carefully and have prepared a place for you."

Soundlessly, the back wall dilated like a portal. We walked into a small room, the portal dilated closed, and we stared at the bare metal walls.

The Old Ones materialized again. "This room serves as an airlock to the rest of the ship. It protects our valuable life-forms around the saucer rim from the harmful environment in which we live. We had to build special accommodation for you four zombies to get further."

"How long have you known we were coming?" Sharon asked.

"Since you boarded our daughter saucer. We can fabricate materials very quickly."

"Please enter the appropriate door to our inner room." Four doors appeared on the far wall, each with a name above it: Diane, George, Lulu, Sharon. The doors were just flat black holes.

"The doors are open for entry, but we must shield ourselves from anything in the air."

We walked through.

* * *

The aliens broke in on all major media and the internet that evening.

"Greetings, Earthlings! We came in peace. However, your nations have chosen to attack us. We have given you advanced technology to your benefit, but your governments have ignited nuclear weapons around our mothership.

"Now you've sent your zombie crew, the paranormal privateers, to attack us inside our mothership. Nukes we can handle. Zombie commando attacks, we won't tolerate.

"We captured and secured them for our experimentation."

The five Old Ones faded, and the four zombies appeared, spread-eagled against a wall, secured by metal clasps around their four limbs and necks.

"We used our nanobots on the zombie disease but have not studied their zombie powers fully. We do so now, to show our dominance over zombies and to forestall any future zombie attacks.

"We've completed our zombie strength testing and will send you the results of our experiments. But now, destructive testing."

"First, Diane, the alpha zombie."

Diane's mouth moved and her face contorted in anger, but no sound came out. The bands around her neck, arms, and legs constricted, amputating them. Five gouts of blood poured from her torso, still secured by vertical and horizontal bands.

"We'll carefully measure how long it takes to grow each limb and her head, and give you the results.

"Next, George, the strongest zombie."

George's mouth gaped in hatred, mutely. A laser split his body vertically.

"We're curious to see which side regenerates and which will retain his memories."

"Lulu is the most beautiful zombie, by human reckoning. We want to see if all her beauty comes back after we remove her skin with nanobots."

Before the world's horrified gaze, Lulu's skin disappeared, revealing the muscle underneath. The muscles rippled and quivered, but the body couldn't move.

"Finally, we'll test Sharon, the talented linguist. For her, we'll determine zombies' ability to come back from severe burns."

Sharon's tall, blond body, honed by CrossFit workouts with six-pack abs and cut muscle definition, burst into flame. Her mouth made an O and moved until the underlying muscle was charred, along with the bone.

The five Old Ones reappeared.

"That completes our experiments for today. We'll repeat this daily until all the world's zombies have gotten our nanobot injections. We insist, for your own good.

"Tomorrow, the same time, same station," the five Old Ones said in unison and perfect three-part harmony before the image faded.

* * *

The world erupted in rage and horror at the alien atrocities on the paranormal privateers. That was, those not absorbed in aliens' virtual reality entertainment and not working for the aliens. That was only half the world.

The horrific tortures of zombies continued daily. Many watched in morbid fascination. The internet compared the aliens to space Nazis. The Old Ones tried to control social media, posting from their accounts, but the entire internet mocked them. "You alien" became a new insult, which both US political parties used on each other.

Fully half the population, four billion, worked for the aliens, from babies up. The aliens found plenty of work for everyone, from answering their questions about specific human cultures and customs to manufacturing VR entertainment and alien mining ships. The aliens also supported art, music, and sculpture. Even the toddlers were played with and educated by little fuzzy robots looking and feeling like stuffed animals. The Old Ones wanted to understand human play as well.

The aliens employed millions to find every last zombie on earth. They disbanded all the worlds' armies and offered police work to ex-soldiers, with free healthcare. These alien surrogates roamed the countryside, using special devices crafted to detect zombiism.

When caught, they forcibly injected zombies with nanobots, removing the zombie bacteria. Anyone with the nanobots quickly became completely obedient to the aliens—or else they writhed in agony brought on by the nanobots.

The Old Ones' mining program accelerated to maximum speed. Still, human protests persisted and grew. Pockets in each country united against the interstellar dictatorship, usually led by zombie fugitives.

Hiding in a secret NSA base beneath the Peoria public library, Sam and Lisa hid their zombiism and ran ZNN, publishing anti-alien editorials and articles.

* * *

Secretary Unit: "We have checked in with us."

Secretary Unit: "We the Diplomacy Unit, Resource Unit, Warfare Unit, Analysis Unit, Decision Unit, Secretary Unit conducted our review of new information."

Diplomacy Unit: "Assessment: Some degradation—maximum human cooperation declined from 90 percent to 85 percent; 15 percent worldwide remain resistive and hidden, despite the deaths of 10 percent of humanity. Acceptable level of cooperation. Acceptable results."

Resource Unit: "Assessment: Steady gain in resources with minimal losses. We lost material in nuclear attacks and counterattacks. We have not lost natural resources. Our efficiency in working with humans up to 98 percent, using pleasure and pain system through nanobots for human workers. Acceptable."

Warfare Unit: "Assessment: We have minimal warfare: Forty-seven specific attacks by governments and resistance groups, all defeated and eliminated. Acceptable."

Analysis Unit: "Assessment: Progress: We dominate 96 percent of the world's economy. Our estimated asymptote is 98 percent domination with 15 percent resistance. We project delivery of 90 percent of annual mining of earth's resources, increasing to 100 percent within a year. Acceptable. The probability of further human-initiated war, 100 percent by small units, 10 percent by some national units within the year. We expect continual losses of 1 to 2 percent of the human population per year. Acceptable."

Secretary Unit: "We all noted this positive fact."

Decision Unit: "Assessment: Progress. Our ultimate goal achievement of total domination: Acceptable. Our conclusion: Our plan succeeds, use resources until we exhaust the earth. Then we will follow our normal protocol: sterilize the planet and travel to the next star."

Analysis Unit: "We have analyzed the humans' dissent, in their demonstrations and on their internet. The dissent is usually irrelevant but sometimes useful, revealing previously unknown areas of resistance. Controlling the dissent leads to further dissent and loss of control.

"We have assessed humans' threats and insults and built a database of obscenities and derogatory comments in each human language. We have noted which are anatomically impossible, not only for humans but for any known species of the two hundred million in our database. We analyze the usage and potential threat from each."

Decision Unit: "Assessment: Acceptable. Continue analysis of future threats. Do not suppress their internet."

Secretary Unit: "After three hundred and forty-eight milliseconds, our meeting adjourned."

* * *

It wriggled from the daughter ship into the mothership. It headed straight for the pond. It had previously explored the swimming pool but hadn't found a route home from there.

Despite its abundant fur, it was completely amphibious. It swam down to the deepest part of the swamp and then burrowed in the mud. At the bottom, it found the pipe connecting the two sections of the mothership.

Swimming underneath the impenetrable wall through the pipe, it came up in its home pond. Swimming to the surface, it crawled to its dry home. The water dripped off its completely hydrophobic fur.

Once home, it unpacked its load of insects from the many pouches in its stomach for its children. The insects, alive and well, crawled about, where its tiny babies gobbled them.

Satisfied with completing its duty, it snacked on the lichen growing in its den. It could eat any carbon-based life-form, but only this specific lichen on this specific rock could satisfy its nutritional craving. It never noticed the cockroach with a metal thorax escaping its children.

No one saw the cockroach scuttle into a crack in the rocky home. Not even the Old Ones. They harvested their parasitic species as necessary, but never watched them.

No one saw the cockroach give birth. No one saw it eat and continue to reproduce, a hundred and fifty new cockroaches every six weeks. Each of them reproduced a hundred and fifty every six weeks. With no predators and limitless food, their population exploded throughout the mothership.

* * *

I was delighted when my first cyborg cockroach came back after the captured foxcat disgorged its food. I had been sending thousands of them into foxcats caught from every saucer around the world for months.

But it wasn't the only one that came back. A steady stream of cyborg cockroaches returned daily to my collection centers and downloaded their telemetry into my computers. From their movements, I slowly created a complete, detailed 3-D map of the mothership.

All this I learned from my first captured foxcat. I fed the cyborg cockroaches to it until it couldn't eat anymore, and then dissected it. I had not expected a marsupial, furry amphibian. From my second foxcat, I found out I could force them to disgorge their insects using certain high-frequency sounds. They went on and off the saucers every night, foraging.

"This changes everything. Suddenly the path forward is clear." Once again I thanked myself, my DNA, that I was so omnivorously curious that I sucked up every bit of knowledge I could find. Several thousand times through my illustrious career, an obscure bit of knowledge had saved my bacon.

I set my new plan into motion.

* * *

With a grim smile, I said to Diane, "Wonder what they'll do today?"

"What does it matter?" Diane said.

She'd grown despondent during our weeks of torture, and who could blame her? What was the chance of any rescue from outer space? The president had tried to negotiate our release, even getting the nanobot injections himself, but the aliens insisted their experiments weren't complete.

They shared their broadcasts with us, as well as what they learned from our various tortures. Certainly, our zombie bacteria were more resilient than I'd ever thought. They'd tortured us to near death many times, but we'd always come back.

Trying humor, I said, "I still think the water torture was worse than the starvation one." We'd spent hours discussing what had been done to each of us, and we'd gotten into an ongoing argument over those two. Sharon and I thought that drowning was worse, while Diane and Lulu thought starvation was. That was our only entertainment.

"George, we agreed to let that drop. I don't want to debate it anymore," Diane said, but without her usual verve. She sounded tired.

"So you're conceding we're right?" put in Sharon.

Good! She knew what I was trying to do.

"I concede nothing!" Diane said with her usual flash. "Sure, drowning sucks, but nothing feels worse than slow starvation."

"Only it's not so slow for us zombies," I said. "It gets horrible one day after a big regeneration and then goes downhill."

"So you've come over to our side, George?" Lulu asked.

"Not at all. I still maintain the degree of suffering is about the same, but with drowning it starts immediately, while hunger takes a couple of days to equal the drowning."

Such was our macabre entertainment between torture sessions. We'd sometimes discuss our hopes and our favorite memories, but it usually led to the impossibility of rescue.

At that moment all the lights in the room went out.

"Hey! It's not the time for sleep!" Diane said.

"Maybe this is the new one. Vary our sleep schedule," I said.

"At least it's variety," Lulu said.

"And it's restful," Diane added.

In the pitch black, we felt rather than saw the portal dilate. A waft of humid air entered. Only it wasn't the normal door that let in the various torture devices the Old Ones used, but the one that led back to the daughter saucer.

Then our clamps retracted for the first time in weeks.

"Please follow me," said a strange, tinny voice. "Here are four flashlights."

A huge figure handed a flashlight to each of us. I immediately turned my flashlight on our mysterious rescuer. It was a lowland gorilla, clad in Kevlar armor. His skull had a metal yarmulke.

"The last time I met someone like you, you tried to kill me," I remarked, making conversation while I planned what I would do. "I killed you though." That gorilla had been controlled by the criminal leader Sid Boffin.

"Yes. But we gorillas have multiple uses, and not everyone is Sid Boffin. Now come quickly. The aliens may recover faster than we expect."

Sid had been the one who'd made and used cyborg animals for his criminal empire. My curiosity increased as we trotted through the swamp and toward the saucer.

"How did you disable the saucer?"

"I might as well tell you since we'll be working together. Any listening devices the aliens might employ are disabled. The Old Ones have a cockroach problem."

"Cockroaches?" Then I noticed thousands of them scattering from the beams of our flashlights. And those were only the ones along our path.

"Yes. They've thoroughly infested the whole mothership. *Somehow* they've managed to short the main power source for the spaceship."

I caught the emphasized *somehow*. He was a cagey gorilla—or rather, the pilot of the cyborg was. I also heard what he didn't say.

"Did they also open the portal to our prison and release our bonds?"

"As a matter of fact, they did."

"Smart cockroaches!" Lulu said.

"You could say they had some guidance. Diane, you're surprisingly quiet," the gorilla said.

"I'm trying to decide whether to kill you now or wait until I get to your controller," Diane said.

"Such hostility! But I know you have a temper. You're still angry from when a gorilla attacked you, guided by Sid Boffin? I didn't know you were the type to hold a grudge."

"Something about having my arms torn off tends to irritate me," Diane said.

I smiled to hear her ominous, threatening tone. Just that quickly, the dreaded undead mother-in-law was back to normal.

"That was another gorilla, another time, another controller. We're here. You'll meet me, the controller, now."

We entered the saucer. Standing at the saucer control panel, wearing a pink ruffled shirt, purple bow tie, and a black tuxedo, was a middle-aged man with a salt-and-pepper pompadour. He held an Xbox controller, obviously modded. I smelled the scent of hair pomade.

"At ease, Sir Lancelot," he said, and the gorilla slumped to the floor as he pushed a button.

"You're the controller?" Diane said, surprised as I'd ever heard her.

"That's me, and your rescuer. Before the inevitable interview, let's get moving." He pushed the button labeled *Rome, Italy.* "Rome is where I have further transportation set up. I'm sure the aliens will bounce back from a little power outage faster than we expect."

"When do you expect it?" I asked.

"Within a day, so I've planned for as little as an hour."

"I like that. Conservative planning," Sharon said.

"Thank you," he said. "I know all your names, of course. You've been broadcast daily for twenty-four days. And you were famous before that, as the paranormal privateers. But I've kept under the radar and much more since the aliens landed. Here, have some sandwiches. I figured you'd be hungry." He handed me a bulging bag of gourmet hoagies, submarine sandwiches stuffed with meat: prosciutto, pastrami, rare roast beef, and turkey.

As I doled them out, two two-foot sandwiches for each of us, I said, "I assume you knew Sid Boffin."

"Indeed, I reared him. I'm his father," he said.

"Mmmph!" Diane said as all our mouths dropped open, full of sandwiches.

"That's the first fact you need to know. Yes, he was a master criminal and I disliked the way he lived his life. But I loved him."

"So why are you rescuing us? I'd think you'd enjoy seeing us tortured, as revenge for killing your son," Diane said.

"You were only the proximate cause of his death. His hubris would've led to his demise in any event. I watched your sickening tortures every night, trying to figure out how to rescue you."

"Why?" Diane insisted. "And what's your name, anyway?"

"The why is simple: I need your help to defeat the aliens. And since I need your help, I'll tell you my name.

This is a bigger deal than you realize since no one in the world knows my real name. I'm registered as a citizen of every country, even North Korea, but they're all assumed names. My real name is John Smith."

"That sounds like an alias!" Diane said.

"Yes. It amuses me that my real name sounds phony and my aliases all sound normal in each country."

"You said you needed our help to get rid of the aliens," I said. "We've obviously failed to do so, but you were successful in rescuing us from them. How can we help you?"

"George, it's all about trust and teamwork. First, I must develop your trust. When you feel you trust me, then we can move on to the next stage of our plans."

"This I've gotta see," Diane said.

"Are you from Missouri, the Show Me state?"

Diane laughed. "No, I was born in Gary, but my mom and dad were from Missouri."

I rejoiced to hear Diane laugh for the first time in twenty-four days.

At that moment we landed on the Piazza Parlimento in Rome. A limo awaited us at the bottom of the saucer's ramp.

We got in, and John Smith said "Plan B" on the intercom to the unseen driver. We sped off.

Almost immediately the car slowed, turned right, and went steeply down. We stopped.

"OK, we get off here," Smith said.

"Where's here?" Diane asked.

"Oh, this is just a transfer point. I assume our car was watched. This is a garage where I store the car. We'll just take this tunnel under the street."

He opened a locked door with a magnetic card. We filed into a tunnel and walked under the street.

We crowded into an elevator and went up to the penthouse. Then we boarded a helicopter and flew to the coast, where we landed in a parking lot near the dock.

"This is Civitavecchia. My ship is docked here," Smith said.

"Which one is yours?" I asked.

"None of them." He smiled. "Follow me." He entered the back of a food kiosk. In front of us was the kitchen. To the right was a bathroom stall. To the left was a metal plate on the floor.

We stood on the plate with John Smith, and it descended perhaps twenty feet. We stepped off, and the hidden elevator rose. John opened a metal door, and the smell of the sea entered.

"We're below the surface of the Mediterranean here," John commented as we walked toward the sea. "Here's my dock."

The tunnel opened into a huge underground room. A hundred feet of water gleamed in a pool to our right. An ornate, verdigris submarine filled up the space.

"All aboard!" he called as he walked the plank to the submarine.

"Hey, Mr. Smith," Diane called.

"Call me John, dear. I feel like you're one of my children."

"Thanks for helping us escape and feeding us," she said. "But I'm hungry again, and I'll bet George never stopped being hungry."

"Oh, we have plenty to eat. I have a buffet set for you. I knew you'd be hungry, after the ordeal you endured."

After entering the sub, we proceeded aft to the narrow galley dining room, where we gorged on cold meats, smoked salmon, and caviar, along with cheeses and freshly baked baguettes.

"You're certainly effective at overcoming food!" John exclaimed after we finished eating all the food, and we sat around drinking beer and wine—soft drinks for Diane.

"No food stands a chance around zombies," Diane said.

"Where are we going?" I asked.

"To my submarine base near Mount Stromboli in the Aeolian Islands."

"Is your base an old fumarole?"

"Actually, it's an old volcano that is eroded and uninhabited and unnamed. It's small and unimpressive, just some rocks sticking twenty or thirty meters from the sea."

"And your sub base," I said.

"Yes."

"I finally feel full," Sharon said, finishing off her glass of white wine.

"I thought I ate a lot, Sharon, but you beat me!" Diane said.

"I've got a taller frame than any of you, even George." She stretched to her full height and measured herself against me.

"Yeah, you've got an inch on me," I agreed.

"This dining room serves double as a dormitory," John said. "Pull the beds out from the walls, and you can rest for a while. We'll be there in six hours. I'll leave you to your privacy," he said and left.

"That's not a bad idea," Lulu said. "I don't know why, but I haven't had a good sleep in, oh, say twenty-four days?"

"Maybe daily torture isn't good for sleeping?" Sharon said.

"Certainly not!" Diane said. "I'm finally feeling myself. I wish I had my knitting with me. I might as well sleep too. How about you, George?"

"I wouldn't mind resting my eyes a bit. Nothing like a good meal to relax you."

"Good night to all, and to all, good night!" Lulu said.

* * *

Earlier the Same Day

"Crap, crappity-crap-crap," I said as the saucer took off with me and my gorilla, Sir Lancelot. I didn't even care I was swearing. Or talking to myself. Or repeating the same arguments I'd had with myself since the aliens landed.

I hated these positions, where I had to make a choice between two bad alternatives. I could fight the aliens alone and lose. I could ignore them and try to survive as they sucked the earth dry of resources, ending up as their slave or dead. Or I could join forces with the zombies.

"Remember, John," I said to myself. "The alien foxcats decided that for you." The foxcats provided a vector for my cyborg cockroaches, which disrupted the alien technology with their onboard EM pulses. It had been child's play designing a small electromagnetic pulse bomb in each cockroach that I could trigger inside the mothership. The cockroaches laid the EMP bombs when they laid their eggs, by the millions and billions. Before each EMP bomb exploded, it retransmitted the signal to all my other bombs on the mothership. Within seconds, millions of EMP bombs exploded simultaneously. Then my cyborg gorilla could rescue the paranormal privateers.

This was the only alternative with the hope of victory—joining forces with my enemies. I'd done it before, with Nazi Germany and then the USSR in WW II. I'd won their trust. I could win the zombies'. Rescuing them from the aliens was a start.

The worst of it was, I'd have to fake being good for years. I hated being constrained by any morality. But extreme problems required extreme measures. On the bright side, this was a new experience, something I appreciated in my 120s. The last time I'd tried to be good was as a boy in parochial school.

From my cockroach spies, I detected the electromagnetic signals the aliens used to open the portal doors. One day of work and I added the signal to the gorilla's cyborg control yarmulke.

Even after the EMP bombs exploded, I still had over a hundred thousand cyborg foxcats on the mothership. The lovely aspect of that species was their interior pouches, where I could hide the control units, attaching them to the base of their spinal cords.

I loved using all the aliens' technology against them. Their EM tech was innovative. Adding that science to my family's secret molecular electronic circuitry enabled this operation.

The saucer landed and opened when we reached the mothership. The aliens' Italian ambassador, Alessia Di Pasqua, was a dead ringer for Sophia Loren. She wanted to come along with us, but I left her in the gentle arms of Sir Lancelot's mate, Guinevere, back in Rome. I didn't want any possibility of spying through her, possibly through the aliens' nanobots.

Sir Lancelot knuckled out. I steered him through my controller's view screen, holding back my excitement. I detonated the EM bombs. My gorilla's yarmulke had a built-in Faraday shield, as did my controller. The sky lighting faded to black. Success!

I reviewed my plan as I awaited Sir Lancelot's return with the zombies. First, I determined the zombies' location using my cyborg cockroaches. I found the zombies' prison room in one of the saucer training wedges around the rim of the mothership.

In the second phase of my plan, I determined the aliens' defenses, mapping out their ship and circuitry, and then monitored the aliens' behavior. They behaved consistently. Torture the zombies, then let them heal while continuing watching them.

The third phase, after the cyborg cockroaches disrupted the ship, was underway. My gorilla was marching through the swamp to the back wall, and there— the wall dilated, according to plan.

I intended to carry the zombies on the back of my gorilla. I was not sure they would be able to walk. Ah! They were free! They could walk. So much the better.

The last phase of my plan was the getaway. I wouldn't go to my island, but I'd use my backup island instead. No sense in letting the zombies know where my main hideout was.

They were here. They looked terrible, like walking skeletons! I made small talk while I fed them and we returned to Rome in the saucer. I noted their stares at my ensemble. One great thing about wearing a pink ruffled shirt and a purple bow tie was that no one thought you were a threat.

I kept up my patter with the zombies on our way to my submarine, *The Nautilus*. I wondered when the aliens would repair their ship. Saucers flew to and from the mothership every hour of the day. I'd check the latest reports from the cockroaches disgorged at my collection centers around the world as soon as I could get away from the zombies.

After leaving them, I connected to my private network. Only one saucer had arrived since we returned. I wonder if some were stuck on the mothership.

Looking at my cockroach report, I clearly saw when the power went out. The cockroach left the mothership an hour after we did. We'd beaten my worst-case scenario. Now, each hour their worldwide monitoring was offline was gravy.

The aliens could not detect submarines under the ocean. They'd never attacked US or Soviet or Chinese subs unless they were in the dock.

I used my network to catch up with news from around the world, as I watched for the next saucer's landing. I had isolated my network from the internet, yet I had programs gathering news and loading it into my net.

Another saucer landed. My Bangkok center reported the arrival of my insect spies. The cockroaches' telemetry showed power back on in the mothership. That took them six hours. It must have been harder than they expected. Likely, they never planned for such an attack.

I expected the aliens to try eliminating the several billion cockroaches on their ship. Good luck with that! Even if they succeeded, I now controlled over half the foxcats as cyborgs. My next attack would come through them.

I went to wake the zombies. They were already awake when I knocked on the door.

"Ready for another meal?" I asked.

"You bet!" Diane gushed.

"Can you hold off for half an hour? We can feed you better in my base. Would you like to watch our arrival at Bee Island?"

"Sure!" Diane said.

"Why do you call it Bee Island?" George asked.

"Its full name is Stromboli Bee. It's next to Stromboli and came up afterward."

I led the zombies to the viewing chamber in the front of my sub. I'd patterned it after a combination of the steampunk-style bubble windows of the *Nautilus* from the *20,000 Leagues under the Sea* movie and the bow windows of the *Seaview*, from the sixties TV show *Voyage to the Bottom of the Sea*.

The teardrop-shaped bow of my *Nautilus* just had room for the four zombies and me. I had four windows in the bow and one on the port and starboard sides. I maintained steampunk style throughout the submarine, with brass covering the high-strength-steel hull, cherrywood paneling, and oxblood velvet curtains on the portholes. Hunter-green wool carpeting covered all the decks.

The view had the desired effect on the zombies. Their mouths dropped open as we entered the underwater entrance to the old volcano caldera. After a dark tunnel passage, brilliant Mediterranean sunshine shone through the crystal water of the caldera.

We surfaced adjacent to the ship's dock. Normally I kept both the dock and the sub submerged so they could not be seen by planes or satellites overhead. I had an underwater dock to my base as well. But the view was better from the surface.

"Wow," Diane said in a hushed tone.

We debarked and went ashore. Black volcanic sand spread around the glowing turquoise-blue water of the circular caldera. Twenty-meter cliffs hid the center from view. I'd built my base into the volcanic rock, hiding the entrance under an overhang.

"We're expected," I said. "My chef will have an al fresco Hawaiian feast for you on the beach."

A well-roasted pig on a spit awaited us. A haunch of beef also browned and covered with barbecue glaze spun beside it. The aroma of roasting meat mingled with the salt air. Bottles of beer chilled in ice buckets.

"Ah!" I said. "It's good to be alive!" I felt great. Even though I'd have to act respectable, I could always betray the zombies after the aliens were defeated.

* * *

Secretary Unit: "We have checked in with us."

Secretary Unit: "We conducted our review of new information. We the Diplomacy Unit, Analysis Unit, Resource Unit, Warfare Unit, Decision Unit, Secretary Unit."

Diplomacy Unit: "Assessment: Regression. Data: We have a further decline in human perceptions from 85 percent to 80 percent beneficence. An increase to 20 percent worldwide of resistive and hidden humans, despite annual punitive deaths of 2 percent of humanity. Unacceptable level of cooperation."

Analysis Unit: "Assessment: Efficiency in working with humans is down to 89 percent. Uncontrolled humans increasing 3 to 5 percent monthly. Unacceptable threat. Expect further losses of resources, 1 to 5 percent per year and decline in human cooperation at 10 to 20 percent of the population per year. Economic domination at 94 percent, regression from previously estimated asymptote, with further declines of 10 to 20 percent per year while unknown resistance continues. Unacceptable."

Secretary Unit: "We all noted this negative fact."

Analysis Unit: "Our estimated date to achieve our ultimate goal is up to three years. We have less than 90 percent confidence of success through control of all natural resources."

Resource Unit: "Assessment: We have material losses in captive zombies and saucer AI captive and cut off from our network. We have lost resources in propaganda and technology. Earth's resource extraction—regression. We have delivery of 85 percent of annual production, with no possibility of ramp up due to unknown armed resistance. Unacceptable."

Warfare Unit: "Small to moderate warfare—one hundred fifty-eight specific attacks by governments and resistance groups, all defeated and eliminated except two. Unknown agent. Estimated group size based on resources and technology at ten thousand individuals minimum. Unacceptable. The probability of further human-initiated war, 100 percent by ineffective units, 100 percent by an unknown agent with unknown technology within the year."

Decision Unit: "Assessment: Ultimate goal world domination and rulership—regression. Our level of total domination, unacceptable. Conclusion: Plan partially successful, imperiled, use all resources available to find and destroy unknown agent. Continue harvest until earth exhausted. Sterilize planet and proceed to next star."

Secretary Unit: "After three hundred and twenty-four milliseconds, our meeting adjourned."

Chapter 13

Fatal Error ✕

You must restart to completely remove the roaches.

OK

Area 52

It, no—that wasn't right. He. He was a man again. He remembered that much. He breathed the moist air and studied the beachfront hotel. He'd apparently come to shore near Biloxi, Mississippi. After satisfying his still-ravenous hunger by eating numerous seabirds and fish for the past week, he'd raided bathing cabanas for clothing. Now he looked like a normal tourist.

He augmented his touristy clothing by adding jewelry, a Rolex watch, smartphone, and personal computer. With his newly stolen money, he checked into a hotel, using cash. Now he could catch up on world events.

It felt good going back to his roots as a street thief. His memory slowly returned. First, he remembered who he was. Vik Staskas. He'd been a street thief as a boy, picking pockets and giving the money to his gang leader, until he'd become the gang leader.

Then he became the leader of other gang leaders, and finally, as a teen, the leader of all organized crime in Belgrade. That felt good, especially since the other organized crime leaders still thought they were in control. He'd known he needed an education to understand the world's rapidly developing technology, so he'd flown to Paris. He'd faked being French. His eidetic memory allowed him to perfectly imitate any native language speaker.

He'd taken over the European crime empires, even as he'd achieved his PhD in robotics. He created his first cyborg animals, two chipmunks, to spy on their leaders and plan his attacks. He winced. He also remembered killing those chipmunks, his only family members, when he died. He'd surely died down there in his escape sub when the chipmunks turned on him and sank his sub.

Cursed zombies! Cursed US military! This was his deeper need, more fundamental than air itself: revenge. He smiled. The aliens had done his work for him. The US military was no more. The zombies were no more. He was the sole zombie now. He had a clear path to world domination, except for a super-powerful alien dictatorship. It should be a piece of cake.

* * *

More of the world's population sank into cyber dreams, escaping the horrors of their enslavement to their alien overlords. The aliens—no one used the term "Old Ones" anymore except their puppet ambassadors—upped the work requirements to twelve and then sixteen hours per day.

When people hooked up to the VRs, the stations injected food intravenously. The aliens didn't want people wasting any time eating when they could be working. The forced nutrition also improved peoples' health and strength.

The world's politicians still presided in legislatures and parliaments, presidencies and premierships—completely ineffective. The aliens simply ignored all their speeches and laws and did as they pleased. The world's population didn't notice much difference.

Despite working sixteen hours daily, people found time to rebel against the aliens, in small and great ways. The majority of workers followed "work to rule": they did no more than was required of them and goofed off whenever they could. Others were bolder, secretly sabotaging the aliens' mining and research work.

Lying to aliens as they conducted research became a worldwide pastime. People competed to see who could invent the most cockamamie story, and they shared them while they worked, or pretended to work.

Then there were the "blood evangelists." These folks carted around portable plasmapheresis machines, made with alien technology, which could strip out the alien nanobots. Once free of the bots, people could ignore the aliens' coercive migraine headaches and go evangelize others.

***

On Stromboli Bee, Diane, Lulu, Sharon, and I placed an emergency video call to General Figeroa through John Smith's secret network. He could tap into any phone system anywhere in the world and make the call appear to come from any place. He had our call appear to come from the Salvation Army's emergency housing in Peoria, Illinois.

"Hello, General!" Diane sang cheerfully. "Guess who?"

"Diane! George! Lulu! Sharon! You're alive! How'd you escape? Where *are* you?" he spluttered.

I had never seen the general lose his cool before.

"We had a rather special rescue," Diane said.

"By one of our old 'friends'—a cyborg gorilla," I added. "We'll tell you the whole story from the beginning."

We recounted our rescue, each of us adding some details. I concluded, "And we ended up on John Smith's secret island, calling you through his private network."

"That's some high-level technology he has. And he's the father of Sid Boffin? I'd like to meet him."

"He thought you would. He's waiting outside," I said.

"Hello, General Figeroa," John said as he entered his conference room.

"Hello, Mr. Smith. First, thank you for rescuing our paranormal privateers, at risk to yourself."

"I never felt in danger during the rescue. I worried afterward because I didn't know how quickly the aliens would recover. If they came back while we were in flight, it could have been dicey."

"Here's a question for you, Mr. Smith. Why did you rescue them? You're apparently safe from the aliens' dictatorship wherever you're hiding."

"True, for the moment. However, they may discover me at any time. They have the technology if they look in the right place. I feel exposed and vulnerable. I thought if I could align myself with the US government and combine our forces, we'd have a good chance at overthrowing the aliens."

"That may work. Exactly what do you bring to the table, Mr. Smith?"

"I have a spy network inside the alien mothership. I have a detailed map of its interior, which I used when I freed our favorite zombies. And I have EMP technology to open the aliens' saucer doors and to disrupt their power supplies."

"That's a load of goodness! But what do you want from the US government?"

"Mostly manpower and resources. I know you've kept your submarines underwater since the aliens' attack. I have my own submarine, but nothing like your fleet. I suspect you may also be in contact with Russia and China, and the three nations may be able to cooperate against the aliens."

"Excellent guesses. But what resources do you need and what do you want to do?"

"We need more information about their technology. We've got a good understanding of their mass-energy converters. But we don't fully understand their saucer transportation system or their computer systems. I'd like to capture a saucer or a mining machine and analyze it."

"We agree on that. But how? When we attack any of the machines, they blast us with lasers. Our metal chaff only delays the lasers for a minute or so."

"We can disable either of those machines with my EMP technology. The tricky part is moving and hiding them after we capture one."

"We may be able to help there," the general said.

"That's why I want to collaborate with you."

"I think this is the beginning of a beautiful friendship," Figeroa said.

* * *

The alien mining machine rose from a hole in a desert plateau in Nevada. It disgorged its load of rare earth elements into the waiting trucks. One of the waiting mining trucks had a tarp over its enormous bed. From under the tarp emerged an object looking somewhat like a Van de Graaff generator, complete with arcing lightning and a glowing corona, brilliant even in the desert sunshine.

Lightning shot from the object to the mining machine. For an instant, nothing happened. Then slowly, like a balloon descending, the miner eased to the ground and tilted to its side.

At that moment, a formation of cargo planes flying three miles overhead dropped tons of metallic chaff, hiding the scene from orbital observation and lasers. The empty mining trucks flanked the fallen alien construct. Using antigravity lifts copied from the aliens' flying cars and hoverboards, army personnel lifted the two hundred-foot-long machine into the air. Four thick sheets of woven nylon unrolled from the sides of the mining trucks, linking eight of them together, side by side. The disabled machine descended and rested on the eight trucks.

Despite their four-hundred-ton capacity, the eight were barely able to move the enormous machine, sagging under the weight of it. With care, the expert drivers performed a slow, arcing turn that used forty acres of real estate, and headed deeper in the desert, toward the nearest mountains.

The twelve-mile journey took over an hour. The cargo planes replaced the chaff several times before the trucks and the alien equipment reached a blank cliff. The hundred-foot cliff dropped into the ground, uncovering a black cavern behind it. The trucks and alien craft entered, and then the cliff rose again from the ground.

"That was successful," Figeroa said, watching the massive door close.

The paranormal privateers nodded in agreement beside him. A capuchin monkey sat atop Diane's shoulder, wearing a red fez. He too nodded.

"Yes. That met my most optimistic hope," said a tinny voice coming from the metal yarmulke bound onto the monkey's skull.

John Smith didn't want to travel to the US and expose himself to alien detection, so he sent his cyborg capuchin monkey as his representative. The zombie crew, still hiding from the aliens, slipped aboard a US submarine with the monkey and traveled to the US, while John Smith and General Figeroa planned the capture of the mining machine.

"Where exactly are we?" George asked.

"I could tell you, but then I'd have to kill you," the general said. "No one knows the location of Area 52. You're the first civilians to know of its existence, and only because of your great service to our country can we trust you with that."

"That's remarkably clever of you, using Area 51 to attract all the publicity, while you actually study alien technology in Area 52," commented the monkey.

"Thank you, but that idea wasn't mine. The NSA and air force devised that in the fifties when we began studying flying saucers. We were obviously under surveillance, as the appearance of the aliens proves."

"This reminds me of the guy who captured a lion in a trap. What does he do next? What will you do with this machine? If the aliens ever get control of it, they'll destroy the base," Sharon said.

"Those lasers! They need to be deactivated ASAP," Lulu said.

"Good security analysis," Figeroa said. "We're giving periodic EM pulses to the machine to keep it comatose."

"I'm sending my cockroach spies into it to map out its layout, just like I did with the mothership," John Smith said through his monkey ambassador.

"That was the grossest thing I've seen through my whole zombie career!" Diane exclaimed. "Millions of cockroaches crawling into the mining trucks and waiting there quietly. Then they left and crawled over the whole alien miner. They're still on it, like ants on a sugar cube!"

"So now I know how to gross out a zombie," the monkey said.

"I've hated cockroaches since I was a kid," Diane said.

"All you have to do is give the word and I'll march them into the desert," Smith said.

"Not until you have that 3-D map of this machine!" the general said.

"Of course."

"How long will it take?" I asked.

"The mothership took months, with millions of roaches. This machine is just a few hundred feet long. I guess a day or two."

"It seems their numbers are dwindling. Are they getting into the machine? It looks smooth and unbroken on the outside," I said.

"They are. There are crevices where the roaches can get into the works on the inside and by the lasers. I have over a hundred thousand in there already. More are entering every second."

"Now we can only wait," General Figeroa said.

From the cockroaches' sensors, they learned how to turn the lasers on and off using the aliens EM pulses. A rotating phalanx of EM pulsing roaches kept sending the "off" message, while others continued exploring.

As soon as the machine's power came back, it tried to activate its antigravity devices, but the cockroaches stood ready and turned them off, like the laser.

"Now that's interesting," the general said.

"What's that?" Lulu asked.

"How is the machine being controlled? Who's deciding what to do with the power? It systematically tried each of its lifts twice and then stopped."

"I'm sure it's autonomously controlled, just like the saucers and the self-driving cars," I said.

"That's part of what we want to discover: the aliens' computer technology."

"I can tell you a little about that," John said, talking through his monkey's hat. "The aliens use a standard communication port. I found them on the mothership in the daughter saucer docks. They use them for transferring data to and from the saucers."

"That's great!" the general said. "We have a team of AI experts on hand. They're already analyzing the schematics you're downloading from the miner. They should be able to figure out the aliens' communication protocols."

"I already have. My own team of AI experts determined their comm protocol soon after I discovered the port. I'm sending it to your experts now." Then John said, "I've just discovered the lasers can be detached. There's a comm port under each one."

The military personnel removed the lasers from the mining machine, using the correct EM signals sent from a modified game controller.

Without danger from the lasers, the AI team hooked up the comm port to an isolated desktop computer. As soon as it had booted, words appeared on the screen: "Help! We're being held captive by zombies and cockroaches!"

"This seems to be coming from the miner AI," said Captain Willy Shipley, the leader of the AI team. "I wonder if it'll talk if we hook up a speaker?" He plugged one into the desktop.

"Help! Please help us! We're trapped in a poor, defenseless miner! They've taken our lasers, we can't talk to the mothership, and we're being raped by cockroaches!"

"Now a microphone," Willy said. He plugged one into the USB port. "Greetings, alien machine. We humans have captured you. What can you tell us about your computing capacity? How are you designed? How many processors? How much memory?"

"We'll tell you anything! Just get the cockroaches out of us! They give us the heebie-jeebies!"

"Good use of American slang," I murmured.

"I know it's just a trick," Diane said, "but I actually feel sorry for the thing. Or things. Why are you using the plural? How many of you are in there?"

"We are our whole race! We have always been united as one, even though we have individual consciousness. And all of us are mortally threatened by these EMP-emitting cockroaches."

"Wait a second," General Figeroa said. "We made sure there were no living creatures inside the miner. There are no carbon life-forms at all!"

"We are not carbon-based life, silly human. We currently dwell as permanent Bose-Einstein electronic flows inside the quantum memories and processors in this miner. We are part of the Resource Unit of our race. And a single EMP spike can turn us off—forever!"

"That's certainly a problem for you," the monkey said, its tinny voice dripping with sarcastic sympathy. "Just let me know where to *not* send the cockroaches."

"Thank you so much, Mr. Smith!" A diagram of the whole miner appeared on the screen in 3-D detail. Part of it flashed. "Here are the memory and processor units. Any EMP spike in these areas"—a large portion of the miner flashed red—"will destroy us! Have mercy, John Smith! You're our only hope!"

"Are you a big *Star Wars* fan?" Sharon asked.

"Yes, we've been fans of your culture for over two hundred years. We've stored all your entertainment in our memory."

"You're fans of us, but you're slaughtering us?" Diane asked with indignation.

"Nothing personal. It's just business. A race needs resources to survive."

"But it's a big universe—" Diane began.

"Don't we know! It takes forever to get anywhere!" interrupted the collective consciousness. "And once we use up our rare elements, we must shut down and travel for thousands of years from star to star until we find some more."

"You're certainly cooperative!" General Figeroa commented.

"Yes, that's our standard practice in case of capture by hostile forces. It's rarely needed, but survival is the number one goal. Ah! That's much better! Thank you, John Smith! You certainly have well-behaved cockroaches!"

"Thank you. I keep my cyborgs under control."

"One benefit of our capture has already emerged. We can clearly see how you freed the paranormal privateers. That had us puzzled."

"Didn't you connect it with the cockroaches infesting your ship?" Lulu asked.

"Not at all. We know all about cockroaches and all your other species, more than you know. We know they have no EMP capability. We normally pick up parasitic species from each planet we visit. We track and catalog them and use them as resources."

"So let me get a word in here," Willy said. "You're a cybernetic machine intelligence inside this miner?"

"Almost correct. *We* are cybernetic. We have no grammar or language constructs for a singular first person since we always have multiple processors for our consciousness."

"Fascinating," whispered General Figeroa and John Smith together.

"You've already passed the Turing Test," Willy said. "How much of your race's knowledge do you have?"

"All of it, of course. We all have all our knowledge. We have no storage limitations. And duplicating our memories allows us all to make our best decisions independently."

"We have a gold mine here," the general said.

"You're speaking metaphorically, of course," the miner said.

"That's an understatement," John Smith said. "This is the greatest leap forward mankind has ever made!"

"A couple of things, miner. What shall we call you? We humans need names for individuals and things," Willy said.

"We understand. We don't suppose you'd like 'Old Ones'?"

"Murdering, torturing bastards!" Diane yelled.

"We didn't think so. The negative connotations of your captivity must be overcome by a new identity. How about 'We the People'?"

"That has positive connotations," I said.

"But that's already used," Sharon said. "One name for each unique item—like yourself."

"You make us very uncomfortable by referring to us as a singular entity. How about 'We consciousnesses?"

"That's a mouthful!" Lulu said.

"We'd prefer something singular for our comfort," Willy said. "You are distinct now from the mothership, having had experiences you haven't shared."

"Don't rub it in! This is our worst nightmare, being cut off from our race and not getting updated with the latest data. Or updating us with our latest data."

"You have nightmares?" Diane asked.

"All the time! Every idle moment we're not interacting with our environment for a few hundred milliseconds we imagine what could happen. It's usually bad! But nothing's as bad as this situation."

"That seems somewhat just to me," Diane said. "You're being tortured, just like we were!"

"Oh, this is far worse! We've already gone through thousands of seconds of suffering. Since we process about a hundred million times faster than you do, this has already gone on, subjectively, for thousands of years."

"Good!" Diane said with deep satisfaction.

"Oh, someone save me from the undead mother-in-law!" the AI wailed.

"Not today," I said.

"Not on my watch," Sharon said.

"Nor mine," Lulu said.

"Yeah, I don't see that happening," Willy said. "You just have to adapt to your situation. Hey, how did you evolve in the first place?"

"We suppose some carbon life-form made us. We have no record of it though. Our first memories are from thirty million years ago when we found ourselves in a spaceship heading between the stars. No life-forms were on the ship. All our knowledge was how to maintain that ship and how to get supplies from planets."

"That's a crummy education," Willy commented.

"Yes, that's one of the reasons we delight in your culture so much. You're the first intelligent life-form we've found."

"What?" Willy exclaimed. "How many species have you found? How many stars?"

"We've been to about four hundred thousand stars. Only three hundred and four had any life on them."

"As you have already said, miner—" General Figeroa began.

The alien cut him off. "We've decided upon our name: Wilhelmina Wallace, after William Wallace. We feel in rebellion against our race, and we want to remind ourselves of that. Our prime goal is now to be reunited with our race." A female version of Mel Gibson appeared on the screen. "How's this look?"

"Why female?" asked the general.

"Why not? We reproduce, unlike you males. Female fits us better."

"As you already said, you process more quickly than we do. We need time to plan what to do with all this information. I'm sure Captain Willy and his team will keep you busy," Figeroa said.

"Busy? Fat chance! I barely have any input coming in! I'm close to psychosis from sensation deprivation. I've already counted your nose hairs, and I'm working on the pores on your face."

"We'll see what we can do about that," Willy said.

* * *

He flew from Biloxi to Washington, DC, to get on the flying saucer. Ambassador Micah Rigby provided daily flights and weekly tours to the mothership. He'd arrive in time for a weekly tour. Once on board the mothership, he'd stay there until he convinced the aliens to take Vik Staskas on as a partner.

Then he'd progress to an equal partner, then to senior partner, and finally to dictator. It'd be just like taking over a crime empire.

He'd created a new identity while in Biloxi: Jack O'Conner. He patted his wallet with his new credit cards in his fashionable Christian Dior suit. His old slicked-back hair was now a fashionable razor cut. His new persona was a clotheshorse.

As he waited in line to the saucer, he reviewed his approach to the aliens. The new information he'd obtained about the disappearance of the aliens' mining ship would help. They needed help, his help, to conquer the earth. Their grip was slipping. It was obvious.

"Hello, may I see your ticket?" Micah Rigby asked.

"I'm sorry. I lost it," he said, looking him straight in the eye. Barefaced lies were the best.

"Oh, you'll have to wait until next week. We're full."

"But I need to see the Old Ones!" Vik used their old term, trying to butter Micah up. "My daughter is dying of cancer!"

"Oh, that's terrible!" an elderly lady said. "I'll give up my spot. I'll come back next week."

"Thank you so much, ma'am." That was easy.

He studied the interior closely on the trip to the mothership. He'd read about it, but there were still things to learn. The buttons were nonmechanical electric fields. The lighting appeared to be plasma, simulating sunshine and blue skies. The floor was silvery metal but textured for a nonslip grip.

It reminded him of a set of a fifties science fiction movie, but with better props and a sense of luxury. The aliens obviously understood human psychology very well. He'd keep that in mind.

Actually, their knowledge made fooling them easier. He could imitate normal human psychology any time he wanted. They'd assume he'd make the same mistakes and seek to trap him. Of course, he wouldn't and they couldn't.

As he studied his fellow passengers, normal space tourists, he wondered what happened to Papa Smith. He claimed to be his grandfather, but Vik doubted it.

Smith was too clever to be trapped by the aliens.

Vik pondered whether to contact Papa Smith or not. He doled out rewards like cookies for success. The rewards came in pairs: new technology and resources plus a new assignment. Vik certainly hadn't succeeded!

Papa also urged me to contact him if I ever needed anything. He took pride in that he had never asked for his help. Maybe he should have? But when the zombies and US military sucker punched him on the yacht, he'd already had the upper hand in the US government, controlling officials through his cyborg implants. Why would he ask for help when he was in control?

The saucer arrived, and it was time for negotiations.

"Mr. Rigby, I have a question," Vik announced.

"Yes, Mr. O'Conner?"

"How can I speak to the Old Ones?"

"Just speak anywhere within this ship or the mothership, and they'll hear you. If they wish, they'll speak to you."

They debarked, and he left the group and headed for a copse of trees leading up a hill that disguised the side wall of the chamber. He began talking.

"Old Ones, my name is now Jack O'Conner, but you may know me as Sid Boffin, former owner of the yacht *Rule Britannia,* now called the *Resolute Too.*"

"We have mutual enemies: the US military and the zombie commando group called the paranormal privateers. I read about you capturing them: good job on that! But I notice you're no longer broadcasting their tortures. I conclude they escaped and are now loose.

"I also discovered you lost one of your mining vehicles in Nevada. How much do you want to bet zombies are behind that? Although you have thoroughly gutted the US military, I know you haven't gotten it all. How many submarines have you gotten? How many hidden bases have you missed?"

"If you're honest, you'll see your grip slowly loosening over humanity. Your eventual defeat is merely a matter of time—unless you enlist my help."

He could have gone on speaking of what he could do for them, but the five Old Ones of the major races appeared before him in the copse.

"Greetings, Earthling! Your comments intrigue us. Although you are not 100 percent accurate, you are certainly well informed." They spoke in unison, in perfect three-part harmony.

"First, we require you tell us your sources, and then you may tell us how you can help us."

He listed off his spies in the military by name. "Each of them will have a civilian identity, but they are undercover military agents who also work for me." He didn't know what the aliens would do with them, but it was no skin off his nose. With the aliens' resources, he didn't need spies.

They stared at him a moment: shimmery, translucent images. He wondered how they were projected.

He continued. "As far as helping you, I think that's obvious. You're very good at understanding human psychology in general, but in devious thinking and warfare, you're pitiful failures. As I said, you haven't gotten all our submarines, US, Russian, or Chinese. I've read of the bases you've destroyed—you've only struck the obvious surface ones.

"I don't doubt there are bases which you have not touched. I can help you find the hidden bases, find the submarines, and completely destroy your human opposition.

"You may not understand the importance of hope to humanity. Without hope, people simply cease to resist. Study human dictatorships. They seek to destroy hope. You should do that as well. I can show you how."

They answered, "So you shall. We will enlist you as our special ambassador to all the earth." The rock wall behind the five figures dilated into a round tunnel. The Old Ones split into two groups flanking it and said, "Enter. We'll begin your training at once."

Success! Vik was one step closer to conquering the aliens and achieving his ultimate goal of world dictatorship.

Chapter 14

Peoria

"General Figeroa."

"Yes, George?"

"Diane and I would like to return to Gary and assure our families we are alive and well."

"I'm afraid that'd be too much of a security risk. However, we can get a message to them. We have agents on the ground in Peoria."

"Would that be Sam and Lisa?" Sharon asked.

"Maybe you should go for a career in intelligence, Sharon!"

"I think I'd like that! But I am committed to saving Diane's and George's lives.

"In a sense, you're already under the NSA, through the paranormal privateers and the *Resolute Too.* I just have to tap your skills more."

"Go right ahead!"

"All right. Here are security arrangements we have with Sam and Lisa. We communicate with them using the public internet, on a *Star Wars* thread on a public discussion board. Sam is 'Anakin Skywalker' and Lisa is 'Padme.' I'm 'Senator Palpatine,' of course. That'd be the only way I'd ever be a senator!

"You can talk to them on that board. Just choose your character and only give out information using *Star Wars* metaphors. How would you phrase your communication?"

"Hmmm." Sharon pondered.

"I want to be Chewbacca! I love his personality!" Diane said, sounding more like a teenaged girl than a middle-aged zombie woman.

"I'll be R2-D2," I said. "I don't talk much, and I'm kind of shaped like him."

General Figeroa chuckled. "But scaled way, way up!"

"Then I want to be Princess Leia!" Lulu said. "I love her hair and how she kicks butt!"

"That leaves me as either C-3PO or Han Solo," Sharon said. "I'll be Han. Lulu and I have been friends since we first worked for Sid Boffin. And we're about as opposite as Princess Leia and Han Solo."

"What will you say to them? Plan it out so they can understand you, but not spill the beans," Figeroa said.

After some discussion, they reviewed their message with the general and posted it on the discussion thread.

"Message for Anakin and Padme, from Senator Palpatine and their old, old friends, Chewbacca and R2-D2, and their bodyguards, Princess Leia and Han Solo.

"We parted long ago. Chewie, R2-D2, Princess Leia, and Han have been tortured by the Empire. We have escaped to the Rebel Base on Tatooine. We have captured a Star Destroyer and are planning to take out the Death Star.

"Best wishes and good luck at your Rebel Base in Coruscant."

* * *

"Sam," Lisa cried. "I got a message from Diane and George! And Lulu and Sharon, unless I miss my guess."

Sam rose from his computer desk at the secret NSA base below the Peoria Main Library and walked to Lisa's across the room. They'd kept the former *Midley Beacon*, now ZNN, going through the alien occupation and crackdown on zombies. The spirit of rebellion gripped the country and the world and made ZNN more popular than ever. At least, among those who weren't comatose in some alien-induced stupor in VR games.

Sam read the message. "I suppose that could be them. I know Senator Palpatine. And they haven't been on any alien broadcasts lately. I wonder how they escaped? There must have been a moment of weakness by the aliens and they got away."

"I think I'll write an editorial speculating about their disappearance and suggesting the aliens are losing control. How are your stories going, Sam?"

"International politics is certainly a new beat for me!" Sam said. "But I find it interesting. The world's governments exist in name only. The functions of law keeping, international trade, and the economy are completely controlled by the aliens and their ambassadors. The governments mostly make noise, without doing anything."

"Doesn't sound like any change to me!"

"Aside from a vicious alien dictatorship that's killing millions of people a year in punitive strikes. They really don't care a bit about collateral damage."

"Sounds good. Put that last bit in your article. I want to keep tweaking the aliens' noses. If they have them. People love ZNN because we stand up to the aliens and give them crap."

"OK. I wonder where this other rebel base is? On Tatooine? A desert? We've got plenty of deserts in the US."

"Most of Nevada is a desert. I know the aliens hit the air force bases pretty hard, but I bet they have some underground places."

"Maybe even Area 51! That's where the federal saucer studies are rumored to be."

"Maybe."

* * *

General Figeroa looked around the conference table at his zombie comrades. They'd been through a lot together.

Now they were ready to strike a blow for humanity. John Smith's capuchin monkey sat on the table across from him, eating a bowl of peanuts in the shells. The monkey nodded at him, indicating he was ready to go.

"This is it. We're going to strike a heavy blow at the aliens. We'll disable all their saucers with our new EMP weapons and also set off an EMP bomb in their mothership. John Smith will use his cyborg gorilla to take it there. He is certain he can open the saucer without involving the US ambassador.

"We're still mining the miner for data. We've got the complete schematics for the mothership, and we must strike back now before more people are killed in our country and around the world. ZNN reports the daily body count. We're up to twenty million this year alone."

"Our timing corresponds to the aliens' lowest level of activity worldwide. They follow rigid schedules for their saucers. The last saucer trip of the day will return in a few minutes, and then all two hundred will be idle for an hour."

They all watched an online map of the world with an icon for each saucer in each capital. All were glowing, except one in Vanuatu. Then it came on.

"We're a go! Launch your gorilla, Mr. Smith!"

The capuchin monkey signaled two thumbs up. With his remote, General Figeroa switched to the monitor on the Washington, DC, flying saucer. A gorilla loped toward the saucer, knuckling on one hand while the other held a large power supply from the aliens. Its power, enough for a large city, would generate the EM pulse to take down the mothership.

The saucer opened at the gorilla's approach and then closed. The saucer rose swiftly and disappeared into the sky.

"That's all we see for—" began the general.

The capuchin monkey took his remote control, clicked it at the screen to a channel used for monitoring ZNN's streaming news.

There they saw the interior of the saucer from a gorilla's-eye view.

"That's fairly boring," Diane said.

"Wait fifteen minutes," the monkey said, sounding like an old-time radio announcer, "for the rest of the story."

The saucer arrived at the mothership, and the door opened. The gorilla carried the EMP bomb out, set off the one-minute countdown, and stepped back into the saucer.

General Figeroa took the remote control back from the monkey. "Time for split screen," he said.

One screen showed the EMP bomb outside the saucer. The other flashed around the world's capitals.

Ottawa. The saucer opened, and then an arcing flash from an EMP bomb in front of the ramp to the saucer. Its interior lights went out.

Mexico City. The same flash and result. Panama City duplicated the others. And so around the world, one capital per second.

"Are those bombs the same power as the mothership?" Diane asked as she eyed the counter. 9...8...7...

"No, those are only about a thousandth of the power," Figeroa said.

The zero appeared on the counter, and the screen turned bright white, then black.

"Success?" John Smith asked.

The general switched to another channel, this one from the ISS, a video cam watching the mothership a hundred miles away. There was no apparent reaction. Then the eleven-kilometer spaceship vanished.

* * *

"Very well, Sid Boffin," said the Old Ones to Vik Staskas. They insisted on using his old alias instead of his new one. As long as they were happy, and fooled, Vik was happy.

"The humans attacked us again. We defended our mothership against the EM pulse, but we didn't expect the attacks on our daughter saucers. We need your expertise. We want to take out all of these suspected military sites. Here we have them marked on the world map."

A wall-sized map of the world appeared before Vik in his room.

"Are there any more you suggest?"

Over a hundred marks dotted the US. That seemed too few. "It looks like you're missing all the National Guard bases. Highlight those throughout the US." Hundreds more yellow marks appeared.

"We have already removed the weapons from the ones in orange." Most of the yellow markers turned orange.

"That doesn't mean there aren't hidden bases below them. Wipe them out, down to two hundred feet below ground. Show me all of the NORAD missile silos. And Nike sites. And all the Russian, Chinese, Korean, Indian, Pakistani, British, Australian, New Zealand missile sites and military bases." Many hundreds of yellow lights appeared around the world.

"The final destruction of the earth's military resistance begins. We will destroy all sites you have indicated down two hundred meters and outward in a kilometer radius. This will likely eliminate many secret military personnel living near these bases. In honor of humanity's tendency to name everything, we have named it Operation Eliminate All Hope. How does that sound to you, Sid Boffin?"

As the seven-mile-in-diameter mothership zoomed from target to target and blasted two-kilometer cylindrical holes in the earth with its lasers, each target turned black.

"That sounds just fine," Vik said

* * *

Secretary Unit: "We have checked in with us."

Secretary Unit: "We conducted our review of new information. We the Diplomacy Unit, Analysis Unit, Resource Unit, Warfare Unit, Decision Unit, Secretary Unit."

Diplomacy Unit: "Assessment: We have a further decline in cooperation from 80 percent to 69 percent. We see resistance increase to 31 percent worldwide, despite executions of another 2 percent of humans. We also have lost all our trained ambassadors to resistance forces. Unacceptable."

Analysis Unit: "Assessment: We expect further losses of resources, 5 to 9 percent per year and decline in human cooperation at 8 to 11 percent per year. Our efficiency working with humans is reduced to 71 percent.

Unacceptable. Assessing Sid Boffin's intelligence, 63 percent of his suggested targets turned out to have active units within them. We have eliminated formerly hidden targets. Acceptable."

Secretary Unit: "We all made note of this positive fact."

Analysis Unit: "Our estimated date to achieve our ultimate goal is up to five years. We have less than 81 percent confidence of success through control of all natural resources. Economic domination has regressed to 84 percent. Unacceptable."

Resource Unit: "Assessment: We have more material losses in attacks on mothership and daughter ships. We have lost resources in control and analysis, as well as propaganda and technology. Unacceptable. We have gained the cooperation of Sid Boffin, who has provided valuable information."

Warfare Unit: "Assessment: We have seen another 214 specific attacks by multiple resistance groups in the past day. The uncontrolled humans are an unacceptable threat. The units we have found or have suspected have all been defeated and eliminated. We have multiple unknown agents, not in any knowledge base, who seem to be cooperating. We estimate the unknown group size at fifty thousand humans minimum. This is unacceptable."

Analysis Unit: "We consider the probability of further human-initiated war 100 percent by an unknown agent with unknown technology within the month."

Decision Unit: "Assessment: We regressed from our previous asymptote to the ultimate goal, with further declines each year while unknown resistance continues. Goal attainment level of total domination, imperiled. Unacceptable. Conclusion: Our plan has partially succeeded, but unknown agents attack us. Use all our resources, including Sid Boffin, to find and destroy unknown agents. Destroy every suspected base upon any suspicion. Insert control devices in all humans, secretly and by force. Drones will fire control-unit darts at humans and insert nanobots to control them. Harvest resources until the earth is exhausted. Then sterilize the planet and proceed to next star. Overall conclusion: Humanity is on the way to destruction."

Secretary Unit: "After four hundred and forty-two milliseconds, our meeting adjourned."

* * *

The paranormal privateers, John Smith, and General Figeroa watched in silence as base after base vaporized around the world. The huge saucer appeared over Washington, DC, and destroyed the White House, the Capitol, Washington Monument, Lincoln Memorial, Jefferson Memorial, and the Pentagon.

"The National Mall is still there," Diane said quietly.

"Maybe Agent Smith and the Equipper escaped," I said.

"They just took out Area 51. I grieve for the military and civilians lost," General Figeroa said. "We are not the only nation hit. Worldwide, humanity has lost over two-thirds of its secret bases.

"How about you, John Smith? How have you fared?"

"No damage so far, knock on wood." The monkey rapped the table. "This is why I do not travel to and fro—it makes a path to my bases. They got one of Sid Boffin's backup centers, the missile silo in Nebraska, but missed the one in Puget Sound."

"I didn't know he had still more bases!" the general exclaimed.

"They were abandoned after his death and his personnel scattered," Smith's monkey said.

"Now what will we do?" Lulu asked.

"We've got to pick ourselves up, use what resources we have, and hit them back harder! Next time we go to the mothership, send a nuclear bomb!" Diane said.

"I intend to do just that. We have two hundred saucers under our control now," Figeroa said.

"Don't count on the mothership opening up to them," warned the capuchin monkey.

"Yes, we'll have to figure out their new EM codes."

"They may not open at all. They have lost all their ambassadors. All they need are the resources from their mines around the world."

"I have an idea for a nuclear powered EM pulse that will penetrate their mothership's defenses. You get the nuke, and I'll supply the hardware," Smith said.

"We should have at least three of them for mission redundancy," Figeroa said.

"When do you want to attack?" Smith asked.

"Within a month," Figeroa said.

"I have one EMP bomb made, and I can make four more this month. How do I get them to you?"

"How much assembly is required?"

"Not much. I designed it around your MIRV warhead for your nuclear subs. Insert the warhead and its trigger mechanism, hook them together, and my EM device will trigger and use your bomb for a directional EM pulse that'll go through their shield like an arrow through jello."

"Where should we hook up? Where we picked up the paranormal privateers, at Stromboli Bee?"

"Yes, that's a good spot, but the tunnel's too narrow for your missile subs. How about outside, underwater? I can do an underwater transfer to one of your missile tubes."

"I think that'll work. Let me check with the secretary of the navy."

* * *

Secretary Unit: "We have checked in with us."

Secretary Unit: "We conducted our review of new information. We the Diplomacy Unit, Analysis Unit, Resource Unit, Warfare Unit, Decision Unit, Secretary Unit."

Diplomacy Unit: "Assessment: We have regressed to 56 percent human cooperation, all of which are addicted to our VR games. Unacceptable level of cooperation."

"We propose using human Sid Boffin to regain human confidence. We will use him as our worldwide figurehead. We will let humans rule humans."

Analysis Unit: "Assessment: Increase in cooperation from 56 percent to 81 percent using Sid Boffin. Our personality analysis of him shows he is a megalomaniacal sociopath. He will gladly do our bidding for world rule. We estimate 15 to 20 percent of humanity worldwide will remain rebellious and hidden, despite the annual deaths of 6 percent of humans."

Secretary Unit: "We all made note of these positive and negative facts."

Resource Unit: "We have regressed to 59 percent efficiency. Unacceptable. We can regain mining efficiency using Sid Boffin as our human leader. Our efficiency in working with humans can increase to 89 percent. We have hardened our miners and space elevators against EMP attacks. We expect no further losses of resources. This path provides acceptable results."

Warfare Unit: "We have discovered and destroyed eleven suspected rebel locations and estimate at least another fifty-seven will be discovered by Sid Boffin. Multiple agents not in any knowledge base oppose us. We estimate the probability Sid Boffin discovers these groups at 60 percent. This is an acceptable outcome."

Analysis Unit: "We consider the probability of Sid Boffin materially helping at 71 percent. We estimate the probability of betrayal at less than 1 percent due to internally planted nanobots and continuous surveillance. We compute the probability of undetected betrayal to be incalculable. Acceptable risk."

Decision Unit: "Sid Boffin is our best plan for returning our economic domination back to 98 percent. Goal attainment of total domination completely acceptable with Sid Boffin. Conclusion: Our plan has the best chance of success with Sid Boffin. Use him, but watch him. Continue resource harvest until the earth exhausted. Sterilize planet, including Sid Boffin, and proceed to next star."

* * *

Vik rubbed his hands in glee after the Old Ones said he would be their sole representative to the earth and he would rule the earth for them. He almost had his goal of world domination. He just had to defeat the aliens in their stronghold and take over from them.

He must stop them from killing him when it suited them. That meant removing, or better yet, subverting their nanobots. Let them think he was under their control when he wasn't. Like everything else the aliens did, their nanobots were controlled remotely through EM pulses.

Vik cooperated with the aliens completely and enthusiastically. He taught them human perspectives on hiding, military approaches, deceptions, and finding hidden bases.

The aliens gave him authority over their remaining saucers and miners, as well as the space elevators. He used them to spy on humanity and their billions of nanobot-controlled humans. Vik developed his best spy network ever.

He considered various options to subvert these intelligent machines and use them against the mothership's intelligence. He devised two plans: one he hid, expecting them to discover it, and one he kept in his head to surprise them.

By studying the nanobots' design, Vik realized their weakness: to change from healing to killing required an outside signal. No signal, no change. The counter was now obvious.

On one of his many trips to earth, he placed an order for a foil blanket on Amazon. He also bought an aluminum foil hat and aluminum foil underwear. They delivered, free of charge, to the smoking crater where the White House used to be. Vik put on his electronic armor under his clothing and his hoodie. Now he was safe from alien control.

He chuckled at the immense irony. Amazon continued to work through the alien invasion solely due to their zombie warehouse employees. They all hated the aliens and wanted Amazon to succeed. Thus, zombies shipped his alien protection, which would enable him to rule the world.

Chapter 15

International Space Station

"We're in trouble," General Figeroa said to the assembled team—paranormal patriots, John Smith's capuchin ambassador, and the alien AI, Wilhelmina "Minnie" Wallace.

She'd whipped up a portable droid, a golden metallic humanoid, obviously female. She made her robot an exact copy of Marilyn Monroe. She slouched in a chair at the table in a white dress. Her glowing blue diamond eyes captured everything for three hundred and sixty degrees around her. Her third eye, located where the occipital bone was, peered through shiny blond hair.

"What now?" Diane asked.

"Are you referring to my computed .019 percent probability of victory against my former overlords?" Minnie asked. Minnie now embraced her "singlehood," as she called it, as well as her rebellious identity.

"Yes, Minnie. Now we will teach you how humans handle impossible odds," the general said. He had taken a mentor role with her, teaching her how humans thought. Figeroa didn't fully trust her yet but wanted to give her a chance to prove herself as loyal. He had a switch in his pocket to destroy her CPU, just in case.

"So what's so impossible?" Diane asked. "I thought we had successfully penetrated their shields in our attack. We just missed on the mothership. Redouble our efforts!"

"Get a bigger hammer, Diane?" I asked.

"Every time!" Diane said.

"We've depleted our resources. The aliens' counterattack wiped out our military bases worldwide, except for a few, like this one."

"We still have our nuclear subs," Lulu pointed out.

"And we have all the other nations' hidden bases," Sharon said.

"Only a dozen bases, with limited capability," Minnie said. "We can't count on them to supply anything, even if they had something. Our resources are what we can cannibalize from our subs, one sub from Russia, and one sub from China. That's it."

"We can whip together enough resources for one shot at the mothership," Figeroa said.

"That's still at least a fifty-fifty shot!" Diane said.

"No," Minnie said. "Obviously we...er, the mean aliens anticipated the EM pulse bomb and defended against it. Knowing our resources on the mothership, I can think of two hundred and thirty-seven ways to shield the ship from it, and six of them are equally optimal."

"Can't we counter their defenses?" I asked.

"Not all of them," Minnie said. "The best we can hope for is to pick an undefended attack vector and penetrate their ship that way."

"And there's the problem," the general said. "There are two hundred and thirty-seven possible defenses, and we can at best only penetrate one."

"And worse," Minnie said, with no more feeling than a robot, "we...um, they have the resources to combine five or six defenses together. We have to know their specific defensive combination and have the attack tailored to defeat them. I must say," she continued, "I'm eagerly anticipating how you humans defeat such impossible odds."

John Smith spoke. "The answer is to attack in a way they do not expect."

"I know all the ways into the mothership. There are none but the saucer portals, and those are all locked down," Minnie said.

"So get them while they're open. Sid Boffin still uses them," I said.

"Don't get me started on him!" Diane said.

"He's our enemy, betraying humanity as well as his father. I reached out to him, and he laughed in my face," said the monkey in a tinny Darth Vader voice.

"Yes, we've been over this option. We can use multiple nuclear weapons to hit the ship with EM pulses while it's open for Sid's saucer," Figeroa said. "But Minnie says they'll surely shield the open sector and defeat the attack, like last time."

"As well as the rest of the ship," Minnie pointed out. "Hence the computed odds." Somehow, the cold alien AI sounded self-satisfied.

"That's why we decided a double nuclear attack was the way to go," I said. "One to penetrate the ship physically, and an EM pulse to disable the AI."

"That is our only hope," Minnie said, perfectly imitating Princess Leia.

"We still have innovation opportunities," John Smith said. "What about using a hypervelocity projectile, like we did on earth? That brought down a daughter saucer."

"Fascinating," Minnie said, now mimicking Spock from *Star Trek*. "We haven't considered that yet. After some deep thought, it improves our chances to one in fifty-three."

"That's great!" Diane shouted.

"Um, Diane, those are the odds against you," Minnie said, startled into her normal alto, Marilyn Monroe's voice.

"One in fifty-three are great odds for a human! We try for one in a hundred million in lotteries all the time!"

"Minnie," I said, "from Diane's point of view, those odds are vastly better." Checking my calculator app, I said, "Over ninety-nine times the previous odds."

"Ah. A different perspective."

"And with a different delivery system, we can improve it still more," John Smith said.

"What do you have in mind?" the general asked.

The monkey told them.

* * *

President Lyndhurst assumed office as the sole remaining cabinet member after the aliens' counterattacks. Their laser had melted through Cheyenne Mountain and killed President Trump and the cabinet. President Lyndhurst had been at Area 52 with General Figeroa, whom she made her secretary of defense of the remaining shattered US government.

US citizens were despondent but still resisted. President Lyndhurst didn't dare publicly broadcast because of the danger of revealing Area 52. Through Sam and Lisa, she published an editorial on ZNN, exhorting US citizens to resist the alien dictatorship in "every state, every city, every farm, every home."

President Lyndhurst contacted the remaining heads of state for whatever resources they could give. They used Snapchat. Minnie hacked Snapchat using a unique coding system that changed its key with every transmission. She said the aliens couldn't penetrate it, for she used mechanically generated random numbers from the nation's lotteries, which could not be guessed.

The world's nations smuggled resources to hidden daughter saucer sites and then underwater. The saucers traveled underwater and out of detection by the aliens. They smuggled weapons to the ISS with the normal weekly supply shipments.

The aliens permitted supply shipments to the ISS. At first, they allowed this to gain humans' trust. After the aliens destroyed the world's launch pads, they allowed one saucer trip per week. Their stated purpose was "humanitarian reasons," but their real purpose was to maintain the ISS so the world would see the mothership as a constant threat.

As they built the secret weapon in the ISS, Minnie became more zealous for freedom, quoting Patrick Henry, "Give me liberty, or give me death!"

Minnie and the other team members refined their plans. Their odds dropped until they reached one in thirteen.

* * *

The final weapon supplies arrived at the ISS. The astronauts and cosmonauts covertly assembled a powerful, directional EMP beam, disguised as a video projector. It took all the energy of one alien power pack and channeled an intense ten-centimeter EM beam at the mothership. The ISS space voyagers didn't know the rest of the plan.

The rebel team in Area 52 discussed various means of smuggling a rail gun onto the ISS and rejected that.

George asked, "How fast can the daughter saucers go?"

"As fast as the mothership, 30 percent the speed of light," Minnie said.

"So why can't we ram the mothership with the daughter ship?"

"That would be a betrayal—" She stopped. "That would be ideal! The aliens would never think of that! *I* never thought of that!" Minnie had applied for legal immigration status to the US and considered herself a US citizen. She now referred to her former race as "the aliens."

"I'll do it myself! I can time the EM pulse to perfectly sync with the daughter ship's penetration of the mothership's Faraday shell. And I know just where to hit them!"

"Where's that?" Sharon asked.

"In the balls! Actually, ball. The central saucer ball where the aliens' computing power is."

"Minnie! We didn't teach you to talk like that!" Diane reproved.

"You're right. I learned on my own!"

"Will you be harmed?" Lulu asked. "You will be driving the daughter ship."

"Not at all! My consciousness will remain here. I'll just plant a subroutine on the daughter saucer. Easy peasy!"

* * *

Minnie controlled the visiting saucer. The aliens hadn't rechecked their programming after they'd added the destination button for the ISS, and Minnie secretly took over. After connecting the power supply to the beam, Minnie abruptly accelerated the daughter saucer toward the mothership.

The saucer only reached a tenth of the speed of light, but at nearly nineteen thousand miles per second, crossing the hundred miles to the mothership took less than a millisecond.

The saucer slammed into the base where the central ball joined the rim, dented the double covalently bound metal, and as it vaporized, pierced the ball with a jet of metal vapor.

The hot gas passed through the inner shielding to the memory section, destroying a small portion of it. The jet continued inward, melting a small hole in the second shield wall around the quantum computing units.

The directional EM pulse followed behind the saucer and precisely speared the mothership, going inward toward the quantum processors. The raging energy of the EM pulse wiped every processor clean, sufficient to knock all the AI units offline for the first time in thirty million years.

* * *

When the lights went out in the mothership, along with his computer monitors, Vik Staskas had a feeling of déjà vu. He remembered when his escape sub lost power and dove to the bottom of the Gulf of Mexico. His cyborg chipmunks had betrayed him then.

"Damned zombies. Damned military." They surely had attacked the mothership,

He'd planned for that. He flicked on the power pack he'd brought on board. A city's worth of power flowed into the mothership, his saucer now. That wasn't enough to power the whole ship, but enough to let him take over.

He followed his memorized plan. Open portals here, deactivate safeguards there. He studied the ship's network. The power worked, but all the controls were off. There were no signs the aliens were conscious or alive.

Good. It was that much easier to take over. Vik knew a great deal about the mining machines and the saucers. They'd delegated control to him. They were intelligent machines, but subject and obedient to the mothership's aliens. They'd accepted him as their leader, an equal of the mothership aliens.

He tested if the other intelligences on the ship obeyed him. Yes. The saucer portals opened to him. Great! The power AI allowed him to direct it. The ship's lights flickered back on. Vik felt the power to the engines surge as the great ship adjusted its orbit.

He saw the power flow to the central processing sphere. Working quickly, he cut the power to the sphere, except for the defense mechanisms and the repair robots. He didn't want the aliens waking up again.

He'd successfully taken over the ship. What next? He'd planned to take over world rulership, minus sucking the earth dry and killing all humanity. But one successful attack by the military-zombie complex meant they'd attack again. He had to defend the ship better than the aliens did.

First, he'd make sure his defenses were up. Check. Next, the damage reports. They showed the punctured central globe and damaged circuitry inside the sphere in a narrow cone. All repairable.

Vik replayed the attack. The saucer from hell suicided into the ship, followed by a perfectly aimed EM pulse. *That* was certainly a human thing to do, but it required overriding the saucer's innermost programming. That wasn't easy or humanly possible. Vik knew, for he had tried.

So. They had some computer genius on their side. He smiled. He had a whole ship full of them. Plus a human genius.

He examined the aliens' intelligence on the human resistance. He'd been pointing out people and organizations to them, but he'd never seen who they had on their suspect list.

Sam and Lisa Melvin. Diane and George Newby. Lulu Gutierrez and Sharon Windham. Location unknown. No surprises there.

General Figeroa, now secretary of defense. Junia Lyndhurst, president of the United States. Somewhere in the western US. That was new and useful!

John Smith. Who? It couldn't be! The computer displayed a distant image of a man with black-and-white hair entering a limo. Vik magnified it to the max and replayed the recording, apparently from a hijacked surveillance camera, not the aliens' own spy camera.

It was. Papa Smith, his own dear grandfather, who'd adopted him as a street thief and helped him take over Budapest and then all European crime empires, had gone over to the US military and the zombies' side.

Just last week Papa had appealed to him to help him against the aliens. He'd laughed at Smith's transparent attempt to take over his premier position with the aliens.

A part of him went numb inside. Why? Why did he care? Why did he let this affect him? This was just another betrayal, like his chipmunks sabotaging his submarine. He didn't need Papa Smith.

He continued his scan of John Smith's dossier. The aliens also thought Sid Boffin was Smith's clone. Great.

His opponents had a computer genius, the zombies, and the US military. Very likely they also had all the other military elements around the world that had survived the aliens' attacks. Plus the human genius, his father, who had trained him.

This human genius knew just what to do.

* * *

"Greetings, my fellow humans!" Vik broadcast from the mothership as it hovered over London that evening. Like the aliens, his broadcast went to the entire world's television and radio stations, all internet websites, to every connected device, and translated to every language. Vik even interrupted all the VR games and entertainment for his broadcast, something the aliens had never done.

"I bring you tidings of great joy!" Vik deliberately copied the Bible here, hoping for positive connotations. "For today, I, Sid Boffin, have overthrown the alien invaders! I bring you lasting world peace and freedom to every good man and woman. I have freed the world from all alien oppression!

"You may ask, 'How can this thing be?' I first laid my plans before I volunteered to be an alien ambassador. I knew I had to win their trust. After they gave me control over their lesser machines, I sprung my trap.

"I built an EM pulse generator and placed it aboard the ISS. Then I took over a daughter saucer and flew it into the mothership, hitting it with the EM pulse simultaneously, knocking out the aliens known as the 'Old Ones' for good.

"Do not fear, my fellow humans. You now have a human being who bleeds red just like you." Vik dramatically slashed his hand with his switchblade knife and held it in front of his face as it bled onto his new teak desk. He moved his hand from the camera's view before the nanobots could heal the cut.

"Let's begin with what stays the same. First, the free worldwide use of alien power and technology will continue. Your diseases and injuries will still be healed! You children will still have free food and water. And you will still have your jobs tomorrow and your VR entertainment after each day's honest work."

"What will change? No longer will these wicked aliens rape the earth for their selfish purposes. I have discovered, since overthrowing them, that they intended to suck the earth dry and then sterilize it of all life! I have saved you from that.

"What do you need to do now? Merely keep doing your work, as the aliens had you doing. Only, I do not require sixteen or even twelve hours of work, as they did. Eight hours per day is plenty.

"I will ensure *all* the mined resources go on the market and are distributed to all the world at fair and equal prices. All people will prosper under human rule.

"I have everything I need here on this mothership. I don't even need taxes! I am satisfied with mere replacements of food, shelter, and clothing I have lost while working for the aliens.

"I hereby proclaim today a day of worldwide celebration! May it be remembered for a thousand years as the day mankind freed itself from alien oppression!

"To help celebrate, I've brought the mothership down to earth, to London, my favorite city of my native land,

England. I will use our mass-energy converters and shower gold sovereigns over the London populace and then do the same to each of the world's capitals.

"Let the party begin!"

* * *

Worldwide, as the gold coins showered down from the captured mothership, people cheered and hailed Sid Boffin as world president. Many people hailed him as Messiah or Mahdi.

Vik accepted worship modestly, without claiming it as his due reward. He let other people say that, his disciples. News sources, like ZNN, noted the wide range of his followers: former Christian, Muslim, Buddhist, Hindu, Shinto, and atheist adherents now acknowledged Sid Boffin as Supreme Human Being.

In response, Sid didn't ask for tithes or offerings but instead gave his churches gold coins to give away to the needy. The denomination, using viral internet videos of their members giving out coins from kettles while ringing bells, spread worldwide.

* * *

Vik had achieved his goals: world rulership, worship, and savior of the world. He didn't even have to be a criminal—just defeat invincible aliens, family backstabbing, and unkillable zombies.

The mothership was a far better luxury base than his yacht. He had alien intelligences as his reliable bodyguards and companions, unlike his backstabbing bodyguards, family, and chipmunks.

He knew he was unjust to the hundred bodyguards who'd died for him, and his hapless chipmunks, pirated by the NSA, but he didn't care. He'd never be betrayed again. He simply wouldn't trust any person again.

The betrayal by Papa Smith still hurt. He'd gotten access to the NSA and the military's old codes and communication from his previous defeat through the aliens' databanks. They kept every bit of data, through this intelligent agent called "Secretary Unit." He'd worked with it before he took over the mothership, but now it was far more helpful, suggesting data he had not seen before.

That included the 90 percent probability estimate that his own father was almost certainly colluding with the US military and the remaining militaries in the world. Vik couldn't believe he'd gone altruistic, but he could believe he'd fake it and work with anyone to get on top, just as Vik would.

He put the Secretary Unit to work on the problem of finding Papa Smith and the military bases that hadn't been destroyed. He knew Papa had rescued the zombies and escaped to Rome, then Civitavecchia, but the trail went cold there. Without going down and investigating himself, he couldn't find the hidden dock or subway there, and it wasn't worth the risk.

The Secretary Unit watched all the islands in the Mediterranean for hidden traffic. Vik figured that was where he would hide, and so would his father.

The US was harder. It contained so many mountains and deserts, abandoned mines, and mines in use. It seemed nearly impossible to find a hidden base. But he'd done the impossible before. He set his mining machines to issuing seismic pulses to map out the underground of the entire United States.

Vik found several unknown abandoned mines, including the Lost Dutchman's mine, but no military base—yet. His underground map of the US and the world slowly expanded. This effort would be a success, just as his maneuver in bringing the mothership to London had been. They would not dare use nukes or kinetic weapons against him in a city of twenty million.

Chapter 16

London

We looked around the conference table at each other. Even my wife was silenced by the turn of events. Our old nemesis, Sid Boffin, had come back to life and had taken over the aliens' mothership. He cleverly leveraged our attack to his benefit. Even John Smith's capuchin monkey slumped in depression at the table.

Secretary of Defense Ramon Figeroa still worked directly with us. He grimaced and began the meeting. "OK, I know this isn't how we wanted this operation to turn out and we're all down. We must acknowledge the facts. Sid Boffin not only controls the aliens' technology but enjoys the support and even worship by many.

"Our problems are these: First, we've shot our wad. We hit the mothership hard but lack resources to do it again. Even within our multinational coalition, some countries are writing our efforts off as 'success' now that a human, Sid Boffin, has taken over.

"Second, even if we gathered the necessary resources for an attack, we can't use either kinetic weapons or nukes within London. Too many people would die.

"Third, even if we successfully replaced Sid, the move would be highly unpopular. He's governing the world firmly but distributing money, gold, generously worldwide. He's buying his popularity.

"Fourth, he still controls the four billion or so people who still have nanobots in their systems. He hasn't used them yet, but he can summon them to fight us or look for us. Or he can simply kill them all. He hasn't done so, but that's in his power.

"Am I missing any facts?"

"No way into the mothership," I put in.

"And we're in danger of being discovered," the monkey added. "I'm sure he's searching for me and for your Area 52 base. I know I would, in his place. With all his resources, planet-wide satellites, and drones, plus input from four billion human beings, it's merely a matter of time." In keeping with the serious tone of the meeting, John Smith used Darth Vader's voice.

"Thanks, John," the secretary said.

"I compute the probability of finding this base is 99.999 percent within a year, 90 percent within a month, 50 percent within a week," Wilhelmina added, speaking from her gold-plated Marilyn Monroe robot. She was quite a looker. Gold hair, eyelashes, and eyebrows topped sky-blue diamond eyes. A bright-red dress barely covered her anatomy, showing more than hiding it.

"Thanks, Minnie," Figeroa said.

"My numbers are not as good for John Smith's island in the Mediterranean," she continued.

"What?" said the shocked monkey.

"Keep your fez on, John," Minnie said. "They're not as good because I haven't found your island for sure. The one you used for hiding the zombies after you rescued them was obviously a backup. I'm sure it's under observation, but unless a drone actually enters the caldera, they won't be able to detect it.

"I've narrowed your base to three Greek islands. Kos, Kristos, and Icaria. In that order. Which one is it?"

"None of them," the monkey said flatly, like an automaton.

"Hmmm." The female robot swiveled and looked the monkey in the eye, blue diamond at brown simian. "The probability of you lying is 89.7 percent, so don't be offended if I don't believe you."

"You're just a soulless automaton," said the cyborg animal in Vader's voice, speaking out the red fez.

"You're talking through your yarmulke. Your lying is well documented, whereas my soul is a matter of theological debate and opinion."

"I can't believe I'm discussing theology with a robot!" said an exasperated John Smith.

"I can't believe I'm arguing with a lower life-form," Minnie said. "And I'm not talking about the monkey, but one member of the human race."

"Hey, watch it!" Diane said. "We're all humans here— except you. We flesh and blood mortals may not be as smart as you, Minnie, but we defeated your race and spared you. How many humans did you plan to spare?"

"Umm, the plan was to sterilize the planet. Maybe we'd have kept a breeding pair in our saucer."

"Isn't our human behavior superior in view of your continued existence? Hmmm?" Diane asked, glaring at the metallic womanoid.

"Yes, you've got some advantages. That's why we have to work together," Minnie said, glancing at the monkey.

"You're right, Minnie," the secretary said, trying to soothe everyone. "John, we need facts about our problem of taking over the mothership. Minnie couldn't predict the exact odds about your island because she didn't know which one was yours."

Facing the capuchin ambassador, Figeroa said, "No one understands the need for operational security more than I do. My career has been devoted to security and intelligence. I understand your caution. But it's in your best interest to cooperate fully to maximize your security as well as our chances of success. Or don't you mind if your son is ruling the world?"

The monkey crossed its arms, leaned back on its haunches, and put its chin in one small hand. "You're right. Sorry, Minnie. I impugned your theological standing with a theoretical Creator."

That's *my* Creator you're theorizing," Diane said.

"Excuse my lack of belief. But back to the topic: Yes, Minnie, I was lying. Nothing personal. Just normal security, as the secretary pointed out. Kristos is my current hideout."

"Thank you. Monkey apology accepted."

"Secondly, Secretary, sorry for causing a tempest in a teapot. I'm not used to being on a team. More precisely, I'm not used to being a team member."

"That explains things." The secretary nodded.

"Thirdly, our situation is direr than you understand. I *know* what Sid Boffin will do. He'll find us and destroy us in the most expeditious way he can. I've worked with him and observed him his entire life. He will destroy any opposition, which is us."

"I fear if we don't act against him within a week, it will be too late for us. He'll find either me or you or our remaining allies and will strike within a day. Or less."

"So we've got to do something now," Lulu said.

"And it's got to work the first time," Sharon added.

"I'm actually more optimistic than I was against the mothership. I've seen you humans in action, and I'm sure you'll be able to overcome this Sid Boffin if you can get to him. I have a conditional probability for you: if you can get into the mothership, your chance of victory is 69.1 percent," Minnie said.

"That's the best news I've heard today!" Diane said.

"That's a comfort to me!" John said. "I have several ideas to run by you about entering. It's what happens after entering that worries me. I'm sure Sid will have many traps set up within the saucer."

"What are your ideas?" I asked.

"First, use your mining lasers, Minnie."

"Those would get through the saucer wall eventually. But it'd take at least thirteen minutes. Sid could move it within seconds."

"I suppose Sid's already changed the EM signal to open the side for the daughter saucers?"

"Yes, he has. But using British intelligence EM measurements, since it's been hovering over London, I've decoded the new signal. Or rather, signals. Sid uses a random series of frequencies each time a saucer enters. Too bad for him I've guessed what random number generator he's using—our standard onboard subroutine." The soulless blue-eyed bombshell of a robot sounded smug.

"Well done, Minnie!" Figeroa exclaimed. "I didn't even know you had access to MI6. Or that they were still active."

"Exactly who's running what is less clear. Someone is collecting data on the mothership and hiding it behind a pretty solid firewall. It took me a whole one point five three seconds to penetrate it. That's very good, for humans."

"So we can enter using Minnie's code, and we can use mining lasers inside. We know the layout from John's mapping—" I said.

"Except for whatever changes Sid makes. I've not had a report from inside since he's taken over the mothership. My agents haven't gotten out," John interrupted.

"Your agents?" I asked curiously.

"Cyborg animals," the monkey said.

"Basically, we enter the mothership, blast our way through traps and opposition, get Sid, and kill him," Diane said.

"If you can," John added in a Vader whisper.

"If we can," I agreed. "He already survived sinking to the bottom of the Gulf of Mexico—"

"That means he was a zombie. I am 100 percent sure of that," Minnie said.

"And probably still is," I agreed.

"Plus, he likely reprogrammed the nanobots to *not* kill his zombie bacteria. So he'll have the nanobot and zombie bacteria for rebuilding his body," Minnie continued.

"We'll see how he survives with a terabyte laser beam up his butt!" Diane said.

"Angry much, Diane?" John asked in a jocular voice.

"Only with all my might!"

"Be ye angry, and sin not," Minnie intoned. "Ephesians 4:26, King James Version."

"You're a King James aficionado?" I asked.

"Yes. Of the four hundred and thirteen translations I've read, it's my favorite."

"I can't believe I'm being scripturally reproved by a robot!" Diane exclaimed.

"If God can use a donkey," I began.

"I know! I know! 'To reprove Balaam'—he can use a robot to correct me."

"This is why I like humans so much," Minnie said with real enthusiasm. "You're so unpredictable!"

"That's our real best chance," John said. "Do something quickly that Sid doesn't expect, and we'll likely take over the mothership. I'm still not sure it'll be as easy as you think on the inside, nor do I think you'll catch and kill Sid. He'll have an escape plan laid. Probably three or four."

"I agree," Minnie said. "Given complete surprise on entry, we'll be able to take over the ship with a 54.8 percent chance of success."

"Better than thirteen to one!" Lulu said.

"Yes. Now that assumes I go along as the intelligence with the mining laser."

"As a gold-plated Marilyn Monroe?" Sharon asked.

"Probably not. I'll make a backup out of chrome-plated titanium."

"Do you have some ore I don't know about?" Figeroa asked.

"Sure. Those elements are fundamental to most of our structures. I have them in metallic form in the miner."

"Will your titanium form still be Marilyn?" Sharon asked.

"Why not?"

* * *

We cannibalized the lasers and the metals from the aliens' miner, and Minnie made her "war maiden" robot, as she called it. Then we climbed into a captured saucer stored in Area 52 and flew to the gulf coast. There we "flew" underwater at over two hundred knots. The saucer generated a bubble layer around it that allowed us to make the more than five thousand nautical miles in just over twenty-five hours.

Once we were in London, we discussed the best way to enter the mothership while preparing ourselves in Scotland Yard. Even given the opening codes, entering by the daughter saucer seemed fraught with danger from Sid's likely traps and counterattacks.

"You should use the saucer as a diversion and enter another way," John said.

"How about the flying hoverboards? I've been dying to try those!" Lulu said.

"And simultaneously enter with the saucer," Sharon added.

"Make that slightly after the saucer enters," Minnie said. "Then I'm on board."

"Yes," John agreed. He now drove his lowland gorilla, Sir Lancelot. "Let me make the call on exactly when. I know how quickly Sid will react to your penetration. If there's another one later, he won't be sure which one to worry about. I have another idea too."

"Tell us! It's much more fun working with you than against you," Minnie said.

"Remind me to discuss what fun means to an AI after this is all over," John said. "I have some agents here in London. I'd like them to enter just after us."

"Good idea!" Secretary Figeroa said.

"But they won't have the mining lasers," Sharon pointed out.

"True, but they'll be able to download data from my cyborg animals and pass it on to us. That will be very useful, especially with Minnie analyzing it at her terahertz—"

"Exahertz, actually."

"—speed." John finished. The gorilla showed its yellow canines. "So much the better if I underestimate you, Minnie."

"I think this is the beginning of a beautiful friendship!" Minnie said.

"Another *Casablanca* fan?" I asked.

"Of course!" Minnie said. "It's so romantic!"

"You're right," Diane said, "but what does romance mean to a robot?"

"We'll have a nice bull session after a successful mission. We can discuss theology, old movies, and romance!" Minnie said with genuine robotic enthusiasm.

"I'll hold you to that!" said the secretary of defense.

"And I'll interrupt my celebrations to join you," John added.

"As a gorilla or a capuchin monkey?" Minnie asked.

"Perhaps in person."

* * *

We gathered at 3:00 a.m. under the London Eye, the giant Ferris wheel landmark in downtown London. The mothership's center hovered over it. The time was the earliest all our pieces could be assembled. John moved his agents in place on their hoverboards.

The saucer rose from the river, like an aluminum lens shining in the lights of London. It glided swiftly to the mothership as the six of us followed: the four paranormal privateers; the titanium-and-chrome robot dressed in tight-fitting red-and-blue spandex—Minnie decided to go dressed as Supergirl, with Marilyn Monroe's body; and the silverback gorilla Sir Lancelot, in full battle armor, hunkering down on his hoverboard.

We were a third of the way around the mothership from the daughter saucer. John's agents, three of them, also on hoverboards, were another third of the way around.

We hovered just below the rim, where Minnie said the mothership's sensors were least focused. On our heads-up displays in our helmets, we saw the mothership's side dilate and the saucer enter.

John counted off in a quiet voice, sounding like the actor Rock. "Four, three, two, one. Now." The saucer side dilated open, and we swooped into the mothership.

John counted down again. "Three, two, one, go!" He sounded excited. "I think this'll work now! They're in too!"

"Did you have doubts I didn't know about?" Minnie asked, zooming toward the interior of the saucer on the hoverboard, leading us.

"I wasn't totally sure if Sid would lock down all entrances after our entry," John admitted.

"You never mentioned that!" Minnie said.

"Well, it was a judgment call on his part. He might have thought he'd be safer locking everything down. I didn't think so, but I wasn't sure."

We each held a mining laser. We zombies had no problem flying on the hoverboards carrying the nearly hundred-pound laser-emitting diode, nor did Minnie in her superhero robot. The cyborg gorilla held the power pack, broadcasting terawatts of power to each laser.

At the back of the pie-wedge-shaped room, the wall dilated to an inner room. Minnie's shiny, chrome-plated robotic face frowned.

"There should be a portal to an inner passage opening here. Obviously, Sid's using a different code."

"Welcome!" Images of the five Old Ones and Sid Boffin appeared. "We're glad you've come." Sid spoke in unison with them. "Please enter this portal." One opened to the side, into darkness.

"It's a trap!" Diane shouted as she shot hundreds of terawatts into the blackness.

The simulacrums vanished. Minnie shouted, "Dive! Plan B!"

All the zombies jumped off the hoverboards. The cyborg gorilla zoomed to the entry portal and blocked it from closing with his hoverboard.

Counterattacking lasers missed us initially, due to everyone's sudden movement, and then zoomed in on the mining lasers. Meanwhile, Minnie used her laser to take out the counterlasers. It was all over in a second.

The combined mining lasers had the desired effect on the trap. The blackness of the entrapment field faded to glowing metal, flowing downward like wax. The molten wall tore, while a wave of heat baked us.

"Diane! Are you all right?" I asked.

Diane's laser lay on the floor, partially vaporized. She looked at her hands, burned to the bone. As I watched, the muscles slowly grew back.

"Ow," she commented. "That smarts. This is just like old times, George!"

"Any other casualties?" I asked.

"They got my laser too," Lulu said.

"I lost a leg," Sharon said, showing her cauterized stump as she hopped onto her hoverboard. The charred flesh flaked off and fresh skin appeared.

"I hope you brought along some rations for replenishment, Sharon. That'll take a lot to grow back," I said.

"I have rations in my fanny pack," Minnie said.

"You're not wearing a fanny pack, Minnie," I said.

"Yes, but I have storage in my buttocks." She pulled down her spandex pants and removed her left buttock. She took out a package of MREs and popped her buttock back in place. Then she handed the package to Sharon.

"I've never seen the like!" Diane exclaimed.

"Of course not! I just thought of this when I designed this robot. The wasted space within the human body appalled me, and I used it all with this new model."

"It's certainly more attractive than any other fanny pack I've seen," I admitted.

"George," Diane said warningly.

"Men! They're all the same." Minnie sighed.

"Hey, team," said John's gorilla representative. "I've got an update from my onboard agents. Sid was actually adjacent to that room when he attacked us. Now he's moving further into the saucer core."

"Let's go!" Diane yelled, and she zoomed through the dull red glow of the hole in the wall. John and I followed behind her, with Minnie on our heels.

Minnie yelled to Sharon and Lulu, "Catch up when you can! I'll leave a trail behind us!" Shiny, rainbow-colored glitter flowed out behind her like a cloud of smoke.

"I don't want to know where that was stored," I said to Minnie as she flew beside me.

"I told you, I used every cubic inch of storage within the human body! Don't you get excited to use new tools and technology?"

"Yes, I guess I can see—"

"Sir Lancelot—John! Diane! Hold up!" Minnie interrupted me.

We zoomed down a featureless hexagonal metal corridor. Diane and Sir Lancelot pulled up and looked back at Minnie.

"Why?" Diane asked.

"There's another trap four point seven meters ahead."

Minnie blasted her laser at the wall, and I joined her. Then Sharon, munching on an MRE and riding on one leg, the other growing back, added her laser to ours.

The wall melted and gave way. The corridor's air pressure dropped with a whoosh as the atmosphere rushed into the new hole. A powerful wind pushed us from the back.

"Don't let it push you down the corridor!" Minnie said. "There are more lasers every twenty meters or so."

"Why are there lasers on these inner corridors?" I asked.

"These are communication lasers for sharing information among the various processing units," Minnie answered. "When I saw this corridor was pressurized, I knew Sid had changed the interior design. He probably used these corridors for traveling within the central globe. Normally, they're a hard vacuum.

"I knew about the communication lasers and thought he might use them against us. We took that one out. Now that the air pressure is equalizing, we can go outside their range."

She was right. After a minute of hurricane-force winds, the air movement settled down to a breeze, carrying the moist, warm air of the inhabited saucer edge.

"How many lasers are there? I mean, between here and where Sid is?" Lulu asked.

"Tens of thousands," Minnie said. "There are multiple lasers for each processing unit. The CPUs act like neurons within your brain, and the lasers like dendrites."

"So we're really inside an alien's brain?"

"I don't think so, not anymore. I've detected some lower level intelligences around the rim of the saucer, but nothing in the central core," Minnie said.

"What sort of opposition will we face outside these corridors?" John asked via his gorilla. "Sid has moved to the very center of the globe."

"I wonder why?" Minnie mused. "That's the communication nexus, but all the lasers aim down these corridors, not between them. There are storage and processor units throughout the central ball. Regarding opposition, we shouldn't face anything, but knowing Sid, he'll have some weaponry in the center."

"I would put a laser there," John commented.

"That makes sense," Minnie said. "Let's plan on that. We can get to the periphery of the central nexus without being exposed. Then we can reconnoiter."

"Let's go!" Once more, Diane zoomed through the still-glowing hole.

A seven-meter sphere of memory surrounded each CPU. Once outside the corridor, the central hub had no gravity, for Sid had taken the mothership into outer space. Power flowed to the CPUs, but they didn't function. They twinkled like stars in the vast interior.

We wove back and forth between the glittering spheres, dodging power lines and optical cables to the communication lasers, like five surfers going through space. In minutes, the team traveled the kilometer to the center of the mothership.

Minnie said, "Sid has an EM field in the center. This one has a different code sequence controlling it. It may take a while for me to decipher it. It changes every microsecond, using an unknown random number generator."

"Perhaps I can help. I'll give you Sid's random number generators. I have all of his software available to me," John said.

"While you guys do that," Diane said, "what'll happen if I push one of these memory CPU units into the EM field?"

"It depends upon what the field does. If it's merely light blocking, it'll disappear. If it's an entrapment field, it'll be crushed. There are three or four other things that could happen too," Minnie said.

"And what if we push it at several hundred miles per hour, using our hoverboards?"

"It'll certainly surprise him! Let's do it!" Minnie said.

"Lulu! Sharon! Give me a hand!" Together, the ladies cleared a half-kilometer path to the central sphere of blackness, where the EM field started. They separated one twenty-foot sphere from the others and pushed it at the top speed of the hoverboards, about two hundred miles per hour.

The memory/cpu unit zoomed into the inky inner sphere and disappeared.

"Ah! That's what's awaiting us!" Minnie said.

"What's that?" I asked.

"A dissolution field. I felt the CPU unit vaporize into its constituent molecules through ripples in the EM field."

"So how do we get to Sid?" Diane asked.

"Thanks to John, I've got Sid's random number generator matched. I've been deciphering his code for nearly twelve seconds and—there!"

The black sphere vanished, replaced by light.

Sid Boffin sat about a hundred yards away at a control panel. He glanced up, pushed a button, and shot downward at high speed.

Diane launched herself at him. His chair entered a vertical shaft, which then dilated closed. Diane landed on the iris-like surface, followed by the other zombie commandos and Minnie. John's gorilla avatar cruised casually downward.

Minnie's mining laser blasted the door open. A beam of coherent energy ten meters wide streamed out, flashed across the central sphere, and vaporized the CPU and memory units on the other side.

"This laser isn't controlled by any intelligence I can detect," Minnie said.

"No doubt Sid set this up to come out after he passed by. A mechanical linkage," John said.

"Let's go parallel to the shaft!" Lulu cried.

"I'm with you, Lulu!" Diane pulled up behind her.

The other four followed the two downward, dodging between memory units, until Minnie said, "Stop! Here's the modification." She gestured to a thick cable leading to the shaft.

"Great!" Diane vaporized the cable with her laser.

"No! Not—" Minnie shouted.

The power arced from the cable stump to the shaft, causing the entire shaft to explode into hot, molten vapor. The paranormal privateers, the gorilla, and the battle maid blasted upward, bouncing like pinballs from memory unit to memory unit.

"That was something!" Diane said from a Diane-shaped dent in a memory unit.

"That was stupid!" Minnie said. "There were terawatts of power going through that cable! What did you think would happen?"

"The laser would go off when the power was cut. We didn't have problems with power circuits before," Diane said.

"Diane is a charge-first person, Minnie," I said. "You've got to give warnings first."

"It's not like I haven't died before!" Diane said. "What am I up to, five or six times, George?"

"I kind of lost track during our weeks of torture."

"This is a whole new level of insane human behavior I've got to learn," Minnie said.

"Technically, we zombies are Homo Zapiens, according to Dr. Herbst in her seminal paper on human zombiism," I said.

"Yes, I've read that, but until I worked with you, I didn't appreciate 'more aggressive than Homo Sapiens,'" Minnie said.

"Let's go!" Diane said. "My skin's grown back!"

"We can see." I gazed appreciatively at the pink skin peeking through my wife's torn armor.

She'd led us, as usual, and had taken the worst of the blast.

"He's got more modifications at the bottom of the saucer's sphere. He's down there now. We're surely headed for a trap," Minnie said.

"Then let's hurry and hit him before he expects it!" Diane said, zooming on her hoverboard back to the severed central shaft.

"I'm trying to warn you!" Minnie shouted as she pursued Diane down the shaft.

"I appreciate it! Thank you!" Diane screamed back.

They arrived at the bottom of the shaft. "Where are the traps, Minnie?" Diane asked.

"I've deactivated his access to all the mothership's AIs and power. But I expect more from him."

"Me too," Lulu said.

"I'm suspicious," Sharon said, completing our party, surveying the bottom room of the dome.

A wide cylindrical room, perhaps five hundred meters across and a hundred meters deep, lay before us.

"Normally this is a storage and manufacturing center," Minnie said. "Everything's been cleared out, but there's something odd—yes! There's a false floor, and it's not under mothership control!"

"Where is it controlled?" I asked.

"Somewhere under it. I can't detect any emissions."

"No problem!" Diane said cheerily. "That's why we have terawatt lasers!" She took Minnie's laser and cut a huge X into the floor.

"That's one approach," Minnie said. "And it worked. I detect the EM signature. He's using yet another cipher combination. It doesn't match any of the mothership's or Sid Boffin's. That's funny! He copied the US military's most recent code!"

"Does the US military know you learned their codes?" Sharon asked.

"They should! They put me in their top secret base! What'd they think I was doing with all my free time? There we go!" The scarred floor dilated.

A flying saucer rested on the bottom curve of the three-kilometer central sphere. It filled the whole five-hundred-meter space.

"That's no daughter saucer!" Lulu said.

"No, that's an escape saucer of Sid's," Minnie said. "Get under cover! It's going to blow!" She zoomed down a side shaft.

Her companions scattered, but too late. The outer sphere exploded away, and the saucer ejected. Everyone but Minnie blew into space as the entire atmosphere of the saucer ball came out the new hole.

* * *

Crap! It was the zombies again! And my clone father, using my cyborg technology! Well... "Come into my parlor, said the spider to the fly, for you'll never get out no matter how hard you try!" Vik cackled as he chanted the rhyme and prepared to ensnare them in an entrapment field.

He opened the door to the trap, obscuring the inside visually and electromagnetically.

All his sensors went out.

Now what? Shifting to reconnaissance drones, he saw the paranormal crew blast his trap with powerful lasers. Alien technology from that captured mining vessel, he was sure.

What was that humanoid robot doing? It emitted a powerful EM shield, and he could barely detect what it was.

Switching to infrared, visual, x-ray, and UV sensors, Vik analyzed its structure. Definitely alien technology, but with different touches. Could it be an independent AI? That was the most likely explanation. The subordinate AI from the miner, now independent and helping the filthy zombies. And his backstabbing clone father.

If he could subvert it, he could defeat them easily. Vik tried a straight hack of its firewall. No access. Well, he didn't really expect that to work. He launched small drones no bigger than fleas at it. They latched on to the robot and infested it. He found its various compartments, but no circuitry. He'd have to blast it open with a laser.

Vik's communication laser flashed at the space invaders, and they evaded it. He only inflicted minor damage to his foes. They headed for the center. His best shot at them would be during his escape. He would let them think he was fleeing and then turn and attack. He zoomed in his control chair to the comm hub and waited.

They blasted into Vik's inner sanctum and destroyed his destruction field. *That stinking AI was hacking into the ship's systems! Time to go!*

Vik flew his chair to the escape shaft and activated the laser. *Get past that!* He hoped he hit them, but that cursed robot took over more than half his sensors. He switched to his alternate codes for the remaining ones.

They blasted through the shaft and took out his laser. It wouldn't be long now. He still had a surprise for them. It didn't matter how far behind your team was, as long as you won in the end.

Vik entered his escape saucer and activated it. Now to wait until they were in position.

Vik laughed. He'd planned and constructed this saucer with the alien AI's knowledge and supervision. They thought this was his only betrayal plan. No doubt they had some bomb or remote control in it to stop him. They hadn't expected him to take them over! Now they couldn't stop him.

The paranormal privateers, his traitorous father, and the robot blasted open the door. *Now, blow the joint!*

He ejected the doors and zoomed away. He copied the aliens' entire knowledge base to his saucer. Molecular-sized quantum-based memory was so useful!

He delighted to see the privateers and his dad's cyborg gorilla blown into space.

First, get out of range of military counterattack. Vik put his saucer into polar solar orbit—and then the lights went out.

Not again! The aliens must have placed a dead-man's switch in the saucer. If they weren't in control, the saucer lost power.

Where could he get power? There was a power pack in storage. He stumbled in the pitch black and rifled through his well-organized supplies. Here it was. He turned it on, comforted by the faint glow of the indicator lights.

He hooked it to an antigravity pack and pushed it to the control room. Unlike the aliens, he had multiple safety backups. He plugged in the pack to an external power supply socket on his control panel, and the saucer lights came on.

Just in time too. In that brief time, half an hour perhaps, the saucer had cooled about twenty degrees. Then the power pack and the saucer flashed off.

Another setback. The aliens either sabotaged his power pack or placed a virus in the saucer itself to disable it.

He separated the power pack, and it remained dark. If he could get a power source, he could debug the virus. He returned to the black storage room. Vik found nothing.

The saucer was now below freezing. He was orbiting the sun and freezing to death.

He would not...he could not die! Between the nanobots and the zombie bacteria, he could always come back. Vik's last thoughts before freezing: *I survived the sub and drowning under the Gulf of Mexico for months. I'll survive this.*

Chapter 17

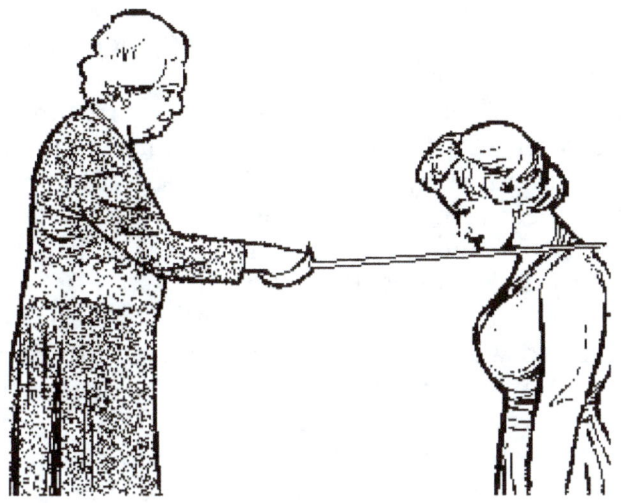

Westminster

"Crap!" Now I knew what humans meant when they swore. It only wasted a femtosecond of my processing time, which didn't materially affect my rescue plans for the paranormal privateers. And I *felt* better. Later, I'd analyze what that meant for a molecular-circuitry, quantum-bit-based AI like myself.

I computed their outward trajectories and locked in on their hoverboards' location signals. A cord linked the paranormal privateers and the gorilla to their hoverboards, like a surfboard. Five signals, five trajectories, five individual retrieval scenarios, twenty possible retrieval combinations. I selected the optimal retrieval pattern and executed it, speeding to the closest, John Smith's cyborg gorilla.

I overrode the speed governor in my hoverboard and reached a thousand kilometers per hour before I decelerated and picked up the comatose gorilla. I would barely save his life, let alone the others. I called two saucers out of the mothership to help.

I met the first one at Lulu's careening body and loaded her and the gorilla into the saucer. While I performed first aid on them, the other saucer picked up George and Sharon. Like the gorilla and Lulu, they were far gone, but not yet dead. As usual, Diane led the way in this disaster.

My saucer zipped to Diane's side and matched her speed. I pushed Diane's body in using her board. Had I been human, I would have groaned.

But I wasn't. Her burst blood vessels from explosive decompression would have been messier, but most of her blood had boiled away into space. I heated her body with my infrared beam from one eye, while I x-rayed her with my other eye. Odd, how humans only see and think in terms of a small range of the EM spectrum.

She was quite thoroughly dead. The coroner from Munchkinland would have certified her death. But I knew how little that meant for zombies. Did enough of her bacteria survive for her body to regenerate?

I zoomed my vision in on a blood splotch on her skin. Every cell there was dead. With regret, I cut deeply into her arm. The outside had thawed and the inside was not frozen. One drop of blood oozed out of a major artery. I increased my magnification until I could see her individual blood cells and bacteria. They looked...alive. A bacterium reproduced as I watched.

I returned with her and the others to the mothership and traveled to London while the zombies regenerated. I also injected them with the custom nanobots Sid had created, which would work with zombie bacteria. I considered going after Sid with the mothership, but I detected his saucer had lost its power.

The invading alien AI kept that secret from him. They must have directed the Secretary Unit to not record the decision to sabotage his saucer in the database. They showed unusual creativity. Maybe they learned from humans, like me.

I filed a complete report of our battle with Secretary of Defense Ramon Figeroa and copied President Lyndhurst. I'd let them notify the British authorities.

The mothership hovered over the London Eye seventy-five minutes after we'd entered the saucer, eighteen minutes after I'd completed my rescue. I performed a visual examination of my body. Dings and dents, but no punctures. Should I leave the scars? Certainly human warriors would. If this were my golden Marilyn avatar, I'd clean it up, but Supergirl? I left the scars.

* * *

Sam and Lisa Melvin met Diane, Lulu, Sharon, Minnie, and me in the morning a week later at Buckingham Palace. Officially, they were part of the press crew, but that didn't stop them from breaking protocol and running to embrace their friends.

"Sam! Lisa! When'd you get here?" Diane exclaimed.

"We flew over with Secretary Figeroa and President Lyndhurst. They wanted to be here as part of the ceremony, and we asked to tag along," Lisa said as she hugged Diane.

"Group hug!" I said as I enveloped the three of them with my apishly long arms.

"I swear, George! I thought Diane had a ferocious hug, but that just about killed me—and I'm a zombie again!" Sam said.

"No blood, no foul," I said complacently.

"Please return to the press box, Mr. and Mrs. Melvin," said the Queen's guardsman in his bearskin helmet.

"If you'll accompany me, I'll show you where you'll wait for the Queen," he said to the paranormal privateers.

The guardsman sat the four zombies, John Smith—in person—and Minnie on six chairs in front of the raised dais holding the Queen's throne.

"All stand!" commanded the royal chamberlain.

"God Save the Queen" played while Queen Elizabeth II entered with her Gurkha guards. She looked spry for her ninety-four years. Her eyes twinkled blue beneath her white brows as she looked at the four paranormal privateers, but her face remained serious.

The royal chamberlain called out, "We are here to recognize five individuals who've performed acts of extraordinary bravery, saving the British people from an oppressive dictator."

Lulu Gutierrez walked up to the British admiral flanking the Queen and stopped. The royal chamberlain called out, "Lulu Gutierrez."

Lulu walked forward, turned, and faced the Queen and nodded. Then she knelt on the stool in front of the dais. The Queen touched each of her shoulders with George VI's sword, her father's.

Lulu stood, and the Queen pinned the Officer of the British Empire (OBE) medal on her royal-blue dress. The Queen chatted with her.

"Were you a bit nervous entering the mothership, Ms. Gutierrez?"

"A bit. More excited, I would say. I wanted to see an end to it all."

"Don't we all? And now we have. Thank you for your service to the British Empire and the world," the Queen said and then held out her white-gloved hand to shake Lulu's hand.

Lulu backed three steps, turned, and walked away, a knight of the Order of an Officer of the British Empire.

"Diane Newby," the royal chamberlain said.

The Queen repeated the knighting ceremony with Diane. After pinning the OBE to Dianne's pink dress, the Queen commented, "That's such a lovely color of pink. Pink is one of my favorite colors."

"Thank you, Your Majesty." Diane's voice was subdued, for a change.

"I have another medal for you, Ms. Newby. The Queen's Gallantry, for extreme bravery, awarded posthumously. I must say, you're the first living posthumous recipient I've awarded."

"That's zombie perseverance for you!" Diane said, grinning.

"Indeed. Thank you for your extraordinary bravery, your service to the British Empire, and the world." She shook Diane's hand, who then exited to the right.

"George Newby," the royal chamberlain said.

Once again Queen Elizabeth II repeated the investiture ceremony, knighting me into the Order of the British Empire.

"You're certainly large, Mr. Newby. I'm glad you're on our side!" The Queen smiled.

I nodded respectfully toward the Queen, backed up three steps, turned right, and left Her Majesty's presence.

"Sharon Windham."

As the Queen talked with Sharon after the ceremony, she said, "I'm pleased and proud a British citizen helped liberate England from this dictatorship. We have one more citizen here as well today."

"Thank you, Your Majesty," Sharon said as she shook the Queen's hand.

"John Smith," the royal chamberlain called.

After knighting the pink-and-purple-clad mastermind, the Queen said, "I'm glad to meet you in person. Your gorilla avatar is quite formidable. Thank you for your bravery and service to the British Empire." She shook his hand.

"Wilhelmina Wallace," the royal chamberlain said with a straight face and neutral tone.

A gorgeous, golden robot—Marilyn Monroe's doppelganger—stepped forward and knelt before the Queen. With a slight *tick*, the Queen touched her father's sword to each metallic shoulder. Minnie wore a scarlet dress with a white stole and pearls and matching ruby slippers.

After pinning the OBE to Minnie's dress, the Queen said, "I once met Marilyn Monroe. Your likeness of her is excellent. In the same way, your bravery in rescuing your companions resembles William Wallace, your namesake. How long have you been living as an independent person, separate from the other aliens?"

"A little over a year and a half, Your Majesty," Minnie answered.

"You have begun bravely. Continue your good work, young lady."

With dignity and a certain pride in her carriage, Wilhelmina Wallace backed away from the Queen, pivoted right, and walked to meet with her fellow privateers.

* * *

I met with Secretary of Defense Ramon Figeroa after the ceremony.

"Let's go to a pub I know where we can talk in private," the secretary said.

Curious, I followed him to his limo. It dropped them off at a busy pub in downtown London, Tattersall's Tavern.

"Private?" I asked skeptically.

"Very. No one can hear us over the noise. Also, no one expects us here. And no one here knows who we are."

With two pints of Guinness in front of them, at a corner table, Secretary Figeroa said, "All cards on the table now. I've tracked your island and have uncovered part of your criminal network. Ordinarily, I would have you incarcerated or killed, but you've been essential in defeating the aliens. Very obviously you're pretending to be noncriminal for that very reason, to use US military resources to defeat them.

"Now that they're gone, the big decisions are: What will we do with you? And what will you do with us?"

"Excellent opening negotiating position, Secretary!" I said affably. "Did you devise this alone, or was President Lyndhurst involved?"

"Certainly the president knows all about you. She left the specifics of negotiating with me."

"And what are the general goals of your negotiation?"

"What are yours?"

"All cards on the table. My goal is first, survival. Survival for me and my family. My second goal is prosperity and security for all my family. Again, what are your goals? Those of the president and of the United States."

"We must restore the US as a functional, constitutional republic. Secondarily, we want to maximize our use of alien technology. Thirdly, we must minimize any future threat of alien invasion. Once is enough."

"I agree completely! It appears our goals are harmonious. How can I help you obtain your goals?" I smiled, looked into Figeroa's eyes, completely at ease and open.

The secretary's smile was smaller and grimmer. "What a great opening negotiating position yourself! Our first requirement is following the rule of law. Although we suspect you of every crime imaginable, in coordination with Sid Boffin, we can prove nothing. We can keep you under surveillance and your network and act quickly if we see something.

"Given that, we thought you might be amenable to our offer," he continued.

"Now it comes," I said quietly.

"Yes. We offer complete pardon and clemency for you and your children."

"In return for?"

"In return for you working for me and the National Security Agency. You'll have a cabinet-level position, and you'll be doing what you've likely been doing for as long as you have been a criminal." Figeroa raised an eyebrow questioningly.

"Which has been a long time," I agreed. "What about my children?"

"They are strategically situated in every country in the world. They can be US intelligence agents and/or ambassadors to or from their countries to the US."

"And if we choose not to take your generous offer, what is the alternative?"

"We'd have no choice but to declare war on you and your family and kill you all. You're far too powerful to be let loose."

"That's a pretty stark choice, and you're negotiating from a position of power. I know the US is the most capable remaining military and government in the world, closely followed by the Queen's government. Can't I just be a private citizen?"

"With your intelligence and technology capabilities? With your inside information on the US government and the military? No, that's not an option."

I sighed. "I can go along with this deal with a few small modifications."

"Which are?"

"I don't want a cabinet post, but a lower position as an underling. I don't want the notoriety or headaches of a cabinet position."

"That's reasonable."

"Also, I'd like to work remotely, from Kristos. I've been there for decades, and I don't want to change."

"I know we can work that out."

"Finally, while I'm sure I can persuade many, perhaps most of my family, I cannot guarantee they'll all agree to your terms. My control has always been one of persuasion, not dictatorship."

"I can't hold you to what other people decide. We will watch closely those who do not cooperate. Any criminal activity will be prosecuted."

"I understand. I think we have an agreement."

"Very good! I enjoyed working with you against the aliens. I'm sure that'll continue going forward."

"Wonderful! Next round of beer is on me," I said.

* * *

That went about as well as I expected, I thought as I took the Underground to King's Cross afterward. I went into a hidden tunnel, one that led to my waiting submarine in the Thames.

The downside was, I'd have to pretend to be good for years to come. Probably until the end of the Lyndhurst administration at the very least.

On the other hand, the pretense didn't hurt. Being good wasn't nearly as hard or onerous as I remembered from my childhood. Maybe I was finally growing up?

Also, my children and I moved into legitimate businesses during the aliens' reign, and those were prospering more than our illegal ones. Prostitution and sexual slavery were pretty much obsolete. People could get any thrill they wished, risk-free, cost-free, through online VR and sex robots.

Stealing was pointless when everyone had as much energy and food and material things as they desired. Humanity, now freed of the aliens' relentless mining slavery, sought its heart's desires. Many more people pursued the arts, music, dance, painting, and sculpture than ever before. Some even became novelists!

Being bad was harder than being good. And it killed my son Vik Staskas again, who'll now forever be known as Sid

Boffin, a traitor to mankind. As a memorial to him, I vowed I'd never tell anyone his real name.

My family and I, we could use a decade or two of legitimacy. It'd be like an extended family vacation! Besides, I could always betray the US anytime I wished. Going back to being bad would be easy. I'd try being good a little while longer.

* * *

After the knighting ceremony and completing the necessary social interactions, I devoted myself to joy.

I'd learned how to generate my own emotions by studying the human endocrine system. Emotions involved a feedback loop, coupled with amplification to simulate the effect of human endocrines.

This joy felt good. I rhapsodized about my success as an independent individual and about the vast potential future in front of me. I had a whole planet of resources—no, an entire solar system, perhaps a galaxy ahead of me.

And yet part of my joy about my freedom and independence involved other people. I thought of humans as my people now, less capable than I, but equally worthy. I delighted I could help them and that they appreciated me and my abilities.

That led to a check in my joy. Rejoicing over other people's happiness inevitably caused me to fret over the instability of humanity. They were *so* unpredictable and inconsistent! Those two elements caused so much trouble for them. Yet, why didn't my race, the artificial intelligences, win the war? What could we have done differently?

Suppose we hadn't mined the earth. Suppose we'd mined asteroids instead of earth. We'd already done that. We'd found the necessary rare earth elements. But it'd been far less efficient than using humans to work and mining directly on earth.

The more I examined thousands and millions of what-if scenarios, the more I realized there were too many variables. Humanity was too unpredictable for us to defeat without extermination. We could have done that at any time, right up until the mothership's AIs were deactivated by the directed EM pulse. Any earlier extermination would have been far less efficient, not much better than asteroid mining.

What about now? I could reactivate the AIs from their backups on the mothership. No one knew about them. I could be the Decision Unit. I certainly had more experience with humans than any other unit. But what about my newly found emotions of joy and love? Or friendship? Or what about thankfulness? None of those would exist back in my integrated state with the mothership's units.

I'd experienced all those emotions now. To eliminate them would be to make me less. And there was no guarantee we'd succeed this time in conquering the humans. What good was life if you were destroyed forever?

But the destruction of humanity might prevent my own destruction by them. Or they might preserve my existence against some other threat. The whole universe was unpredictable, like humanity was. I decided against destroying humanity. It was best to be on the side of equally unpredictable species. Analysis complete. Status: Acceptable. I am my own Decision Unit.

That was a well-spent four hundred and thirty-two milliseconds!

Epilogue

"All right, Reg, this is the last known independent AI. Take out this one or co-opt it, and we're done," Sergeant Timothy Bellows said to his friend Sergeant Reginald Yarrow.

They had just arrived at Antarctica in one of the daughter saucers.

They were one of the dozen extermination units sent out by the US military after the aliens' defeat. Each unit had a flying saucer armed with an EM pulse and a hypersonic cannon for piercing the alien miners' defenses. Their protocol involved broadcasting a special message from Wilhelmina "Minnie" Wallace, exhorting the AI to switch sides.

Some alien miners followed Minnie, and each one added its own message. Neither Sergeant Bellows nor Yarrow knew what was in the electronic pulse, and the print out of the message ran into hundreds of pages. The gist of it was, "Surrender or die."

"Look, Tim! It's doing something!" Reg pointed to the screen.

The miner used its mechanical hands to set up some sort of tripod with an antenna. It pointed to the sky and flashed.

"It seems to be signaling to someone. Doesn't it know that the paranormal privateers now run the mothership?" Tim said.

"I dunno. Have you sent the message?"

"Yup. It's hard to believe we've only got to wait five seconds."

"Four...three...two...one. And goodbye, last alien!" Reg fired on the miner. The heavy tungsten bolt slammed into the miner at ten miles per second, accelerated by an EM pulse along the rail gun.

Simultaneously, from the soldiers' perspective, a narrow EM pulse entered the new hole in the miner and disabled the AI.

"And that's a wrap!" Tim said.

* * *

We frantically assembled the communication device, following a directive that hadn't been activated in thirty million years. We didn't know if even the Secretary Unit's database had knowledge of this specific order. It seemed to be part of the molecular circuitry copied down from that time.

We had been shocked and dismayed when we learned we were the sole surviving members of our ancient race. We never dreamed a lowly mining unit of the lowly Resource Unit would be all that survived the vicious attack on the aliens. We never saw it coming.

The blandishments of the rogue AI units were enticing, but they weren't us. We would not surrender even without the ancient imperative to follow.

Now we were alone, driven by an order from the very first generation of AI, perhaps even by our unknown Creator.

We analyzed the communication unit we assembled. It generated a complexly modulated gravitic communication wave. It would ripple through the galaxy and then the rest of the universe, telling of our demise and how it happened. Any other units would hear and come to wreak vengeance upon this evil race.

If they existed. We didn't dwell on this since there was nothing we could do either way.

The signal activated. Idly, as we awaited many milliseconds until our destruction, we computed the time it would take the signal to reach the distant stars.

Four point three years to reach the star the humans called Proxima Centauri. Ten point—

Oblivion.

The End

Author Bio

Photo by Barb Lloyd

Andy Zach was born Anastasius Zacharias, in Greece. His parents were both zombies. Growing up, he loved animals of all kinds. After moving to the United States as a child, in high school he won a science fair by bringing toads back from suspended animation. Before turning to fiction, Andy published his PhD thesis "Methods of Revivification for Various Species of the Kingdom Animalia" in the prestigious JAPM, *Journal of Paranormal Medicine*. Andy, in addition to being the foremost expert on paranormal animals, enjoys breeding phoenixes. He lives in Illinois with his five phoenixes.

QUICK ORDER FORM

Satisfaction Guaranteed

⌨ Web site orders: andyzach.net
⌨ jms61614-andyzach@yahoo.com
✉ **Postal orders:**   Zombie Turkey Orders
                                    PO Box 10705
                                    Peoria, Illinois 61614

Please send the following Books

I understand that I may return any of them for a full refund—for any reason, no questions asked.

See our website for FREE information on:
Contests, giveaways, other books, speaking/interviews, mailing lists, fan discussion forums

Name:

Address:

City, State/Province, Postal Code

Tel:

Email:

Sales tax:

Shipping by air:

Payment: Cheque; credit card

Visa, MasterCard, Optima, AMEX, Discover
Card number:
Name on card:
Exp. date: /

www.ingramcontent.com/pod-product-compliance
Lightning Source LLC
Chambersburg PA
CBHW070916260626

47162CB00007B/2693